ZHIVË

B.C. CLARK

Library of Congress Control Number: 2025902206

Copyright © 2025

All Rights Reserved

ISBN: 978-1-966468-63-9

Dedication

To the Clark, Sosa, Villarreal, Sturgeon, Smith, and Garza families.

Acknowledgment

This story could not have been done without the love, care, inspiration, and support of these amazing people:

I'd like to thank my parents for bringing me into this world—not just in this life, but into a specific world where I could find myself getting lost.

Thank you to Nathan Sturgeon. I know we're not blood, but you'll always be my little brother. If it weren't for us staying up late watching movies, I would've never come up with this story.

And a special thank you to my old and new friends: Giovani, Kaycee Melendez, Trevor and Garrett Singletary, Alexis Richardson, Carissa Carlson, Carlos Gonzalez, and Sydney Do, wherever y'all are. Take care and stay strong.

Contents

About the Author

B.C. Clark is a Fast Food Cook, Warehouse Stocker, Maintenance Man, and currently a Flight Attendant and Writer living in Houston, Texas. As a child, B.C. was introduced to the world of superheroes. After watching Sam Raimi's Spider-Man, he was captivated by the art of the film. From that moment, he vowed to one day create a world full of superheroes, inspired by the people and movies around him.

Chapter 1
PROLOGUE

It was the summer of 1997. Cathy Baker was anxious about her senior year and nervous about making bold decisions for her future. Times were different compared to 2015. Once you finished high school, you had to grow up right away and plan for whatever came next, whether it was college, family, or work. Cathy wasn't sure if she wanted to work at her father's business or continue her education and pursue nursing. Her head throbbed from the stress of it all, and she took a break. Her last school year hadn't even started yet, and she was already losing hair.

Across the street was a young man named Tate Clark. He had just finished his semester and was ready to begin his junior year at King's University, a private college in Southlake, Texas, where he was majoring in Engineering.

Cathy met Tate when she first moved into the neighborhood. It was '86, and she had just turned six. (Tate was nine.) They'd play outdoor games together like tag, hide-and-seek, cops and robbers, and so on. Their families knew each other well—family get-togethers, picnics at the park, church services—you name it. As the years passed, Cathy and Tate hung out less and less until she hit thirteen. She became a moody teenager, stuck in a bitter attitude and laziness. Tate was already deep into his high school years. He had no time to play tag or hide‑and‑seek. That was for kids. He wanted the newest video games, the coolest clothes, and to nail that hard skate trick with his friends. No time for childish games. Cathy grew nostalgic for what they once had. Now and then, she'd drop by his house, and they'd share a thought or two about their past, hoping to rekindle it.

About a year later, Tate graduated and was ready to move on to King's University. After the ceremony, when families were taking pictures together, giving hugs, and celebrating, it was Cathy's turn. She wore a white blouse with a black skirt and some messy sneakers because she didn't like heels; she went up to Tate and gave him a big hug. Her arms kept sliding off his wide shoulders because of how sleek and smooth his black gown was. Tate landed a quick peck on Cathy's cheek, and her face turned instantly red. It wasn't exactly her first kiss, but it was the first a guy had ever given her. From there, she formed a little crush on her childhood friend. These feelings were new, strong, and, would she like to admit—beautiful?

Two months later, Cathy was lost in butterflies. She couldn't deny her feelings, and what amplified them more was that it was someone she had a good relationship with, someone she grew up with. On this day, she looked outside her bedroom window to see if he'd go outside—to check the mail, mow the lawn, take his dog for a walk—anything. The hot sun was setting, and Cathy gave one last peek behind her blue curtains. Finally, Tate was outside, waving goodbye to his parents. They drove away in their Nissan minivan for an out‑of‑town meeting and wouldn't be back until the next day. Once the coast was clear, Cathy rushed outside in her gray, baggy shirt, pajama pants, and pink slippers—eager to see her best friend.

"What are you doing out here?" Tate asked, more curious about why she seemed to be in a rush than her being out in the dark.

"Just wanted to see what's up."

Tate noticed her excitement, her lips curling inwards to hide her big smile. He wondered if she was joking or had something funny to say.

Tate shot the excited girl an offer. "Would you like to come inside and watch a movie?"

"Sure!" If she had answered a millisecond faster, she would've looked desperate.

The house looked the same. Nothing had changed. It was a typical suburban home with off-white walls, plain tile, a kitchen with an island, and marble countertops. It looked almost identical to her house, except her walls were white, her countertops dark, not light, and Tate's house wasn't a two-story home. Tate showed off the entertainment side of his living room, rambling about how his parents got the new VHS player everyone wanted. Cathy didn't understand a single word he said—mainly just intrigued to hear him talk, thinking of ways she could kiss him like boys and girls do in the movies. On the topic of movies, Tate wasn't some oblivious kid. He knew what he was doing. He put on a horror flick to set the mood, hoping Cathy would get scared and hold tightly onto him. While Cathy liked her friend, Tate was also a teenage boy. He was more into lust than love (as most boys usually are). He, too, was hoping to kiss Cathy. The scary movie he picked didn't help much, though. It was a slow burn, and it wouldn't get to the jump scares until the second half. It was now a waiting game.

Stupid, he thought.

When the fear-inducing moments finally came, Cathy grabbed onto Tate's wrist tightly; any tighter, and she'd turn his skin red. Another jump came on the screen, and her legs curled up onto his. Tate reached for the remote and lowered the volume on the TV.

"Are you okay?" he laughed, rubbing her shoulder with his other arm.

"Yeah. It's just so scary."

"Nothing to worry about. *Nothing.* Trust me."

Cathy had been staring at his lips. This was the moment. It was time for young Tate to make a move. Their eyes locked for too long. Any longer, it'd be painfully awkward. Cathy was sick of waiting. In her mind, it was torture. She let out a little yelp, leaned forward, and kissed him deeply. Fireworks went off. Goosebumps waved over her body, and her stomach swirled. Her first kiss. Everybody remembers their first kiss—that floating feeling you hope will never go away. Things probably would've escalated if Tate hadn't heard the garage door open. His parents' meeting was canceled due to electrical issues at their establishment. As Cathy snuck out the living room window and out the side fence, she kept thinking of the butterflies, the goosebumps, and the floating. For Cathy, that was short-lived. Tate left for school the following week. Throughout the years, Cathy had a few chances to see him, but the timing was always off. Plus, it never hurt to spend holidays or summer vacations with family.

During this memorable summer of '97, Cathy's mind went to strange places, mostly on the topic of sex. She was in high school—of course, it was bound to cross her mind. Few people knew she was a virgin, and the selective few who did would gossip about how she was prude. Cathy digressed—she knew she could've been with anybody she wanted, but she wanted Tate. She trusted him the most—or at least she thought...

When the moment came, Cathy grew scared. Scared yet ready, she put her mind to it. She was going to see this through with her childhood best friend. As always, she peeped through her curtains and spotted him shooting a few hoops in his long, curvy driveway. This was one of those bold decisions Cathy was going to remember for the rest of her life. Each step toward her front door was a struggle. Slowly but surely, she made it outside, inching closer to Tate's driveway. Suddenly, at the last second, she decided against it and turned around—but it was too late. Tate looked up from his setup. His heart skipped a beat, not realizing Cathy had practically snuck up behind him.

"Oh, hey!" he smiled, exhaling in relief to see an old friend.

"Um... hi," Cathy mumbled.

"How've you been? How's school?"

"Good, I guess. And your school?"

Tate grinned, nodding. "Could be better. I missed you."

Cathy's cheeks turned salmon red. She wasn't good at flirting and wanted to find a way to bring up intimacy without making it obvious.

"I missed you too."

"So... what's new?" Tate said nonchalantly, throwing his basketball into the hoop a couple of times while making small talk. His focus shifted back and forth between Cathy and the ball.

"Not much," she answered. "Been on any fun dates or anything?" The nervous girl hoped the question wasn't too forward or seemed prying.

"Eh... kinda, but not really. You?"

"No."

"You gotta get out there, man," Tate chuckled.

"I actually wanted to ask you about that. If you don't mind."

"Cathy... you can ask me anything."

It was difficult to express everything that came to her mind. Her words tripped over each other, stuttering nonstop until Tate seemed annoyed by her struggle to convey her thoughts.

"Cathy! What is it?" he exclaimed.

"I think I like you. And I wanted to know if... *if...*"

"If what? What is it?"

Instead of breaking the ice, Cathy brought up something that could slowly ease them into the topic. "Do you remember that night? Before you left for King's?"

"Yeah. What about it?"

"Do you think... *Things* would have gone further if we had continued?"

Tate began playing coy, wanting Cathy to say what she was really thinking.

"What do you mean?"

"Like... if we had kept kissing... would we have done more?"

"*Morrreee* what?"

"You know..." Cathy paused. "It?"

Tate raised a brow, acting dubious. "It?"

"You know what I mean."

"Maybe," Tate said, smiling at the idea of what could've been.

Everything happened so fast. Cathy couldn't recall what happened between the words they shared in the driveway and suddenly being naked on her best friend's twin bed. She remembered fragments: their bodies pressing together, the feeling of him becoming a part of her, and each breath they shared. Her heart beat fast as her memories jumped to random events—*playing tag, hide-and-seek, having a family picnic, cops and robbers, both families spending the Fourth of July together*—all memories involving him. The love was intense, and while it was painful for Cathy, she couldn't help but enjoy it.

"I love you," she moaned.

Tate was too focused on the moment to respond. Cathy felt an uncontrollable urge. She begged him to keep going no matter what. This was her second boldest decision, one she would never forget for the rest of her life. This wasn't a one-time ordeal. Their affair continued on a few times until the new year (1998).

When Tate left to return to King's, Cathy was in an odd state. She was pregnant. Initially, she was in the first stage of grief: *denial.* She couldn't believe it—she didn't want to believe it. A teenager like her couldn't hide this forever, and she had no idea what to do.

Her parents didn't take it well at all. They immediately contacted the Clarks' residence (too frustrated to go there in person) to see what was going to happen and if their son knew about their daughter's situation. To the Clarks' surprise, they had no idea, and neither did Tate. What shocked Cathy's parents the most was that the Clarks didn't seem distraught about the idea of having a grandchild. They explained that they had overheard their son say he didn't plan on having kids at all and was likely going to *"end his bloodline,"* whatever that meant to them. The point was—they wanted grandkids, just not *this* soon. It broke their hearts that their son had no plans to bring children into the world.

The Bakers weren't feeling generous. Claiming their *"hands were tied"* and they had "no time" to deal with this, they decided not to support Cathy. They didn't believe in abortions, so they took other measures... they kicked her out. Even when things seem darkest, there's always a light. The Clarks welcomed Cathy with open arms. They were an Albanian family, traditional in their beliefs and family values. Although Cathy was just across the street, she never once saw her family outside their home—no one leaving for work or even going on a grocery run. It was as if they were avoiding her. It was hard, but deep down, she knew she had to move on and embrace her new family. That took time, of course, but knowing the Clarks helped speed up the process.

As the months went on, Mr. Clark always looked after his daughter-in-law. He hoped for a grandson, one who would love photography just like him. While it was fun to talk about what the future held for this child, Cathy was afraid. But she was never alone. When the question came up about the baby's name, Cathy felt honored to announce that she'd be naming him after the man who took her in and had been a second father to her growing up: *Samuel Connie Clark.*

When the day came to bring little Sammy into the world, it bothered her that Tate was nowhere to be seen. Throughout Cathy's pregnancy, Tate had stopped by whenever he could. Sometimes he seemed invested, while other times he shut down, wanting to focus back on school or hanging out with friends. This time, he had to be there. It was a special day. He *had* to be there. Cathy asked Mr. Clark if he had tried calling or if Mrs. Clark knew where Tate had gone the previous night. They were *clueless.* Cathy pushed through until she heard those little cries. From that day on, everything changed. Everyone's lives had changed. A new age had begun. Welcome to the world, *Samuel Connie Clark II.*

Chapter 2
NO BIRTHDAY PARTY THIS YEAR

People often seem to forget about Texas. The only time strangers want to know about it is when they're nearby, watching a western or rural movie, or when it's mentioned in casual conversation. Texas has the best of things—food, culture, lifestyle, and, of course, the people. Some may roll their eyes and scoff in disbelief, but if they were truly open to Texas, they'd see the love people have there.

On this journey, a particular young Texan had stayed up almost all night doing homework and taking pictures of various objects outside his bedroom window. He was a kid among the people of Dallas, Texas. Specifically, Fort Worth.

Click! Click! Click! His Canon AE-1 camera sang.

Click! Click! Click! Three more shots captured.

As the sun rose, cardinals chirped in the mid-November air. Only God knows how great the cold will be, fun and cuddly until it shifts into an icy hell mixed with cabin fever.

The boy taking pictures was Samuel Connie Clark II (mostly known as Sam). He lived in a dingy apartment on the second floor, his rusty door labeled "2B," as apartment signs usually go. He didn't live alone. The other tenant in the home was his mother, Cathy Bakers.

The year was 2015. Today, November 16th, was Sam's 18th birthday. Cathy spent her Monday morning preparing a birthday breakfast for her son. She called it her *"breakfast delight"* – crispy sunny-side-up eggs, hot waffles, and sweet maple bacon, all neatly arranged on a white plate.

Holding back her excitement, she stood ready, surprised that Sam hadn't come out of his room yet. Before heading toward his room, Cathy poured a reasonable amount of medium-pulp orange juice into a narrow glass. She knew he preferred something other than pulp-free juices.

After preparing the meal, she picked up the plate and cup, leaned forward, and knocked on the door with a modest, soft fist.
"Sam? Happy birthday!" she called, entering without much concern for privacy. Luckily, Sam wasn't like other teenagers—he wasn't too particular about locked doors or quiet mumbles, nor did he keep a bottle of lotion and napkins on his nightstand.

Sam hadn't noticed that his mother had walked in. He was too busy taking pictures from his window, trying to improve his shots.
Click! Click! Click! Three more pictures taken. Most of Sam's photos were of birds, buildings, or nice cars passing by. He seemed stuck in a particular position because of his hand

pressing against his lower back—sore but committed. "Happy birthday!" she cheered again.

Sam lowered his camera, the lanyard around his neck pulling it down to rest on his chest. He gave his mother a gentle smile. "Thanks, Mom."

"Also, don't worry," Cathy assured, "The boys are on their way to pick you up. They're just running a bit late."

"I should be fine. I don't think I'll be able to finish the rest of my homework, though," Sam said, looking down at the stack of papers on his dark wooden desk.

Cathy set the plate down beside the stack of late homework. "It's okay. It's still early. Just eat. But finish it right after, okay? I don't need to hear from the school that you're late on it again."

Sam, now feeling hungry, towered over his mother. His attention shifted to the strong scent of the food on the desk, and he ignored the time. He usually found it hard to eat in the morning, often becoming nauseous. This time was different, considering he'd barely slept due to homework and taking pictures. His appetite kicked in.

"So... any plans today?" Cathy asked.

Sam had no immediate response, still tired and barely wiping the crust from his eyes.

"*Sweetie?*" Cathy waved her hand to grab his attention.

"Huh, w-what?"

"Any plans for your special day? Are you going to throw your usual party? Or something different this year?"

Still processing her questions, Sam slowly moved across his bedroom, stacking some other pieces of possibly unfinished homework that lay on top of his unkempt twin bed. "Oh! Um. Yeah, maybe."

"Maybe?" she questioned. "Well, let me know. I know you prefer to wait until you're off work. Just don't tell me at the last minute, okay?" Cathy gave him a quick hug, wrapping her arms around her lanky son before leaving so he could enjoy his meal.

Sam usually threw a little party each year, inviting a few friends. For those who showed up, they'd eat, play games, and relax. He'd kept this tradition for the past six years, knowing that if he skipped the party this year, his friends would be disappointed.

There were two reasons for his final decision. First, there was an upcoming event at work, perfectly timed for Thanksgiving break. Sam worked part-time at a magazine company called *Inferior Times Magazine* as an editor and assistant photographer. They were holding a raffle to pick three photographers to travel to London for a photoshoot and display their work on another popular magazine's cover. Sam was optimistic, but he knew the odds of being chosen were slim.

The second reason for not hosting the party was that he and his mother needed to catch up on bills. They had recently been late twice on their light and water bills, although they'd just managed to pay them off. They couldn't afford to be late again. Groceries were tight, so most of their meals consisted of old sandwiches, snacks, or fast food. Their situation was different from most families around them.

It had been just Cathy and Sam against the world. Cathy and Sam, the dynamite duo. Sam's father, Tate, wasn't in the picture, and Sam didn't know him. Though curious about his father, he refrained from asking. Cathy had planted a story in his head, telling him she left Tate when Sam was three and that things simply didn't work out. She said Tate lived elsewhere because of work. But in the back of Sam's mind, resentment lingered. For a hormonal teenager, that sense of frustration only grew, as he struggled to understand why she had left him. Yet, he never pressed for more.

Cathy and Sam had lived in Apartment 2B for the last 13 years. When Sam turned 16, he felt it was time to pull his own weight regarding essentials like food, electricity, water, transportation, and occasionally, luxuries.

After thinking it over, Sam was confident about his decision.

No birthday party this year...

After breakfast, Sam stuffed all his paperwork into his dark gray backpack. He was a busy boy, often that one kid in class who always turned in homework late (not intentionally, of course). Between multiple projects for work and seven classes—Science, English, Geometry, History, you name it—he had his hands full. Some assignments were for extra credit, as he hoped to get into a good school like *A&M* or somewhere in Dallas. However, his chances were waning, considering the last thing a school wanted was a student who always turned in work late. In a final, frantic effort, Sam tried finishing his history project before class. It wasn't a good look... and to make matters worse, the project was already three days overdue.

Getting dressed for school, Sam quickly brushed his dark brown, wavy hair into a messy pompadour and slipped on a rugged white t-shirt that was fading into a stale color. The outfit included brown corduroy pants, along with a pair of classic Chuck Taylors. Something was wrong—something was missing. Sam took note of what was important.

I got my clothes. My homework. My backpack is hanging on the doorknob, and—oh!

He reached his long fingers into the drawer in his small desk, clutching some oversized silver aviator glasses that glided effortlessly onto his thin face. They sat crooked in front of his cinnamon eyes, with one leg lifted slightly above his ear, and a thin crack sweeping over the left lens.

On the way out, Sam snatched his old black-and-white film camera from the top side of his desk and stood by the front door to grab his olive green windbreaker off the coat rack.

HONK! HONK! Blared a beefy truck horn.

It was a usual routine, like a catchy song Sam had memorized every beat and bump of.

"Bye, Mom!" he shouted, locking the front door with the spare key Cathy kept hidden in a flowerpot in the balcony's corner. From there, he spotted the red truck his best friends were in. The balcony was attached to a long set of stairs that hovered above Apartment 2A. Sam slid down the rusty metal railing, letting gravity carry him down the stairs.

"Woo!" he cheered, sticking the landing at the last second.

Once again, the truck blared: HONK! HONK!

"Yeah, I see you!" Sam adjusted his glasses, glancing over at his friends, the Sings brothers, Trevor and Garrett. Goofy twins, now the same age as Sam, the three had been best friends since third grade. Together, they were as thick as thieves and as funny as classroom clowns (even though Sam wasn't the funniest of the trio). It was the only time Sam felt he could be a little comedian.

Although the twins hardly looked similar, they shared the same traits, some similar mannerisms, and obviously the same parents. It wasn't difficult to tell the difference between the two.

Trevor had a square face and a stocky body, with short, combed, neutral brown hair and a natural cattleman cowboy hat. He always wore various colors of flannels, boot-cut jeans, and umber brown boots. Trevor was a couple of inches shorter than his brother, had a lighter shade of blue in his eyes, and three beauty spots on his face.

Garrett, the 14-minute-younger brother (sometimes called *"Gar"* for short), had a round face and was chunky (mostly muscle over his fat). His eyes were a darker shade of blue, and his face had no spots. He wore his hair long, dropping to his shoulders, and, like Trevor, always wore a hat, though his style was caps—any type of cap was his signature look. From trucker caps to baseball caps or snapbacks, Garrett wore them backwards, forwards, or sideways, just to be silly. He also sported random zip-up jackets and hoodies in various colors, along with the same boot-cut jeans and boots.

Sam climbed into the truck—a vintage beauty, a Candy Apple Red 1970 Ford F-150. Anyone could bet the twins worked their butts off day and night, blowing every penny into restoring that gorgeous beast. The truck was the boys' most prized possession, and they'd flip if someone else even drove it, let alone wrecked it. Only Trevor or Garrett could get her up and running. Sometimes they took turns driving to both school and work, and other times they'd flip a coin to keep things fair.

Besides the truck, Sam's mind returned to his plan: school, then work. To him, it was just another day in paradise. Nothing new. What made things easier for Sam was that the twins also worked at Inferior, all in the same editing department. Rarely did their schedules get tangled up over who had to go to work first or who had to pick up whom. Sam desperately needed a car, but he lacked a license and experience behind the wheel.

The boys looked out for each other. Every Friday after work was payday, and every two weeks, Sam would take money out of his bank account and give both friends $20 each. It wasn't just for gas money, but also a big *thank you*. That was one of Sam's most respected traits—the twins admired his mindfulness and caring nature. Sometimes they'd reject his money, but they eventually gave up, as Sam would just hide the dollar bills in their truck.

Inside, Sam took the middle seat, trying to get comfortable on the black bench. Most of the time, he leaned against Trevor, mainly to annoy his personal space. Garrett was driving this time, heading straight to school.

West-Made High. Home of the Falcons. During the 15-minute drive to one of their least favorite places, Trevor pulled out a fresh pack of minty menthol cigarettes.

"Here, Sam," Garrett smirked, passing him a matte black Zippo lighter. Trevor handed Sam a cigarette.

"Happy Birthday!" both the twins cheered, lighting up their white sticks one by one, spark by spark, and inhaling the sweet taste of nicotine at almost eight in the morning.

"Thanks, guys," Sam grinned, inhaling deeply.

Trevor brought up some news, his tone eager. "Did you guys hear what Inferior said this morning?"

"Huh? What?" Sam squinted. "What about?"

Trevor explained, pulling out his phone to show an email. "Inferior announced they're doing the raffle early and will announce the winners at work today."

"Really!?" Sam exclaimed. "Like—you're not messing with me?"

"No, they just announced it a couple of hours ago."

"Imagine if we all won the raffle," Garrett chuckled, still driving.

"I know," Trevor replied. "That would be so cool."

As Sam reached into his narrow pocket to pull out his cracked phone and view the email, Garrett brought up something he'd been thinking about since he'd wished him happy birthday.

"Hey! So—the usual birthday thing this year? What do you say? Our place? Your place? What's the plan?" Garrett continued in his thick Southern accent. "I got some stuff I could bring over and set up. Whaddya say?"

The email distracted Sam, so he barely listened to Garrett's question. "Eh. I'll just finish it up later. Whatever you say."

"Huh? What?" Garrett looked over, momentarily distracted from the road.

"The birthday party!" Trevor emphasized.

Sam looked away, not knowing how to break the news without sounding like the bad guy. "Well... I don't think... there's no birthday party—"

Garrett slammed on the brakes, nearly sending them all flying from the bench. Trevor tightened his seatbelt, forced back into the leathery seat. Garrett pressed his foot back on the gas before they caused an accident on the freeway.

"Bro! What the hell was that?!" Trevor shouted, then turned to Sam. "And what did you just say?"

"I can explain..."

"Please."

"This year's been hectic. I don't mean to make excuses, but I'm busy with work. I have to put in more hours to pay for the electricity and water. Mom hasn't been able to work overtime lately, and I need to help her out. Plus, I need to get back on track with all the homework piling up. We're almost at the end of the semester."

Silence fell over them, until finally Garrett spoke. "No, I understand, man," he said. "You're busy, and you need to help your mom. I get it."

"Yeah," Trevor added, his tone annoyed.

Garrett was understanding, kind, and hopeful. He knew when to cut off a joke and when to keep it going. Trevor was also kind and loyal, though a bit pessimistic. He'd always have Sam's back.

"Whatever," Trevor grumbled.

"Maybe next year," Sam said, though he internally felt guilty despite the smile he forced.

Trevor looked away, craving another cigarette. Garrett gave his brother a look, silently telling him to let it go.

"You know everyone at our table isn't gonna like it when I tell them you canceled, right?" Trevor added.

"I know..."

Chapter 3
FULTON'S STORY

The local gas station on Main Street was lit up. An elderly man (who happened to be the owner) raised his hands above his head, quivering with fear at the sound of a deep voice yelling, *"GIVE ME EVERYTHING IN THE REGISTER! NOW!"*

In front of the owner was a robber, a man wearing a camo-green balaclava and a black hoodie, pointing a *Glock-19* right in between his eyes. *"HURRY UP!"* The robber pointed the firearm so close to the old man's face that he could smell the gun polish. Carefully, he opened the register and emptied everything. Even with a description from the police, it was hard to point out any physical attributes of the gunman other than the mocha skin color around his desert brown eyes and wide lips from the holes in the mask. The robber wasn't alone. Behind him was another goon, a female by the look of her slim body and posture. She, too, wore a ski mask, but instead of her partner's green cover-up, she wore a black one with an airsoft face cover with goggles on-top, along with an orange puff jacket. The woman stood by the door, ensuring no one was coming in or out. If they did the math right, the cops wouldn't show up for 10 minutes. They'd make it home with no troubles.

"Here's the m-m-money. P-please, don't shoot." The cashier's voice shook as he handed about 270 dollars to the gunman.

"Okay, let's go!" The two ran out of the store with no eyewitnesses hanging around. They ran around the store and into a black van with orange trim on the side skirts, rear bumper, and front. It was a company van with a logo and title printed beside it, *Summit Peaks Industries.*

"Go, go, go!" The female voice shouted, the other pressing his foot on the gas and hauling ass into the city to blend in with the crowd of cars.

The man in the camo mask was *Fulton Rockefeller Bruning.* (Some refer to him as Fult.) In the passenger seat, the accomplice was *Georgia Fezz*, but she simply went by *Jo.*

"Did we make it?" Jo asked, throwing the mask off to reveal her slender face and big green eyes. Her fair skin was sweating through her jacket from all the adrenaline. She fixed up her golden-blonde hair and acted as normal as possible. She believed they had made it with no problems. So far, no sirens have been wailing within Downtown Dallas.

"I guess so," Fulton answered.

Fulton's story was like Sam's. They had key differences, of course- but one *big* difference between them was that Fulton was a bit of a momma's boy. Over the years, he grew a robust and clingy bond with her, eventually becoming protective of her.

At seven, Fulton had to grow with the weight of the world on his shoulders. Being seven that year was something Fulton could never forget. That was the age when he lost his father to a stroke. It left him feeling down. Pushing his emotions in a direction that led him to his mom, *Donna Bruning* (*Ma*, as he'd call her). Together, they grew distraught, hopeless, borderline homeless, and with no doubt, it wasn't all fun and games. Donna had to get her act together and put all her time and energy into supporting her only child. She pushed on and on until her son came of age to put in his own efforts. By the time he reached 13, Fulton had to learn how to take responsibility. He made his own food, getting to school on time, and selling his own things just to earn a few bucks. This kept on until he turned 15. From there, Fulton got a job delivering newspapers to local neighborhoods. He'd wake up at four in the morning, bright and early, and prepare his rounds to whatever streets he had to deliver the papers to.

At 16, he finally saved enough money to afford his first car (an old, salvaged hatchback.) Throughout the year, he continued to save, able to fix the transmission and afford new tires for the hopeless heap to keep it running. He drove back and forth to school and would often help take his mother to work when her own vehicle wouldn't work. This continued until he graduated high school the day after his 17th birthday. His graduation gift was a custom-made letterman jacket from his Mother. It was all black with black and white stitched patterns on the neck, wrist, and waistline, along with a patch of his first initial stitched on the chest. He practically never took it off, even in his adult years. Fulton's track record was outstanding. Awarded with a scholarship to the University of Dallas, pulling all-nighters, summer classes, quick wit, and ambition. Before he knew it, he graduated with his Masters in Engineering. He saved himself the eight years, getting shit done in six.

Fresh out of school, he returned home and searched for jobs matching his education and experience. He found little work once he turned 24.

A couple of years later, Fulton had landed on Summit Peaks Industries through an ad in the newspaper. The company was founded in 1950 in Tokyo, Japan, and soon expanded all over the globe. It established most of Dallas' foundations, from stores to estates, restaurants, air conditioners, and even smoke alarms. With all that sounding like music to the man's naked ears, he applied for the job immediately when he saw that the company worked with engineers. Fulton hoped he could fill in any gaps for wanted workers. It is sad to say that they only needed people willing to perform tasks in the Warehousing Department. Although it wasn't much, Fulton had hoped to move up within the job.

During his time there, he started waking up two hours early before his shift, waking up at five in the morning to prepare himself for the day before proceeding to the loading area. He started the job by slapping delivery labels on the packages flowing through the workbenches. Soon, he was scanning products and tracking orders on the racks in the aisles. It was nothing but easy money and honest work.

A year after working in the warehouse, he signed off on an apartment just a few minutes away from work. Fulton also put down a loan for a pre-owned vehicle (a 2010 Toyota sedan). It was smooth sailing for the rest of that year.

Following up, his Mother fell into a depression. She felt nothing but loneliness in her empty home. When Fulton found out, he offered her to stay with him, but she rejected it. Donna told her son that living with him in his small apartment made her feel claustrophobic. When Fulton heard those words, he worked over 40 hours a week to make his Mother feel anything but depressed. He went from day to night, from dawn to dusk. All that hard work paid off. He could sign off on a vast apartment complex, a calm two-bedroom and bathroom. Something adequate but not so small.

Ever since Fulton was young, he carried a certain mentality regarding hard work. A pair of words that stood by his heart intrigued him. *One day.*

He believed that *one day* he'll have a lot of money, give his mom a good life, and be successful. All he could say was, *"One day."*

Now at the prime age of 35, Fulton saved up a handsome amount of money. Hundreds of thousands of dollars, buying an expensive condo on the top floor with his mom, treating her to glorious meals and delights from the work he put in. Most recently, Fulton made it to the manager position in the warehouse, forgetting all about his desired position in the beginning. Fulton focused on moving forward with where he was at. There was no more struggling, no more scraping by life.

What people didn't know was that there was a lot more left in the dark with Fulton, and deep down, he knew if people found out how he'd make his easy money, he'd be an outcast. Fast money causes fast problems. The only problem was that it was harder for him to stop doing these specific things- but Jo convinced him to continue what he does... *robberies.*

Speaking of Jo, not much could be said about that woman (From Fulton's perspective). There were rumors here and there about how she came from an abusive family or that she was born in a mental institution. The list of stories continued, but she didn't care. But if they really knew the truth. They wouldn't dare speak about her or her little tendencies. (Quite the mystery with *that* one.) She's unpredictable. She is so quiet and mischievous that it seems she could snap at any moment. The only thing people knew for sure about Jo was that she loved *fire.*

Back home in the Condo on McKinnon Street. Fulton's body became riddled with chills. The inside was much colder than the air outside. Quickly, he shoved his only available hand into the pockets of his sentimental jacket. From a stranger's point of view, the jacket looked small on him. He still clung to that thing like a child. Donna once tried to convince him to throw his old jacket away, but Fulton got defensive. His attachment grew as he aged, and throwing the jacket away was out of the question. Fulton tried to stay warm. His other hand was carrying a bag of late breakfast from a retro-themed restaurant a few blocks away: *Doe's Diner*. He got two orders to-go for himself and his Mother.

The whole condominium building was grand, luxurious, and sleek, with silver and sky-blue windows. It went up about 30 stories. On his floor (Level 25) was his nosy neighbor waiting for him. *Gloria Glenn*. She and Fulton met about a year ago. Gloria was eager to meet her new neighbors the moment she saw stacks of boxes coming through the hallway. She kept looking through her peephole, hoping to get a glimpse of the newbie. When her eyeball caught sight of the man, she was amazed by how handsome he was.

She thought. *I have to meet this guy.*

As Gloria watched him walk closer, she stood straight and greeted him kindly, "Hey, Fulton! How's your day?"

"Wassup, Glenn. Can't complain. Just another day. Also, were you waitin' on me?" he raised, grabbing his keys to unlock his front door. She rolled her eyes and pointed her short index finger with long, white fingernails at the silver elevators a few feet to her left. "Noisy elevator. I can hear you coming a mile away."

Fulton scoffed, still trying to grab hold of his key.

Gloria's voice shifted into a concerned tone. "How's Donna? Her cough sounded bad last night."

"You heard that too?"

Gloria slowly nodded, not leaving her eyes off her neighbor.

"She's feelin' better... at least, I think. I might take her to the Doctor or somethin'. I don't know yet."

"Well. Lemme' know."

As Fulton entered, he locked the door behind him and called out to his Mother.

"Ma! I'm home. I brought breakfast!"

The room sparked colors of bright white, cold and clean floors, and high countertops. The interior design was laid out like an architectural home. The designers plastered art onto the blank walls. They even had a glass balcony.

When Donna was offered to live with her son, she declined. She wanted to see her boy succeed and move forward rather than have her son have someone to worry about. He gave her little to no choice. Providing for her the better life he dreamed of.

"Ma?" He called out again. There was no such response that squealed from the parent, leading Fulton to see where she was. He checked the kitchen. Empty. Now, moving along to the guest bedroom- nobody. Finally, he studied her bedroom, the main suite of the wondrous home. There she lay. Tired and looking sick in her blank, queen-sized bed. Donna coughed like a broken generator. A mushy gurgle followed every cough.

"Damn. Ma? Do you think I should take you to the Doctor this week?"

Donna looked up and groaned, "Oh, hush now, boy! I'm fine. I don't need a damn Doc."

He raised a brow, staring her dead in the face for reassurance that she was okay.

"It's just a small cough, Fuller. It's nothing."

His body cringed at that name. He hated being called that. The only time he was referred to as *Fuller* was when his mother was angry with him.

"Ma! I'd rather be called by my whole name. That'd suffice!"

"Honey, I don't have the time nor the patience to yell out your full name just to get my damn food here," she sassed. "Now. Can you please bring me my food?"

Fulton shook his head. "Ma, you gotta *try* to get out of bed today."

She laughed, not wanting to move an inch off her comfortable palace. On some occasions, she wouldn't move from the bed for a week straight, other than washing up in the mornings, "Did you or did you not get my food?"

"Nah. I didn't," he replied as his voice shook, scrunching his nose, "Are you sure you're okay?"

"Well, if I'm being honest here… you're right. I'm not well. I feel so lightheaded and weak whenever I walk out of this bed. My stomach feels so empty…"

"Why didn't you tell me?"

Donna closed her eyes, wanting to avoid the topic of conversation. Fulton attempted to bring the conversation right back.

"Tell me, and I'll get ya' your food. Please?"

His Mother shrugged, "I'm just scared of what it could be. I've never been sick like this before. I'm already old, so hell– *everything scares* me."

He chuckled at the sound of her emphasis, looking off into space, hoping she'd stay on topic for a while longer.

"WELP! I'm taking you to the Docs tomorrow. I don't need you feeling like shit–"

"Language." she interrupted, then gave him a limp thumbs up regarding the previous comment. "Now. Where's my food?"

Fulton rolled his eyes, walking over to his kitchen and grabbing the bag of food.

"I hope you feel better," he told her, carefully handing her the plastic container full of scrambled eggs, bacon, and hash browns.

"I hope so, too."

Leaving the room, Fulton went to his office space and sat in front of his glass desk, reviewing some reports he meant to sign off. His desert eyes looked through the inked letters, catching on that there were essential products stored within the warehousing units that needed to be put out for delivery during the next couple of weeks. Since Fulton was the new warehouse manager for Summit Peaks, he'd needed to put in many more hours than he expected.

"Hey, Ma!?" he called out.

"Yeah!?"

"I'm going back to doing overtime at work. Possibly even more! I'll leave ya some money for food and other shit tomorrow. Is that good?!"

"Again! Watch it with the language!" she warned.

Fulton paused, "So is that a *yes* or–"

"Yes!"

He continued to peek through the reports, not missing a single grammar remark, seeing over any additional information and details for the shipments.

Delivery Time: One/Two–Day Delivery.

Secured Containments.

Shipment MUST arrive on time.

High Urgency.

The products being shipped out were mainly furniture, tools, parts, electronics, etc. It was all part of the job. Fulton almost considered looking back into the engineering department for a split second. Alas, it was too late to back out with how far he'd come.

He returned to his mother's room and explained more about the hours at Summit Peaks. "I'm sorry I'm not home as often as you'd like. Ma. Work has been a drag, and I'm just tryin' to get by now."

"Son, you don't have to worry about gettin' by. You're already there," she said with a welcoming smile as she placed a hand on his warm cheek and trimmed beard, "What's there to stress about?"

"It's work... it's all this work, and then the hours I'm puttin' in, along with you feelin' sick and all the stuff I've been doing–"

"Hold on, hold on, hold on," she said abruptly. "You're *fine*. No one's making you do overtime. And don't worry about me. I'll be alright."

"Yeah... I guess."

"Also, what have you been doing?" She questioned.

Before Fulton could answer, he shook it off, "N–nothing." His voice was shaking, and his nose was scrunching again.

"Fuller. You know damn well I could tell when you're lyin'." Donna turned sternly, folding her arms.

"How?"

"Wait." She paused, turning to a sarcastic tone. "How? How old are you again? I've wiped your ass for 5 years, fed and took care of you, and you don't think I can't see you scrunch your nose and hear that voice shake every single time?"

He looked away, feeling the guilt seep in, not just from lying but lying to his Mother, the last bit of family he had left.

"I'm sorry, ma."

"If there's something you want to talk to me about, I'm right here."

"It's nothin'."

"Well, alright then. But whatever is done in the dark can always be brought into the light."

"*Ma!*"

"I'm just sayin'. I love you, Fuller."

"Love you too."

Chapter 4
WEST MADE HIGH

West Made High was an ordinary school. Home of the Falcons and stress-inducing schoolwork, tense environments, and aggressive faculty. Only a few teachers could have a docile attitude among their peers. From the outside, the school looked beautiful. The red bricks along the exterior made it feel comfortable, along with the white frames that stood out more than their royal blue and gray pride colors.

It was almost time for dismissal. Sam felt relief creeping over him as he didn't have to be as nervous anymore. Nothing abnormal, of course- he was just another scared kid around other scared kids. The only difference was that they were better at pretending to be confident, faking about putting on a social act rather than showing off an anti-social act.

Get it together. It's just school. He thought to himself.

His last class was basically a free period. It was audio and video production with Mrs. Smith. Sam was the only student in that room that was top of the class. He already had experience in photography, videography, and editing, so this was nothing new. Of course, many strangers around him would call him a know-it-all or a teacher's bitch because his intellect thoroughly impressed Mrs. Smith on the topics. Sam didn't let those comments get to him. He'd get most of his pain from Felix Rade. The school's neighborhood is an all-star football player. Also known from time to time as *Sam's second asshole.*

Felix was the stereotypical jock you'd seen in the movies. You know- the ones that play hard (possibly a roid freak) and always wear their letterman even when it's hot outside or during inappropriate occasions. Felix wouldn't always wear his blue and silver-gray team jacket. Sometimes, he'd wear a plain jacket or a hoodie from a local store. Felix had almost every athlete's usual short, slicked-up haircut. He usually wore baggy jeans and the newest shoes every sneaker enthusiast wanted. Felix had always been on Sam's case from the second semester of their freshman year to their current senior year.

At first, the rivalry started with a small comment or two, with mean names such as Loser, weirdo, and freak- soon he pumped up the name-calling to ten: Dick, bitch, fag, and eventually moved up to rumors and little white lies. Now, it was at a bigger stage... Physical attacks. Those were minor but would sometimes leave Sam easily bruised or scraped.

Fortunately, Sam knew the problem but didn't have the confidence to confront Felix about it. He knew he felt threatened by Sam's intellect. The bully also felt offended by his relationship with Mrs. Smith. It was all personal for Felix because Mrs. Smith was his second cousin. The bully felt threatened that a total stranger had a stronger connection with his family than his own. In his mind, he wanted to be liked by everyone. He needed to be. It didn't matter if they were strangers or family. He just needed to be liked and respected, and the ones that didn't were only maggots to him.

Before the bell rang for dismissal, Sam was putting a new lens on his AE-1 camera that his friend Alexus Rich Sands got as his birthday present. It barely fit, but it wasn't a problem as long as it did its job. Sam aimed it steadily at Mrs. Smith and called out to her from his desk in the corner.

"Hey, Mrs. Smith!"

Her head turned urgently, not realizing a camera was being pointed at her face until Sam yelled, "Say cheese!"

She threw an awkward smile and let him take the shot. *CLICK!*

Sam looked at his new lens one more time, admiring it. *Thank you, Alexus.*

Alexus Rich Sands was the chill, artsy girl in his friend group. What was unique about her is that her looks were deceiving. Mostly because her voice didn't really match her appearance; her carmine-red hair and fair skin looked marvelous in the sunlight. Her outfits were cute yet straightforward, and she looked like someone you could just pinch their cheeks like one's grandmother would do to their grandchild. She's ambitious and as caring as Sam's Mother; she'd never give up on him. As for her voice, she mostly sounded as if she were more southern rather than northern. Heavier than Garrett's accent.

BEEEEP-BEEEEP! BEEEEP-BEEEEP! School finished for the day. Sam waited on the concrete stair-steps in front of the entrance. He'd usually wait around five minutes until the twins could pull their truck around.

Trevor met up with his friend, informing him that Garrett couldn't make it to work today because of football practice.

"It's just me and you today," said Trevor.

"Oh." Sam hoped the tone didn't sound disappointed. He cherished the twins equally. Even if a gun was pointed at the back of his heading to tell him to choose, he wouldn't. He accepted them both as they were.

"Wait-" Trevor paused, "Sonny wants to talk to me about an upcoming internship he wants to do. I'm gonna talk to him real quick before we head out."

"Alright. That's fine, man."

Sonny Marcos was a foreign exchange student from Bogota, Columbia. He moved to Dallas in 2014 and plans to graduate with Sam and his friends by the summer. Since his accent was so thick and hard to understand, Sonny sometimes needed to work on talking. (It might be a speech impediment of some type.)

Sam spotted a familiar face leaving school. He squinted through his worn-out aviators and could finally see. Alexus Sands was walking by. Sam waved his arms up to see if she could notice him, waving on until he figured she couldn't see him with her head low to the ground.

Is she upset? He thought, glancing at her again, hoping to see her face.

As she continued to walk, his head followed her movement. She was near Felix Rade. Sam's body tensed, praying Alexus wasn't in Sam's similar situation. When she passed him, Felix spun around and strutted beside her, poking at her and tugging at the ends of her red hair. Sam stood up, carrying his backpack and camera, rushing to her.

"Hey!" the boy screamed, trying to call Felix's attention over. Sam threw off his backpack and camera, sprinting towards him.

"Whatcha up to, Freak?" said Felix, still tugging on the poor girl's hair, "Aren't you that wannabe cowgirl? Right? Don't you live on that weird farm of yours? Do you ever pick up horse shit? Or just dog shit?" Felix gave Alexus a slight shove on her shoulder, further belittling her.

Alexus raised her arm up and backhanded the douche. As the hand met face, it stung with a painful vibration. Her hand was now numb, throbbing away in pain.

"Leave me alone!" she snapped. Felix's face turned red, not just from the slap but from the embarrassment and stares from his peers. Suddenly, a push from behind shoved his frame forward, inspired by Sam. The shove had little to no effect on the bully, and with a quick, bold thrust from Felix's fist, he knocked Sam's head into the rigid sidewalk. Students were shocked and moved in to get a closer look at the fight.

One kid shouted, "Beat his ass, Felix!"

"Kill that nerd!" another yelled.

Felix pulled Sam up by his collar, teasing him, "What are you? Her boyfriend?! Hahaha! You're such a faggot, Clark!" One more punch was thrown into Sam's jaw, nearly knocking him out. Before another cross, Trevor pulled up to the sidewalk in the red dame truck, stomping on the brakes, screeching the rear tires as loud as possible. This alerted Felix, causing him to back away. He knew one twin was strong, so he imagined how much stronger the brothers were together. In his mind, he hoped Garrett wasn't around.

Trevor ran out of the truck and picked Sam up, removing him from the crowd so he could feel less embarrassed or ashamed of what he had tried to do.

Sam's stomach was in knots, and his body shook from the rush of adrenaline mixed with a dash of anxiety. He felt like he was going to throw up. He stood hunched over, leaning against the red dame and facing away from any crowds. Trevor threw his hat off with such anger, walking briskly towards Felix and grabbing him by the letterman, also grabbing Felix's chest skin, too, ready to start another bout.

"Hey- hey- hey- hey- he started it!" Felix stuttered in fear, flinching from the punch Trevor was about to throw until Mrs. Smith came outside and shouted, *"Hey! What is going on?!"* Trevor immediately let him go and explained his story before Felix could play the victim. "The prick was fighting Sam. I stepped in. That's it."

Mrs. Smith didn't have to question it. She knew her cousin and how much he terrorized Sam, as much as Felix deserved after all these years. It doesn't mean anyone can hurt him and get away with it.

"Felix! Trevor! Come with me to the principal's office. Now!"

Sam, who had a slight limp, walked over to Mrs. Smith, ready to defend his best friend.

"Mrs. Smith! Trev didn't do anything. It wasn't his fault."

"He was about to hit me!" Felix yelled in a whiny tone.

Mrs. Smith turned to Sam. "Is any of this true, Clark?"

Sam looked down at the floor for a second, mumbling, "Nothing happened. Trevor did nothing. Can we all just go home?"

Mrs. Smith sighed in annoyance. "Sam, I can see the side of your cheek swelling... Do you need to see the nurse?"

"No. I'm fine."

"Then I'll ask again. Is whatever Trevor said true?"

Sam paused for a moment, then nodded profusely. Feeling both guilt and embarrassment.

Mrs. Smith folded her arms and turned to the two. "Like I said. Both of you go to the office. Now!"

As Felix walked away, he spotted Sam's bag and gave it a kick. A sound of glass breaking alerted the poor boy with the swollen face.

Alexus followed Sam as he went to retrieve his bag and patted him on the shoulder.

"Thank you, Sam."

"Welcome," he grunted.

"Are you okay?"

"My jaw is a bit swollen, but- I think I'll be fine."

"A black eye might be forming." She spotted.

"Shit..." Sam exhaled. It was going to be a long night of phone calls to the school and parents for Cathy.

"It'll be fine," Alexus cheered optimistically. "Just put some ice on it. Here- I think I have an ice gel in my lunch bag."

Sam clarified, "No... it's not that. Felix kicked the lense you got me... it's broken."

"Don't worry about that. It's fine, Sam," Alexus grabbed her ice pack and gently put it on Sam's cheek, "It's kinda melted, but I think it'll help."

"Thanks."

"You know- you don't have to save me, Sam. I appreciate it. I really do. But Felix isn't a bother to me."

"I know… I just wanted to help."

Alexus messed with his hair, hoping to bug him out of his sad mood, "Next time. Don't be a hero. I'm okay. Thank you."

A few minutes later, Trevor came out with a grin on his face. He seemed to be vindicated. Before Sam took off to work, Alexus put the ice pack back in her bag, leaned in gave the boy a hug, and whispered in his ear. "Happy Birthday."

During the ride, Sam was quiet for most of the time. Trevor couldn't figure out if he was quiet because of the pain in his face or if it was from the humiliation.

"Sam?" Trevor called out, patting his back. "You okay?"

"I'm fine."

"So- What happened exactly?"

"I tried to say hi to Alexus. She ran into Felix. He was bothering her- I guess you can fill in the rest."

"Oh. Um..." Trevor wasn't sure what to say next. It was awkward- how would one respond to something like that? Trevor wanted to say sorry, but what would there be to apologize for? He did nothing wrong. Was he sorry because his friend got his ass beat? Sorry for not helping sooner? Sorry, out of pity? Empathy? The questions were endless. For the rest of the drive, it remained silent.

Things would've for sure been worse if Garrett wasn't at practice. He would've beaten the shit out of Felix with no remorse. Sam didn't want to think about it anymore.

"Let me know if he bothers you again. Okay?" Asked Trevor. Sam was paying attention to that last remark. He was stuck in thought about Alexus's words.

"You don't have to save me, Sam."

I wish I could. The boy thought.

There's nothing a good, late breakfast can't fix. Trevor took a short detour to Doe's Diner. It was the trio's spot. Most days, they'd be lucky to get a booth. Specifically, their booth. It was in the middle on the left side wall. The reason was because that specific seating area had the most expansive window with a decent view of Downtown Dallas' city skyline.

It was a retro themed diner. An old, timely place that carried an essence of the '50s. The only thing missing was some preppy cheerleaders and greasers. Even the staff's uniforms looked vintage, covered in pastel colors. The whitest pants on the men and the pinkest skirts on the women.

Outside, Doe's had a large L.E.D. sign on top that glowed bright red, almost impossible to miss. A diner that was truly immersive. Customers really felt like they were being brought right into the old days. The only touch of modernity within was their registers. Obviously, most people carried cards rather than cash and pennies.

Inside, the two high schoolers took a load off in the red and white striped, cushioned seats, waiting until their favorite waitress arrived at the table to take their orders- not that she needed to anyway- Mrs. Buffers was already familiar with the boys. She was so close to them she memorized their full names, birthdays, and work schedules.

"Hello, Kids! I Haven't seen y'all in a week. I usually see y'all boys every couple of days. What's up?" To her, not seeing the teenagers meant something was wrong, or they were up to mischief, and other times, they didn't crave Doe's.

Mrs. Buffers had a heavy southern accent and was chunky, with a belly more prominent than her breasts and her dirty blonde hair was shifting to gray. She was close to retiring and saying hello to her vacation time with her husband. The boys would never see her outside the diner, meaning they'd only recognize her when she was sporting her white and pastel pink uniform.

"Not much, Mrs. B. We're just busy with work and shit," said Trevor.

"Ha! Honey, it will get increasingly busy from here on out. Don't worry! It'll get easier."

Looking over the colorful menu, Sam sighed, "That's reassuring."

"Gar is at practice?" She asked the remaining clone.

"Yes, ma'am."

"Knew it." She cracked a smile and turned her attention back to Sam, who was glossing over the food items.

"Hey! Whatcha lookin' at the menu for, boy? I already know what you're going to order!" Mrs. Buffers grabbed the menus off the table with her thick, white hands, clicked her plastic pen, and wrote their orders down on a little yellow notebook.

Sam felt offended, smiling. "Excuse me? How do you know I won't order something else this time, ma'am?"

"Well, are you?" she put.

"Can I see the menu?"

Mrs. Buffers rolled her eyes, sliding one on the flat, smooth, white table. She was almost convinced one of them would get something different this time.

"Umm– No. Just kidding! I'll have my usual, please."

Mrs. B took it back, her hand resting on her wide hip, "Chicken and waffles with chocolate milk. I already wrote it down. You almost had me, though."

Mrs. Buffers turned her attention across the booth, sarcastically asking what the twin was craving. "What about you? New? Or the usual?"

"Same thing as always– except– instead of coffee, can I get orange juice? No pulp."

"Yes, sir. One short stack with eggs and bacon. I'll be back with y'all's meals soon. Relax now, sweet peas." Mrs. B trailed off to the kitchen with a pep in her step.

"Ew, no pulp?!" Sam gagged.

"What's with you and the pulp in O.J.?"

"It's just liquid sugar,"

The clone pointed out the hypocrisy, "How's the chocolate milk, then?"

He snorted and pushed the thought aside as he watched Sam get lost in the view outside. Trevor was glad to see his friend shrug off the feelings he endured moments before going to Doe's.

Chapter 5
INFERIOR

After the late breakfast, it was time for work. Just a short ten-minute drive from the diner. Depending on the area, Dallas has the most convenient spots. Retail stores, hospitals, clothing shops, you name it. It was easy to get around (unless you were in the middle of rush hour.)

Trevor parked on the side of the building. It was narrow, but the parking wasn't for everybody.

Employee's Only! The sign stated.

About four months ago, the twins got their truck towed for not having the company's sticker on their front windshield. Trevor was so pissed that day that his face looked like he was gonna pop a blood vessel.

Sam looked up at the building. It was almost time to watch their logo light up. A white L.E.D. sign with its initials, *I.T.M.* (Inferior-Times Magazine.)

"Wow," Sam whispered, taking another glance.

"Yeah," Trevor agreed, "Speaking of which- what if Ellie is there, huh?!"

Sam's mouth opened a little gap, not wanting to deal with the jokes and theories again. "Shut up, man."

"Come on! It makes sense. Ms. Ellie *Juniperrr*!" he teased.

"Shut up!"

Ellie Juniper was one of the top models for Inferior. She hailed from France, migrating to America when she was 21. At 18, her growth spurt got a crazed amount of attention as her beauty was unmatched. Her heavy accent and dreamy moon-colored eyes were a sight for sore eyes, and her voice was a beauteous ring for the ears.

Soon, she wanted to get deeper into modeling, and the offers and contracts came in. Not just making *her*- but also her parents wealthy. They became millionaires within a couple of years. It was unlikely that she would be at Inferior. She's never had the time of day to settle down, constantly traveling to Europe, Australia, Brazil, and other exotic countries.

Inferior wanted her. And since she'd be the company's bedrock, they made a generous amount to sign off on. Nobody knows how much. Only left to the imagination. Eventually, they pulled her into the pages of the magazines at 27. Since then, Sam has been one of the few photographers she has been allowed to take pictures of (at least in America). The Twins gave poor Sam so much shit about it. Kept on hinting that she might have a crush on the boy. Or maybe he had a crush on her.

"Just because I sometimes take pictures of her whenever she comes by doesn't mean she likes me. That doesn't make any sense," explained Sam.

"Yeah, but rumor has it she only lets *you* take pictures of her."

"Repeat that word again," Sam demanded.

"What?"

"*Rumor.*Meaning hearsay. Meaning that it's possibly *not true.*"

Trevor shrugged, teasing his friend still. "*Possibly.*"

The twin quickly changed the topic, pointing out Sam's forgetfulness. "Hey! Make sure you get your phone. This is the fourth time you've left in the truck."

"It's not the fourth... It's like the second."

Trevor groaned, explaining all the times that led up to number four. "Also, put in a passcode. Last time I couldn't stop Garrett from making a whole picture album dedicated to his hairy ass."

"I'll try to make one. Although I don't think I'll be able to remember my code, Trev. For now, I'll have to deal with the ass pics."

"Yeah," He laughed, "Just wait until Ms. Juniper asks to take a picture from your phone, and you'll have to stare at two sets of cheeks."

The two continued to joke around as they entered the building. They clocked their time on the little tablet before the receptionist's desk. Trevor turned his head to the side, greeting Mr. Crosby (the security guard) by the elevators.

"What's up, Mr. C?"

"Hey, how's it hanging, kids?" he smiled, nodding his round head underneath his black baseball cap. Everyone at Inferior knew Mr. Crosby. The building's guard for potential looters, unauthorized personnel, and occasionally paparazzi. Crosby was a good man, but he made things personal. He was very talkative, and it often disrupted everybody's time during work hours. It's not like the man cared much. He treated everyone with the utmost respect, just not with timing.

"Sorry, we'd love to continue to chat, but we gotta go," Trevor waved, entering the elevators with Sam.

"It's alright. Y'all have fun." Crosby smiled.

Sam pressed the fifth-floor button when the doors slid closed. During the ride up, someone broke the gas.

Sam gagged, covering his nose, "Ew!"

"Silent but deadly." Trevor snickered.

The boy wanted to get out of there before a whiff of the gas slipped further into his curvy nose.

When the doors opened, he gasped for clean air, stating, "I swear, if you or Garrett do that again, I'm not riding in there anymore."

Trevor wheezed like crazy, which eventually caused Sam to laugh, not minding the incident anymore. He was all for fart jokes but not in confined, closed areas.

The boys wheezed, then coughed to contain themselves from being clamorous.

It was supposed to be a simple job for the day. It takes about six hours (five on a good day) of editing and then home. The office was busy with traffic, people strolling or running back and forth from the boss' office or hurrying and printing out labels for the shots they either sent or took.

Sam was one of the few that received little recognition for his work. He'd get taken advantage of, and on rare occasions, his work would be credited to someone else, but it came with perks. Perks of a few additional bucks in his next paycheck, or at least buying the pictures off of him. He wondered if it had to do with his age. Was it because he was too young and easy to take advantage of? Sometimes, it made sense because everyone else (other than the twins) was between the ages of 21 and 40. It was a shame- Sam wanted to take a stand but didn't want the risk of losing his job. He loved taking pictures- photography was his best gift. He was a pure natural at his shots. It was no wonder why few wanted them.

Two hours into editing one of their model's thigh gaps, the big hoss stepped in, *Kendrick Grafton.* Everyone on the floor had to refer to him as *Mr. Grafton* or *Sir.* He strutted into the center of the tables, looking around– spying, sniffing everyone out. His usual rounds, as Sam would say. The rounds of complaining, bitching, and sometimes throwing a snarky compliment to a few workers in the area. It was a game of–

Who is Kendrick going to belittle next?!

Sam understood that most managers aren't friendly in the world, but he got a strange feeling. A feeling that Mr. Grafton doesn't show him the most common courtesy. He couldn't understand the sense of style that Mr. Grafton was attempting to achieve. Was he trying to go for a rich, snobby look? Or a complicated hipster type of style? His glasses would sometimes throw him off whenever he was working. They looked tacky. The cheetah print design all over the frames did not look well. Out in the world, many know that a boss is a boss, and nobody really *likes* their bosses.

"Clark!" Mr. Grafton shouted.

"Um. Yes, ma'am– Sir! I mean– Sir?" he stuttered, turning his squeaky rolling chair towards Grafton's direction. Mr. Grafton eyeballed the teenager from head to toe, groaning for odd reasons. "Ms. Juniper is here for the evening. Since Artie isn't here today, you're no longer assisting today. You're the backup. In 15 minutes, you're needed in the stage room. Got it?"

Sam paused momentarily, comprehending each fragment that slipped his mind.

"...Got it, sir!"

"Good."

Turning his chair back to the computer, Trevor poked his sides, taunting and tickling him, "Ooh, Ms. Juniper *wants* you!"

Sam slapped off Trevor's hands. "Stop it already."

"I dare you to ask her out. Please, bro." The twin begged.

"What makes you think I like her? Let alone *her* to *me*."

Sam shook his head in disbelief, preparing to head to the stage room down the hall. This was a lot of pressure for the boy, considering he only ever helps take pictures. Was this a type of promotion? Or was it just for today since his partner, Artie, didn't show up? Something he'd ask Mr. Grafton later.

The stage room was relatively small. Able to fit in about nine queen-sized beds with a delicate squeeze. The lights flickered and buzzed; it seemed the fluorescent bulbs could pop at any moment. The voltage to them was too high; buzzing sounds played on as if it weren't quiet enough. Sam noticed the camera had been set up. Below the lights was the stage, hiding behind tall, thick, black curtains.

"Good. But not good enough," the young man noticed.

He needed to fix the camera settings, and the angle on the tripod was off, leaning to the right.

The shots would look ridiculous.

Sam extended each leg on the tripod. "*TSSS*," each leg hissed like a snake from the extension. Everything was looking as well-done as a steak. Last, the lighting in the room had to change. He grabbed the control panel on the cart beside him, tuning to a peaceful, natural light. A warm aesthetic approach to the scenery while making the side lights cold.

A moment later, the sound of a door creaked open. Sam guessed it must be the back door for maintenance to come through. That wasn't the back door- it was the dressing room door. The nervous boy carefully lifted his head from the magnifier, and the realization kicked in faster than a light switch.

It was the one and only Ms. Ellie Juniper.

"God..."

She looked more gorgeous and rich and, dare he might say, the sexiest French model in the state. Maybe even in the world. She walked out of the room wearing a maroon silk robe with her initials *E.J.*sowed into the left side of her robe. Her hair just got done for the evening, all for the shoot. Now, it was all on the kid. All faith was in him.

"*Bonsoir* (Good evening), Sammy!" she greeted, waving her smooth hands and smiling brightly.

"*Sammy*. Heh." He grinned. She'd always call him that. She wouldn't say Samuel or Sam. He'd always be "Sammy." He grew used to that sobriquet. He loved how the name slipped out of her lips. The thickness of her accent filled his ears with such vibrant sounds of music. The poor boy lost his train of thought.

"Oh! Hi, Ms. Juniper."

"Please, Sammy. No need to be formal."

Sam had again lost his focus, instantly clearing his throat to get back on the task before he got complaints from Mr. Grafton.

He walked up to the front of the set, pulling the heavy curtains back, using the advantage of the springs to roll them across the ceiling brackets and set the scene.

This was all new. Someone had switched everything around. The set designers made a mockup of a beach (or at least a portion of it), covering the floor with real sand. It smelled of an actual beach. Salty and strong. Long striped towels sprayed across the floor. Behind the set was a wall painted green to add a background image for an editor to fill in. Sam put the pieces together, remembering how Mr. Grafton sent the twins to South Padre Island to take pictures of the ocean's landscape. Sam was most likely going to drop the image in for the background after taking the pictures. He guessed that the Inferior was going for a different approach. An image that tells people, *Hey! We know you miss summer. And even though it's practically winter, here are some pictures that will make you crave the heat even more!*

"Ready, Sammy?" Ms. Juniper sounded excited, untying her cover and letting it drop to the floor, revealing her body in an alluring two-piece. He thought to the near max, spotting every curve, crease, and miraculous length of her hourglass figure. Sam looked down at the tiled floor, hoping his stare wasn't creepy.

Just don't look her in the eyes. He jokingly thought.

Ellie pulled a pin out of her jet-black hair and walked onto the scene, lying and posing seductively on the white and blue striped towel. The lights above helped shimmer her black bathing pieces.

"You okay, hon? You seem uncomfortable?" She asked, concerned for her photographer's well-being.

"I'm fine. Just thrown off. I need to check the uh- stuff-adjustments."

Sam had never been so confused in his life. He'd never seen what was underneath her designer threads. Ever since she had signed with the company, he'd rarely taken her picture. The times he did were mainly in summer dresses or formal attire. Nothing like this.

Suddenly, Ellie's assistant cleared her throat to snap Sam out of it.

"Whenever you're ready!" Or, in layman's terms, *Get it together, shithead!*

The boy stumbled behind the DSLR camera, biting the edge of his lips as his finger was on the narrow shutter button.

"*CLICK!*" That was one shot. Sam's eyes widened. He forgot to turn the external flash on.

"*CLICK– FLASH!*" Sam grew a smile. *Thank youuu Artie.*

In every third picture, Ellie would switch up her position. Posing like a goddess. Some with her legs crossed, or for others, they'd laid open. Sam couldn't bear the thought of sustaining a terrible erection in front of her.

"Focus, Sam. Focus," he whispered.

Finished, Ms. Juniper threw her robe back on, tying the dark, silky ribbons around her waist to hold it in place. She winked at Sam and blew him a kiss.

"*Merci!* (Thank you) *Au revoir* (Goodbye)."

Sam's hand shook, trying to pull the SIM card out of the device. His face went from pale to a cotton candy color.

"*Wow.*" he shook.

Back at the desk, Trevor smirked at his friend, noticing the color in him and the spark in his eye. There was no time to joke around. They had about three hours left to kill to get started on editing and formatting- but because of Sam's excitement from what happened in the stage room, he needed to take a leak badly.

Sam started his trek, noticing the bathroom looked tidier than usual. It was just about time they cleaned it. Most people in the building didn't care to aim appropriately or flush their damn piss.

After his long whizz, he soaked his hands in the melon-scented soap that fizzed in his palms, deep-cleaning the sweat and dirt underneath his fingernails.

Just outside, Sam felt a harsh itch develop in the right corner of his head. There was a feeling of unease, delay, and warning. It was as if time was literally slowing down. Somehow, that itch provided all these feelings into one. A second later, a leg of a metal tripod whacked poor Sam's head.

"OW!" he moaned, turning around.

It was one photographer. A tall man carrying a stand lazily. "Sorry, boss. Ya' good?"

"It's fine. My bad," replied Sam, taking the blame as his hand covered the area of pain, rubbing some dirt in it.

Trevor looked up from his desktop, glancing at Sam as he walked back in.

"You okay?"

"Yeah. Just tired."

Mr. Grafton walked up to the young man to ask him how the session went, but he had to get one question out of the way before he forgot, "Excuse me for interrupting, Mr. Grafton, but is this a promotion? I think you mentioned how I'm now a backup for Artie?"

Grafton let out a little snort and judging by that same snarky look on his face; it was looking least likely, "Haha! What?! No, you're not promoted. Well- sort of. You're going from assistant to backup photographer in case of times like *this* where Artie is absent."

"Oh..." Sam's excitement died within two seconds.

"Now. How'd the pictures go?"

"Good, I think-"

Grafton cut Sam off before he could get another word in. "Great! Now, finish up what you can! Bye."

Not a minute after Sam sat down, Mr. Grafton stood in the center of the office to announce the big news, "*ATTENTION EVERYONE!*"

The whole floor looked up from whatever they were doing. All peers, family members, and associates.

"As you know! We are having a big trip down to London! All the way to dear old London! Yes! You heard me correctly!"

Commotion spread, whispers of excitement spreading like a yawn, hearing the tiny wisps of curiosity and joy, and the obvious questions: *Who is going? Are we all going? What's going on? Why?*

"Now!" Mr. Grafton clapped, grabbing the attention back, "We were only taking five, but as of now, we can only take *three* with us to take some new shots at the new fashion festival!"

All eyes bugged, now their attention couldn't break. Sam couldn't care less. Well- that was a lie- he was pessimistic about the odds of him winning that trip. Sam wasn't so interested in fashion. He'd instead want to take simple pictures of whatever piqued his interest: landscapes, people, animals, and such. To make it fair, he listened to the news that was brought forward.

"We have randomly selected the three on this floor! Don't be a pissant if you didn't make it!"

All ass cheeks were clenched, and fingers crossed. Tons of *please-be-me's* could be seen by the looks on their faces.

Mr. Grafton pulled a list on his phone, and no one around could see if the list was biased, bullshit, or, for all they knew, a stupid *spin-the-wheelful* of names.

"Jessie Garza!"

A round of applause for the 27-year-old woman was given when she pumped out of her to take a bow.

"Reese Stellar!" Mr. Grafton called out.

Another wave of claps went. Trevor and Sam were packing and closing up their stuff. Trevor had doubts after the first name was called. "Well. Maybe next time?" Trevor shrugged.

Sam had a feeling that it wouldn't happen. It was time to go home anyway and see what was left for the rest of his birthday.

"Artie Beltran!" Grafton yelled the last name. "Oh– he's sick. My bad! Clark!"

The boys froze in place.

Why did he call my name? Sam questioned. *Am I missing something? I didn't pay attention.*

"Since Artie is sick for the time being, plus since you're now his backup, please take his place in going on this trip."

"*YES!*" Sam cried out without hesitation. At first, he didn't know what he was saying *yes* to until he realized Grafton was done with the winners' names.

"Okay, everyone! Have a good night!"

Before Sam could walk out the door with the rest of the employees, Mr. Grafton stopped the kid and pulled him aside to give him a little disclaimer.

"*F.Y.I.*, Clark. This isn't special treatment or any form of favoritism. But you can consider this either your birthday present... Or just dumb luck."

"Oh- thank you! Sir, you don't-"

"Alright. Get the hell outta here." He dismissed.

Outside, Trevor was smoking and rubbing his palms together. He inhaled almost to the tip, wanting to feel the heat near his perky lips. The city was colder at night, and it didn't help that winter was closer than a man attached to a dick.

"Congratulations." His friend grinned, giving his shoulder a friendly pat.

Throughout the drive back to the Apartment, Sam thought about the opportunities that could grow from this trip. A way to help him and his Mother out. He dreamed of getting a house in a nice neighborhood and not having to deal with annoyed landlords or a cluster of bills or maintenance issues.

"You know what's crazy?" Sam pointed out.

"What?"

"I've worked at Inferior for about two years. And I've only been credited a few! Just a *few*."

"Really?" Trevor's eyebrows raised.

"It's weird. I've taken *sooo* many pictures. So many."

"I'm surprised you haven't said shit yet."

Sam dragged on, "It's fine, I guess? Sometimes I want to say something, but- I don't know."

Trevor listened closely to those last words, hoping some few words could inspire him. "Well, I hope you'll find the courage and confidence to take a stand someday. I don't mean to sound gushy, but you took *a* stand today with Felix. You're braver than ya' know, Sam."

"Thanks." Said Sam as he smiled weakly, looking at the road pass beneath him.

The Apartment appeared frigid at night. Most of the building's bulbs were out. New tenets' eyes would have to adjust until they could notice any of the unit's numbers on their doors. Sam and Cathy lived there long enough to know they didn't need to see the label on their door. It all came naturally. It was also easier, considering the gate around the community hadn't worked in over three years. It always stayed open.

Sam hopped off the truck. His left foot stomped into a puddle, soaking his calves.

"Ah, shit!"

The puddle was as cold as ice. Sam slammed the passenger door shut and b-lined it to his home in desperation for warmth and new pants.

Reaching into his pockets, he struggled to feel the metal texture of the door key. Since the door was rusty, he had to pull and turn the lock as hard as possible.

"*CLICK!*" it unlocked.

"Happy birthday, again!" a voice screamed.

Sam looked up, frightened as a startled cat, not realizing it was his sweet mother.

"Hi! You're home early?" he questioned, tossing his windbreaker jacket on the coat rack.

"I just got off. I couldn't miss my baby boy's big eighteenth!" she reached forward, pinching his cheek, still treating her son like he was ten. Sam trembled in pain as his face was still in pain from Felix's punch. The pinch also made him howl.

"Ow! Ow! Ow!"

"What? What happened?" Cathy's eyes widened, witnessing the red irritation on her son's features.

"N–Nothing. I was messing around with the guys, and I fell." Sam lied.

"Ugh. See what happens when you boys play around too much." Cathy strutted into the little kitchen, grabbing a sandwich bag and a handful of ice cubes from the freezer and making a homemade ice pack. She gently raised it towards

Sam's cheek, slowly pressing against it. Sam grabbed it from her small hand, keeping the pressure.

"Thanks, Mom."

Cathy's eyes trailed down her son's frame, spotting another flaw.

"What happened to your pants? They look wet." Her head peaked behind Sam, and a thin trail of water followed behind.

"Sorry, Mom. I accidentally stepped into a puddle before I came in."

"Seriously!" Cathy exclaimed, rolling her eyes. "We have a floor mat outside for a reason!"

"Well, I was hoping to get to my room before any more water got on the floor, but you surprised me."

Cathy threw some paper towels on the floor, letting them soak up the excess water.

"It's fine. Just leave your shoes here in the front. Don't take them to your room. The carpet doesn't need to get stained again."

"I know. Again, I'm sorry, Mom."

"It's fine," Cathy reiterated, wiping down the floor. Sam was ready to call it a night until a little shout from Cathy made him halt.

"Wait!" Cathy ran back to the kitchen and got something from the fridge, hiding the mysterious item behind her back. When she stood in front of her child, she pulled her hand away from her back, revealing something humble and in awe. A chocolate cupcake with a blue candle stuck on top.

This was it. It's perfect.

Perfect.

It was the little things that could give Sam such joy. He didn't need a cake or a party. This was all he ever needed.

Cathy sang. "*Happy Birthday to you! Happy birthday to you! Happy Birthday, Dear Samuel! Happy birthday to you!*"

Sam blew out his candle, hugged his mother, and was ready to sleep. Before he trekked to the bedroom, Cathy stopped him, informing him about one last surprise: she had up her gentle sleeves. She twisted around, reaching behind the kitchen counter, revealing to him a box wrapped in gold foil with a black ribbon.

"Huh?" He questioned the peculiar package, noting the obvious that it was a gift.

Cathy reached her arms out like she was presenting a treasured token on a silver platter. For a split second, she stopped, almost as if she was hesitant about giving it to him. Her arms slowly retreated, and she looked down in dismay at the homemade gift wrapping.

"Thanks, Mom." Sam smiled, grabbing the gift. "What is it?"

"Well, you gotta open it, obviously." She giggled slightly.

Before Sam tried to pry through the foil, Cathy stopped him and insisted he open it in his room. She reminded him he needed to get some rest and to clean himself up.

Sam wanted to check on any updates from work. Thankfully, he took his work laptop back home and was greeted with two emails in the inbox as he moved the golden gift on top of his dresser. *I'll open it later.*

The first email was the booking information and seat reservation. The seat was in the business class, and while Sam appreciated it, he thought it was unnecessary.

The last email was intriguing. It was a message from Ellie.

Thank you for the pictures, Sammy.

Here's something for your troubles. You'll find it in your account. ;)

l'amour (Love), Ellie.

Sam logged into his bank account and found a transaction notification. A grand total of ten thousand dollars slid into his checking.

"Holy shit!" He yelled in shock.

Flabbergasted by the amount, however, Sam couldn't accept. It didn't sit right with him. It wasn't fair. He couldn't take that money, especially from her.

The boy thought: *Ellie is a well-respected woman. I am grateful for the payment, but it feels wrong.*

Scrolling through the options, he sent the money back. Sam wanted to earn that money. He didn't feel comfortable getting things handed to him. Anyone would've taken that money in a heartbeat. Not Sammy-Boy, though. Not him. That was all good- but also too good- stupid even.

Chapter 6
SUMMIT

Another day, another dollar. Fulton's rectangular alarm clock had to remind him to get up and go to work. The man was already used to his days off. It was hard getting back into the swing, having to wash off the weekend high and treat this new week like one.

Fulton stretched his arms and legs, shaking like a rattlesnake, as his face twitched from all the stress. Fulton just had to see his face in the lit-up bathroom mirror. He ensured his hair stayed neat and checked for any blemishes on his face.

None present. Good.

The soap he used to wash his face smelled of strawberries and passionfruit. It was something he couldn't get enough of. Rubbing that scented sensation once again in his face.

Before walking out the door, he wanted to check on his ma. The grown man nearly started tip-toeing down the hallway to check on her. He tried his best not to wake her. He looked like a child, wanting to sneak into the kitchen for a late-night snack.

She was asleep. Of course, she would be. It was five in the morning. Donna usually wouldn't wake until nine. She didn't need to get up at four or five in the morning. No more taking her kid to school or work. She did her part, and now she could relax for the rest of her life.

"Good morning, ma," He whispered gently as he kissed her thin, wrinkly cheek. He couldn't see it, but she had a little smile. She accepted all of her son's love. She'd always love him, no matter what.

Retreating back, he smelled food. It was the food he'd gotten from Doe's. It was still wrapped in a plastic bag. There was not a crease on the foam box. Not opened once.

She didn't eat? Fulton grew concerned for her health.

It was cold as hell outside. The screaming wind didn't help, especially with no sun. Fulton bolted to his black luxury sport sedan, ready to blast the heat and go to work.

The streets weren't as busy. The only people out at 5 a.m. were band kids and athletes going to school for practice, drunks heading back home with whatever sense they had left, or others going to work around the exact time.

Fulton could go past the 45-mile speed limit if he wanted. Eventually, he would start pushing towards 60 to help arrive a few minutes before clocking in.

With fifty floors in the air, the Summit Building stood tall, about 27 stories shorter than the Chrysler Building in New York. On the exterior was their company name, at the center of the building. A clean, bright yellow sign: **Summit Peaks Industries.**

Fulton pulled his car to the south side of the establishment, around the entry booth, to access the warehouse. The bald security guard waved, making small talk.

"Hey there, Bruning. Here early?"

"Man, I'm always early."

The guard scanned his ID and unlocked the gate to go through. "Alright-alright. You're good to go. Have a good day."

While the outside parking lot was quiet enough to put a baby to sleep, it didn't mean the inside was the same. Once the side door opened, beeping, sawing, crashing, and the breaking of objects echoed within the department. Loud enough to get many angry neighbors to bitch out their windows and scream, "Shut up! Some of us need to work in the morning!"

Workers were everywhere. Everyone had a job to do, no matter how big or small. Fulton's office was in the back. The room was almost soundproof when the doors were shut. Only hints of screaming, sawing, crashing, and beeping remained audible.

His office had been a blank canvas since the previous manager, Phillip Garth, claimed he was retiring. The day he announced it, he packed all of his crap away with a bitter attitude and left it up to the newbie to decide what he should do with the office. To Fulton, it sounded more like fired than retired.

The man didn't put up pictures or any tacky kitten wallpapers. Just a wooden desk, silver desktop with an old modeled keyboard, mouse, and a rolling chair, all in the center. Surprisingly, Fulton had good internet. Most of the time he had, he spent by himself, constantly thinking about family — Mama's boy.

There was little to do for the next eight and a half hours except to sort and file paperwork from all the trucks that had come in. Sometimes, when he'd peek out from the shutters, Fulton could see workers on forklifts, screwing around with frail wooden pallets full of orders.

Fulton had to go out there himself to help stock up the delivery trucks and ensure that things moved forward. As the email said, today was urgent, and everything had to arrive on time. He hoped he would be able to pull some overtime today.

No one questioned what was in the boxes. The crew suspected they were full of furniture, couches, and glass, even though they were heavier than usual... Even confirmed by the CFO himself, ever since Summit got a new chairman, packages had been discreet and heavily secured.

Jo was stationed at the far end of the house, in the parcel department. She was messing around with the buzz-saw, cutting up cardboard corner slabs for the packages. She worried less about the boxes and more about the cutting. Sawdust sprayed all over her brown jacket, turning it into a moldy-looking color and making her smell like a robust lumberjack.

Apart from her was a newbie, Johnny Plaza Jr. He sat in a rolling chair, kicking back and staring into space like he had nothing else to do. It's definitely a great start to a new job. He turned that attitude up a notch by pulling out his phone to play a quick game of Tetris to pass the time.

Fulton saw him killing time and walked carefully to that area to see why he didn't get up.

"Excuse me, sir?" Fulton waved, tapping Johnny's boot with his.

"Yeah?"

"Could you get up?"

Johnny rolled his eyes, and some flakes fell down his shoulders as he scratched his bushy beard and hair. Fulton pushed the rolling chair back into the slot of a desk nearby and locked the wheels.

When Johnny attempted to pull the chair back from its place, Fulton stopped him. "What's your name, man?"

"Johnny. Johnny Plaza." he scoffed, "What's yours?"

"Boss."

The smug look on Johnny's face disappeared.

"Oh…" the man turned embarrassed, walking away and pretending to work. In the background, Jo was hysterically laughing her ass off, pointing at Johnny like a joke.

"You should've seen your face." she chuckled.

Johnny glanced at her. The type of glance that told you to *shut up or else.* She instantly shushed and continued to play around with the saw, with a wide, smoldering grin stuck on her face.

"Get back to work." Demanded Fulton.

Traffic in the warehouse picked up. Fulton decided to step in by throwing the boxes into the last delivery truck; even Jo decided to help and stopped fooling around. Before throwing in the last few, Fulton scraped the base of his right hand onto the paneled walls of the truck.

"Ah, shit!" he yelled, looking down at his hand.

The one time he decided to not wear gloves, a rigid scrap of wood stabbed into the back of his hand. Blood slowly poured out. Fulton stumbled out of the truck and burst into his office to pull a first-aid kit from his desk to tend to the vile wound. A sharp pain waved over the spot — he was thinking he should head home already. The job was done, and everything would go as planned, according to the delivery instructions.

After he had addressed the minor wound and doused the area in heavy peroxide, Jo barged into his office nonchalantly.

"Hey, Boss. Whatcha up to-"

"Wait!" Fulton alerted, pulling his hand up, to keep her away.

"Just gimme a moment. My hand hurts like a bitch."

She smacked her lips, retreating slowly from the room.

"No. No, you can still come in. I was just tryna' tell ya to take it slow." Fulton reassured.

"Oh. Okay!" Jo pulled up a plastic chair, planting down on the uncomfortable surface. It was the type of seat only middle schoolers could fit in.

"So, are we going to go over those plans?" she emphasized, leaning closer to the desk. She was curious about what their next job would be.

Fulton wrapped a small bandage and gauze around the surface of the pain. "I'll talk to you about that later. Ma's starting to feel better, so... Plus, I should be fine with the overtime."

Fulton's mindset was bipolar when it came to the idea of more jobs. One day, he'd be okay with sticking up a few people, and the next, he was right with the honest work. Something that wasn't enough for Jo. She frowned, kicked back against the left wall beside Fulton, and played with a random lighter she had found near the delivery trucks. It probably belonged to a driver who was a heavy smoker, with hardly any fluid left in the plastic gadget. Jo hoped she'd be able to have some type of fun again.

"Maybe, next time. Maybe." he winked, still wrapping up his hand.

"Maybe?" She questioned, looking down at her feet, "Yesterday, you were just pointing a loaded gun into a stranger's face, and now you're the employee of the month?"

"Girl, stop."

Jo giggled. "You do this every time. You're a selfish Robin Hood one day, and then you're an average Joe the next. No pun intended, by the way." She relaxed her eyes, hoping they'd looked like convincing puppy-dog eyes.

"I'm goin' home. You can head out, too."

"Wait!" she called out. Fulton had barely taken a few steps outside his room, and her odd callout sounded like he was leaving forever.

"What?"

"Could we bring a third guest into the group?"

Fulton scooted back into his office and slammed the door.

"Not out loud, idiot!" Fulton hissed, "Look, Jo. We'll talk more later. 'K?"

"Can I at least tell you who?"

He nodded, hoping it would shut her up for a few hours.

Jo lifted one of the shutters and pointed at the lazy, curly-headed, bearded man.

"Johnny?" Fulton raised in a tone of disbelief. The audacity to bring in not only a total stranger but also someone who was incompetent with work.

"Yes."

"The dude that doesn't seem to do shit and looks like he has the worst time here?"

"Yes," Jo answered blankly.

"Why should I bring him in?"

"He already knows what we do. He may not be a good worker here, but he's enthusiastic about jobs."

"You told him?!"

"Fult, He's good with money. Have I ever done wrong by you?"

"Why did you tell him?!" Fulton yelled, half-pacing his office, worried about what would happen next.

"Like I said, he's good with money."

On the way to the condo, Fulton had his left hand on the eleven o'clock edge of the steering wheel, and he noticed blood on his right was seeping through the gauze.

Is it as bad as it looks? He wondered, pressing his foot on the gas, speeding home to clean up the red mess before it deteriorated.

When he got off the elevators at the condo, he expected to see Gloria outside her door. This time, however, she was in the middle of the hallway, a few feet away from her door.

"Hey, Fult!" she waved.

"What's up." he waved back, the bandage on his hand looking more red than pink.

"What happened to your hand?" she gasped, walking closer to examine him.

"Just a small accident at work. Nothin' crazy."

"You sure? That looks bad," she informed, carefully taking a look.

"Yeah. I noticed. Has ma' been feelin' well? Was she coughing again?"

Gloria smacked her tongue, knowing her neighbor hoped to hear an ounce of good news, "I don't want to sugarcoat it, but... she's still coughing. She stopped about an hour ago."

Fulton bit down on his upper lip, continuing down the hall to his door.

"Thanks, Gloria."

"I think we should call a doctor."

"We? Thanks. I appreciate the help, but I got this. I'll let you know if anythin' happens."

The home was quiet. The condo felt empty. Donna was still in bed, wasting her hours watching pointless reality shows. Fulton knew the news should broadcast any moment now, and she never missed the reports. He thought he might even sit in and watch with her. First things first, he needed to check on her.

"Hey, ma'?" he called out, creaking the door open.

"Yes?" she responded. Her voice sounded raspy, like someone had choked the life out of her. After clearing her throat, her voice sounded less polluted, "Yes, Fuller?"

"Just checkin' on ya. You good?"

Donna coughed again. Her coughs sounded like a hardened nicotine user who'd smoke about 15 packs daily, blowing their lungs to shit. She coughed again, shoving a tissue over her mouth. She doesn't want her son to contract anything if she was really sick.

"Mama, I think I need to take ya' to the docs."

"I'm fine. Don't worry about me."

"How can I not? Your cough sounds worse and worse by the day!" Fulton held her tender hand with his injured one.

"Fuller, wait, what happened to your hand?"

"Just a work thing. Don't worry about it, Ma'."

She rolled her eyes, getting out of bed and into the kitchen. Fulton followed, keeping a safe distance.

She looked through their new fridge, hoping to find something delicious with her name on it. She didn't care for leftovers; she wanted anything fresh that could catch her dark, hazel eyes.

She's okay for now.

Fulton went to the bathroom to examine the problem he endured at work. He groaned in pain when peeling the sticky bandage from his skin as it pulled out the little hair on his fingers and wrist. He examined every detail of the injury. His eyes dilated to the spot. A splinter gashed in his skin.

*I need to get that little **sonofabitch** out.* He cried and reached into the mirror cabinet to grab a pair of metal tweezers, sitting beside a bottle of rubbing alcohol. Luckily for Fulton, he was ambidextrous. Handling the little plucker with his other hand wasn't a problem. He hovered the little tool above the wound. Then, the tweezers seeped into the hole. Fulton could almost feel the little prick. He tried his best to not make any noise. There was no need to alert her of something as small as a stupid splinter. Finally, he squeezed the picks together, grabbing the head of the wood.

"Got it." he brooded, pulling the tool upwards and the splinter outwards. He saw the little stick rise from his slimy skin and thick blood. Strangely, it didn't hurt him; it felt rather weird. It was difficult for him to explain.

Back in the kitchen, Fulton asked his ma if she was hungry.

"Hell, yeah. I haven't eaten anything all day."

"Why not?! You should've called me. I would've gotten you somethin'."

"Nah', I don't want to bother ya' with that." Donna shooed him away, watching her son retreat from the cold fridge.

Fulton then came up with an exciting idea, "Why don't we have a movie night? Like how we used to. Just us two... Get a pizza and watch an old, cartoon movie."

Donna rubbed her eyes, beginning to feel exhausted, "I– Don't you have work tomorrow?" she yawned.

"Yeah, but I just wanted to spend some time with ya'. Come on, Ma'. Let's do it."

"We haven't done that since you were little. I don't know, maybe... maybe next time... tomorrow."

Fulton leaned against the counter, knocking his fists against the surface out of boredom, "Alright, then."

She yawned again and suddenly coughed viciously. She instantly covered her mouth with her bare hand. For a moment, she stopped, still covering her mouth. Before her son could get a word out, she let out a violent cough and gag, spitting chunks of blood into her palms and dripping onto the floor.

"Ma'! Oh my God!" he screamed while running to her room and grabbing her by her shoulders.

"I- I'm f- fine, hon'..." she falsely assured, sounding delusional, almost as if she didn't know what was happening.

"I- I'm fine..." Donna coughed out more blood, spilling a bit on the floor.

Fulton attempted to reach for his phone but realized he left it in his bedroom. He had no intention of leaving his mother alone. Fulton screamed for his neighbor, "Gloria! Call 9-1-1!" hoping she'd hear him through the walls.

The scared man turned into a boy. He wanted to scream as he held his mother tightly, ensuring she was upright and okay, "Hold on, Ma'! Hold on!"

Donna continued to cough, spitting blood again, trying to reach for the box of tissues on the counter.

"I'm fine... I'm fine."

Chapter 7
C IS FOR:

Half a day in the hospital didn't do justice. Fulton should've brought his jacket. His body jazzed in the cold, shaking every other second. He reached over to grab a magazine—a sleek paperback of one of *Inferior-Times'* new copies. His eyes scanned the women and men in selected poses, some with their hands covering their goods and some half-naked. He looked over a page that displayed Ellie Juniper in her new two-piece. It was the same picture Sam had taken on that fake beach set.

"Eh. She 'ight for my taste," mumbled Fulton, tossing the book away.

His mind was confused and worried as he remembered his mother's horrifying coughs—the amount of blood she spilled and the agony she sang traumatized him.

With most of his money, he paid a high price for one of the best doctors in the city, overhearing about a man named Aussie Ground and all the work he'd performed for the past 15 years. He made the call and got a quick spot open for his ma.

Leading up to this, he sat in the waiting room until it was okay to see what was happening. He'd been waiting for hours, and God only knows how long until the anticipation of waiting could kill him.

Fulton had found the cafeteria and grabbed a small cup of coffee to keep himself energized and warm. His head rotated in meditation, and the knots around his neck and back throbbed as he continued drinking.

When he arrived back in the room, he made it in time for one nurse to call out to him.

"Fulton Bruning? Is there a Fulton Bruning here?"

He raised his hand, rushing to the nurse. "I'm here. How's she doing?"

The blonde attendant left no response, beckoning for him to follow. The hallway felt colder than the other rooms. Fulton shivered, covering his hairy arms. They walked on and on until they were at the far end of the building.

The nurse opened the door for him, and he saw his ma there. She was sitting in a plastic chair, looking up at Dr. Ground. This was the first time Fulton had officially met him, besides hearing his voice over the phone.

Dr. Ground turned to face him, greeting him, "Hello, Mr. Bruning. Nice to meet you."

Aussie lifted his bulky hand open, waiting to shake his hand. Fulton was too cold. He couldn't bother moving an inch.

It wasn't long before he noticed and offered him a warm coat in the other room.

"Please. Thank you," said Fulton.

Aussie was a bit of a hefty man. He had muscle for sure and some weight, but he was far from obese. It might've been bulking season for him. It was clear the man had been to the gym a few times. He had no hair on the top of his head but did sport a clean goatee.

When he came back with a covering, Fulton could finally greet him politely, shaking his hand and noticing the Doctor's complexion was darker than his own.

"Alright, Mr. Bruning. Have a seat."

The introductions were over, and it was time for business. Time to see what was wrong.

"So, Doc. What's wrong? Why is she coughing so much? Why is she not eating?"

"I'll answer all of those momentarily, I'm afraid."

Donna raised a brow. "Afraid?" That remark didn't sound too good.

Dr. Ground pulled up a file on the counter, looking through her symptoms and scans again before finalizing a solution. He wanted to be positive before proceeding.

"I'm gonna rerun these tests. It won't take too long, I promise."

Before the two could get a word in, Aussie had already left the room. Whatever he saw definitely wasn't something good. They fell quiet, thinking of their own conclusions about what it might be.

Could it be? Could it really be something terminal?

Their guesses were just the tip of the iceberg... it could've been anything.

Donna held her son's hand. Her palm was sweating with nerves, and she just wanted to be home in bed. She felt no need to deserve what was coming. She coughed again, covering her mouth with a scented tissue, spitting out drops of blood that hurdled up.

"Do you need me to get somebody, Ma?" he asked, gently rubbing her back.

"I'm– I'm fine. I'm fine. Let's just wait for now."

Those words exploded like a grenade. Something he didn't plan on hearing again.

I'm fine.

Hearing those words sent up a form of PTSD Fulton didn't know he had. The grown man had to cover his ears if she wanted to state those words again. She wasn't fine... It was apparent she was less than that.

"They did a biopsy on me," said Donna.

Fulton's head shook in disbelief. His back shuddered into a deep dark, where his mind flowed.

Could it be?

He felt better off not knowing what she just told him. It was another thing to add to his list of worries.

Half an hour passed, and Dr. Ground returned with that same beige folder resting between his armpits, grabbing a stool to place his hunky body in to explain.

It was now the moment of truth. What is going on?

Dr. Ground cleared his throat, glancing at Donna as she cleared her blood-filled throat.

"Mrs. Bruning? How is your family's medical history?"

Donna couldn't say. She gave him a dubious look, not remembering much of her past. It was so long ago she couldn't define it.

"I'm not sure how to tell you this... but I believe you are showing signs of having breast cancer."

For Fulton, time froze, and his mood became mellow to the deafening brink of collapse. His hearing had become muffled, as Dr. Ground explained.

"We found a lump and—"

Just those words were in the aftermath. It was confirmed, and that sickening wave of depression went over.

The following things the Doc had to bring up were the expenses and treatments. It was more money that had to be pulled out of his pockets.

Before leaving the hospital, Aussie pulled Fulton aside, informing him, "Mr. Bruning, I will not be in town for the next week, but I have a partner in this facility who is willing and will be able to continue treatments for your mother. I'll inform you of my return, but until then, you'll be in good hands. Alright?"

"Yeah. That's fine," he mumbled.

"Great. Oh! And before I forget," Dr. Ground pulled the man closer. He wanted their conversation to be between the two and no overseers. "I understand how you feel. I know this is the toughest fight you'll both have to endure, and I have a friend who will guide you. He works at this center near downtown. Just ask for Terrance Balle. He'll be there if you need to talk about anything. Trust me when I tell you, Mr. Bruning, that your mental strength and emotions will be tested. Going to that center will help."

Aussie gave Fulton a pamphlet and a business card with details of the center. It was an offer—a little something to take into consideration.

The drive couldn't have been more uncomfortable. Donna didn't speak or turn on the radio to drown out the bitter mood or silence. It was as quiet as getting caught doing inconspicuous things—like throwing a party and your folks coming home, getting walked in on during sex, or when you're a child, and you curse the worst words in front of your parents. That special awkward silence.

The only sounds that filled the misery were the heavy breathing and clicking mouths of all the yawning they suppressed.

When they returned to the condo, Gloria was waiting outside her unit, giving Donna a gentle hug and asking if she was okay.

"I'm okay," Donna teared up, her eyes becoming pink and her voice shaking with each syllable.

Gloria turned to Fulton and attempted to hug him, only to be turned down by the man. He walked away into his home.

The two leaned against the cold kitchen countertops, standing there until one broke into a topic. Donna carefully moved her eyes to her son, noticing he was silently crying and clenching his jaw as tight as he could to not sob or break down. Instead, he moved his dry palms to his face, covering himself up.

The mother rushed over to his side, hugging him, and suggested something, "Hey, why don't we—you know—order some pizza and watch a couple of movies like we used to? You're off work tomorrow, right?"

Instead of an eventual and soft social night in, Fulton pulled away. He trailed off into his room and slammed the door behind him.

The man spent the last few hours crying himself to sleep. His poor, old mom could hear the sobs and screams as he shoved his face into his soft pillows. His screams and small tantrums made it seem like he was a child stuck in an adult's body.

Fulton cried later that night until he fell asleep again.

The next day, he didn't bother going to work. He left the building around five in the morning to drive off to Jo's. He needed some advice or a plan of attack to get rid of her cancer. He didn't mind the drive to Kennedale. With all the pent-up emotions and frustration, he was wide awake for the 40-minute drive.

Kennedale stood in the south area of Fort Worth, near Forest Hill. Tons of green in that area. Trees, leaves, and land, some would say.

Jo's house wasn't hers. It belonged to her grandparents (grandmother mainly, as her grandfather had already passed). She moved there at a young age and seemed to have made it apparent that the home would be hers forever until the day she died.

The house color had turned to a faded white, and the wood panels along the frame of the home were cracked. The shingles were peeling, exposing dirt that had been living since 1980, when Jo's grandfather built it. The house also sat on two and a half acres of land, with plenty of wide-open space. Most of the grass was trimmed, and since it's holding a senior citizen and a 30-year-old lunatic, they had the time to water it, leaving patches of it to yellow and wither away.

The green surrounding the home was bushy (up to four feet). Fulton felt blessed, comparing it to what he had back on Wolf Street.

Fulton approached her door with anger and eagerness. He banged on it until she'd answer.

Jo ran up to the door, yawning like the sound of a humpback whale. She was wearing pajamas—blue basketball shorts and a charcoal-black tank top.

"Jesus, Fulton, it's five in the morning. What do you want?!"

"Ma has breast cancer. I can't afford it alone, Jo."

Still tired and processing, the pyro-girl rubbed her eyes and listened closely.

"Wait. What are you saying?"

"I'm sayin', 'yes.' And I'm sayin' my mother has cancer."

"Yes to what? Stop being so vague! Also, I heard about the cancer part. I can't believe that's happening… Damn."

Fulton sighed, hiding his tears and shamefully admitting, "Let's do another job."

Those words woke her up like an early morning cup of coffee. Her eyes gleamed joyfully, and the hairs on the back of her neck stood up.

As she hugged him and jumped up in the air, Fulton became depressed, wondering how his mother would feel about the things he was planning on doing in her name.

"We're not doing it now, though. Just give it some time, and we'll do it. Got it?"

Jo agreed, rubbing her eyes. "Okay. Got it. Do you wanna come in so we can talk more?"

Fulton walked inside, careful not to wake up her grandmother.

The inside of the house was old. It was all built by hand with loads of bricks, wood, concrete, and nails. It smelled like plywood and paint, and everything looked dull. It was cozy and western.

She guided the man up the creaky steps and into her room.

When Jo cracked her bedroom door open, he glimpsed a peculiar object. He couldn't quite sense what it was, only noticing a pair of thick gray gloves attached to the ends of a cylinder shape.

"What's that?" he grilled, peeking over Jo's little yellow head to get a better look.

"Nothing," the woman answered blankly, throwing a blanket over the subject. "It's a little... project. So what's the plan?"

"I don't know, man. I'm thinkin' it should be somethin' simple. Just a couple of stores or three until I make enough."

"I'll think of a few places we might hit. Under one condition, though."

Fulton laid down on Jo's questionably clean twin-sized bed, getting comfortable enough to fall asleep. "What?"

"If you want a big pot, we bring a third guest into our group. If we do this, we need all the help we can get," she explained.

"Yeah, and that more help means more split cuts," Fulton replied, closing his eyes. "Look. I'll think about it. I just need to rest my eyes."

During his shut-eye, Fulton would lapse in and out of sleep. Each time his eyes opened, he'd witness something odd that Jo was getting up to.

He didn't know whether it was just his mind playing tricks on him or if he was having a lucid dream. He'd wake to her using a torch on the mysterious objects on her table. Other times, his eyes woke up to her touching her body around the blue flame. Sometimes, she'd be breaking up metal frames, along with what seemed to be parts of a motor.

Fulton assumed he'd been so fatigued that he hallucinated such strange things.

A few hours later, he was now well-rested, and ready to head back home. From his car, he could hear Jo rushing downstairs. She intended to remind him of the condition she mentioned earlier.

"Hey! Don't forget what I said!"

Rolling his eyes and groaning, he drove off, wanting to get home before either his mother or Gloria noticed he was gone.

Within the week, Fulton's problems were cooking. He fell into a trap of depression and debt.

Fulton had to attend therapy sessions at the Downtown Dallas Center. He'd go every other day whenever he felt empty. He'd walk in feeling alright during the session, only to feel alone walking out.

The man could only describe this feeling as walking into a room full of sorrow and bipolar (or lack of a better term)—fine in one moment, but not in the next.

At first, he was nervous and often embarrassed just for showing up. His mind wasn't alert and focused on his visits but more attentive to how he would afford all the treatments his mother had been undergoing.

Fulton laid down on a slim, burgundy leather couch with his hands folded behind his head to offer comfortable support. He spilled his emotions to his shrink—Terrance Balle—who wore the flashiest and tackiest suits any therapist would ever wear. His fiery red hair and trimmed beard didn't do justice. Today, he wore a forest green suit, beige tie, and red oxfords. Fulton took one quick stare and thought the man was a tall leprechaun.

"I don't know how I can just let her lay in bed and rot, Balle. There's not one moment where I can't stop thinkin' about her. She's dying," spilled Fulton.

"Please, just call me Terrance, Mr. Bruning. It's alright to think of her. She is indeed your mother, and you are her son. You care for her. I'm sure all she requires from you is your love and care."

"I don't think I can afford more treatments. I'm not sure what to do. It's so much stress buildin' up," Fulton whined.

Terrance wrote notes on his clipboard, taking action and details on how Fulton spoke, acted, and behaved.

"How is your job treating you? You told me earlier that you officially became the new manager of the Summit Peaks warehouse. Is that right?"

"Yes."

"Would you say you're earning more? How is it treating you so far?" Terrance asked.

Fulton sat up and scratched his head, still stressing. "It's alright. It's not much, but it's gotten me far. I just hope it'll continue to do so. I have other ways to get money, but it's not fair."

"Other ways? What do you mean?"

Fulton digressed, "Nothing... Sorry, I spoke too soon."

Terrance made a note of that statement.

"Mr. Bruning. You can tell me anything. Anything you say in here does not leave this room. This is a safe place."

"Yeah, I know. Maybe next time I'll say somethin'. Tonight, I have a job to do. It's stressful, and more shit that's addin' up. But it's all for her—my ma. I'll see ya' in a couple of days, Doc. I—I mean—Terrance."

"Have a nice day, Mr. Bruning."

Out in the cold, Fulton continuously rubbed his hands together while walking to his car to stay warm. Jo sat in the passenger seat, playing with one of her zippo lighters to create a fun-size fire for herself.

Down the road, the city was building its annual Thanksgiving Parade. From afar, Fulton could see the giant floats of cartoon characters, objects, and such. The one that caught his eye was a baseball. He reminisced about the times when his father would sit outside in front of his driveway and toss the ball to him for hours, talking about pointless things. The way his mom was sick reminded him more every day about his father.

A cold breeze flew past Fulton's face, and he broke out of his trance, focusing on the main task.

The man got in his car and started the engine with the heat on full blast. Fulton turned over to Jo, who unknowingly burned her index fingertip into a crimson-red mess.

Fulton's jaw dropped as Jo remained still.

"Huh? What is it?" she probed.

Fulton then shrieked, "Dude, your finger! You're going to burn your damn finger off!"

Jo quickly looked forward and clipped her lighter down. She didn't feel any pain. She felt nothing. It was like she was immune to the works of fire.

To cool her throbbing finger down, she stuck it in her mouth, swirling and drowning it in her saliva.

To reiterate, she loved fire.

Fulton turned his head away, paying attention to the road ahead. The streets were cold and wet, and accidents would become an all-time high in Dallas. (It would be worse with December's sleet and snow coming in.)

The two were on their way to meet up with Johnny Plaza Jr. It was about time Fulton had met him properly.

He asked Jo if he needed to know anything about the guy. She gave none but a shrug. Jo wanted him to share his opinions and fair judgments about the guy.

From the start, Fulton knew this guy would be a hard case. At work, he noticed Johnny was a lazy bum, not wanting to do any work at Summit. Not to mention, he had an arrogant attitude, but it left an opportunity. He could be a cunning warrior if he was an arrogant worker and socializer.

Johnny was waiting for them at the Summit parking lot. From time to time, Johnny would throw gambling parties and steal most of his opponent's money. He couldn't give two shits about someone unless they had something valuable in their pockets.

The lot was long, comprehensive, and dirty. It could fit around 350 vehicles of any sort. The industry was receiving tons of applicants—people waiting to score an interview—so much so that they were planning on building a parking garage beside the establishment.

From afar, Fulton and Jo could see Johnny sitting under a light pole, warming his hands up. His body was shaking, and it seemed he had been waiting outside for a long time. Cold snot ran down his bushy mustache and beard.

As Fulton pulled the car beside him, he rolled the window down.

"What's up, Johnny? How are you?"

"C-c-could you-you let me i-in?" he shook.

"I'm sorry?" Fulton teased. "I can't understand you. Did you want to get in the car?"

"L-let me in the—GODDAMN CAR!" Johnny yelled loud enough for a stranger to look in their direction.

Fulton groaned and unlocked the car door, hoping the random man would look away. Johnny rushed inside and embraced the warmth. His skin thawed like ice cream, and his breathing went normal.

"Also—I'm—fine," he answered, taking off his puffy coat and red beanie.

Fulton shivered at those words.

He turned back to get a clear view of the man. "I know we've met before, but this time, I want to meet ya'. So tell me somethin' about yourself."

"Didn't Jo tell you anything?" asked Johnny.

"No. She didn't. So tell me somethin'."

As he grew comfortable with the temperature, Johnny slipped his fingerless gloves off and played with his brown curly hair, focusing more on his well-being than anything else.

"Well... I've worked here for about a month and a half. I've known Jo for two years, and I'm just in this for the good stuff. Is that enough?"

"Not sure," said Fulton. "Is it? I can already tell you're a bit much. That's why I'm gonna ask again."

Jo giggled, looking at the men beside her as she felt the tension turn rocky.

"Do you like him so far, Mama's boy?"

Johnny rolled his eyes and continued to mess with his hair. "Look, I don't wanna waste any of my time right now. I just need to know whether I can be with you guys. I'm more of a go-with-the-flow type of guy, if that helps?"

The two in the front looked at each other. They thought similarly, knowing this wasn't Johnny's first rodeo.

Jo trusted the hairy man with her best ambitions. Fulton didn't know what to think about him. He wasn't just arrogant; he seemed to be whiny and careless. One of those reminded him of himself.

It was good to see they were on the same page.

Later, they stepped into Fulton's main office, spreading a map of the city and which town they wanted to head into first.

Johnny and Fulton argued, fighting over cities like Arlington and Mesquite. Fulton wanted something closer and less crowded.

Johnny was smart—suspiciously smart. His arrogance would scream naïve, but he knew what spots to hit.

"I'm telling ya', man. I know what stores have good scores. I know you don't know me that well, but you have to trust me."

Fulton couldn't buy it, putting his hands over his head.

"Please," Johnny begged.

Jo then added, "Fult, we're gonna hit a store or two, regardless. So let's just pick a place and get it on."

A moment of silence passed, and Fulton had no choice but to give in. It was better than nothing.

"Fine!" he shouted. "What did you have in mind?"

"Well, first, I was thinking about doing a couple of spots. Ya' know—just to dip our toes in the water. A small family bank and a convenience store. Something simple."

Fulton didn't seem amused. "That's it?"

"No. That's not all."

"Good. Because ya' had me worried for a bit. A little bank and a store is less than what—three grand? Two?"

"Yeah..." Johnny replied blankly, hoping deep down Fulton wouldn't mock him.

"Then what's your best?"

Johnny

 grew an eerie smile and put his offer down.

"Dallas. Regional. Bank."

Each word that came out sent a shiver down Fult's spine. He and Jo did the little jobs like stores or stands. This next heist was going into expert mode. They needed to get their shit together, or they'd be looking at long sentences.

Chapter 8
CHEW GUM

Thursday morning, Sam was looking over the ticket information. He didn't want to miss his flight and definitely didn't want to miss out on a new opportunity. The plane was ready to depart tomorrow afternoon. It was early-release day for Thanksgiving break—perfect timing.

When Sam told Cathy the news about him winning the trip to London, she gave every worried response that every mother gives, mainly the five Ws: who, what, when, where, and why.

After all those questions were answered, she calmed down, accepted it, and was happy to see her son be presented with an opportunity and hopefully help get the bills paid.

When the twins picked him up, Garrett didn't hear the news. Sam was so excited to tell him.

"Hey, Gar?"

"Yeah?"

"Did Trevor tell you what happened yesterday?"

Garrett shook his head, wondering which part of the day he was going on about.

"About what happened to Felix?"

Sam's face dropped. "No. The other thing."

"About who won the trip?" Garrett asked.

"Yes!"

"No. Who won?"

Sam gave a moment of silence, followed by a smirk and a stare.

"Who?" Garrett wanted to know. He didn't get the hint until his brother cleared his throat and tilted toward Sam.

"You got in?!" he exclaimed.

"I got it!"

Garrett rubbed his friend's shoulder and messed with his hair as he congratulated him. "I'm happy for you, man. I really am. When do you leave?"

"Tomorrow afternoon. Right when we get out of school."

Sam didn't notice, but Trevor was in a bit of a sour mood since he didn't get it. It was crazy to know that his friend got in by luck if Artie wasn't sick. Alas, he sucked up his bitter attitude and congratulated him again.

Everything was all good between the three.

When they got to the table before the first bell rang, Sam announced again to his peers that he'd be gone and busy for the break.

The only one who seemed to be interested in what he had to say was Alexus and his other friend, cheerleader Heather Hagen. The rest (Sonny Marcos, Carissa Carlson, and Abe Cite) were busy having their noses in books and trying to finish last night's homework within the next 5 minutes.

"What's up?" Alexus questioned.

"I'm going to London!"

Heather was confused. "What do you mean, London? I don't get it."

"Inferior—my job—had this raffle thing going on, and whoever gets picked gets to go to London to take pictures," explained Sam.

"That's nice. Like, for real. That's actually cool," said Alexus.

"Thanks. I still need to pack. I'm so excited."

Heather became sarcastic. "Wow. Going all the way to another country just to take pictures? Wow! I don't know anyone who could do that!"

Behind the three-way conversation, Trevor frowned momentarily, thinking that maybe Sam was rubbing it in.

Garrett signaled his twin, letting him know everything was okay. It was all just excitement.

"Well, be safe. Have fun." Heather smiled, tying up her platinum blonde hair into a messy bun.

Finally, the first bell rang. Carissa was covering her ears from the loud echoes. She attended a shindig last night because Sam didn't throw his traditional birthday party. A couple of peers at the table assumed she had a problem, but—despite the underage drinking—she knew how to have a good time. Even with the bell off, the sound continued from ear to ear as she started regurgitating and spitting drops of puke on the clean tile floors.

At the end of the hall, he spotted Felix walking to class. It shocked Sam that he had a black eye and a busted lip. The bully walked tediously. His shoulders hung, and he kept turning his face whenever people were nearby. As much as Sam didn't like the guy, it didn't satisfy him to see him look humiliated.

Sam wondered what had happened to him, but before he could finish, Garrett chimed in to answer his internal inquiry:

"He's not going to bother you."

"You did—"

"Yeah," the twin answered blankly. "Trevor told me what happened after he was sent to the office."

"Gar... you didn't have to do that."

"Don't worry about it, man. Just let me know if he bothers you again."

The first-period class started. When Sam walked in, the history teacher (Mr. McCrown) called him over:

"Mr. Clark! Welcome! Could you come to my desk?"

"Yes, Sir?"

Mr. McCrown smiled. "I'm assuming you got that project done?"

Sam gasped like a drowning victim, reaching for air. He'd forgotten it again.

"Ah. I see... you don't have it." McCrown's words felt like sharp knives. Sam didn't mean to disappoint the guy.

"I'm so—sorry, Mr. McCrown. I finished it, I—I had just forgotten it—"

"Excuses. Excuses..." McCrown interrupted. "I'm sorry, Clark. I need to assign you for after-school detention today, and we'll see what Principal O'Malley says about tomorrow."

"Sir, I can't go."

McCrown's face shifted. He looked angry at first, then confused.

"What do you mean you can't go?"

"I have a work trip tomorrow, and I need to pack up everything tonight," explained Sam.

"Late, late, late as always, Clark. You forget to turn in your homework on time, let alone pack up for a trip the night prior."

"I'm sorry." Sam's eyes went low, having no excuse.

"Don't be sorry. Be responsible. Look, I can't convince Principal O'Malley to let this slide. She wanted to turn this around for this school, but she only made things hostile. If I let this slide, she'll be on me for the rest of her time here," the teacher tore off a pink sheet of paper from one of his notepads to assign mandatory detention for the kid. "I'll see you after school."

Sam couldn't attend that after-school session. If he skipped out on it, he knew the consequences would worsen. It might even affect his current grades, which were barely passing. He's a smart kid; he just had bad luck.

Mrs. Smith overheard great news about Sam in the last class. She went over to his table and, like the others, congratulated him. "I heard you got selected. Congratulations!"

"Thank you, Mrs. Smith. I appreciate it."

"When do you go off?"

"Tomorrow," he answered.

"Really? I thought you'd be leaving on a weekend or something."

"I thought so, too."

Mrs. Smith smiled at her student, proud of his work and choice of study.

"Any advice about plane rides?" he asked. "I've never been on one before. I'm kinda nervous."

"Yes. Chew gum."

"Noted." Sam turned his eyes towards the computer to finish up on work from other homerooms.

On a routine-like basis, Felix would walk into the classroom to take his aunt's paperwork to the front office, and as he passed, he'd sometimes make Sam flinch by pretending to swing at him or smack him in the mouth. In the earlier physical abuse stages, he'd nut-check him or flick him in the head. Other times, he'd make disgusted faces or say something redundant to him. Sam couldn't help but make severe eye contact with Felix, not because of his busted eye or damaged lip, but because of what happened with Alexus. He knew he shouldn't have looked at him, but it was necessary to be cautious. As usual, a comment slipped through the jock's cut-up lip:

"What, Connie?!"

How does he know my middle name? Sam thought. It could've been worse. A snarky comment was better than a crotch shot or a finger flick to the face.

Dismissed for the day, it was time to choose. Take the punishment and get home relatively late, pack up essentials with a slight chance of forgetting something important, fall asleep late, or skip detention and not go to school tomorrow. (It wasn't fatal to ignore an early-release day.) Regardless, Sam had no intention of showing up tomorrow, detention or not.

The twin's immense red beauty pulled up to the curb, ready to drop him off back home to pack up. From the passenger window, Garrett could tell something was up. He rolled down the tinted window, calling out to Sam as he walked close.

"What's wrong?"

"Nothing... actually, there's a couple of things, but I wanted to ask you about Felix."

Garrett scoffed. "What about him?"

"What if he gets on my case again?" Sam had fear in his voice.

"He's not. Trust me. What's the other thing that's bothering you—besides Felix?"

"Would you believe me if I told you I got detention?"

"No," replied Trevor. "Why?"

Sam shrugged, his face leaving a blank expression on their answers.

"No! Are you serious?" Garrett exclaimed, laughing.

"Really?! You got detention... I don't believe it," Trevor cackled.

"I'm skipping it."

"Good—I mean—bad? I dunno' what to say, Sam. I wouldn't worry about it. Just come on." Garrett beckoned, scooting down to the middle seat. It was now or never. Sam did indeed have a choice but felt more lenient about following this opportunity. Now, there was no holding back. He made the choice and got into the truck.

"Are you thrilled yet? I mean—you're going across the ocean, bro!" Garrett hyped, sounding happier than Sam was.

"Yes! I'm just on edge about the plane situation. I've never been in one."

"Chew some gum," said both brothers.

Chapter 9
LONDON: DAY ONE

Forty hours later, now entering the final descent of the flight, Sam woke up in terror. His memory ceased for a few seconds after being brought back to life. The boy sat drenched in his steamy sweat, confused about where he was.

In a blink or two, Sam realized his trip wasn't a dream. It was all true. It was almost time for landing, and everything was surreal. There was no way he was already across the country with paid meals and a room.

He focused back on the nightmare before he'd forget. This one felt real. It wasn't horror movie monsters, sacred demons, or bullies. No, it was something new. The thought of it being something entirely different made it worse.

It was about a car accident. The vile feeling of flipping over and being crushed to death shocked him. Sam didn't have to fret about it for too long. As he predicted, within minutes, he'd forgotten all about it.

Poof. All gone.

Sam groaned. *My ass is so sore. I hope I never have to fly longer than 10 hours back.*

He took a peek outside the window slot, and boy, was it a view. It was something he'd never forget—something that could replace the view of the Dallas skyline forever.

Just from the window, he could see a few attractions. He saw Tower Bridge.

Wow, that looks so much bigger than the pictures.

From that distance, he could spot the London Eye. It wasn't hard to notice that big ring in the air. (It was one of the few attractions he was eager to see.)

There was another spot he couldn't quite make out. Even with his readers on, he couldn't tell.

Ding!

The plane rang, and the Captain on the other end of the P.A. system spoke, "Goooood night and good early morning, ladies and gentlemen. This is your captain speaking. We'll be landing in a few minutes. When we do, please give us a moment to secure and organize your luggage, which you will find in the baggage claim area. We hope you enjoyed your nonstop flight. Thank you for choosing us, and welcome to London."

At the baggage claim, he met up with Jessie and Reese. There was no point in interacting with the two, knowing they were secretly screwing each other every week. For them, all this trip did was further encourage their friends-with-benefits behavior.

Inferior provided the three with a company vehicle and a chauffeur to take them anywhere they needed (with exaggeration), mainly to work and back.

The chauffeur was tall, his voice somber and elegant, and he had an English accent.

"Hello. My name is Robert Jackson. I'm here to take you to the Hotel."

"What hotel?" Jessie asked curiously.

"The Rington Hotel," the chauffeur answered.

He reached into his coat and handed each of them a neat brochure with further information on the establishment, landmarks, and various locations around London's towns, restaurants, stores, and attractions.

"The Rington, huh? That's a nice name," Sam muttered.

The Hotel was about 20 stories high and contained an immense pool that tied together with a hot tub, a sauna, a complimentary breakfast, an office space, a gym, a spa room, and a tanning room.

Everything sounded welcoming, but for Sam, it was a lot to take in. Most of the amenities were utterly unnecessary. Sam knew he wasn't even planning to use more than half of those rooms, anyway.

The tall driver stepped outside the vehicle to pull his passengers' luggage out. When they had their belongings, the man explained the escorting situation to them.

"So, as of today, I will be your driver to and from work. I will also take you wherever you need or want to go. However, I have a schedule to follow. Whenever you need to go, I'll be here. If you're behind schedule, then you miss your ride. Good day."

Robert entered the car and drove away.

"I guess we head inside?" Jessie asked.

Reese moved his blue, rolling suitcase to the front.

The moment the tip of his shoes entered the lobby, they caught the receptionist's attention. She looked up from behind her desk and snapped her fingers, calling them over.

"Are you from Inferior? From America?"

It was hard for Sam to understand her accent, but after taking a few seconds to fully grasp her words, he answered her question.

"Uh—yes? Yes. We are."

"Great. Your names and identification, sir?"

Before Sam could get a word in, Reese cut right before him. He became impatient, wanting to get to his room to screw Jessie's brains out until completion.

"Reese Stellar. What's my room?"

The receptionist batted an eye, concerned with the young man's tone. "Let me see... Ah! Mr. Stellar. You are in room three thirty-one."

She slid his keycard on the marble counter. Reese snagged it away like it was a sentimental item.

"Samuel Clark."

"Alright, Mr. Clark. You'll be on the seventh floor. Your room number is seven hundred and seven. Here's your keycard, and if you need anything, please use the guest phone in your room."

Sam grabbed his card while distracted by the vast design of the Hotel's lobby, dining room, and high-rise ceilings.

"Wow."

Tonight, there needed to be more time to explore the Rington. More time to look at the giant fish tank in the middle of the dining room or throw a coin in the little waterfall against the wall next to the bar.

But unfortunately, Sam was jet-lagged; he needed to get his eight hours first. Then everything could come next. The entire week would screw with his perception of time.

Back in Texas, it was nine. Sam looked down at his watch.

"Jesus... It's already three in the morning."

There was plenty of time to call his mother to tell her he had made it safely. Hopefully, she wasn't too held up at work and could answer.

The phone kept dialing with no answer. Thirty seconds in, and no pickup. Eventually, a robotic voice spoke to Sam.

I'm sorry, but the person you are trying to reach is unavailable. Please leave a message after the tone. Beep.

"Hey, Mom. I made it here safely. Um—I love you, and I miss you already. Call me back when you have a chance. Bye."

Day one out of five.

It was the fourth time in a row that Sam had fallen asleep. The jet lag was getting to him hard. His sleeping schedule was already screwed, but he couldn't imagine how messed up it'd be when he'd finally be home.

An alarm set off on his phone.

RING-RING-RING!

Sam shot straight up from the bed, realizing it wasn't his regular sleeping alarm but a phone call. A call from Mr. Grafton.

"Sam! Are you up?!" he shouted at the end of the call.

"I'm awake. I'm awake."

"About time. I need you up at Hyde Park at ten-thirty. Sharp."

"Okay. Hey! Really quick—can you tell me what time it is? I just need clarification to see if everything is correct in my phone," Sam said.

"It's 9:50," Grafton said blankly. His tone sounded more irritated than usual.

"Got it. Thank you. I'll be there shortly."

Sam checked his laptop to see if any emails had been sent out today. None. There was nothing new from work or personal, except for some spam emails about getting his next fast food order for ten percent off.

It was time to get ready for the event. Sam couldn't decide what to wear. He needed to clear his head and think it over during a two-minute teeth brushing.

Take it one step at a time, he thought.

A quick slip of a gray t-shirt, light blue denim jeans, and his casual sneakers looked decent for today's assignment. Sam grabbed his essentials: laptop, camera bag, jacket, and confidence. Luckily, he only had three things.

The nervous boy started biting at his nails and double-checking everything to ensure he was ready to work, sliding his specs on his face as he trekked down the red and gold hallway.

The silver frames began peeling on the edges, and one arm was crooked—partially off by its hinge from the wear and tear. He had to get a new pair, eventually.

The silver elevator came up and sent the young man down to the lobby, hoping he could grab some breakfast before work.

Sad to say, there were no pancakes, waffles, eggs, or any sort of big breakfast items. Already off to a bad start. Sam grabbed an apple and coffee from the dining counter near the receptionist's desk.

The driver was outside waiting for him, leaning against the SUV and picking the dirt out of his crystal nails.

"Hey, Clark! You ready to leave?"

"Yes, sir."

The driver moved and gave the kid a stern warning. "Remember what I said yesterday? Don't be late. If you're late, I'm late. This affects my job, too. I'm only helping you with this once. I don't mean to sound like a grouch, sir. I'm just letting you know."

"I understand. I'm really sorry. The ride got to me, and the time here is different and—"

"That's fine," he interrupted. "I'm just letting you know. You help me, I'll help you."

Sam nodded, looking down at the ground, disappointed and ashamed for interfering with someone's task.

"Let's go."

During the ride, the man went over a few potholes along the way. Sam nearly choked on his coffee from one of his gulps, going down the wrong pipe and coughing like a sick child.

In the meantime, Sam looked over the brochure the driver gave him. Sam recalled seeing a map included. When he reached into his pockets, he realized he had completely forgotten it in his room. His heart dropped for a moment until he noticed more similar-looking brochures in the back of the driver's seat.

There were three other maps. The first map he pulled out was a standard issue of the trip that he received before. All the go-to attractions that any tourist would wanna see. It wasn't too recent—it'd been issued five years ago.

The next map was far from recent, dating 25 years back.

Why would this be in the back? Sam wondered, picking up the last vintage-looking map from the pouch.

A wrinkled, faded, 40-year-old map of the city lay in his hands, further from 2015. Sam looked at it. Each looks more updated than the newest. It was strange. The previous sketches had shortcuts. Even some that weren't on the latest edition.

Still riding along, Sam momentarily took his mind off work, studying London's roads and old paths. It was something remarkable.

"This is actually cool," he said to the chauffeur and asked why he had these in his car.

The man explained that the maps were for tourists and that they came from other drivers. They kept them there for visitors to learn how updated and improved they've become since then. Just a minor history glance was all. Nothing crazy.

Life screamed at Hyde Park. The wind yelled into Sam's soft ears, tickling the little hairs.

Since the park alone was huge, he needed help to figure out where to go. Sam followed the park's trail, hoping to see someone or something familiar. About 50 feet away, he could see Grafton, Juniper, and a few assistants setting up the lighting and area around her.

He kicked up the speed, approaching the few faster than the flock of ravens above him. Sam went further into the park as Mr. Grafton swayed around, his mind reacting slowly to the boy's face, thinking it was a random pedestrian jogging around.

"Wait—Clark? Finally," he groaned.

"I'm ready to take pictures, sir."

Mr. Grafton pondered, not knowing what to do with him for now. It was almost too late for Sam to get to work. Finally, he came up with a solution.

"Hm. Okay then. Hurry and start setting up your stuff, I guess."

While simultaneously setting up the equipment and looking around, Sam felt eyes locked on him. Someone's attention was being put forth all over. The tension caused him to look around, seeing that the sights were from Ms. Juniper.

He wanted to make conversation with her but didn't want to be a bother. She was practically suffering. Her makeup artist splashed warm colors on her face; all the while, she'd been freezing. That gray hoodie covering her shoulders didn't aid, but God—she looked as beautiful as heaven.

Is that a new dress? Sam studied the scale of apparel as the sun made the maroon in her ensemble shine brighter than the lighting for the photos. Even crazier were the heels that she wore, which made them stand out.

In nothing flat, he stopped staring before it got weird. Sam killed the time by pulling a spare cigarette from his jacket and lighting the end to flames before taking some random pictures of the park. Through the eye lens, he found a bird resting on a little branch with its beak plowed between its wings.

It might be cold.

He squeezed the shutter button, taking a few frames of the little red thing. Sam beamed, looking back at the pictures.

"Awe. Cute!"

Reese stood in the distance, looking through his phone to pass the time. His messenger bag was hanging behind his ass, along with his new Nikon camera behind his arm.

The crew couldn't figure out what Kendrick was going for. Was it more city-style? Nature-themed? Or a more nonchalant kind of approach for the magazine? Eventually, they'd figure it out.

Sam snuck in a few shots of Ms. Juniper when she threw her jacket off. Ultimately, he picked up a pattern. Sam was on the front lines, taking endless pictures of her.

Some looked off-guard, bringing a stunning, authentic, and visual appeal to the set of photos. Sam was appointed to her center. Some pictures had to be taken on a messy bench while pieces of bird-shit mushed into his sneakers.

Later, if he could, he'd try taking them from a nearby hill (not the best idea). The pictures made her seem small. It was back to her center.

Much better.

Suddenly, Mr. Grafton called out to the boy, "Alright! You're good for now. Let's wait for the next steps."

Sam's legs ached, and his eyes were strained. He could feel bags pulling his face down as he leaned against the bird-shit-covered bench.

Cold gales eased his tension. Winter was coming (if not already here), and it was coming fast. The only thing needed was for Thanksgiving to hurry and pass.

It's better than summer, he told himself as he inhaled and exhaled deeply, kicking back on the bench. Sam always hated the heat.

"What's better than summer?" a familiar voice asked.

Sam gently turned his head, his eyes widening at Ms. Juniper.

"It's okay. It's okay," she assured him. "I talk to myself sometimes."

Ellie patted Sam's thigh. A black, fuzzy jacket covered her torso.

Unlike Sam, Ellie loved the heat, despising every inch of the cold. Sometimes, she'd get easily sick if she'd been out in that environment for too long. She missed summer. It reminded her of her home back in France.

"You like the cold better, yes?" she shivered.

"Yeah. Fall and winter are my favorite seasons. You?"

"Love summer," she winked. "You not cold?"

"Me? No, not at all. I love this weather," he answered, removing his windbreaker to let the draft flow further through his shirt.

Ms. Juniper laughed. "You crazy. I can't really stand this type. I wish I was on the beach."

Across the hilltop, Ellie's manager waved her over to let her know it was time to leave.

"Ah. Shame. I have to leave. Bye, Sammy. Wait—you'll be here tomorrow and later to see me at the festival, right?"

"Yes! I will."

"It starts at 11. I guess we'll see you at 10?" she asked in a high tone, excited.

"I'll be there. No way I could miss that."

"Yay! I'll see you later. Bye, Sammy!"

"Bye," the boy said softly.

Sam lifted himself up from the bench and dusted himself off, wiping the bird shit off the back of his pant legs.

"Aww. Dammit," he winced in disgust.

After collecting his things, Sam walked down the same path he came from. He could haul down a taxi or something nearby to take him back to the Rington, but before leaving, he debated whether he should take a grand tour around town. Maybe he would go sightseeing for a few hours...

No. He paid it no mind. The kid was still drained.

Out of the blue, an annoying itch developed from the side of his head. Sam scratched it and turned his head in its itchy direction. He continued to strike at it like an itchy dog.

His eyes looked up to notice a baseball was flying toward his head—quickly. Sam ducked, and the ball grazed the top of his head, landing on the grass.

A stranger was running towards Sam's point of view, calling out to him, "Hey?! Are you okay there, mate?"

Sam cautiously picked his head up, standing straight.

"Hey, sorry about that, my hand slipped," the man explained.

Sam tried to take the blame. "No—no, it's fine. I got in the way."

The man scoffed, walking past Sam to retrieve his ball.

Sam's cracked-up phone vibrated in his pocket. It was his mother calling. He answered without hesitation, missing her and home already.

"Hey, Mom!"

"Hey, sweetie. How's the trip?"

"It's going good so far. I just got done with work for the day."

"That's great," she laughed.

"Yeah... Also, did you just wake up? You sound tired," he questioned, checking the time on his watch.

"Umm. Yeah—yeah. I just woke up. It's barely going to be five a.m.," Cathy yawned.

"Oh, wow. Yeah, I tried calling you yesterday when I got to my hotel. I didn't know if you were asleep or anything."

"Yeah, I saw. I had just seen the notification. Sorry, my phone was dying, and I was working late. When I got home, I just crashed on the couch."

Sam was relieved, hearing the soothing sounds of his mother's voice; he was homesick.

"Well, I'll let you go. Make sure you take some pictures or at least bring back a souvenir or something."

"I will. There's a lot to look at."

"Wait!" Cathy jumped before the call ended. "I just wanted to let you know that I'm proud of you, son. Keep up the work, and it'll all be worth it. I love you."

Sam grinned, sending the call off, "I love you too, Mom. Bye!"

Chapter 10
MANIC HEISTS

Jo appeared to be in an off mood today. Fulton had stayed the night again at her place, and throughout the night, he heard her mumble meaningless nothings to herself. Now and then, Fulton could recall her having some type of bad day, but on this day, she'd usually be excited to do a heist. What was scarier than her odd mumbles was the gut-wrenching scream she let out in the middle of the night. Fulton assumed she probably had a nightmare.

The screaming didn't stop. The man had to assure her she'd be alright, but Jo never believed that. When he asked what her night terror entailed, she refused to answer. More specifically, it was none of his business.

The first job was at a gas station. Jo was taking the lead on this one. This was a simple task—nothing that the three hadn't done before. Fulton grew concerned about Jo. She didn't seem up to the task, but the eagerness in her voice changed his mind. This didn't need to be a two-man job. In, then out. Simple.

Johnny and Fult waited in the van, keeping the engine warm and a foot on the brake, ready to release and run. Jo put on her balaclava and airsoft mask and started towards the front doors. It was nighttime, so few people were out, especially in the ghetto side of town. A simple pedestrian wouldn't have the balls to get that gas station burrito in a neighborhood like this at two in the morning.

The two in the van let the woman do her thing. As long as she got the money, it didn't matter what she did—at least, that's what Johnny believed.

"Why the regional bank?" Fulton questioned.

Johnny turned his head to the boss. "Scared?"

"That's bigger than a little station, dude. Security will be there. Cops will be nearby. I doubt they'll be carryin' a lot of cash in the registers."

"Exactly. There's something better."

Fulton's face squinted, confused. "Like what?"

"I'm working on it. I'll have a plan after we do the bank. Since it's not a big corporate one, they'll be carrying more cash than the average one."

Fulton looked past Johnny and out the passenger window, hoping he could see Jo doing alright on her own. "Then why don't we just do those? Why the big jump?"

"Because by the time we hit the second one, they'll notice a pattern, and then they'll send out more units to look for anything suspicious. The bigger the score, the fewer jobs you can do."

"Got it."

"Amateur," Johnny mumbled.

BANG!

A gunshot went off. The men's heads turned quickly, alerting their attention. They didn't know if Jo shot or if someone else did. There was nothing they could do. Their job was to stay in the van and wait.

A moment passed, and Jo ran out, holding handfuls of cash and a candy bar that was squished in her hands.

"Go! Go! Go! Go!" she repeated, jumping into the big vehicle. Fulton let his foot off the brake and put the pedal to the metal. The tires screeched for a moment, pushing off.

When things looked clear, Fulton glanced at the rear-view mirror, checking in with his friend. "What happened? Who shot?"

"Me."

"WHY?! Did you—"

"No. I just wanted to scare him. He wasn't playing along."

Fulton sighed out of relief. "At least you didn't shoot him."

"Yeah," she whispered.

Jo threw her guise off, glancing at the goggles on the airsoft mask, wiping off a drop of blood that stained it. *What the hell happened back there?*

She didn't know, but Fulton monitored her in the mirror. Something was off.

The next morning, the police reported that a cashier at a local station had been shot in the left arm and found an hour later by a usual customer who made the call to the paramedics.

*   *   *

Johnny wanted Fulton to help him out with the next one. This was light work, but if something went wrong, this was all over for the rest. The plan entailed Johnny wearing a fake suicide bomb vest, which was made with a bulky velcro vest, a digital timer with some flared-out wires wrapped around the stomach and arm line, and pieces of ripped duct tape.

The goal was to get the money, put it in an envelope, walk to the nearest grocery store's bathroom at the far end of the building, hand the money over to Fulton in the bathroom, and leave out the back exit. Easy.

They waited until the evening, minutes before the bank closed up for the day. Johnny didn't want to attract attention, and screaming bystanders would be a dead giveaway.

The little bank was located uptown, not too far from the city. Instead of using the van this time, they used Fulton's car. The van's orange trim already attracted attention, but a black sedan was perfect for blending in. Fulton dropped off Johnny near a local burger joint. It was just down the block—not too far for the walk to be unbearable, but not too close to attract attention or cameras.

After Fulton dropped him off, he went straight to the grocery store. His plan was to shop around, carry a few groceries in his cart, and, after specifically seven minutes, go to the bathroom and wait for Johnny. After the trade, Fulton would walk out, buy whatever was in the cart, and meet the rest at Summit.

Johnny strutted into the bank. He wore a thin red jacket zipped up to the top, a black baseball hat that looked brand new, and some dark sunglasses. This wasn't exactly meant to hide Johnny's identity—just something that covered his prominent features so no authorities could clearly recognize him. Plus, he didn't have a mask, and there was no time to buy one. The whole point of these two jobs was to throw off the police, hoping they'd find an odd pattern to keep them distracted.

The teller at the front was a young Mexican woman. She adjusted her plastic glasses, cleared her throat, smiled, and politely informed him, "I'm sorry, sir. We'll be closing in a few minutes. You'll have to come back tomorrow, and we'll help you then."

Johnny faked a smile. "You can help me right now."

"Sir?" The lady didn't understand. Her intuition was telling her that something was off. She rolled her shoulders back, standing tall, and prepared for whatever this off-feeling was.

Johnny quickly unzipped his jacket, revealing the trashy homemade vest. The timer was counting down from three minutes.

"Money, please," Johnny said, with no emotion expressed in his tone of voice or face.

"Oh, my God..." The lady's face dropped, looking up and down from the vest to his face. She wasn't ready for this.

"Money, please," he repeated. "Now."

The teller's hands shook as she slowly opened the register, grabbing handfuls of bills.

"Can you put that in an envelope, please?" asked Johnny. His tone sounded more giddy as his eyes caught sight of all the green she held. "Also, no dye packs."

"I don't think we have those, sir," her voice raised.

Johnny rolled his eyes. "Heh. Yeah. Sure you don't."

As she shoved the money into a thin blue envelope, her eyes met with the timer. She felt horrified by the two-minute mark and how the robber in front of her had no fear of dying or hurting others. The fear that engulfed her made her move slower.

I can't believe this is happening.

Not once in her life did the poor lady think she'd ever have to encounter this. She thought this was going to be a normal day. She was ready to clock out, head home to her young, energetic husky, feed him his nightly dinner, and eat whatever dinner her grandmother made with her parents. This was clearly far from routine.

A tear streamed down her right cheek. Johnny saw this and noted her nametag.

"Daniela?"

"Yes, sir?" she sniffled, slowly grabbing more bills from the open register.

"You're doing great. I will not hurt you unless you let this timer count down. Just keep going. This'll be over soon. Then you can go home and go about your day. Okay?"

Daniela found his comfort odd. It didn't help; in fact, the comfort he showed made it worse. The timer made it to her line of sight again — a little over a minute later.

When she emptied the register, Johnny snatched the two envelopes away from her and ran outside. Daniela fell to her knees, gasping for air. Tears flooded her eyes as she grasped her shoulders, almost facing God. A mixture of emotions came: relief, shock, anger, and terror.

*　　　　*　　　　*

Out in the back, Johnny threw the jacket and vest in the dumpster and trekked to the grocery store. Instead of running to make it on time to meet up with Fulton, the man fast-walked through the parking lot, zig-zagging through rows of cars. He listened for any sirens, but none went off.

She must still be in shock. Or maybe they're already on their way.

Regardless, Johnny kept walking and tried not to attract attention to himself. He was just a random guy with a hat, glasses, and a plain white t-shirt. Just a boring guy in a boring outfit.

Johnny walked past another parking lot at a shoe store, and suddenly a police siren went off. Not too far away from the hairy man. His brisk walk turned into a jog as the market was in his line of sight.

As he was about to get into the crosswalk that led to the store doors, a cop car appeared right in front of him. No siren, no warning. Johnny jerked back. Adrenaline filled his body, and his only plan was to run.

Somehow, luck was on his side today. The cop car went past and was on its way to the bank. They had no description of the suspect yet.

Inside, Johnny roamed through aisles. It was an unnecessary move. Nobody in the store noticed or cared, for that matter. The man threw his sunglasses and hat into a rack in one aisle. He didn't care if anybody saw or if the aisle was for pampers. Luckily, there were no cameras in the hallway leading to the bathroom. Johnny made it with decent timing—he was only off by two minutes.

Fulton was pretending to piss in the middle urinal out of the three. It was a good call, considering most guys got uncomfortable if they had to stand shoulder-to-shoulder to take a piss. Fulton turned to what he assumed was Johnny. If it wasn't him, it would just be making outlandish eye contact with a random fellow while having your penis in your hand.

"We good?" Fulton asked.

"Good." Johnny pulled the envelopes out of his pocket, tossing them to his partner.

"Make sure you wash your hands," Johnny added.

Shortly after their exchange, Fulton walked out first and proceeded with the original plan: buy whatever he put in the cart and then head to Summit. The money was safe in his signature jacket.

Chapter 11
THE IRISH RIDE

Day two out of five.

RING-RING-RING! RING-RING-RING! The hotel phone rang again beside sleepy Sam.

RING-RING-RING! RING-RING-RING! His eyes gradually opened at the tone. His brain hadn't yet registered that he most likely overslept.

Again, the phone screamed.

RING-RING-RING! RING-RING-RING!

When his eyes fully opened, he pulled the phone off the nightstand and cleared his throat, an attempt to sound like he had been awake for hours.

"Y-Yes? Hello?" His voice shook.

"Sam!" Mr. Grafton shouted from the other line.

The sleepy boy cleared his throat again. "Mhm. Yes, sir."

"Where the hell are you, kid?! You were supposed to be here about half an hour ago!"

Sam's barely waking eyes searched for his phone. He mostly had to rely on his hands to feel its familiar, smooth surface. When he found it, he read the time.

"Sir, it's not ten yet. I still have about thirty minutes. I'll be there, I swear."

"Did you even check your damn email, Genius?!" the man snapped. "We had a schedule change! You were supposed to be here half an hour ago! Tower Bridge. Now!"

"Oh, God..." he gasped, sucking a strong gust of air into his lungs, feeling like he would cough it out.

Sam got out of bed, put on whatever he had in his luggage, and grabbed whatever he could—camera bag, laptop, chargers, phone, etc.—not even bothering to brush his teeth or fix his hair.

Running down the warm hallway, with one arm inside his jacket and the other in his pants to tuck in his shirt, he repeated the location to himself.

"Tower Bridge. Tower Bridge. Tower Bridge."

Out in the front, he stretched his neck, searching for the chauffeur. He remembered again that he was late and that the damn SUV wasn't anywhere in sight. He should've made a mental note of what the driver said to him yesterday.

Sam's thoughts ran, coming up with made-up conclusions. *I'm going to get fired. Where's the guy? Did he drop off Reese? Or Jessie? My ass is grass...*

Sam's breathing became heavy, his chest rising and sinking down. He could even see his heart move in time with his breathing, hyperventilating on the verge of a bad panic attack.

In the corner of his eye, he noticed a mustard shade of yellow passing by—a taxi. He had no choice but to flag it down, waving his arm around like a lost hitchhiker.

"Taxi! Taxi!" Sam yelled.

Its tires screeched. The driver must've noticed his next customer in his rearview mirror. The taxi reversed into the entrance of the Rington Hotel. Before it came to a full stop, Sam grabbed the handle tightly, threw the door wide open, and rushed into the back seat, his equipment dragging behind him, nearly forgetting to close the door.

"Where to, me' good sir?" the temporary chauffeur posed.

"Tower Bridge!" Sam spoke without hesitation, ready for any question. "Tower Bridge! Please! I'm in a hurry."

The operator put the pedal to the metal, making way to get there as quickly as possible.

"How many quick routes are there?" asked Sam.

The man's dark eyebrows lifted, and he adjusted his mirror to look back at young Sam and give him a straight answer.

"Oh, 'dere's plenty. 'Dere's about three quicker routes. Which sounds good to 'ya, lad?"

It was funny how Sam elected to ignore the fact that the driver was Irish. His accent was a little thick, and he had a long mustache with a patchy beard. The man was always smiling throughout the costly ride. He was very kind to Sam, attempting to make conversation to dull the quiet awkwardness.

The panicky boy in the back tried to see any other routes on his phone before he could knock a word in, but his phone was already dying. He'd forgotten to charge it last night. He squeezed the power button, but the little low battery icon popped up before shutting down.

When putting the phone away in his jacket, Sam's fingers knocked against an odd shape poking from within the pocket and another edge rubbing against his stomach. *The vintage map!*

Sam carefully unfolded the sides, looking over them one last time to see if there was a faster route to the bridge.

"Um– is this one good?" he asked, sliding it underneath the Irish fellow's hairy chin and pointing at the specific route. It was a road with no name but a familiar place for the kind driver.

"Oh, 'dat one? Alright then!" he squeaked, turning his wheel almost 180 degrees and now heading down a dirt path.

For a second, Sam thought something might have been wrong because of the driver's response. He grew a pair and asked, "Is there something wrong with it, sir? You seemed surprised."

"No, it's fine, lad. It's just kind of abandoned, is all."

"Abandoned?"

"Aye. Me' lads and I go 'dere to drink sometimes. Mostly to hang out 'dere. It was once a private community. 'Dey tested military weapons. From your country—I assume—American?"

"Yes."

"Ah. I knew it!" The man cheered. "So easy to tell!"

Sam bit his cheek, surprised at the history, which lured him around the shortcut. "When was that? If you don't mind me asking?"

"Weapons? 'Dey stopped after that war in 1975... I can't remember its name."

Sam attempted to figure out which war. Although history wasn't his strongest suit, it didn't hurt to remember.

"Excuse me, sir?" Sam called out.

The operator's big blue eyes looked back at Sam in the mirror. "Yes?"

"I was wondering if you could tell me the time, please? I just don't want to be late."

The driver's long fingers pointed to the top of the car's cracked dashboard. A little past ten.

*   *   *

The vehicle stopped in front of two metal gates. It was the only way to pass through the shortcut.

This definitely isn't weird at all, Sam thought as he readjusted his glasses.

Inside the gated area were a few people chilling around, sitting in the corners, and chugging down a few bottles of Guinness. Some were even shoving tongues down each other's throats, having too much fun to pass the time away. All were dressed in black, and most had long hair that hung down their shoulders. One stood close by the path, pissing a dark yellow stream into the dirt, creating disgusting mud.

Sam assumed those were the friends the Irish gentleman had mentioned earlier. The man tugged off a rusty lock that held the gates together and tossed it far off. He then pushed the gate open for his taxi to pass.

The driver seemed giddy, like a child on Christmas. "No one really drives here. We usually walk right in," the driver smiled, turning to face Sam and pointing at his glasses. "Are 'dose yer' readers?"

"Urm. Yes. Yes."

He nodded, taking a short glance at the eyewear. "Well, aren't 'dose a fine pair of aviators ye' got on, boy."

Sam accepted the compliment. "Thank you, sir."

As the adult slowly drove into the area, he poured out some personal details to the young man. "Ya' know, you're a lot like me, kid. I mean—he's not almost as near yer age or as skinny as ye, but—I'm sure you and he would've gotten along."

Still pulling into the area, Sam noticed debris scattered across the five-acre land. He could almost make out a few large objects embedded into the ground. To him, it looked like the bottom half of an M48 Patton just lying there like a decoration for all to admire.

"What's your son like?" asked Sam.

"Eh—He's... not really here anymore, I'm afraid."

Sam felt an awkward empathy towards the stranger. *Should I change the topic? Stay silent? Something?*

"He was an old weasel. And—hyper as one. Shame on his mother. Lost her too."

All grins disappeared, and the man fell into a depressing tone, almost revealing everything to his passenger.

Sam sat in the backseat, appalled. It sounded to him like this was recent... *Was it?*

*   *   *

While the poor stranger further depressed the tension, Sam's whole head suddenly itched. It felt like all the surrounding skin was cracking. Seconds swished by, and all he could feel was a trembling full force of pressure swaying him back into his seat as splashes of rigid glass smacked his skin, only to get showered with gusts of heat.

The heat was grazing his skin off.

To him, it felt like the car had rolled off its tires and into zero gravity. Although this wasn't the case, the car had flipped over onto its top, the floor hitting their heads.

Before the shock came, Sam could only remember some warm liquid splashing the windows and ricocheting into his face like water would smack at a water park. Only instead of water, it was thick blood.

Everything had gone deaf to his ears. Everything went quiet... *everything went into oblivion.*

Chapter 12
BANK JOB

At the warehouse, Jo was staring at the bit of fire that poked out from the tip of her lighter. She got distracted by its light, putting her in a deep state of mind. Her trance soon broke when she heard Fulton pull his car up outside the office.

For the next job, Fulton reluctantly agreed to let Jo and Johnny do the planning. It was an offer he couldn't refuse. This score, combined with the previous two, was going to be enough for his mother's treatments. All of this had to be done. It had to.

They explained that the job needed to be quick. Jo knew the receptionists had access to all the registers. To top it off, the customers had payday coming up, and most had cash in their wallets. The main goal wasn't the money. Fulton's questions were finally about to be answered.

Why the regional bank?

Johnny got a whiff from someone in the company that the higher-ups had a couple of safety deposit boxes. He didn't know exactly which box to go for, but from what he heard, most of the employees had them. He could practically go for any random box, and something good might be contained within.

Fulton paused and collected all the information.

"So basically, we're stealing from our bosses now."

"Way to sum it up," Johnny said sarcastically.

Jo would grab all the money while Johnny would go for a safe deposit box. They didn't need to go after those hard casings, but Johnny knew a few had something much more valuable in them. He wouldn't explain what exactly, but it was his plan of attack.

Fulton was on crowd control, keeping an eye on the front (just in case) to notify the couple if cops were nearby. Afterward, they'd stay a night or two in a nearby motel. Johnny knew to schedule a room ahead of time. RM 200.

"We can move tomorrow," said Johnny, his tone eager to move immediately. He then turned to Fulton. "Are you down?"

Fulton sighed, giving it a thought. "Yeah. Let's do it."

The mischievous three went down to Summit to grab a few desired items—a delivery van for cover and some disguises. Fulton stuck with his usual camo balaclava. It wasn't much, but it covered the details. Jo used her black and orange paintball mask. It was all she had. Johnny had to leave home to get his own. As eager as he was, he wasn't unprepared.

Later, they all met up at Fulton's office. The anticipation was killing everyone but the Mama's boy. Skittish, Jo knew her buddy would always be prone to get cold feet before any job. In the end, he'd always do it.

"Come onnnn." She nudged. "Think of your mom."

Fulton flashed a fake smile, slipping his sentimental jacket onto his shoulders, ready to go.

"Hell yeah!" She laughed.

Together, they turned their heads to see Johnny finally showing up, wearing the most queer-looking mask on his face. It was a navy blue, full-face balaclava. The eye holes were covered with polarized rainbow retro lenses he'd molded on with frames. What made it worse was that he wore it inside out. It was all out of place, like chicken scratch.

Underneath Fulton's guise was a repulsive face. "What— what are you wearing?"

"It's my mask. I made it." Johnny beamed.

Jo closely examined the strange thing. "Yeah... I can tell you made it."

"What?" His voice cracked, oblivious to their judgment. "I don't know about y'all, but I think it looks super cool. It's also reversible."

Johnny flung his queer mask off and flipped it inside out, revealing to them the same solid color in the correct position.

As Fulton walked away to the van, he yelled, "It's inside out, dumbass!"

Downtown, they circled the bank for about 30 minutes, ensuring everything seemed adequate before storming in. Few customers and employees were leaving the building. One teller at the front looked tired, her eyes drooping as she lay her head on her hand, watching time pass. Another civilian walked out of the bank—Cathy Bakers was going home for the day.

Pulling behind the building, the three tugged their masks onto their faces, showing no emotion or remorse. The only goal in their minds was lucre.

Jo opened the back doors of the van, pulling out three loaded Glock 19s ready to blast. Fulton grabbed a black duffle bag for the loot. Last, she handed Johnny a crowbar and a hammer. He was more focused on the deposit boxes than whatever was in the cash registers.

Before shit went down, the crew needed a couple of minutes to prepare. On and on, they replayed the plan in their heads. Jo lit up a cigarette to take the edge off.

Fulton turned toward Jo, checking on her. "You okay?"

"No," she said blankly. "But I'm ready to do this."

"Jo... I need to know you're alright."

She went quiet. She heard him but wasn't interested in answering any of her boss's questions.

"Ready?" Jo beamed, rolling down the van's window to toss out her cigarette.

Both men nodded. "Ready!"

A countdown went on in their minds: 5... 4... 3... 2... 1...

All three put on their attire, readied their weapons and marched straight for the bank.

Jo busted past the sliding door and fired three bullets into the ceiling.

"EVERYONE GET DOWN!" screamed Jo.

Civilians went into shock, falling face-first onto the floor. They covered their ears and held one another close, not caring if they were family or not. The three had one aim.

Fulton stayed at the front, watching the outside world, while Johnny headed straight to the back, pushing civilians out of his way. Children hugged their moms, dripping tears and snot onto their clothes, while elders could hardly bend down. Some upheld their bodies with metal walkers and wooden canes.

Jo ran up to the receptionist, a blonde middle-aged woman with blue eyes, holding her hands in the air and trembling with fear as Jo held the heavy gun between her eyes.

"Open the registers! Now!" she demanded, cocking her gun back.

This wasn't Fulton's favorite part to look at. His stomach twisted into a full knot, and sweat bled through his getup. He knew Jo would get the money in an instant. Now, he was worried about Johnny.

It was Johnny's first time working with him, and Fulton wondered if the man would take too long to complete his deeds. He only hoped he'd be finished by the time Jo stuffed all the money into the bag. They were in a rush, and Fulton was so pumped full of adrenaline he had to piss. He twisted his leg like a child doing the pee-pee dance.

Another loud burst from a gun rang out.

This time, it wasn't to cause sudden attention. Jo shot at the innocents.

She shot the receptionist twice in the chest and once in the head. Blood and brain sprayed on the floor. Screams continued to echo as Jo shot another victim—an old man. The same man who lifted himself with his cane no longer needed the support. A bullet took his life.

Fulton spun around and ran toward Jo, slapping the weapon out of her hands and pushing her away.

"Why would you do that?!" he yelled, grabbing her face and screaming. "Jo! WHY?!"

She stood still.

Nobody could see it through her airsoft mask, but she was happy.

Fulton tugged the cover off her face to snap her out of it, but all it did was reveal a grin painted from ear to ear.

And she did nothing but kill.

By the time that old man's body hit the floor, Johnny was already heading toward the front, dragging one of the deposit boxes behind him.

"Let's go! Did you guys get the money?!"

Fulton looked at the bag—empty. The woman hadn't even opened the register yet. He slammed the damn thing open, grabbing stacks of whatever cash he could fit in both hands and stuffing it into the bag.

They had no time to rob the customers. That idea went straight out the window.

The blood on the floor soaked Jo's shoes, and the children who held on for their lives were covered in more than just snot and salty tears.

It was time to go.

For Johnny, it wasn't time yet. He pressured the civilians to empty their pockets. Gluttonous, he wanted more than just the estimated score. His eyes didn't register any of the blood. He was more focused on what he wanted, setting his sights on a middle-aged father shaking like a rattlesnake.

The man carefully handed over his wallet to the masked accomplice.

"Thank you very much!" Johnny exclaimed.

Fulton could hear the nearby sirens. The cops would be there shortly.

"Okay, come on! Let's go!" Fulton grasped Jo's hand and pulled her outside.

Before Johnny stepped out, he couldn't help but give a little goodbye speech.

"Thank you for your time, ladies and gentlemen! It's been a pleasure!"

Outside, they tossed the bag and box into the van's bed and booked it.

Johnny stood away from the van and jogged toward the next street.

Fulton panicked at the thought of Johnny ditching them. "Wait! Where are you going?!"

"They're going to be looking for three of us! It's best to split for now!" he explained.

Jo and Fulton drove off into the city and attempted to look casual. Fulton didn't know if it was good timing or just dumb luck. Rush hour had just started, and cars swooped everywhere, jammed throughout the streets. It'd take the police some time to get through. Fulton wanted to get to the motel ASAP.

Fulton looked over at Jo and thought, *I'll deal with her later.*

Even if the heat were to die down along the way, the murders were still on his mind. Fulton couldn't wait any longer to question what had happened.

"Jo. Why the hell did you do that?"

She was in her own little world. Her face was blank, and her eyes trailed off to the other cars passing by. She didn't hear a single word from her friend's mouth.

"Jo! Answer me!"

"Huh? What? What's up?" She paused.

Fulton clenched his jaw, staring at her in disbelief. "You know what's up. Answer me!"

Jo sank into her seat, eased up, and eventually, she finally answered, "I don't know... Honestly, I just don't know. But it felt like a huge urge, and I just... did it."

Fulton didn't understand. Nothing made sense.

At the motel, they never felt so disgusted. The place reeked of mold and dumpster water. They could have rented a more luxurious room at a Hilton, but Johnny had booked a cheap one on the side of the expressway.

The room didn't look prettier than its aroma. It only had one full-size bed lying smack in the middle. The two dumped their belongings onto the filthy bed surface, and dust sprouted from the sheets. Stains of red, white, and yellow colored the mattress.

Fulton stood disgusted, feeling more content with how spoiled he'd become.

"I'm happy I don't live in this shithole," he grunted.

"Same," added Jo.

Fulton gave her a dubious reaction, believing her home was as shitty as the room.

Rain poured outside as Johnny arrived at the motel in a taxi, excited to count the loot. Fulton laid the stolen belongings onto the viridian-green carpet floor, estimating how much they'd retrieved from the registers and thanking God they didn't secretly stuff a dye pack between the bills.

Altogether, they got nine hundred dollars.

But that wasn't all—Johnny rushed over to the side of the bed, slamming the metal deposit box beside the cash. It was time to see what his fuss was all about.

"Finally." He grinned, giving it a harsh slam with his crowbar until he could peel it open. He poured out whatever was in it.

Nothing but glory came out.

Pearls, golden necklaces, and spare change made a colorful waterfall of money. The two fell in love with what they had. Though only some desired it more, Johnny grabbed most of what he could. He knew the deposit box belonged to someone with the benjamins for it. He didn't care who it belonged to or why it was there. He just knew there was something precious in it.

Since Fulton had no intention of starting an argument about who got what, he had to be fair. He understood Johnny got it first and helped with the plans. Instead, Fulton was given the pearls.

He clutched them and realized they were prettier than he imagined; he almost considered not giving them away.

The sum needed to be more.

The three thieves had to sit down again and think about the next place they would hit. They didn't know what place exactly, but they knew they didn't want it to be another bank or some gas station on the side of the road. Fulton wanted it to be another big hit—more money—but he hadn't a clue.

Jo spoke up.

All this time, she was lying in bed, gazing at the wrinkled magazines on the nightstand. She picked one up and called out to the two, "Hey, guys? Did y'all hear about that new tailor shop that's opening up?"

Chapter 13
A NOT-SO-NEW LIFE

Friday. November 25th. Sam was in a coma, lying in a nice hospital bed throughout his Thanksgiving break. He had tubes shoved into his nose, arm, and the tip of his penis. His skin felt tender, and his body fragile. His eyes split open to the blinding fluorescent bulbs that hung on the ceiling. Everything felt different. He wasn't in England anymore... He was back home. A home called the Dallas General Hospital.

At first, he seemed alright. He tilted his head slightly to his left, noticing a flock of great-tailed grackle birds moving as slow as a sloth outside his window. He blinked hard twice, wondering if it was just his vision screwing with him. It wasn't. The birds flew in a slow formation, and Sam's heart felt too big. His breathing became heavy, and his head caught an itch. This time, it was all around, and nothing bothered the kid more than an itch he couldn't scratch. His perception fell, and the black grackles continued steadily.

He couldn't see it, but the young man heard his mother's cries, calling for help. According to the doctors, his heartbeat was at a high of 400 beats per minute. The monitors could barely keep up with the climbing rate. His eyes closed once again, falling into oblivion. He didn't die—just suffered.

*   *   *

The next day, he woke up and sat upright. Sam noticed his mother lying on a soft blue pleather couch before the bed. Beside him was a bouquet of red roses that rested in a glass vase with multiple get-well-soon cards. Alexus left him a small present. The wrapping looked similar to what his mother had made for him. *I still need to open that birthday gift,* he thought. Another present had his favorite colors—navy blue and red-orange—with a bow on top from the Sings twins.

Feeling paralyzed, he scanned the room. His mouth was dry, and he had a craving for burgers. When he moved his arm, he felt a sharp pain develop. His arm was in a bulky cast, and some of his fingers were bandaged. Underneath his gown was a torso painted with stitches and staples.

Soon, Cathy awoke from what seemed to be a nightmare. She shook and kicked in her sleep. Her eyes then opened in worry as she noticed her child sitting up.

"Oh, thank God!" she cried, rushing over and hugging his head close to her chest.

Cathy kissed his forehead and sobbed uncontrollably. "Are you okay? Are you okay?!" she cried repeatedly.

Sam couldn't speak. He was in shock and utter confusion. "What happened to the birds? What happened to London? What day is it?" he finally asked.

As his mom held him closely, someone had already entered the room. It was Aussie Ground, the bearer of bad news to the Bruning family he helped a week ago.

"Ah—good. You're awake. Hello, Mr. Clark," he greeted, carefully shaking Sam's hand. "I'm Dr. Ground. I'm sure you have some questions, and I'll gladly answer them. Also, I'm sorry if I seem to be in a rush. I'm currently back and forth with another family undergoing chemotherapy sessions and another with a broken back. But I promise to take the time for your needs."

Aussie brought out his stethoscope and quickly listened to Sam's heart rate, making sure it was beating at a normal rate. "How are you feeling, Sam? Your heart's going a bit fast there."

A warm wave flew over Sam. He wanted to get undressed and cool down on the tiled floor. His breathing remained heavy. He couldn't help but push himself away from his mother's grasp.

"What—what's happening?" Cathy asked, panic crawling within.

After a moment of silence, Sam finally spoke. "I—I—I don't—I feel like I'm boiling... I don't think I'm—I'm not breathing right. And I have a—a goddamn itch all around my head!"

Aussie put his hand on his chest, guiding him to breathe in and out slowly, waving a clipboard towards his face to fan him. "Just breathe, Sam. Focus on that. Breathe."

"What's going on with him?" Cathy inquired.

"I believe he's going through some sort of panic or anxiety attack," Aussie answered. "Again, just breathe, Sam. You're back home. You're here in Dallas. You were in an accident over there and were in a deep coma for the past week. Today is November twenty-sixth. Everything is okay."

"Can—can I go home?" Sam asked, laying back down.

"I'm sorry, Mr. Clark, but we need to keep you for just one more night for some tests. You'll be able to go home in the morning. I'm sure you and your mom have tons of catching up to do." Dr. Ground gave a kind pat on his forearm before exiting the room.

The moment the door clicked shut, Cathy burst back into tears. Her stress was through the roof from all the burdens that filled her week—work hours at the Dallas Bank, apartment bills, low food, and hospital visits. The crying held no aid, only bringing puffy eyes and harsh migraines to her temples.

*   *   *

In the morning, Cathy helped Sam into the passenger seat of her car. Dr. Ground wanted to talk to her before they left.

Inside the vehicle, Sam was reading the get-well-soon cards from his friends. Almost everybody sent him a card, besides Sonny and Abe. Next up were the gifts. He opened Alexus' present first; it was a pack of t-shirts in assorted colors. He could never get enough of those. When his eyes fell on a white shirt, Sam remembered how he had worn a similar one on the same day of his accident.

The last gift from the twins was hard to open. Sam couldn't pry the wrapping off the box.

"Screw it," he mumbled, ripping the cardboard box in half.

It was revealed to be a new phone.

"Aww no..." he sighed. "The guys really stepped it up."

To a spoiled child, it was considered old because it was a previous-generation model, but to Sammy, it was like a diamond.

Meanwhile, Dr. Ground explained to Cathy about the future effects on her child, handing her a few pamphlets on trauma treatment.

"There's a center downtown. They don't just support trauma but other symptoms such as anxiety, depression, and anger. I'd recommend you take Sam, or he goes himself to this center. At least twice a week. I'm sorry, but he'll see things differently."

"Differently?" Her voice cracked.

"Trauma works in mysterious ways. Teenagers these days like to self-diagnose and assume, but those who actually get this act differently. He'll have mood swings and likely be tense, especially since he's still in school. He may experience panic attacks here and there. All in all, I apologize, Mrs. Clark—"

"Bakers," she corrected him. "I'm not married."

"The father isn't in the picture?"

"Not since he found out I was pregnant with him. I never took his last name."

Aussie turned confused. "How does your son have it then?"

"At the time I was pregnant, I was still in love with him... Took me a while to get over that, but before I knew it, it was too late. Now it's stuck." Cathy paused. "I mean—regardless—a piece of him is still around. Name or not. I love my son dearly."

"I hope things work out." Dr. Ground gave her a prescription for Sam's meds and another pamphlet on other centers around the city.

"Thank you, Dr. Ground. Be seeing you."

*   *   *

At the apartments, everything was quieter. A sense of melancholy filled the space. Aussie was right. Sam viewed things differently. Every detail seemed faded and lonely. It was like he couldn't recognize he was in his own home. He had to return to school in a couple of days. It was a shame. Sam was hoping he'd be able to spend more time in England to take more pictures and stay up past curfew during the entire break.

It's been a crazy week, he thought.

Sam spent the last couple of hours trying to set up his phone. It would cost more because of the SIM card—hell, everything would cost more. Everything he had on him was either lost, burned, or broken. All his money, clothes, camera, and phone. The only survivors were his luggage and laptop.

Later, his mother called him downstairs. She wanted to spend some time with him. Cathy was on the couch watching a hilarious episode of *Family Guy.* Sam came down but was disinterested in watching TV. She saw that his mind was elsewhere, focusing on his new phone and what food was hiding in the fridge.

"Sam?" she called out.

No response. Sam was quiet, still rummaging around in the fridge. He was calm but quiet. Cathy assumed his silence was just the tip of the iceberg in this new change.

*　　　*　　　*

November 30th. Monday morning. Over the weekend, Sam saw himself change—physically change, to be more specific. His complexion was tinted, and his body was rapidly growing. At first, he thought he was gaining weight, but it was muscle.

Some shirts went from loose to regular, and the regular shirts were athletic. Any further, and he'd be unrecognizable. His face looked less thin, and his energy skyrocketed. His eyesight was also cured. He completely forgot about the fact that he needed glasses.

It was a new day. Still, Sam had a sense of low self-esteem. He covered his body with a new windbreaker jacket.

His best friends drove to the front, ready to pick up their pal. Garrett had the idea to go to the front door and escort him. Trevor, on the other hand, wanted to keep the engine running. It was falling below 50, and it was only getting colder.

When Sam stepped outside, Garrett's eyes gleamed with surprise. He noticed some changes with Sam. The first thing he pointed out was that he wasn't wearing his glasses. The next was that he didn't appear too lanky, and his complexion wasn't as pale anymore.

"Damn. Welcome back, man! You look good! Lookin' better!" Garrett cheered.

"Thanks, Gar." The boy smiled.

"Your chest is looking a bit puffed. What did you eat in London? Damn!" he joked.

Sam folded his arms. His friends were too kind, and he hoped no one else at school would exaggerate.

The boys had plenty of time to lollygag before heading to school, taking a detour around town to catch up with an old friend.

Trevor looked at Sam's red cast and bandaged fingers as he drove. "Hey. Are you okay?"

"Yeah, I'm fine."

"Does it still hurt?"

Sam looked down at his arm. "What? My arm? Oddly enough, it doesn't hurt anymore. I don't feel anything in my fingers either."

Other than physical injuries, Garrett studied Sam and had to ask, "No glasses? I know they're just readers, but you usually wear them all the time. Or did you get contacts?"

"No. I guess I just forgot them. I can see just fine, though."

It was a new detail to them, but they noticed Sam was quieter than he used to be. They understood it was a lot to take in and get back into the swing of things. No one wanted to ask about what happened before the accident.

As they neared the school, Sam's palms began sweating profusely. They'd usually sweat a little, but this time, they were drenched. His breathing became longer and heavier, and his sights wouldn't leave the school. The school would usually make him nervous, but not on the verge of a panic attack. He hid his face, closed his eyes, and relaxed his breathing. *I don't have time to panic. I need to focus on getting back on schedule.*

Walking into the cafeteria, Sam's pits swelled with each close step to the big hall. In his mind, all the kids were staring at him. He believed even some of them could read his thoughts. He internally screamed with anxiety, and his body tensed up like a petrified goat.

Getting closer to the group's table, he saw them all: Alexus, Sonny, Heather, Abe, and Carissa. All were sitting there to welcome him back. Sam couldn't do it.

I can't... I can't, he thought, turning around and running toward the restrooms. Sam sped into one stall. His body temperature rose, and he curled himself up, took off his jacket, and rocked himself in a crouched fetal position, thinking about the accident. He thought of that Irish man's voice and how his accent was funny to him.

His smile grew fake, and his mind went real. *This is how things will be if I don't get better soon.*

He pulled out his phone and texted Cathy that he needed to attend one of those sessions as soon as possible. She replied shortly, letting him know that she'd take him right after school.

The first bell rang, and Sam waited five minutes until the hallways were almost empty. He peeked his head around the corner, hoping that none of his friends were around. He assumed the questions would only resurface his problem.

Out in the hallway, the coast was now clear. That was until Sam turned the corner and bumped into Alexus.

She gasped. "Hey! Watch where—Oh! Sam!" Alexus jumped into his torso, hugging him close. One of her eyes teared up a little when she felt their bodies collide.

"Are you okay? Where'd you go? We were all waiting for you!" she exclaimed.

Sam was lost for words. He was still hugging her, his face buried in her red hair and shoulder. He shrugged in response to all her questions, still quiet.

"Here, I'll walk you to class," she smiled, grabbing his arm and leading him.

Continuing to be quiet, Sam walked with Alexus to his class. On the way, she got a good look at his face. She didn't say anything, but she, too, noticed his color and body change.

"I'll see you later," she said, hugging him once more. When she pulled away, she stared deep into his brown eyes, almost as if she were telling him goodbye.

*   *   *

It was the first period with Mr. McCrown, and Sam worried he'd throw too much attention on him. His memories became unfortunate as he remembered he was supposed to go to detention before the trip. Not even 15 minutes into the lesson, one of the office aid members strolled into the class, asking for Sam.

The member passed him a hall pass and a permission slip to visit the main office. All the eyes were on him. It felt like elementary school again, when everyone hyped up the tension just because a kid got called to the office, theorizing they might be in trouble. Only this time, Sam *was* in trouble.

Up in the main office, Sam saw the school's boss, Principal O'Mally. A ferocious woman with a hard-on for punishment. She handed out detentions like candy. Sam understood why he'd be in deep shit this time. He didn't plan on skipping after-school detention just to end up traumatized.

Supposedly, a newcomer was taking her place next semester. When the word spread, O'Malley took it to heart and used her whole power and worth to leave a mark on the school before her time came. Sam knew that tons of kids at West-Made definitely wouldn't miss her.

Sam walked over to the wooden, ominous door to wait for further punishment. When he entered, O'Mally tied up her dead black hair in a messy bun. Her roots were graying, and she had just finished eating a breakfast bagel, wiping crumbs off her blue blazer and European-cut slacks.

"Take a seat, Mr. Clark," she pointed.

Sam grasped the neck of the seat. It was cold and rubber-like—uncomfortable at its touch.

O'Mally cleared her throat, continuing to wipe the crumbs off herself. "Now... First things first." The tone in her voice was bitchy and arrogant; her posture was bold. She puffed her chest out as if she had implants and wanted to show them off to the little world.

"I'd like to offer my sympathy for what happened to you over the break."

"Thank you, Principal O'Mally," the nervous kid replied.

"Second. I also heard from Mr. McCrown that you didn't attend your assigned after-school detention the day before you went on your little trip. Is that correct, Mr. Clark?"

"Yes..." Sam mumbled.

"What was that?"

"Yes, ma'am."

O'Malley gave the boy a cold stare, sinking her eyes deep into his soul. "Then why didn't you attend?"

"I had to go—"

"No, you didn't," she interrupted. "You didn't have to go, and you knew you had detention during that afternoon."

"Ms. O'Mally... I had to. It was for work. It was important."

She began to laugh hysterically, practically going insane from hearing that her rules were irrelevant. Sam might as well have yelled at her and watched hell rain down. She was already bringing the heat.

"Is—that so?" She folded her arms and re-adjusted her messy bun to look more professional. "Since you ditched detention and were out for a day before the break and also talked back, I'm assigning you detention for next week. Got it?"

"Wait—wait. What?!" Sam exclaimed.

"Fine. Then two weeks."

Sam's jaw dropped at the increase. "That's bullshit!"

"Oh, really now? Fine. Detention for the rest of the semester. And since work is more important, you will attend detention during your lunch period instead. You will attend all of them. Fail to do so, and you will be suspended. Do I make myself clear?"

His jaw clenched with panic and anger, and his head started to develop that same itch he got from the hospital. He bit down on his tongue to prevent any vulgar words from slipping out. "Yes, ma'am."

Little did she know the assigned detention would only be eligible for the next three weeks until the beginning of the school's winter break. Sam stepped out, returning to his history class until the period ended. He had no intention of blaming Mr.

McCrown for telling Principal O'Mally—he was just doing his job.

*   *   *

It was lunchtime, and Sam dragged himself up to the second-floor hallway to begin his first day in his lost privilege. He met up with the room, and beside the door was a plastic board labeled *RM 202: L.O.L. (The Loss of Lunch Room).*

The inside of the room was grand and moist. All the desks were separated by seven feet, so students couldn't interact with one another. Sam took the desk in the corner on the left side, and since the lectern was diagonal to the room, he got a clear view of everything.

Across the opposite side of the room was the only other student attending L.O.L. Funny enough, it was a familiar face— Abe Cite. Sam recalled Trevor and Garrett telling him a story about how, during their early-release day for Thanksgiving break, Abe made an airplane with testicles drawn all over it and tossed it around the room. Clearly, O'Malley didn't take it too kindly with his class acts.

Something felt off about the kid. Abe made little to no eye contact with him. Other than a shorthand wave, Sam thought Abe would've been more excited to see him back at school again. He was probably tired, considering Abe buried his face into his arms and slept through the period without touching his food.

Sam couldn't blame him—the food was crap. Nothing but a cold cheese sandwich and a small carton of milk. Gross.

Another 30 minutes in, Sam needed to pee, and the bell rang for dismissal. He bolted out of the room, holding his crotch and running into the nearest bathroom. Sam placed himself in the closest urinal, which had shit stains along its corners. He held his breath and relieved himself, hoping the stench of his urine would suffice over the smears.

As the boy relieved himself, he caught two seconds of entertainment from the gossipy notes on the wall. Some kid had fun with a Sharpie and wrote: *Felix Rade is gay.* Unlikely. This message was either written by one of Felix's punching bags or by a friend on the team making a crude joke. It was also unfactual, considering Felix had already hooked up with a third of the girls at West-Made.

After peeing, Sam went lightheaded, and his eyes strained and burned as if he were staring at the sun. He walked over to the sink to wash his face, hoping that would relax him. When Sam took a gander at his face in the mirror, he had to double-take at his eyes. The color in them was changing. It shifted from his usual cinnamon to a piercing electric blue.

Sam jolted, heading for the exit out of the bathroom. That sudden jolt turned quick—his vision popped, and the senses in his eyes sharpened. The blue hue around his pupils remained. His breath shortened, and his eyes saw clear and vibrant colors coming to life. With the pop in his vision, his perception of time followed.

Sam remembered the grackles flying past the window and how they were so slow. *This was relative.* Everything around him was hindered. Students were everywhere but weren't moving at their usual pace. Sam grasped that not only was time slowing down—he was also speeding up.

No answers came to mind about what he was doing. With another quick jolt, his legs sped up, his arms followed, and he ran down the school's narrow hallways. The hot wind brushed against his frame, the adrenaline within spiked, and life had never felt so carefree. *This is new.* Sam had never felt such a sensation before.

He passed by most of the kids trying to get to class. Not a single one noticed the fast boy. The thrill was cut short when Sam turned a corner and bumped his shoulder, causing his focus to be lost. His perception and vision popped back to normal. His sneakers skidded as he tripped onto the tiled floor, leaving black tracks and rips in the soles of his shoes.

The kid looked behind him in shock and awe at what had just happened. He didn't panic, cry, or cause any anxiety. He felt happy, yet scared. He had run from the far right side of the school to the far left within six seconds. A skid trail wasn't the only thing he left on the floor. He made the tiles lift and rip. With every footstep, he created small potholes all over the floor.

Students around the hall covered their ears from the sound he caused during his run, as well as the messy hairstyles from the large gust of wind he created. Papers flew everywhere, and questions came up. Everything was parallel and broken. The school's fire alarm had also gone off. Obviously, there was no fire, but there was cause for concern.

Sam looked at the mess he made. It was almost... awesome.

"Holy shit!" he laughed. "What?!"

Chapter 14
THE BIGGER PICTURE

Sam was completely distraught. He hid in the boy's bathroom again. He hadn't a clue what exactly had happened, but he wanted to find out. Kids were curious. Truly curious. Not the kind of curiosity about what a certain drug tastes like or what the hottest girl in school looks like nude. Pure, innocent, questioning curiosity.

Cathy picked up her son. Together, they drove to the city to see the therapist. Sam rested his head on the window, still tense about what had happened earlier. He didn't know what to say. The countless theories scrambled his brain.

I'm fast now? What was that? Is it the meds? The accident? Is this all in my head? Am I just hungry? Tired?... Horny? Jesus Christ...

"What's wrong?" Cathy gave her son a gentle massage on his shoulder as she drove.

Sam tensed up whenever her head turned over to look at him. His mind had created a slight phobia of cars *(dystychiphobia)*, and he closed his eyes to ensure he wouldn't feel another attack.

"Sam!" Cathy exclaimed. "Are you okay?"

"Y-yeah. Are we almost there?"

"Yes."

Cathy stopped rubbing his shoulder and changed her hand motion to a squeezing one, feeling Sam's shoulder. She noticed he wasn't as boney as he used to be.

"Have you been working out?"

"Uh- I- dunno."

Sam's inquisitiveness increased. These questions had to be answered eventually. He rolled down the window, letting in a fresh breeze to prevent that warm wave from coming over. "Who's the shrink?" he tried to joke.

"Who?"

"The guy I'm gonna be seeing. My therapist."

"Oh," she nervously chuckled. "Terrance Balle is the guy."

When they arrived, Sam recognized the building. It was one of the usual sights that caught his eye every time he'd sit down at Doe's Diner with the twins. Only this time, it was an up-close view. The office was about 20 feet tall and as wide as two school buses. The colors were sandy, and the labels were brown. Sam assumed this was intentional, knowing those colors were meant to calm and relax others.

Sam entered, glancing around. *This place is bigger than I thought.*

Distracted by the interior design, Sam bumped into a stranger passing by. The whites of the man's eyes were pink, his eyelids strained, and his nose sniffled every second. He looked like he had just finished crying. Embarrassed, the man tucked his head down into his letterman jacket, excused himself, and scooted out of Sam's way.

"Sorry, boss," he sniffled.

"No– you're all good," Sam assured him.

The sad man moved to the front entrance, leaning against a wall and stuffing his face into a tissue he grabbed from the front desk.

Cathy grabbed her son's shoulder and pulled him around. "I have to go. Mr. Balle should be coming out here in a couple of minutes. I love you, and I'll see if one twin can pick you up. Does that sound good?"

Sam twiddled his fingers, still looking around. "Yeah, that's fine."

Cathy gave him a little peck on his cheek before exiting the building. Immediately after she left, a door swung open. Sam looked over to see a tall man dressed in a flashy blue and yellow striped suit that flowed over his body. The man wiped his sweaty forehead and ginger beard with a neon red handkerchief.

Sam walked up to the man, unsure if it was him. "Uhh. Mr. Balle?"

"Ah! You must be Sam. Nice to meet ya!" he exclaimed, shaking Sam's hand. "Sorry for the waterfall above me. The AC in the restroom went out."

"It's alright."

Mr. Balle guided Sam toward his office, ready to start the session.

Like Fulton, Sam sat down on the leather couch. The bottom cushion was still warm, as if somebody had just been in it.

"This might sound weird, but- was somebody just here?" he asked. "The couch feels hot."

"Oh, yeah. I had just gotten done with another session a few minutes ago. I don't mean to rat the poor guy out, but it was the guy you might've seen crying in the front loft."

Sam didn't seem surprised by that answer. "What's up with him?"

"I'm sorry, Mr. Clark, but I'm not allowed to share that information."

"I understand."

Mr. Balle continued for the next hour of the session, listening to Sam's inner thoughts and emotions. To him, nothing was new—other than what Sam had to say next. He was almost eager to explain the new feelings that had swallowed him up that morning at school.

"I felt this heat fall over me. I panicked, and I didn't know what to do. But the next thing I knew, my friend Alexus came to my side and helped me walk to my class. I had this feeling that she was telling me she knew. She knew what I was feeling and helped me calm down. Later, that same feeling came back, and I ran to the restroom, only to feel some other weird feelings. Time felt like it was slowing down, and what felt hot turned into a cold. A cold rushed through my veins... I don't know, Mr. Balle. Things feel super weird now."

Terrance took notes, making direct eye contact with the young man, understanding his pain, and supporting him. He had to. It was what he signed up for.

"Mr. Clark. I'm sorry to interrupt, but really quick—you mentioned somebody named Alexus. Is that your friend?"

"Yessir."

"Got it. Just gathering all the details. Now, if what you felt and told me is nothing but the truth, I believe you may have experienced an anxiety attack."

Sam pulled himself up from the couch, concerned about the words he had just heard. "An anxiety attack? Is there a cure for that?"

"An anxiety attack is an intense moment of fear based on perceiving a moment, triggering threat, or a traumatic episode. As for a cure, I'm afraid there isn't one. Other than temporary medications, these sessions—well—that is, if you want to continue—will help you."

Sam stared at the floor, his palms beginning to sweat and shake.

"Tell me. Are there any triggers? Anything that causes that panicking feeling to erupt?" Mr. Balle clicked his pen, ready to jot down notes.

"Well. My high school. Even before my accident. Just arriving at the school would make me a bit nervous."

"Why is that?"

"I'd say it's because of people. Maybe?" Sam didn't sound sure. It was a guess.

"People? What do you mean?"

Sam got up from the couch and began pacing back and forth around the rug in front of Balle's feet. The therapist brought his legs back further underneath his chair to give the kid room.

"Crowds. People make me anxious. Everybody is looking at me and judging me. Only this time, it feels much worse. Like as if the accident dialed that feeling up to ten."

Sam wanted to know if there was any type of medicine he had to take in order for his attacks to go away. Terrance couldn't really help him out with that but considered an evaluation to take place somewhere else. That was about the only way for the boy to get further treatment. He knew nothing about these feelings, so he wanted to do whatever it took to never feel them again.

*   *   *

After the session, Sam stepped outside, waiting for a ride back to the apartment. He didn't know who'd pick him up, thinking it would likely be the Sings twins or his mother. Or maybe a taxi or one of those Uber rides people are taking now. He leaned back against the rigid, popcorn-beige wall, waiting.

On his right, the crying man was squatting down on the floor against the building, smoking a couple of cigarettes and sniffling to himself. The man had been crying for some time.

"Sir? Are you okay?" Sam called out, keeping a distance so as not to upset him further.

"Y-yeah," the man cracked. "Just thinking."

"I don't know if you remember, but Mr. Balle and I passed by you, and you said 'sorry' because I accidentally bumped you. Do you remember?"

"Kind of. I'm sorry—I have a hard time remembering people and, hell—even the names I have to remember. I suck at it."

"You don't have to apologize, misterrrr?" Sam froze, not catching a name.

"Fulton. Also yeah! Yeah, you're right! I shouldn't have to apologize... I mean, nobody apologized when I found out my ma was sick. No one apologized for how things have been going for me. I mean..."

Fulton stopped ranting to the kid about his problems and switched back to tearing up, his throat clogged with sadness as he looked away from the young man, embarrassed. He didn't know who this kid was, and there was no reason for him to vent.

"Shit. I'm sorry, kid. I didn't mean to get all bitchy on ya'."

"It's fine," Sam retorted. "I'm sure everything you've gone through is rough... Is that why you're going here?"

"It's not fine!" Fulton raised his voice. "Sorry—Yeah. And you?"

"Yes, sir. I went through a bad accident. Trying to look past this thing I have called—anxiety, and I don't know much about it, but I hope it's not contagious, haha!" Sam hoped his little, awkward joke could lighten the poor man. Comedy wasn't his strongest trait.

Fulton snickered, standing up and reaching his hand out to shake the kid's. "I never got your name."

"Samuel. Sam for short."

"Common name. Easy—but I don't think I'm gonna remember it after a few days."

"That's alright." Sam smiled, shaking the guy's hand.

Fulton made out the red cast on the kid's arm. "What happened there?"

"Car accident."

"Here?"

"No," Sam answered vaguely.

"What's your last name?" Fulton wondered. He assumed his last name was something simple and lame, like Jones, Miller, or Smith.

God, I'm gonna make fun of this kid if his last name is Miller, Fulton thought.

"Clark."

Fulton's sad eyes raised. "Ha. Wow, like Superman." That was a shocker for him.

"Yeah. I get that a lot." Sam scoffed and nodded.

Sam pulled a pack of cigarettes out of his windbreaker. Inside the pack was the black Zippo lighter he had borrowed from the twins. He lit his cigarette and inhaled what he thought would be the usual, refreshing flavor of menthol. Instead, he received a sour aftertaste, like rotten milk. Not wanting to make a face or weird the man out, he kept it to himself and acted like it was nothing.

Fulton raised a brow. "Aren't you too young to be smoking?"

"Aren't you too old to be going to therapy?"

Fulton stared blankly at the teenager.

"I'm sorry. Too soon," said Sam, looking down at the floor awkwardly. There was a long silence between them. The kid hoped he could think of a decent joke or at least change the topic.

The man scoffed, disregarded the comment, and moved forward. "Nah, you're cool. I'm mainly doing this for my ma. She's going through this rough patch, and it's just hell... I don't wanna give details and spill my shit into your life, but you strike me as a mature, well-kept person. You're a bit awkward, but still..."

"Thanks," said Sam. "I'm trying my best."

The man dragged on about his troubles. It made little sense to Sam, but to Fulton, it was perfectly logical. Fulton felt an urge to rant to this young stranger rather than pay out of pocket to do it. The two talked for almost an hour about random things: work, school, and growing up. They eventually concluded with a discussion about hard work and achievements.

"Hey, kid... life is hard, and the only way through it is the hard work you commit to. That's all. Nothing more or less than that shit. Bear that in mind with your parents. Especially for mothers. They put up with all the bullshit and are the ones who deal with it."

Sam regarded this stranger as a momma's boy, but it didn't make much difference. He questioned the advice. "Really? Only hard work? No care, no optimism, no dedication, friends, family, love, or anything else in life? Just that?"

"You'll understand when life hits ya'," Fulton said hollowly.

The boy tried to search for a deeper meaning. "I- understand what you're trying to say, but I feel like there's more. I could be wrong, but something tells me otherwise."

"More what?"

Sam continued. "There is more to life than being committed and ambitious. I don't mean to pry—because I understand you want to vent... Are you okay?"

Fulton adjusted his posture, turning fully to face Sam. "Tell me. Do you have a job?"

"Yes, sir."

"What do you do?" Fulton wanted details. He was prying for more information.

"I'm an assistant photographer and editor at Inferior."

"Cool. Now, do you strive for growth at this job?"

Sam answered with confusion. "Eventually?"

"Kid, you gotta know what you want. What is it?"

"I don't know... I never gave it much thought. I do know I want to go to school and get a decent job somewhere." Sam swung his foot against the concrete out of boredom. This was the first time someone gave him a bit of a push to think about his future.

"You gotta think big, man. Life keeps moving fast. Next thing you know... nothing." Fulton sighed and finished his thought. "I guess there's no point in complaining about circumstances. I mean—take it from me, I'm a manager at this warehouse for Summit Peaks, and I- I don't know, kid. I guess we can agree on some things. Even something small—"

Sam decided to finish the sentence, hoping to understand what Fulton was trying to say. "—But with a lot of meaning."

"Yeah. Somethin' like that." Fulton muttered, tossing his cigarette to the ground and burning it out. "It was nice to meet ya', kid. Again—I might forget your name, but I'm sure I'll see ya' again."

"Take care, Fulton."

Samuel continued to wait for his ride, thinking about the words his new acquaintance had left him. He couldn't fully understand them, though maybe one day he would. He was only 18; he had years ahead of him. Not that he needed to take that tip to heart, but it was indeed something he needed to have an open mind for.

After waiting for what seemed like hours, the sun had set, and Sam could no longer tolerate his patience as his mind went bizarre. He thought of his mother and how she probably forgot about him, and he thought about the twins and how they might've had something better to do. Thinking about his pals reminded him of school and what had happened earlier in the afternoon. His palms began sweating again, and his heart pounded like a drum. He knew nobody was coming for him. The only thing left to do now was to walk.

Sam walked down the broad road. Cars passed by left and right, calling it a night and heading home. It was getting late. The boy focused hard on the road ahead of him, so much so that he felt his eyes tingle, and the little hairs on his body stand up in goosebumps. He recognized the feeling. It was the same as earlier at school.

Quickly, Sam pulled out his phone, tapped into the camera app, and flipped to the front view. No—he wasn't taking a selfie. He was checking his eyes. There it was... those shimmering blue eyes glistened in the night sky. His hands shook, and his breathing quickened. He still couldn't understand what was happening to him. He could only summarize one thing—if he were to make any sudden movements without watching his pace, he'd speed up to nowhere in whatever direction his body pointed. It could be a few feet away or further.

Down the street was Dallas West End, a street full of museums and occasional markets. Sam couldn't take the risk of running into a building or a random pedestrian. The boy turned back and, in doing so, caused a swift move to his left, ending up on the opposite side of the street in the blink of an eye. The frightened boy screamed, collapsing onto the sidewalk of Elm Street. He dared not move another inch.

It only took a moment for the rushy feeling to fade away. Soon enough, the unusual change in his eyes returned to his usual brown, and all the hairs on his body fell. For cautious reasons, he decided not to move until it was deemed safe.

Down the street, he heard a familiar truck horn blaring at the stoplight ahead of him... it was the Sings twins. Sam was relieved, carefully standing up and finally realizing he had been sitting in a dirty puddle that soaked his pant legs.

He was disgusted. "Shit."

The boys pulled up, lowering their window. "Hey, Sam!" they said in synchronization.

"What were you doing on the floor?" asked Trevor.

"Urm. I fell?" (Technically, that wasn't a lie.)

They looked puzzled, dropping a rag on the seat so it wouldn't mess up the leather.

"How'd you know I was near West End?"

"Location turned on, on your phone," Garrett answered.

Trevor followed up, "Your mom told us you'd be at the center. We passed by and saw you weren't there, so we checked your phone."

* * *

At the unit, Sam went straight to his bedroom, tossing most of his wet clothes on the floor and changing into something comfortable—gym shorts and a plain tee. When he tossed his wet garments into his closet, he heard something heavy hit the ground.

THUD!

His pants had probably knocked an object down. Maybe a box, his laundry hamper, or maybe his shoes. He looked over and spotted his mother's gift. The gift he never opened—the one with the gold wrapping and black ribbon.

How did it get in there? Sam recalled he had left it on top of the dresser before he took off to London. It was possible that Cathy had put it in his closet, so when he'd change his clothes, he'd be able to spot it. Or, in theory, maybe she hid it. She had seemed uncertain about handing it over on his birthday.

Sam grew eager to know its contents, ripping it open to reveal a large book with a red leather binding.

How could I forget to open this?

He admired the book before flipping through it. It was a list of family records, a type of assorted family tree, complete with history and information. This was something Sam had always been interested in—but there was an underlying feeling now. He had the information, but he wasn't as fascinated anymore. Did he not care anymore?

The only family he really knew was his mother. He never got to spend much time with his grandparents. He'd only interact with them whenever they'd call or stop by. They were getting older, and it was hard to contact them. Plus, they still had a hard time trying to work their way around a smartphone. The reason for rarely meeting was unbeknownst to him.

For Cathy, she assumed she asked too much from the Clarks. They were kind souls and didn't treat the two like a nuisance. She believed it was too much weight for them and that it wasn't their burden to bear. It was hers.

Sam looked at his father's name with a blank expression. At least he could say he knew his full name now: Tate Figen Clark.

Sam never really spent much time with his father's side of the family. Maybe one day, he'd be able to see them (if he ever had the time) and possibly learn more about his family history.

Scanning through the lists, some records were scratched off. Sam minded little of it, but it was something he'd have to find the time to get back to. He discovered he had an uncle down in

Houston (Brandy Clark) and an older cousin who lived on the outskirts of El Paso (Denice Synski).

One part of his history struck him as oddly funny. It said his great-grandfather, Connor Clark, had died at 21 from overeating fish *(mercury poisoning)* and had carried a strange nickname from his love of eating seafood. Since he spoke more Albanian than English to his coworkers, he referred to the mercury in his fish as *Zhivë.*

Chapter 15
THE PLAN

Tuesday, December 1st. Fulton went back to the terrible motel. He'd rather plan this out at the warehouse than this place, but Johnny insisted it was just to be safe. He thought he could never be too careful. Right... careful. More like paranoid. The police were looking around aggressively. They knew this was most likely going to be a pattern. Fulton overthought everything—the plans, robberies, money, the cancer... everything.

Is it too late to pull out?

Fulton paced outside the motel door. It probably wasn't a good idea to drop everything now. They were already in too deep. Soon, he'd gather the right words—something reasonable and understandable.

No... it's no good. It doesn't matter...

He then remembered his ma, who he was truly doing this for—not for riches or power, but for her.

Remember who this is for, he heeded. *Remember.*

Jo then opened the old beige door. She gave Fulton an odd look, wondering what he was doing.

"Nothing," he simply answered. "What do y'all got goin' on?"

"Nothing here. Just waiting for you." Jo opened the door wider so Fulton could walk in.

Johnny was sitting in the motel's desk area, recounting the loot from the previous jobs. Nothing made the hairy man happier than a good old pile of green.

"The money's still the same," Fulton said, annoyed. "You can quit counting."

"I know," Johnny chuckled, "I just like counting it."

The money they had gathered before was more than enough for the three, including the jewelry. Johnny got more than he calculated, but it still seemed to not be enough for him.

Fulton rolled his eyes, then looked over at Jo on the crappy bed, making sure she wasn't up to mischief. He remained worried about her mental health after the last heist. There was still something off, but she elected to ignore him about the topic.

"Just to make sure, we are here until we're done with Beyrou's, right?"

"Yep," said Johnny, staring at the cash.

"Thank God…" Fulton groaned, relieved. "I'm done with this nasty shithole. Let's talk about the plan. Just so we all know what to do and get outta here. I don't think I can take three more days of this."

"You're allowed to go home," said Jo. "No one's stopping you."

"Yeah, then I hear it from Johnny all day. Askin' me what I'm doin' or where I'm goin'."

Johnny put down the money and turned the rolling chair around to face his two coworkers.

"I'm just seeing if you guys are alright. The last thing we need is to end up in prison. Fulton, if it's a big deal for you, then go."

"You gonna bother me all day?"

"I'll be checking on you."

Fulton grew annoyed, groaning at the response. "Whatever. Let's just go through it one more time."

Jo agreed, "Okay."

Fulton stood in the bed's front, facing Jo and beside Johnny in the chair, towering.

"We put the van in the alley. Behind the shop—"

"Yes." Johnny nodded.

"Together, we bust in. Get them scared. Take half the people to the back. The other half will be in the main room. Why?"

This part was Johnny's call.

"Because I will empty their pockets, and if things go bad, we use that portion of the crowd as a distraction."

"Great. Then after that."

Jo was eager to finish the rest off. "I will be on crowd control. You get the money from the registers, and I'll get the rest from everyone else. Everything should be done within five minutes."

"And any longer?" Fulton asked, waiting for someone to finish his sentence.

"Then we leave," answered Jo.

Fulton gave a stink eye to Johnny. He knew Johnny was against the idea of dropping the heist if things went on too long.

Ain't nothin' but a greedy man, he gathered.

"See y'all in three days."

Outside, before Fulton took off, Jo chased him down, wanting to talk to him really quick.

"Boss!" she called out.

"What?"

"You okay?"

"I don't think you should be asking me that, Jo. Are you good?"

The woman curled her lips. No answer or reaction. She didn't want to talk about it.

"Yeah. That's what I thought... Look, Jo—you gotta talk to me about what's bothering you. If you screw this up, then we're done."

"What? You're gonna fire me?" she scoffed, smirking.

"Thinkin' about it."

Her grin got wiped clean off her face. She knew Fulton was being serious. He wasn't joking around anymore. The end of jokes and nonchalance started when his mother got the cancer. No more Mister Nice Guy.

"Fult'... I'm just going through a rough patch. My mood isn't working right. I'll tell you one day, but not now."

"Sure."

The condo was quieter than usual. The only sounds that rang were Donna's coughs and moans of pain. This continued all night.

Fulton cried quietly. His head pounded with stress. He wanted these three days to pass. The money at Summit was great, but not good enough to maintain this specific lifestyle he wanted to live. It was hard enough trying to provide more for his mother.

He feared that Beyrou's would not be enough and that the cancer would linger on for the rest of the year.

What, then? Was it going to be more banks? More heists? Who's to say?

Each cut was supposed to be more than enough. One thing for certain was that it would never be enough for Johnny. He imagined him sticking up people in the street, asking for everything in their wallets. He imagined Jo doing the same thing. The only difference was that she might go on a killing spree if she didn't get better.

Who's to say, right?

After the tear fest, he couldn't sleep anymore. Fulton was now anxious about the job. He couldn't shake off the gut feeling in his stomach that this was going to be the final straw. This was going to be the job that compromised his freedom.

Fulton took deep breaths, slowly inhaling from the nose and exhaling slowly through the mouth. He repeated that process for the next hour.

Remember what you're doing this for... Who you're doing this for.

Chapter 16
EXPLORING POWER

Ever since his first session with Terrance, Sam had gone crazed. He wanted to explore the reasons behind these new sensations flooding his body. This new speed was a huge thrill, and he considered numerous speculations.

Is it anxiety? The meds? Maybe it's because of the accident?!

He couldn't hold in the questions any longer. Sammy got off his little bed, grabbed his windbreaker, slipped on his sneakers, and went outside to test his theory before school. Since then, he no longer needed a ride from the twins. There was no elaboration on why Sam wanted to keep this to himself for now. He didn't know what exactly he was dealing with. This also meant saying goodbye to getting rides to and from work.

By the time he got downstairs, Cathy was in the kitchen.

"Hey! Good morning!" she cheered.

"Morning, Mom."

Then Sam remembered his family book. "Oh—can I talk to you really quick?"

Cathy put her breakfast burrito down. "Of course. What's up?"

"I finally opened the gift you gave me."

"Oh." Cathy's smile carefully withered into a grin. "Well? What do you think?"

Sam walked over to the kitchen and sat beside Cathy. "It's not really what I expected, if I'm being honest. Chunks of it are missing. Some of the ink had been worn off, and the texts were vague…"

"I know. I know. It's all messed up, but it was your father's. I know you've been saying that you wanted to know all about your history ever since you were little."

"Hey? Did you know I had an uncle? Do you know him?"

Cathy paid attention to her son's reaction—his eyes, the sound of his voice, and his ticks. She had no response other than folding her lips. "I didn't."

"How's Grandpa and Grandma doing? I haven't seen them in a while."

"They're good! I don't hear from them often, but last time I checked, they're doing just fine."

"And on your side?" asked Sam.

"They're good too," Cathy said, then mumbled quietly, "I think?"

"What were they like growing up? Dad's parents."

Cathy let out a happy sigh, reminiscing about the picnics, family games, and ridiculous late-night conversations on Friday nights. It had been a long time since she had given them a thought.

"They were fun. I don't remember too much, but all I can say is that they were fun. They were like my second parents to me."

"How about Dad? I know you don't remember too much about him either, but is there something?"

Cathy shrugged. "Honey, I can't really tell you. We had some good memories growing up, but I don't recall everything."

"Oh..." Sam looked down. That same piece of resentment grew in his brain. A damaged section, all dedicated to his mom. He still loved her, but this one thing made no sense. Perhaps it was a question he had to ask her on another day.

"Thanks, Mom. I could give the book back to you. I know it means a lot to you. For now, I'm gonna head out."

She shook her head. "No. It's yours now. I don't need it."

Sam gave her a quick side hug and walked out before his mom could get another word in.

*   *   *

In the parking lot, Sam wanted to forget about the topic of his father or any affiliations with his mother. He went back to his main aim—running. Hoping that feeling would come back. Sam hoped. That's all it took. Just a few random runs, and he'd move fast. There were delusions, and then there was reality. Rushing back and forth in the apartment lot would not make things happen.

Sam thought hard about the events in school. It all seemed like a dream. He concentrated on what he wanted—that rushy sensation, the goosebumps that painted his pink skin, the dilation in his eyes, and how everything became sharp and gaudy.

It has to happen again, he thought.

Again, he gave it another run, doubting it would work. It didn't work. This time, Sam kneeled down on the rocky gravel, his eyes focused on the world around him. They continued to focus more on the area—then it finally came to be. The pop in his pupils and that same grainy, flashy blue hue around his iris sparkled. There was only one guess about what would happen next. *I need to move.*

The trial and error class was now in session. Sam mindfully went forward, figuring out where he would run exactly. He practiced moving to one end of the lot and back to another. Of course, this did work initially, but he had the tendency to move too far and trip over a curb.

The sensation of moving at great speed felt phenomenal. Everything around him slowed down as his body sped up and flew. The wind would turn solid yet soothing at a touch. It felt like he was dragging his hands through water. To the outside world, he appeared to everyone as nothing but a blur.

Something odd happened. When Sam first ran at West Made, there was a loud, exploding sound. This time, when he sped up, there indeed was another loud call but not as strong or ear-ringing as yesterday. One tenant in a neighboring unit stepped out, poking at his ear. It was clear he, too, heard the wild boom. Another closer unit had its windows shattered into a million pieces.

Sam jogged to the side of the lot, not wanting his mother to come out and see what he was experimenting on. The kid's eyes tracked down to the road where he once ran. Potholes the size of watermelons decorated the ground—about ten of them, to be exact. Behind the giant-sized holes were smaller ones that looked similar to a dent you'd see on a bumper or side panel of a car.

It's time to take it outside the lot.

Where would I go? he thought, searching around to see what else was nearby.

An idea popped. Sam recalled a place he wanted to go to—Inferior. It was about ten miles away, but it would do for now. With no preparation, Sam looked around to make sure no cars were coming. It was all clear. He concentrated on the road ahead of him, and in came the neon glow in his eyes. Starting up, his new abilities were getting easier. He bolted off, running into nothingness.

"OH MY GOD!" Sam yelled with excitement.

The wind pushed against his face and clothes, causing high friction to come into play. Before long, he could see bits of smoke overtaking him. He quickly stopped without assurance, making him trip forward and scrape the palms of his hands on a dirty sidewalk. He dusted himself off and dipped his shoes into a small puddle nearby while he scarcely patted down random areas of his body to snuff out any flames. The rubber soles on his sneakers were practically melting off.

"Jesus..." he mumbled, checking over to see how close he was to Inferior.

He opened a map app on his phone, studying the distance between the apartments and Inferior. Far, but not too far. Sam ran further than his desired destination, ending close by at Doe's Diner—ten minutes away.

"Wrong place, but I'll come here later," he chuckled. "I'll try again later."

Sam ran home so he wouldn't miss his ride with the twins. He didn't want to count his chickens before they hatched, but he was already dreaming big. If he continued to practice, he'd never need a car or ask the boys for a ride again. More potholes spawned on the road, and his sneakers collected a new set of friction burns.

That's enough practice for today.

*   *   *

Later in school, Sam sat upright at his desk. He jotted down notes, suggestions, and theories about whether his gift involved slowing down time, superspeed, or manipulating reality.

During audio and video production class, Sam used his time wisely on the computer to research his never-ending questions. The type of questions that were deemed nerdy or strange. Searches such as: "What is super speed? Can anybody get speed? Comic book speed. How to understand superpowers. How do you control speed?"

Sam was anxious about his new abilities and planned on using them more frequently. The power he carried had such potential and was worth the time and energy. So much so that he kept the investigating rhythm going at Inferior. He was lost in unanswered disputes. He craved to go outside and run if he could, but life was keeping him busy. *I'll just have to wait until I get home.*

Not realizing he was still researching specific questions at work, he paused and rubbed his eyelids to ease the tension in his brain.

Ms. Juniper approached his desk, scaring the little, distracted boy. "Boo!"

"Shit! Oh God! Hahaha!" Sam was startled, quickly closing off his search page so as to not draw any attention. "Hey—hi, Ms. Juniper."

"Please, Sammy, I already told you. Call me Ellie." She hugged him, missing him. "I'm sorry about what happened to you during the trip. Ça va?" (How are you?)

DING! The computer behind him chimed.

Sam turned away from her, noticing an email from Mr. Grafton requesting him to step into his office. Sam half-assed his attention on the message, primarily wanting to focus on Ellie before dealing with his superior.

"Yeah. I'm actually feeling a lot better. Thank you."

"That's good. You look different, too, no?" She smiled, lifting his fringe to look at his young face. She noticed the thin scratches and felt more sorrow.

"You sure you alright?" Her accent thickened.

"Yes. I'm fine. Thank you."

Ms. Juniper let his hair drop down and pounded his shoulder. "Good! Because I found out your birthday had passed. How dare you, Sammy? How come you didn't tell me?"

Sam grinned into a blush, looking away from her. "I didn't— I don't know... I didn't think you cared. We don't talk much."

DING! His computer chimed in another message from Grafton.

"Well, I do. So much so 'dat I got you a little something." Ellie reached into her dress on the chest area, pulled out a narrow navy blue envelope, and handed it to her photographer.

Sam took a quick peek at the latest email he received. He didn't read all of it, but it didn't look good, judging by the word "now!"

"What's this?" Sam asked, grabbing it.

"You'll see. Also, try to accept 'dis one, Sammy. Au revoir." (Goodbye.)

Opening the letter, Sam found only two things: a happy birthday card with the word "belated" written in between the words with a pen and a check for ten thousand dollars—the money he rejected before he went to London.

"Are you—what?!" he yelped. There was no way he could return the money now. Sam felt guilty. It was a generous gift, but he couldn't take it. Again, there was no taking it back now.

Albeit, it wasn't as if he didn't need the money, anyway. He had to help pay the bills at home, including the hospital bills.

When Sam reached to put the card on his desk, he accidentally dropped it on the floor. As he retrieved it, he realized his shoes were more screwed up than he thought. The rubber had been scratched, burned, and ripped. The edges between the fabric and rubber pieces were lifting.

"Dammit," he whispered.

This led to further research on shoes, heat, friction, and the physics behind super speed in not only real-life physics but also in comic book culture. Fortunately, Sam had a spare pair of shoes somewhere in his closet. They weren't more so casual shoes—they were boots. Coincidentally, they were exactly what he needed to continue running at a high velocity.

"CLARK!" Mr. Grafton alerted.

"Yes!" Sam panicked, turning his head towards the sound of his boss' voice without hesitation.

"In my office."

That didn't sound good. It was bad enough that the coma caused Sam to miss out on a lot from his job, so ignoring work emails was probably the straw that broke the camel's back.

"Sit down." Kendrick pointed.

The chair looked cold and minimalistic. Just two red cushions held up by brown legs. *I've sat on comfier. I hope this isn't how I get fired. I really need this job.*

Before the man got a word in, Sam had an obligation to plead his case. It wasn't for certain if he was being let go or anything related, but it was better to be safe than sorry.

"Mr. Grafton, I just want to apologize for the times I've been late. The accident in London was very unexpected... I really love this job, and I can do better."

Kendrick had a confused look on his face. "What are you talking about?"

"I just want to apologize for what happened."

"You were in a coma, dude. If anything, you should've picked a better route."

Sam didn't know whether to take that as a serious note or a messed-up joke. His reaction became blank; no response.

"You think I'm going to fire you?" Kendrick grew a wide smile, breaking into an instant laugh. "Hahaha! Nope! Quite the opposite, sadly."

Sam's blank reaction turned both relieved and hopeful. *Where was that leading to?*

"I'm promoting you to photographer. You'll no longer be assisting."

"I... Mr. Grafton—this—this is just—I don't know what to say. Thank you, sir. Thank you so much!"

"Yeah-yeah. You're welcome. Be here tomorrow after school, and you'll be brought up to speed." Grafton leaned back into his office chair, brushing his fingers through his short, graying hair.

"Sir, may I ask why?" Sam was going to reconsider if Kendrick was doing this out of empathy or, worse, pity from the coma.

He sighed in a tone that sounded like annoyance. "Do you want the job or not?"

"Oh—one hundred percent I do. Yes, it's just that—I want to know why?"

Grafton gave the kid a lead-paint stare for what seemed like a minute. Sam waited in the anticipation of an answer. An honest answer out of merit and not pity.

"Double-check if the door is closed. The damn thing has a habit of being cracked open."

Sam moved out of the seat and gave the door a couple of tugs and pushes before sitting back down for the revelation. "It's closed," he assured.

"Good." Mr. Grafton cleared his throat. "Look, Sam. We found some of your belongings in the taxi... or what was left of it. Anyway, one of the serving items was the SD card in your camera. I took matters into my hands and went through the pictures."

"Okay?" The boy continued to listen. Waiting.

"You have a good sense of direction. You know how to take a picture. That's for damn sure, kid. Not just of Ms. Juniper but of other things, too. Plus, the ones you took at Hyde Park were far better than whatever shit Reese took."

Sam was afraid to ask, but it had to come out eventually. "Is it partly because of what happened to me?"

The boss shrugged. "I don't know. Maybe. Maybe not. I'm not that big of a dick."

Sam gave a slight roll of his eyes.

"But you have a gift. Plus, you've been putting in the work. You deserve it."

I do have a gift. "Thank you."

Throughout the days, Sam experienced the ongoing wear-and-tear look in his clothes. When he wore a white shirt, the aftermath of his speed made the color appear ashy, and little charred holes appeared randomly. His jackets crumbled, with threads rippling off. His wardrobe would continue to fall apart if he didn't do something.

Sam found more information on fabrics with one of the newest foundations opening up—a new tailor shop, Beyrou's. Word around town was that they sold almost any fabric known to man. Another word around was that it'd be expensive as hell.

An idea popped into Sam's mind. He used his new gift to run back home, trying his best to dodge most of the cars passing by. But his motions caused damage to the car windows he'd run past—they'd shatter, and the doors would dent.

Another thing to add to the list of research: Taking control of my speed.

There's a lot more to gaining a gift, such as super speed. It's not like what you'd read in the comics or see in the movies. Sam's bones didn't break because he had already attained some type of control. The muscles and bones in his body thickened to provide durability. Therefore, he wasn't such a scrawny-looking nerd anymore. He didn't need the cast on his arm anymore. He probably never needed it right after he awoke from his coma. His arm never ached or stung with pain. Sam figured it was best to make it removable rather than shock others with a magically healed bone.

Everything has a basis in science. It's not magic.

His body's healing process quickened. That didn't mean he was invincible, though.

You might also wonder: What about the loud noises? How about the potholes in the ground? Blurry perception? Why isn't the friction burning up my skin?

Ready for the answers? The ear-deafening claps were from Sam breaking the sound barrier, as loud as a harrier jet. Loud? Clearly. Ear-damaging? Maybe so. Sam was smart. These things could be dulled. He found a way to boost off without going from zero to six hundred, avoiding civilians needing a trip to the doctor. Instead of instantly running at such speeds, it had to be taken slow. *You have to walk before you can run,* as the saying goes. Build up the momentum. Sam would jog a step or two and only then boost off without alerting everyone within the vicinity. If it were an emergency, he'd still have to move carefully.

The potholes were from the force and pressure of his speed. It's a shock that the holes weren't craters the size of a cargo ship. This was likely to be a prerequisite from the day he received his speed—otherwise, the science would remain valid.

Sam's perception during the use of super speed was fixed the day he stopped wearing his readers. Whenever he ran, he could perceive where he was going in a matter of an attosecond. If his powers hadn't fixed his eyesight, everything around him would look worse than a 3D movie without glasses.

Remember, Sam's speed wasn't always past sound. It was an option to run that fast—almost like riding a bike or skateboard. The more you push, the faster you go. Part of that also made him tired. So much energy and force were being used that it eventually took a toll. Metabolism, energy, strength—everything was put into use.

Finally, the friction. The boy wasn't perfect. After running the last few times, red, blotchy pieces would randomly appear on his skin, more prominently on his arms, face, hands, and legs. These weren't just burns—they were also the impact of flies swatting against his skin. Painful. They healed fast, but it hurt getting them. The only way to stop it from happening again was to either vibrate his molecules every time he ran or to wear heat-resistant clothes.

Sam switched out his shoes for a pair of dog boots hidden deep in his closet. They were still new, worn only twice when he helped the twins set up a fence on their family's farm. The steel toe in the boots helped with durability as well as longevity if he wanted to continue running.

Was it hard to run in boots? Most definitely. But this was a benefit if I wanted to run carefully and not go through multiple pairs of sneakers.

Speaking of steel, the thoughtful teenager furthered his new studies. Besides fabrics and abrasion, he looked into other materials that could withstand friction, like metal, silver, and gold—eventually landing on the wonders of tungsten. Tungsten has a high melting point of 6,192 and can withstand high friction (also fireproof) to total perfection.

Sam flipped through many websites before ordering a few rods the size of a thin pencil.

I think about forty pieces should do, he thought.

Since Sam had no access to a factory or tools to melt the rods, he found improvising to work best. He could squeeze some stronghold glue to mold them in place. If that didn't work, he might sew them together (taught by his mother). The twins knew a family member who worked at a smelting industry called Baron's, but the property had foreclosed.

Sam put the order in. "And now we wait..." he mumbled.

Back on the topic of fabrics, was it possible to find an equal? Something—anything—that could withstand the damage? Sam hoped to God that Beyrou's would have the resources. It's possible he could sew it into his clothes. On his laptop, search results brought him to abrasive fabrics. Most orders were sold by rolls or by sheets. Everything needed to be more precise. Sam waited a few days until the shop officially opened.

Cathy reminded her son to take his medicine and head to bed after finishing his homework. To him, life never felt better. No more anxiety attacks, a blessed gift, and a promotion.

An hour and a half into homework for Algebra II, Sam worked up an appetite. He said earlier today that he was done using his speed for the day, but somehow, he couldn't help it. Part of obtaining speed was the fast metabolism. The hunger was never-ending.

Maybe a big slice from Milano's Pizzeria will do the trick.

Cathy was already in bed. She thought Sam had already gone to bed. This was wrong to do, but Sam had the urge to sneak out and eat a good meal. He grabbed his olive windbreaker and steel-toe boots, ready to make a dinner run.

The stupid, rusty door almost blew Sam's cover. It creaked the loudest at night. Sam thought about using his speed at first—but what good would that do? Break a floor tile or two? Make the smoke alarms go off? Possibly shatter all the windows to the unit, including downstairs? Not a good idea at all. At least not until he understood how to make his speed stable. For now, the rusty door had to sing.

Outside, Sam dug his hands into the big pockets of his jacket. The weather was getting colder by the day, and the slaps of the wind for sure didn't help.

No time to waste. Sam's stomach growled, getting hungrier. Soon, he was going to have to calculate his caloric intake. In the meantime, it was reckless spending on food. Hopefully, this new promotion would aid with that.

Sam bent his knees into a running posture. He was ready for takeoff and ready for that delicious, cheesy pizza. He focused on the area ahead of him. He knew exactly where to go and how to get there. His eyes flickered into that blue color. Sam could feel the warmth of the blue rub against his eyelids. He accepted its familiar greeting, as if it were saying hello to an old friend.

Suddenly, the color flickered. Something was off. The warmth flashed on and off like a broken lightbulb. He tried his damn best to focus on his surrounding areas. The flick died down, and his sharpness and vibrancy of colors faded away. Before it ceased, Sam dashed forward, paying no mind to the blue anymore. This time, he didn't move in a blurry motion or make any loud sound-breaking noises. He was just a normal kid running across his parking lot.

Gasping, "What the hell?" Sam's run progressed into a limp jog before giving up.

He clenched his fists and stared at the floor. No more blue. No more gifts...

My powers are gone...

Chapter 17
SEEING DOUBLE

How could we forget about the twins? *The Twins.* They had a life right outside of Sam's issues. They weren't just chauffeurs or a charity. They really gave a damn about their best friend. And why wouldn't they? They'd only been friends since they were kids. No bad times or bad vibes—well—there was one time when the trio was hitting the start of their puberty years, and the twins decided to look up some raunchy type of content on their parents' computer.

Adult content in 2010 wasn't a secret. It was just a simple search away. Kids were curious, and clearly, this wasn't the right thing to be wondering about. Kids were also stupid. Amateurs. The twins forgot to close the tab, minimizing it instead and turning off the computer when they heard their parents, John and Stacy Sings, come in through the front door.

It wasn't long before their father had to use the computer for his recreational online gambling. John blew a fuse, his face turning a lava-red state. Who else was there to blame? His wife? Their dog, Bozo? Or was it the mischievous kids who were already making a name for themselves as class clowns at school? Out of fear (they truly didn't mean to), they put the blame on their best friend.

It didn't quite sound believable at first, but the twins swore it was Sam.

The Sings called up Cathy later that night, going on a tyrant about how their son could end up perverted or addicted. The whole nine yards of what a usual parent might rant about. It could've been worse—the Sings could've blamed Cathy's parenting style or her living situation. But luckily, they didn't make it personal.

Sam pleaded with his mother, telling God's honest truth that it wasn't him. She believed him but used this as a learning experience and took his electronic privileges away for a couple of days. Sam didn't take this lightly.

Who dares to take away our dopamine?! How dare those boring parents not let us have fun?! How could they?!... Can we have Dino Nuggets for dinner, please?

Another attribute of kids was that they held technology or any type of fun close to their hearts. The twins made it their life's goal to make it up to their friend. They really didn't want the disciplinary action—the hard kiss of a belt on the ass. Anything but that.

Children also forgive and forget easily with friendship. This wasn't anything life-altering—just a small debacle. This was where the three boys learned the old saying: *Taking one for the team.*

The trio was coming to a small fade, specifically one man out—Sam. Throughout their days, they noticed the hangouts becoming short, and from short, went to dead nothing. No calls, texts, or the usual late breakfast spots at Doe's. At first, the Sings knew their buddy was going through a rough time mentally. But the rare times they talked, Sam seemed just fine. Fine from the neck down, that was.

Trevor was more concerned with Sam compared to his brother. He wondered where he was going off to. Trevor suspected Sam might've found a girl and was choosing to be discreet about it. He second-guessed himself for a minute—he recognized a pattern of the constant bothers of trying to set Sam up with a lady. He pondered the idea that maybe Sam wasn't even into girls.

Nah. Sam ain't queer, Trevor thought. Then he jumped to a ridiculous idea that he was going out with Ellie Juniper. *Nah. He's got no balls.*

The brothers lived a ranch life not too far from the school zone. Any farther, and they'd have to transfer somewhere else. But not a single chance in hell would that ever happen. Fort Worth was home. It was better than the other two schools they went to. For clarification, the two didn't go to West Made until their second semester of sophomore year.

There was a period in which the trio didn't think they'd be friends growing up. They separated in the eighth grade. During that time, John was trying to buy a ranch in Fort Worth, but that needed time and more money. They had to sell their original home and move to a small spot in Mesquite. Mesquite Petite. Also known as Mesquite Poteet, as the local kids called it.

The following year, they had to move to the edge of Terrell, near a small town called Forney. In 2010, it was a nice place to live, with no care in the world. You could ask your neighbor for a cup of sugar or a cashier at the local supermarket for their secret recipe for some irrelevant side dish. Now, it's a place where new people move in to bring their new problems, involving wannabe gangsters and white kids who were raised right to turn into whiggas.

Forney was alright for the twins. They missed seeing Sam regularly. When Stacy notified her sons that they bought the ranch, it was good news. But when she also added that they were moving back home, that news was better.

Trevor relished the thought of being a kid again, the three of them running around in their backyard with curved wooden sticks, shaped to be pretend-guns. (*Somewhat similar to how Cathy played with Tate when she was young.*) So he deemed it right to have a cause for concern. Garrett, on the other hand, didn't mind much. It's not that he didn't care or anything like that. His primary focus was his future. He hoped for a good football scholarship to A&M or anywhere nearby Texas. Hell, he'd even take Louisiana.

Today wasn't gonna be all fine and dandy for one of the boys. A bad fate awaited one. The question was, who?

It was late. The Sings regretted getting breakfast at Doe's. They both ordered a full plate—the works. Everything you could fit on it: eggs, bacon, pancakes, sausage, ham, hash browns, and so on. Trevor's stomach was bloated, and the black coffee started to not sit right with him. Garrett, too, was also bloated but not as bad as his stocky brother.

"That's the last time I order with my eyes," Trevor groaned.

"Yep. Lesson learned," Garrett agreed, rubbing his stomach through his baggy hoodie.

"Think I might pass out on the ride home—"

"Nope," his chunky brother interjected, tossing him the keys. "You're driving."

"Come onnnnnn. Please?"

"No. Double no. Triple no. Hell no!"

Trevor groaned, sluggishly dragging his body while swaying the keys around.

Before they got into the red dame, Garrett suggested they burn off some of the calories by walking around Doe's a couple of times. Not a bad idea at first, but later, it would be.

The first walk went smoothly. Trevor shared his inner feelings of remembrance with his twin. His feeling of missing Sam almost sounded like worry—worried that Sam didn't care to see them anymore or that something might've happened to him again. Garrett was a constant being of reassurance. *Everything is still the same*, he said.

The second walk followed up on the conversation about their futures. Would they still talk to each other after graduation? It wasn't for another five months, but the underlying world of adulthood awaited.

The third walk was where they got lost. But soon, they'd be found in the back lot of Doe's by Felix Rade. He wasn't alone. Beside him were two other guys from the football team— Charlie Welsh and EJ Thompson. Garrett knew them. They were a team... or so he thought. The pair beside Felix had one arm behind their backs. The look on Felix's face was evil. He wore a big smirk, and his eyes screamed trouble.

"Hey. What's up, guys?" Garrett greeted, his tone slightly annoyed.

"Nun' much," replied Felix.

The twins stood in awkwardness, waiting for the conversation to continue. Trevor had a bad gut feeling, and it wasn't the breakfast.

Garrett placed a hand on his brother's shoulder, guiding him back towards the front side of Doe's. "Well, guess Trev and I will be headin' out. We all have school in the mornin'. See y'all!"

"Wait!" exclaimed Felix. "I want to talk to you for a minute."

"What about?" asked Trevor.

"I'm not talking to you, kid!" the jock shouted.

"Woah, woah, woah. Calm down. That's my brother you're talking to. Let's be civil," Garrett said, always the one to de-escalate a situation.

"Civil, like the black eye you gave me?" Felix snarled. He never forgave or forgot. When the kid held a grudge, he meant it.

Garrett explained, "Because you kept bothering Sam."

"So?!" Felix raised his voice.

Trevor leaned towards the side of his brother's head, mumbling, "Gar, I think we should go."

"Why is he such a threat to you?" Garrett asked.

Felix shook his head. "That's nun' of your business!"

Garrett's face of concern shifted into a little grin. "I know why, Rade. You're jealous. Not just because he's smarter than you, but because your own family favors him more than you."

The players beside Felix took a slight step away from their leader, scared by the shade of red growing on his face.

"Mrs. Smith, was it? Aunt Smith?" Garrett teased. "I get it, man. I do. But that's not a reason to harass our best friend. Why can't you just move on and go back to focusing on playing ball?"

Trevor grew more worried, not taking his eyes off the three.

Meanwhile, Felix bit the inside of his cheek, figuring out what his next words should be. "You know what, Gar? I think I might switch to another sport besides football."

The bully reached behind EJ, grabbing what was hidden in his hand—a baseball bat. "I think I might go with baseball. What do you think?"

The next word that came out of Garrett's mouth sounded guttural. "RUN!"

Both b-lined for the truck. They dared not to look back or stop for anything else. They ran like their lives depended on it. They weren't able to sprint as fast as Sam's super speed, but it was as fast as humanly possible. Trevor wasn't the fastest runner, but he was most likely safe from Felix's rage. They were there for his brother, not him. And he didn't care. The Sings were big on pride, honor, and respect. He was going to fight for his brother no matter the crime.

Just before the key could unlock the truck, both EJ and Charlie caught up to Garrett and pulled him away from the passenger door, throwing him to the ground. His thick face slapped against the sharp gravel. Crumb-sized rocks and debris sunk into his cheek and temple. The pain was just beginning—what came next was worse.

The other two stomped on Garrett's back and waist area. They even landed a couple of kicks to his ass and the back of his muscle-over-fat thighs. Each stomp sounded harsh. Pounded skin made an odd noise.

Trevor stood in shock for a hot second before snapping himself out of it.

"GET OFF HIM!" the 14-minute older brother yelled, running over to his younger. Trevor pushed Charlie first, managing to shove him a few feet away, and then socked EJ in the face. The guy ate the punch, but it hurt—it hurt his nice face and Trev's wide knuckles.

Fighting isn't what it looks like in the movies. It hurts. Fights don't last over five minutes with intense camera angles and smooth movement. They're demanding and tiring. The two goons dropped their bats, tired after stomping Garrett for the fifth time each.

Interesting... Why would they bring bats if they weren't going to use them on him?

Garrett moaned, moving carefully to his side. His back joints ached with every squirm. Meanwhile, Trevor attempted to throw another punch at whoever was closer (EJ) but missed badly. Felix came in close, ordering his friends to do his bidding.

"Hold him!"

Charlie and EJ rushed Trevor, holding each arm back with every ounce of strength they had. Of course, this was all thanks to the training they had during practice and the school's gym.

Felix walked past Garrett's limp body. The heel of his Nike high-tops grazed Garrett's pinky finger. Another millimeter closer, and he would've put his whole weight on it. It was lucky—but lucky wasn't the right term to use in a situation like this.

Felix's eyes studied Trevor in a judgmental way. Then, he slapped Trevor's cowboy hat right off his head, deeming it stupid. Like he was saying, he always hated that hat.

"This is none of your business," said Felix. "So, this is your warning."

The kid pulled his arm back, balled a hard fist, and thrust forward with every ounce of exertion, landing a strong uppercut to Trevor's gut, right between the ribcage. Trevor let out a nasty gasp for air, as if he were drowning. The breakfast in his stomach curdled, and soon he puked on the floor.

The goons let him go, leaving him to crawl on all fours.

"T-Trevor—it's f-fine," Garrett coughed. "This i-i-isn't your f-fight. My fault... it's m-my problem."

"Shut up!" Felix snarled, giving Garrett's ribs a quick kick. The tip of his sneaker almost pierced through. Nothing was broken, thankfully, but something else was about to be.

Felix stood beside his old teammate, lifted his arm, extended it out, and placed his heel on Garrett's elbow.

Across the street, a man witnessed the fight, called the authorities, and shouted—hoping to grab their attention and maybe stop the craziness.

When Trevor looked up from his vomit, catching his breath, his eyes widened in realization. "Wait... WAIT!"

It happened just like that.

The yell from the man didn't distract them. Trevor's screams didn't stop them. Felix's foot didn't hesitate to stomp the joint.

It was too late.

A loud pop echoed through the street, and a wailing scream from Garrett followed—something Trevor hoped he'd never hear in his life. Not from a friend, a stranger, or family.

As he witnessed the horror, Trevor realized this wasn't a street fight. No, this was a jumping. An unfair fight, if anything—three against one, technically. Trevor was just at the wrong place at the wrong time. They weren't there for him. They were there for Garrett.

One detail that was left out was the baseball bats. Oh, how could we forget those wooden things?

The damage was only halfway done. Charlie, EJ, and Felix picked up their bats and moved past Trevor (who now put two and two together on what the bats were truly for) and swung at the truck.

The red dame dented and shook with each swing. Charlie smashed the left rear taillight, and EJ proceeded to hit the driver's side door panel. Felix moved to the front of the dame and smashed both headlights.

A strong hate boiled inside Trevor — A hate so deep and uncontrolled that intrusive thoughts flooded his mind. All the possibilities of what he would do if he ever got his hands on Felix.

He had no idea what sparked all this violence.

Was it Garrett's mistake? Was this really all because he took a stand for Sam? Was this revenge out of hurt pride? Why?

As the three athletes continued to beat the truck, Trevor wanted nothing more than to get up and shove the ends of their bats where the sun doesn't shine. But he was still gasping for air. That punch and the snap of the arm had done as much damage to him as they did to their ride.

In a messed-up, poetic kind of way, they were now triplets.

All three hurt. All three damaged.

Felix gave one last swing to the windshield. A large crack sprayed across the glass. It was bad, but not as bad as Trevor thought it would be. Honestly, it could've been worse. The glass could've shattered.

The dame was still strong, even under attack.

The three took off right after the final beating.

Trevor crawled on the floor, tears flooding his eyes as bits of vomit and spit dripped onto his bottom lip.

Help was on the way...

Chapter 18
HOSPITAL

On the hospital bed, Garrett took a peep at the X-ray of his arm on the wall.

"Wow. That's almost a clean-cut. What are those guys eating at school?"

John and Stacy didn't take this as a laughing matter.

"Are you okay?" asked Trevor.

"Yeah. I still got my other hand. Ha!" he joked. "I'm just happy it wasn't my right hand. I still need that one." Garrett was all high on pain medication. He would feel nothing until tomorrow morning.

"I heard your arm snap," said Trevor. There was a numbness in his voice—depressing.

"Yeah. I don't know how to describe the noise, but I heard it loud and clear... shit, I know I felt it."

"Language," said John. He wasn't fond of cursing but was for sure not going to tolerate it in front of their mother.

Sam walked into the room. His eyes met the family, and he was glad to see his best friends were alright. The boy walked up to Trevor and landed a side hug. When he moved to Garrett, he gave him a full-front one.

Sam misplaced his hand on the back of his shoulder, and Garrett slightly grunted.

"Ah!" That was where most of the bruises and scrapes were.

"Sorry!" Sam said quickly, removing his arm from that area.

"You're fine."

"Be careful, Sam," Stacy demanded.

"I'm sorry."

"It's fine, Mom," Garrett assured. "He didn't know. Plus, I don't feel it too much."

Sam wasn't really close to the Sings. He may have been close with the boys, but the parents would hardly hear or even see their friend, especially after the blame for the adult content when he was thirteen.

Sam was familiar with the hospital. It was the same one where he had laid in a coma. The smell of the hallways was also too familiar, and the cold temperature sent shivers down his arms. Even with his windbreaker on, it was still cold.

"How've you been, Sam?" Stacy asked, scratching her curly red-brown hair.

"I'm taking it one day at a time. Just living and working." Sam was awkward, not knowing how to interact with adults, let alone the parents of his best friends.

"How's work?" she asked, folding her arms.

"Good. Well—could be better. I just got promoted the other day."

"Wow. I bet they're going to work you to the bone after graduation, huh?"

"You never told us that," said Trevor, staring blankly at his friend.

Sam gave a weak smile, not wanting to think about that at the moment.

John gave his son a pat on the shoulder. "We'll be outside. I'm sure you three want to catch up. Plus, there are too many guests in here."

The parents left, leaving the trio to reunite again. Sam was unsure what John meant when he said, 'Catch up,' but then he couldn't recall the last time he went out with the twins.

Was it last week? More than that? Sam tried to think about it. *There was just no way it had been that long. Maybe it just felt that long.*

"Hey, look," Garrett laughed, raising his casted arm up. "We're twins."

Ironic. Sam laughed for a moment, and the humor would've continued, but Sam felt like a liar. He didn't need the cast. He was just wearing it so as not to look suspicious about how a hairline fracture could heal within a couple of days. Sam wanted to tell them about the new things he'd been experiencing, but tonight was officially not the right time. *Maybe tomorrow.*

"How've you been? We hardly see you," said Garrett, his cast still raised up.

"Good. Just been busy with work and helping Mom around the house."

It was now beginning to feel like a dialogue only between Garrett and Sam. Trevor didn't seem interested in joining in. At least, not yet.

"How's your mom?" Garrett continued to ask more questions. He missed his friend.

"She's good. Not much is different. Just working. Also, Gar— you can put your arm down."

"Oh." The twin giggled, putting it down.

"How about y'all? I don't see you around Inferior as much anymore."

"Because we quit," Trevor finally spoke. His eye contact connected with Sam's, and then he trailed away.

"Why? When'd y'all quit?"

"Well—" Garrett got cut off by his brother answering for him.

"When you didn't need rides anymore."

"Oh…" Sam was lost for words. He guessed it really had been a while since he saw them. Trevor now had this notion that Sam had been using them for free rides. But how could that be true if he'd been paying for them? The money didn't matter. Sam cut them off after he learned to use his super speed. *He left them in the dark.*

Garrett explained, "I was about to say that I didn't quit."

"You didn't?"

"Well—not yet. I work a couple shifts here and there, but it's just to build my savings for college."

Sam looked at his friend's cast, then back up at him. "You still gonna play ball in college? If so, I hope your arm is all healed up by the time the season starts up."

Garrett shook his head slowly. "Nah… I'm done with football. I don't need it anymore."

Trevor's face went shocked. This was news to him as well. "What about your scholarship?"

"I don't need it. I'm moving on, Trev."

"Please tell me this isn't because of Felix…"

"Mmm... yes and no," Garrett answered. He was telling the truth. It was easy to assume it was because of Felix, but it was more than that. Garrett explained his own team betrayed him. That loyalty could always be a facade. He told him that high school was cruel and that there was more to life than sports.

Sam reflected on the words *"more to life than..."* Similar to how he told Fulton that there's more to life than hard work, ambition, etc.

Trevor didn't want to believe the words he was hearing. He stormed out of the room without hesitation. Out in the hall, he passed by Cathy. She greeted him but was ignored by the kid. She hadn't a clue why, but could tell it had something to do with his brother.

Garrett sighed and gave Sam a little smile on one side of his lips. "It's not your fault, Sam. You know that, right?"

"It feels like it is."

"It's not," Garrett said sternly. "He just missed you, is all. You know, Trev. The way he gets. It'll pass."

Sam swayed at the end of the bed, appalled by what he'd heard from his friend's parents. "I still can't believe Felix did that to you."

"It's alright, Sam."

"No! It's not!" The boy shouted.

"Shhhh!" Garrett hushed, not wanting to alert anyone outside the room. "I got him, then he got me back. Simple. You know I'd do the same if it were the other way around."

"But he didn't have to break your arm, Gar!"

"Shhhh!"

Cathy stumbled into the room. She held a Milky Way bar (Garrett's favorite) and presented it to him like it was a gift. She'd attempted to get a cake, but nothing was gonna be open at this late hour. It was the thought that counted.

"How are you feeling, Gar?" she smiled.

"I'm alright. Just high." He joked. Cathy gave a genuine laugh. She'd never seen Sam's friends like this before.

Stacy walked into the room to check on her son. "Oh. Hello, Stacy. Hi, John." Cathy greeted, not expecting to see the boys' parents. "I got Garrett a candy bar when I heard what happened. I tried cake, but there was nothing available."

"That's alright. Thank you for that. How've you been, Cathy?" Stacy asked.

"Good. Just busy. I haven't seen you both in a couple of years. What's new?"

John entered the conversation. "Just working. Staying busy as well and making sure our boys finish school. It's crazy how much time has passed since their late elementary days, right?"

"Big time!" Cathy smiled. "I remember picking them up every Friday for a pizza night. Those kids would never sleep."

"Oh, yeah." Stacy scoffed. "Could we take this conversation outside and let the boys wrap up their conversation?"

Cathy paused. "Sure. Yeah—yeah, no problem. Hope you feel better, Gar. I hope this is the last accident for you and Trev."

"Thank you." Garrett smiled, his cheeks turning pinker than usual.

Sam turned his head back to his friend, and Garrett's next words were the most outlandish but funniest thing he'd said in a while.

"Dude... I know I might have told you this before, and I'm going to say it again... your mom is so hot."

"So, is that the lie you and Trev are going with?"

"What? About your mom being hot?" Garrett mused.

"No. Car accident."

Garrett exhaled through his nose. It wasn't appropriate to make a joke right now. "Yeah. That's what I told them."

"And Trevor just has a couple of bruises while you have a broken arm?"

"I'm not a snitch, Sam... I don't want my parents to worry. This is my issue, and I'm handling it. Can't run to our parents forever, ya' know."

Sam let his buddy rest. He needed to reconsider how he was spending his time. Before he turned in for the night, he wanted to find Trevor and explain himself, but he looked too busy talking to some lady with messy, golden-blonde hair. Sam assumed it was probably a nurse or some girl he found good conversation with. *Terrible timing to be flirting with a girl when your brother is in the other room, all high as a kite.*

"I guess our conversation will have to wait until later," he mumbled.

Chapter 19
CLASS CLOWN

Friday. Sam placed his focus elsewhere besides anatomy class. He needed to plan. It wasn't right, but he wanted to get revenge on Felix for what he did to Garrett. And not just for him but for the anger and pain he had caused Trevor. He had to time it just right. In about 20 minutes, he would proceed to his next class, Audio and Video, with Mrs. Smith. This was the last chance to do something. Sam had no intention of waiting another day. He hated seeing Felix's stupid smile. He hated how Felix walked around the school, thinking he was untouchable.

This isn't like me. Sam didn't hate. He never hated. But this ongoing feud between Felix and him had dragged on for too long. *It's time to give the kid a taste of his own medicine.*

What do I do? The possibilities. All the possibilities with his speed. It most likely wouldn't be safe for Sam to move the big guy. He didn't know for sure, but it wasn't something Sam wanted to test right now. *Maybe another day.* He thought about pushing him around, but that would just be another way of moving him. *Maybe I'll remove all his clothing?* That's another way of moving him. He had to think of something else. Something that didn't require too much motion on a regular human being.

Twenty minutes passed. It was time to head to Audio and Video. Sam contemplated giving up. Revenge wasn't his thing. He continued on with his usual schedule.

Maybe tomorrow. There were other things he needed to focus on. His primary concern was the return of his powers.

When Sam woke up, he recognized a difference. The flutter in his eyes had returned. The boy practically cried with relief. He'd been afraid that the powers were only temporary—or worse, gone for good. Thankfully, he needn't worry anymore. They were back. *Hopefully, this time, for good.*

Along with Sam's long list of theories, he added another. This time, there was something that might get answered within a twenty-four-hour period. *I'll test it for sure later in the evening and await the results.* He considered the possibility that it might be the medicine—the pills he'd been taking. Not that they took his powers away, but maybe they dulled them. *My gifts wouldn't be as powerful as they once were.* It was a reach, but it's always better to be safe than sorry.

For now, the powers are back. That's what matters most.

In Mrs. Smith's class, Sam forgot about his revenge plans and focused on his homework. Here and there, he'd use his speed to cheat. Not the type of cheating where he'd look off someone else's homework. The type of cheating where he'd finish his homework faster than the top student in class would, thanks to his gift.

Well—let's not kid ourselves. If anyone could go as fast as the speed of sound, you'd try all kinds of mischievous things.

Sam cheated once during a quiz in Mr. McCrown's class. After that, he had no plans to do it again. Not only was it wrong, but it also caused a commotion in the class, with papers flying everywhere and desks being shifted.

An itch developed in the right corner of Sam's head. That damn itch was annoying, but it was the least of his problems. The itch warned him that there was trouble nearby. Trouble that was about to happen. Sam turned his eyes far to his right. If Mrs. Smith had been in front of him, she'd have seen nothing but the whites of his eyes. Sam spotted that arrogant jock, Felix, closing in on him.

An addition to Sam's powers was "speed thinking"— thinking faster than the average human. Pretty self-explanatory. He gathered from the surrounding area that Felix was going to be a bother. There were only a few ways he could torment Sam.

Maybe he'll shove me in my seat, right? Slap the back of my head? Pull my chair back? That'd be too easy. *Wait... I know. My camera.* Sam's eyes moved away from Felix and panned over to his Canon AE-1. It sat on the edge of the desk, close to his elbow.

At this rate, Felix was looking pretty predictable. He would act like he was passing by and pretend to bump into Sam's desk, when really, he'd slide his hand on the corner to push the camera off and break it on the floor.

Easy. Sam prepared himself. He watched as things played out exactly as he predicted. Felix strutted past, swiped his long hand out to the camera at the last second, and let it fall.

Sam couldn't see it, but Felix had a big smirk. The smirk rapidly changed to something dubious. The camera didn't hit the floor. There was no thud or crashing sound. The all-star player turned around, searching for anything broken, but was left disappointed when he saw Sam gracefully catch the camera.

Sam stared the bully down as he gently placed his vintage possessions back on the table.

"How'd you do that?" Felix asked, his tone rising in surprise.

Sam turned confident. "You're getting predictable, Rade."

Felix took a big step, now only a foot away from his victim's face, and whispered, "Did you catch what happened to Garrett?"

Sam's confidence plummeted, and his little grin turned into an angry expression.

"Better watch out, Connie." Felix loved teasing him by using his middle name.

That was the final straw. That was the nail in the coffin for Sam. From once dropping the idea of revenge, he now refused to stand for it. Sam needed to think of a way to get back at him.

The plan wasn't perfect. The principle of this so-called prank was to invoke humiliation. The whole school didn't need to see what was going to happen. All it took was a few kids and a couple of phones—they'd do the rest. Sam overheard from one of the football players that Felix was going to be at the school's gym after classes instead of heading to tutoring. Typical.

Sam's plan was simple: wait until Felix was in the boys' shower room, take his clothes from his locker, leave him naked with nothing but a towel, and lead him on a type of wild goose chase in search of his clothes. Drop the clothes into one classroom, provide a silly twist, and then watch the rest unfold.

Simple, quick, and humiliating.

BEEEEP-BEEEEP! BEEEEP-BEEEEP! The dismissal bell rang as usual. A fair amount of students stayed for tutoring classes. Others had extracurricular activities or a late ride.

The more, the merrier, Sam thought. *Further the embarrassment.*

Was his plan too far? Maybe. But this seemed like a slap on the wrist compared to what happened to Garrett. *Maybe in some messed-up way, this is justice. Not vengeance.*

Felix took his time at the gym. Kids were heading home by the minute, and things weren't going according to plan. Luckily, Sam didn't have to wait any longer. Felix made his way to the showers, ready to call it a day. *Such a busy day*, Sam thought mockingly. *Nothing says hard work, like being an asshole all day, terrorizing smart kids, and not paying attention in class. America's hardest worker, for sure.*

Sam used a hint of his speed to gather everything from Felix's locker, purposely leaving a trail of dirty socks that led to the gym's doors. Felix grabbed a beige towel, wrapped it around his slim waist, and was ready to call it a day. But this time, his program was interrupted by a silly scavenger hunt.

"Where's my bag?!" Felix shouted, frantically searching the locker room, shivering from the cold air after his warm shower. The single, thin towel wrapped around him didn't help. Felix snooped around other players' lockers, but none contained extra clothes. After flipping through a few more, Felix spotted one of his dirty socks on the floor, then another, and another, until he realized it was a deliberate trail leading somewhere.

"Charlie?! Is this you?" he called out, skeptical.

Felix went through the gym doors and squinted down the hall. He caught sight of an arm (Sam's arm) sticking out, clutching a clean pair of boxers. The arm beckoned in an odd way, almost like it was teasing: *Come here, kid. Want some free underwear? Come and get it.*

Felix grunted. "Charlie, this isn't funny! Give me those!"

The arm flicked away, sliding past the wall. Felix gave chase, running down the hall. He needed to get his clothes back fast before any theater kids or band geeks came out to witness him in his nude glory.

"Dammit, man!" he groaned, pissed off and still cold.

When Felix turned the corner, the plan fell into perfect execution, just as Sam had wanted. Simple. What happened next was quick. To the normal eye, it would've seemed like a blink, but for Sam, it took time. Sweet time. When Felix rounded the wall, he ran straight into a clique.

It wasn't band geeks, nerds, teachers, or theater kids. It was a large group of cheerleaders on their way to practice for a show before winter break. Felix wouldn't have minded flexing for them after a shower, but not in a situation like this—wearing clown makeup, a puffy red wig, and missing his towel.

Sam had used his speed to apply pasty white face paint, a lipstick-red nose, and the wig with supplies from the theater room. The makeup seemed childish enough, but as most guys know, if you're fresh out of the shower (or pool) and standing in a cold room, *certain things* might appear smaller than they actually are.

The girls laughed in unison. One even pointed. A student in the hall pulled out their phone to record. Felix tried to show off his arms, but within a millisecond, realization struck. Felix covered his penis with one hand (that's all he needed), his face collapsing in fear, embarrassment, and humiliation.

He hunched over, still covering himself, and shuffled back into the locker room. The kid in the hallway kept recording until Felix was out of view. One cheerleader begged her peer to send the video to her phone, and from there, she shared it with another student, and so on.

Soon, word traveled fast about Felix's little appendage, making him the laughingstock of West Made.

As said before, kids can be curious. Kids can also be cruel.

Chapter 20
THE TURN OF EVENTS

Later in the evening, Sam saw on the news that another workplace had been involved in a robbery. A few were injured and hospitalized, with plenty of money taken. Cathy hyperventilated when she saw the reports. It was crazy knowing that, about a week ago, her job had been attacked. Sam had to hold his mother close to calm her down.

"I'm just glad I got off— I mean— who the hell knows what would've happened if I had to continue to work?!" she cried.

Soon, relief settled over her as she realized she was going to be fine.

Sam brought up the time when the bank was robbed. "That woman. Did you know her? The teller that got shot?"

Cathy slowly pulled away from her son's embrace to answer his question. "I didn't... I never got to talk to her much. She mostly worked on my off days."

"Are you sure you're okay, Mom?"

"Yes. Just shocked. I'll be fine."

Sam hugged her. "I love you."

She smiled and got up from her soft couch. "Go take your medicine, okay?"

"On it."

Sam didn't take it. He enjoyed keeping his powers. He remembered to check the scuff marks on his jacket. The windbreaker material was strong compared to his cotton clothing, but it still wasn't good enough.

Tomorrow, I need to look at some fabric materials. I need to head to Beyrou's tailor shop first thing in the morning.

The store was making quite the buzz since it had just opened up. Tons of people were constantly shopping there, buying expensive suits and fabrics galore. Sam bit his lip, checking out the prices on the website's bold text.

"Pricey, but I believe I'll manage," he mumbled, looking down at his watch to read the time: 7:40.

Sam got undressed and hopped into bed.

Sleep is an important part of one's health. The body and mind rest, resetting for the next day.

That would usually be the plan on any other night, but not on this one.

It was one in the morning, and Sam fell under anxiety's grasp. *The walls feel like they're caving in on me. Nothing's going to get better,* he thought. *It's like the world is suffocating me.*

His body radiated heat as though a comforting hug would only make things worse, shrinking the world even further. He whimpered in bed as his breathing grew heavier with each inhale. There weren't any signs of this attack— no triggers, scares, or hype.

Through the thin walls, Cathy could hear the cries of her offspring. It was her motherly instinct to get out of bed to comfort her son, but unfortunately, this was something she couldn't help. It was a part of her child now.

*   *   *

Saturday, the 5th.

The sun had risen, painting the sky with vibrant pinks and blues, complemented by the high, cooling beams of the sun.

BEEP! BEEP! BEEP!

Sam's alarm clock rang, startling him awake as if he'd been shaken out of a nightmare. He slammed his fingers on the snooze button, silencing the annoyance. After quickly stretching his limbs, he got up and washed off the sleep to get ready for the day.

When he flipped the light switch on, there was no blooming light to illuminate the bathroom. He sighed in disappointment. *We need to catch up on our light bill.*

His mother greeted him, "Good morning, sweetie."

"Mornin', Mom. How'd you sleep?"

She took a short sip of her warm coffee, scanning recent emails from work. "I slept fine. Did you take your medicine last night?"

"Yeah," he lied, quickly changing the topic. "Also, what's with the lights?" He pointed upward.

"Well... we need to pay the light bill, obviously."

"What's gonna happen?"

Cathy yawned, exhaustion catching up with her after so many days without rest. "I'm not going in for the next couple of days. After what happened, the city closed some banks in the downtown area. Just until everything clears up."

"That's good. Right?"

Nodding profusely, Cathy took another sip of her coffee, her eyes scanning her son's attire. "Going out? This early?"

"Urm. Yeah."

"Are you off today?"

"Yeah, Mom. I'm just hanging out with Trevor and Garrett. Running errands."

Sam walked over to unhook his jacket from the coat rack, only to be stopped by his mother.

"A package came for you, by the way. It's on the nook. What'd you get?" She examined the box.

Sam bit his cheek, quickly thinking of a believable lie. "Just some... camera equipment. That's all."

She glared at his eyes briefly; her sharp gaze pierced right through him. She wasn't that naïve.

"Son, I don't know much about cameras, but I doubt it requires me to forge a couple of your signatures for the order."

"Well—these new lenses are kind of expensive. Uh... they're an international order. They don't sell them here, and they're rare," explained Sam.

"How many did you order?" she questioned, her eyes widening.

"About twenty?" he lied.

Once he reached the frame of his bedroom door, Sam slammed the door shut, ripping the cardboard box wide open.

"Wow," he whispered under his breath, amazed.

The metal shone off his eyes, casting a slight glare on his smooth face. Sam reached into the small, cornered area, grabbing a soft piece. They looked like magnets. Each rod he held between his fingers had a bit of weight for something so small.

"Welp. I can't return this now," he muttered to himself, tearing off the information sticker from the side of the box.

Officials are serious about stuff like this, I guess.

His mother had written three neat signatures on the forms and receipts. Sam grabbed the pieces, stuffing them inside his backpack and boots, and walked outside.

His mother caught him at the last second. "When will you be back?"

"Mom, I'm just going to Beyrou's with the guys, and I'll be back soon. It's barely ten o'clock; I'll be back by two. I promise. You don't have to worry about me."

She looked down at the tiled floor, exhaling slowly. "Just be safe. Those people that did the bank are still out there. Get home before sundown. Okay? Oh! Wait!"

Sam raised a brow. He guessed she might have had a surprise up her sleeve or maybe a snack. He hoped it was a Stripes gas station breakfast burrito.

Sadly, there was no burrito. Instead, Cathy returned with a treat. She held a gray mug filled with water in one hand, and two white pills rested in her other palm. Medicine.

"I don't want to ask about last night, but I assume it wasn't pretty," said Cathy.

"Oh..." Sam hesitated, reluctant to take it. He didn't exactly want to test out the medicine-killing-power theory today. Maybe tomorrow or another day.

At least she didn't ask why the pill bottle was practically full. Ever since Sam discovered his new abilities, medicine was the last thing on his mind—more so now, since he lost his powers the other day.

He reached out for the mug and pills, taking them both. It took a hot second for the boy to swallow his meds. He considered hiding them under his tongue or on the side of his teeth, but if Cathy asked him to open his mouth, it'd look worse for him. She'd figure out he wasn't taking them at all. Every parent wants to see their child get better.

Sam quickly kissed his mother on her thin, rosy cheeks and walked out of the unit.

Excited, he ran down the steps leading to the first floor, leaping over the last three steps and onto the concrete. He nearly tripped over his own foot.

Sam moved his head around the lot; nobody was in plain sight, and everything was clear. He pulled out his dog boots and replaced them with his comfortable every day sneakers.

He got into an adequate running position, focusing his eyes on a specific detail ahead. Soon, he felt his eyes spark, zooming in on the molecules in the road.

BOOM!

He took off. He ran so fast that he appeared as nothing but a blur, seizing the moment of the cold breeze flowing throughout his body. The sensation was almost *orgasmic*, like a cigarette buzz.

Sam noticed at the last minute that he'd miss the tailor shop by a few blocks. He shifted his body weight towards the next block, sharp-turning into Childress Street. That wasn't where he needed to go. He needed to get back on Elm Street.

Slowing down, Sam found himself propped in the back alley of Beyrou's, avoiding being seen. He hid behind a dumpster to change his shoes. The pungent smell made it difficult for him to tie his shoelaces.

Ahead of the alley, a van pulled up behind a clothes store beside Beyrou's. It was reversing and creeping up back and forth. Sam worried they might've spotted him, but there was no reaction.

"Hmm?" He squinted, trying to read the logo on the strange, dark van. *Summit—Peaks Industries.*

Sam didn't give the vehicle much thought, walking further down the messy alley and making his way around to the store's front entrance.

Inside Beyrou's, he studied everything around him. It was vivid.

The carpet was a pleasing black shade, with the walls covered in assorted fabrics and tall, jet-black mannequins wearing slim suits. It reminded him of a shoe store, only cleaner and more organized. The room had an expansive, calming feeling and smelled like a new car.

What made things uncomfortable was knowing the store's primary customers were high-class citizens from the city.

A clerk spotted the young man walking into the flamboyant store and greeted him.

"Hello! Are you new here, sir? Welcome to Beyrou's. Founded in 2005 by Dennis Beyrou. How may I help you on this fine afternoon?"

"Hello. Stop me if I'm wrong, but is it true y'all sell all sorts of fabrics here? At least that's what the word around town says... and the website."

"Yes, sir," she answered happily. "We sell many fabrics and materials for any occasion necessary."

Sam looked around as she explained what was on sale, still astonished by his surroundings. *Wow!*

"Were there any fabrics, in particular, you were looking for, sir?"

His head snapped back to attention, focusing on her. "Oh—uh, yes. I was wondering if you had any sturdy, abrasive, reliable materials?"

"Is there a specific name, sir?"

Sam paused, confused by her question. "What do you mean?"

The lady reached underneath the desk, pulling out a long, brown template with a list of fibers. "Well, we have similar items such as nylon, spandex, polyester—"

"Oh! Do you have something like Kevlar or nylon? A heat-resistant type of fabric. The thin kind specifically."

She licked the tip of her thumb, flipping through the white pages until her eyes landed on the title he desired.

"Ah, indeed we do! How many yards for your suit?"

His eyes squinted as he tried to calculate. "I believe I need four yards?"

She moved over to the register, tapping her pretty fingers onto the digital screen to add his order. Then she looked back up at the young man. "Would you like to be fitted? We have a tight schedule this afternoon, but we can squeeze you in this evening."

"Actually, I'd just like to have the fabric itself. If that's fine?"

She nodded in understanding, glancing back down at her screen to review the suggested color options.

His eyebrows raised in surprise. "There's a color choice?"

"Well, of course!" She giggled. "How did you think this worked?"

"Well, I—I thought I'd just order and go and all that stuff," he dragged out.

The friendly clerk walked toward the corner of the desk's interior, pulling out a glass palette with shaded color variations. From every single color of the rainbow, Sam could only pick one.

"I'm not sure what to pick," he gasped.

"Well, sir, customers here usually go with the usuals— black, blue, gray, white... something plain. Or they just go with their favorite color instead."

Biting his tongue, with his palms beginning to sweat a bit, he found the decision harder than picking donuts. Finally, he went with the former option.

"Are there any navy blue colors available?" he asked nervously.

Flipping through the screen pages, her eyes landed on a green checkmark, indicating that the specific color was in stock.

"Yes, sir. Would you like me to ring you up?"

"Yes, please."

Sam admired the store's architecture as the clerk walked toward the back room. A few people roamed around the store's racked aisles, searching for shoes or checking out the suits and fabrics. This place had an atmosphere that widened eyes.

"This is probably how rich people feel," he joked to himself.

The woman returned with the dark blue fabric, rolling it into a matte black gift bag and tying the handles together with a beautiful silver bow.

"Alright, sir! Your total is $750.00! But lucky for you, since you're a first-time shopper here, you get a glorious discount. Now totaling up to only $600.50."

"Wow." Sam was appalled by the price drop. He pulled out his leather wallet and handed her his debit card to pay.

Afterward, he shoved the black bag into his backpack, zipping it shut as it touched the bottom. Beyrou's had a table station for personal sewing. Sam brought the tungsten rods with him, hoping to attach them to the fabric before resorting to using super glue.

The table was on the left side of the room near the leather samples. Sam took off his bag and dumped the rods out, excited to work on the suit.

A sudden itch developed on the back of his head, one that ached as hard as the moment the accident in London happened.

A loud bang shattered the store's calm, the sound blasting through the front doors like a thunderclap. It sent everyone jumping many feet in the air, their eyes and ears snapping toward the entrance.

A loud male voice screamed, "EVERYONE ON THE GROUND! NOW!"

Heads ducked, and bodies hit the floor as people dropped to their knees. A few women in the back screamed bloody murder.

Sam's adrenaline spiked, activating his powers. Anxiety coursed through him as he watched the robbers slowly invade the tailor shop. To make matters worse, everything in his vision seemed to move as slowly as a sloth. His pupils fluttered like a broken light bulb, and his perception of time returned to normal as the anxiety medication kicked in.

"No. No. No. Not now," Sam said frantically.

One of the robbers, Johnny Plaza Jr., wore the same queer-looking mask he had during the bank and store robberies. Sam scooped up whatever he could into his bag, unknowingly dropping one of the tungsten rods on the floor.

The masked man pushed Sam toward the backroom, aiming his firearm at other innocent bystanders to herd them into the cramped space.

Another robber, Jo, violently screamed at the hostages. Her ferocious glare burned through her orange-tinted goggles. "MOVE IT! GET BACK!" she yelled.

The last robber, Fulton, guarded the front doors, gripping his Glock-19 in his gloved hands and serving as the lookout.

In the chaos, Sam caught a glimpse of the front desk clerk pressing a big gray button under the counter in his peripheral vision. It appeared to be an emergency contact button.

Johnny turned hostile, forcing Sam and several others into the storage room.

One by one, the hostages squeezed between racks, shoving one another to avoid the armed suspects. Johnny pushed everyone as far back as possible. Personal items scattered across the floor—wallets, watches, jewelry, phones, and even Sam's backpack.

Someone accidentally stepped on Sam's bag, causing the zipper to break and rip open.

While Johnny was in love with the valuable items on the floor, a man pushed the barrel of his gun away from the crowd and tackled Johnny into a wall. The heroic man slammed his head against the drywall, eventually taking him down into the metal racks, slapping the mask clean off Johnny's hairy face, and knocking him out cold.

Sam froze in deep fear, lying against the side of the wall as stiff as a nail. Everything was happening so quickly.

A small group of people found their way toward the back end of the room and into the emergency exit. A pregnant woman gasped as she pushed the handle, and everybody quickly evacuated. A loud alarm rang like a police siren.

"The police will be here soon!" said one stranger.

Sam was the last person to run out to the exit, but before he could leave, he wanted to check if the nice woman in the front was okay. The itch in his head seemed to pull him. His conscience told him to return, trying to let him know where the danger was coming from.

He crouched low on the sleek ground, trying his best not to make any noises that could cause suspicion in the room's direction. He peeked through the crack of the door, focusing his eyes to see what was happening from the other side.

"Please! Please don't hurt me! Don't hurt anyone!" the host begged as she tried to avoid looking at Jo.

Crazy Jo aimed the barrel directly at the woman's head, her finger steady on the trigger. She had a big urge to kill again.

Fulton was still at the front entrance, scoping out the rest of the store and avoiding looking at the cameras. He didn't know what Jo was doing; if he knew, he'd ensure she would not kill again.

Sam whined in fear, wanting to help the clerk, as she was nothing but hospitable and courteous toward him. Nobody deserves to go through this.

Quick! Think, Sam! Think! He thought aloud. His breathing pumped swiftly. Sam bit his tongue, nearly causing it to bleed. He picked his backpack up and quickly slipped on his modified running boots.

This is stupid! Crazy stupid! But kids were stupid that way.

There was a pause—a moment that seemed like forever. The boy stopped and thought about his idea, which led to overthinking. Thinking about the past, the fear, the power, and the emotions within seconds of whatever amount of speed he had to use his speed-thinking. Sam thought about Alexus and how he couldn't stop Felix from harassing her, or the Irish man who died transporting him to work. The burdens and support of his mother, and the broken arm that Felix gave Garrett.

That was all he thought about... *Doing nothing and feeling powerless.* Only this time, the boy wasn't impotent, and most teenagers do stupid things in the heat of the moment, despite all of Sam's thinking. He was almost hopeless.

This time, he knew he could do something different. Was it a crazy idea? Definitely, but it was a risk that was exactly like the type he took to protect his friend. Sam shook with fear and acted on it by taking out his boots and putting them on.

The only wise choice in this decision was that he didn't want to be seen and wanted to avoid all the eyes being set on him. He decided he needed to cover his face, and fast. His eyes shifted around the racks, finding anything he could slip on his face. A facemask, sunglasses, anything.

His eyes turned to a red wool beanie that was for sale. It was long enough to stretch onto his face. He draped it over his head, but there was no point. He couldn't see, and there wasn't any time to cut eyeholes in it.

Sam dropped his bag, and a few tungsten rods rolled onto the floor.

"Shit!" he exclaimed, quickly kneeling and scooping them up. After grabbing the last one, Johnny's mask lay before him. It was odd. It was half-folded (inside out) and looked different. Sam carefully grabbed it and pulled the rest of the mask out. Another idea popped into his head.

This is really stupid. What is it possible that this was an act of cacoëthes? Sam would disagree. *Was it a hero complex? No.* Sam just knew it was the right thing.

In comic books, the hero usually has to suffer or have a loved one die under their name. But this wasn't a comic book. Sam grew up with hardship, while most kids around him grew up with the simple life. Two parents and siblings, some fed on a silver spoon, some taking things for granted. Not Sam.

The last thing he'd want was for someone to end up like him. Everyone deserved better. And these were the cards he was dealt with—including the powers.

Sam put on the queer-looking mask, popping vibrant colors of the dark shades of navy blue. The lenses were attached but were nearly hanging by a few threads.

"This smells weird," Sam whispered as he remained crouching low. He huddled into the main area, carefully moving closer to the shoe racks.

"SHUT YOUR GODDAMN MOUTH! MONEY! REGISTER! NOW!" Jo yelled violently.

The clerk shook anxiously as she opened the register. The container was filled with hundreds, fifty, and tens of dollars. Jo's eyes sparkled green, greener than her usual color, as she looked over at Fulton.

"We got it, boss!"

Fulton nodded. "Hey, where's Johnny?"

Jo looked back up at him, shrugging as she lowered her gun to her hip. She grabbed chunks of the money and stuffed them into a black gym bag.

Quietly, Sam leaped across the other side of the shoe racks and into the opposite aisle, still feeling hot and sweating through his white t-shirt. Sam fanned himself before things could escalate. He felt now wasn't the time to panic.

What good is the medicine if he was still panicky? Shock. Nobody witnesses this on a daily basis.

As Jo was about to snug the last bit of cash left, her hand shook compulsively, and she dropped the bag on the floor. Her urge felt like an itch, a craving, if you'd call it. She wanted blood. She needed to see the blood splatter from someone's body.

Fulton noticed her stiff body and called out to her, "Jo! NO! Don't! Just finish the job!"

Her head shifted to his line of view as she glared at his face, still stiff. She immediately pulled her gun up, aiming it closely at the hostage.

"Come on," Sam begged, forcing his speed to come out. The color in his eyes flicked but couldn't remain. The scared kid clenched both his fists (any tighter, and they'd break the skin), not caring if he gave himself crescent moons. "COME ON!"

Jo cocked the hammer back as the woman looked up into the barrel with horror.

The next second, a voice called out from behind the racks, "NO!" the young tone yelled, but it was too late. The gun fired two rounds, and everything slowed down.

The voice that screamed was Sam, jumping out to help the poor woman. Everything slowed. Sam had the time. He didn't notice that his powers had started up and had dialed everything down. Sam saw the bullet move slowly, slower than anybody had ever seen. He shoved through the wooden aisles, running toward her as he gently grabbed the bullet with his fingertips.

"OW!" Sam cried. The bullet was hot. His perception was fading in and out. Things sped, then slowed.

It's the pills, Sam thought. *They're dulling my abilities. I need to hurry before things become normal.*

Instead of grabbing the tiny, hot gun blow, Sam pushed the bullet with the tip of his index finger. It was still hot, but it was better than grabbing it.

Still moving, he found a stopping point a few feet away from the two. Immediately, once Sam stopped moving, his perception returned to its everyday reality, and all eyes were on him. Deep down, Sam felt much calmer knowing he wore a mask to hide his face. The bullet burned his fingertips, but that didn't matter to him. He was pumped full of adrenaline and nerves. He felt nothing.

"Put the gun down, please!" he pleaded.

Jo froze for a second, riddled with confusion, as was Fulton.

"Wait—what the hell?!" Fulton exclaimed.

Unexpectedly, Sam used a small burst of his speed to dash forward and push Jo away from nearby hostages, sending her flying a couple of feet in the air as her body impacted a tall mannequin.

Fulton backed out of the room and exited through the front door. He had a feeling that they might fail at this job.

Sam was still anxious and continued to hide his face. He turned to the group of innocents behind him. "Are you all okay?" he asked gently.

There was no response. Everyone continued to stay low as the crowd was in shock or discombobulation.

Outside, Fulton ripped the balaclava off his dark face and slipped his jacket off as he heard the sirens closing in by the second. He found the van, jumped into the front seat, threw his items in the back, and hoped he didn't look suspicious. His breathing spiraled, and his heart pumped through his broad chest plate. Fulton was frantically scoping his surroundings, wiping the nervous sweat off his forehead.

"What the hell happened in there?" Fulton then slammed his fist on the dash, annoyed by the failed attempt. "Hold up. Where are the keys?"

Back at Beyrou's, Johnny dragged himself outside the backroom and into the lobby. His head felt woozy, and his words slurred. "Hey, guys... W-what happened? Did you—y'all—you get the cash?"

His vision was doubled, noticing Sam's figure standing a few feet away. Soon, the cops rolled in from the front of the store, cautiously waiting to see something from the inside. When Johnny's vision cleared, his sights locked on the boy.

"Hey?! That's my mask!" he yelled, pulling out his gun.

Sam ducked down behind the front desk, spotting the cops from outside. He tried his best to focus on starting his powers up again, but he couldn't concentrate. His primary focus was trying not to die, not to mention his inner battle with the medicine. *It's like trying to run underwater. Nothing's functioning properly.*

The police hid behind their vehicles, firing at the store's windows, hoping to hit the one responsible for opening fire toward the civilians. One bullet grazed Johnny's shoulder. The agonizing pain caused him to drop to the floor and cry, wincing like a frantic child.

As Sam cautiously rose behind the desk, an officer noticed the boy, but his first thought was to fire, not question the stranger with a mask.

He aimed his pistol toward him. "YOU! GET DOWN ON YOUR KNEES AND PUT YOUR HANDS OVER YOUR HEAD!"

Sam stormed out of the main hall, grabbed his backpack and jacket, and hurried out the backdoor before anyone could see him.

Outside in the back alley, Sam noticed the van still parked in the back. The boy kept the mask on, not showing a single piece of skin. He looked closely at the van again, suspicious.

Fulton and masked Sam locked eyes, and the moment felt awkward. Fulton's energy became hyper as he finally found the keys in his jacket. He started up the van, immediately backing out of the alleyway and into the city's streets.

Sam threw his belongings behind the dumpster, shocked at who was a part of the violent acts throughout the week—all the robberies and all the fear that had been put upon the people of Dallas.

"Wait? You?!" Sam said in disbelief.

He followed the van. His eyes locked onto the back of the vehicle, focusing on every detail before taking off, triggering that blue, zoomed feeling and speeding into the streets. Sam ran faster than earlier; the van had no chance of outrunning him. It only took about four seconds before Sam's shoulder rammed into the side of the dark vehicle.

Upon impact, the van tilted, leaning toward its right-side wheels, losing the passenger door, and eventually tipping over. Sam fell to the ground, a chunk of his sleeve ripping off and a mild bruise forming on his shoulder. Bystanders could only see a messed-up boy with a strange mask and a damaged vehicle.

His legs gave in as he tried to stand up. He looked at the van, and his eyes widened through the mask.

"Oh, my God!" Sam limped over to the damage, and people recorded and took pictures of the accident. No one dared to call the paramedics; they only watched.

Sam limped on his left leg, building the strength to budge the van's back doors open, revealing a bloody man hanging sideways from his seatbelt.

He whispered to Fulton, "Sir, are you okay?"

"My... my... m—" Fulton mumbled, his mouth filled with thick blood.

"I can't understand you. I'll go get help."

Fulton continued to make out his words, spitting out the excess, "My—my... ma... mom."

Sam took off the mask as the crowds slowly dispersed, trying to drag Fulton out. The man could only see half of the young boy's face, trying to focus on remembering him.

Sam pulled out his phone to dial for help. "Hello, 9-1-1? I need paramedics here at, uh—"

While Sam talked to the authorities, Fulton stared him down, hoping he would turn his face fully to see every expression. His eyes trailed down to study his figure, ending on the cast on the boy's arm. Fulton could've sworn he'd seen a cast like that before.

Was it on that one kid? I don't remember. Should I remember him? What's his name again?

"All right, Fult—I mean—sir," Sam slipped the flamboyant mask back onto his pubescent face. "Help will be here soon. They'll be here at any moment. Just—just hold on, okay?"

Sam couldn't believe it. Part of him didn't want to think that the sad man he met a few days ago was a deceiver. *Was this his idea of hard work? Was it?* Total disbelief. The young man felt ashamed and worried about the damage he had done to poor Fulton.

Still on the floor, Fulton continued to say nothing. He only stared at the mask's lenses, watching him dash away.

Soon, the paramedics and Dallas police caught up with him. They circled around Fulton, closing in on him and taking certain precautions. The emergency team followed behind to tend to their suspect.

Chapter 21
GOT NO ALIBI

Back in the alley, Sam tugged the mask off and gathered up his items. A grumble in his stomach roared, and he needed to get some calories into his system. About a block away was a McDonald's. There's nothing wrong with downing a couple of burgers and some nuggets. It was a perfect meal for the time being. The more Sam used his speed, the more his metabolism boosted. Sam scarfed everything down within minutes, charging up like a battery. He'd almost forgotten about Fulton and the crazy event today. From there, his mood went from delighted to sour. It was still unbelievable. He wondered why Fulton would do something like that. Granted, he didn't know the guy enough to call him a friend, but at least he said the man had a good alignment. At least, that was until a few minutes ago.

Sam didn't have it in him to run again. If he did, where would he go? Would he run to the twins? Run out of town and leave everything behind? Go to more therapy? Then, he took notice of the positives. He figured if he didn't have these gifts, then Fulton and his gang would continue to rob stores and possibly hurt more people. If he didn't stand up for himself and the victims at Beyrou's, then they all might've died. It was highly likely because of Jo pulling the trigger. Alexus was wrong. At that moment, he needed to be a hero (of some type) and maybe not the whole savior of the world type of act, but at least looking out for the people nearby who needed help. Who's to say?

Adrenaline was still flowing through Sam's system, and he didn't know how to wash it out. His hands shook, and the cold weather didn't help cool him down. The boy paced back and forth outside the McDonald's, hoping the nerves would wear off quickly.

Luckily, the twins wanted to meet Sam for another late breakfast. Something that Sam couldn't resist. All the food in the world couldn't satisfy the boy's appetite.

It was another usual at Doe's. The three ordered the same thing, but Sam gave Mrs. Buffers a curve ball this time and added a second plate. It was a shocker to see a boy so young and not so frail eat so much. Trevor made a concerned expression as he watched Sam down everything within minutes. It was like giving a poor child a whole entrée.

"Starving, Sam?" Garrett asked, staring.

"Oh, yeah!" He exclaimed with a stuffed mouth. "I've been doing a lot of cardio."

"Cardio?" Trevor questioned. "What else have you been up to?"

When it was time for the bill, Sam got up from the booth, ready to bail and get started on the items in his bag.

"Do you guys got this? I'm kinda low on money at the moment."

"Yeah, it's all good," Replied Garrett. Trevor had some hesitance. How rude for a friend they hardly see just stop by for a free meal without a proper hangout. "I guess- it's fine?"

"I hate to ask, but-" Sam hesitated, "But can y'all spare me a few bucks? I need to help pay for one of the apartment bills."

"How much?" Garrett asked.

"Just ten. Maybe?"

"Sure." Garrett was about to pull out his wallet when Trevor stopped him before he could pull it out of his pocket. "Hold on. What's the money for?"

Garrett reminded his brother. "He just said it was for one of his apartment bills."

"Which one?" Trevor questioned, almost not believing his friend.

"Water bill."

This wasn't a shocker to Garrett. He remembered Sam explaining why he couldn't throw his birthday party the other week because of the lack of payments, and it wouldn't help to add on by using more electricity, water, etc.

"It's fine, Trev," said Garrett, handing Sam 30 dollars instead of 10. "It's the least we could do. You've already paid for multiple dinners and given us plenty of gas money."

At five o'clock in the evening, the pills fully wore off. Sam was unaware of the time, remembering that he promised his mother he'd be home by two. As he walked through downtown, cop cars passed by with their sirens wailing. Probably to further investigate the crime scene at Beyrou's or something.

Sam ran back home. When he arrived, he tripped over a concrete slab in front of the apartment, scraping his elbow and palms. "Ahhh! Ow..." he cried from the pain and the sprain in his shoulder. He wiped the bits of blood and skin on his pants and dusted himself off before going in.

Cathy wasn't home. Where was she? He didn't know. This gave Sam time to look into his shopping products. He raced to his room, throwing everything in his bag onto his small bed. The tungsten rods, rolls of cloth, and Johnny's queer-looking mask sprayed along the soft blue blanket. His Mom taught him how to sew. She didn't teach him how to do a full suit, so Sam had to improvise on this. He tried to take his mind off Fulton and what had happened earlier. The boy flipped his laptop open and played some Ella Fitzgerald jazz to clear his mind.

It didn't take long before Sam would poke his fingers multiple times with the needle. "Ouch! Okay. Got it- Ouch!" he poked multiple times, focusing hard on lining up the edges of what seemed to be a sleeve for one of his arms. All improvise. All sewing and poking.

"This better work." It was too late to take it back, even with the receipt crumpled on his bed. Beyrou's would likely be closed and under investigation and construction until everything goes back to normal.

Since Sam had no direction, he did not know whether to make the suit into one or separate pieces. The original idea was to sew the abrasive fabric into his everyday clothes. Still, it needed to make sense to him to wear a bulky t-shirt or thick pants. The shirts would still have some wear and tear effect until he'd understand or control whatever his unique gifts were. In the meantime, a complete, covered, gimpy-looking suit would suffice.

The torso section was now finished. Sam slipped it on and stared at himself in the bathroom mirror. It looked similar to an ugly Christmas sweater, just without the pictures, glitter, or weird ornaments all over it. It was a perfect length. He could stretch his arms up, and the fabric wouldn't ride up or look shrunken from the washer and dryer. The sewing practice sped up because of Sam's patience being tested. It was strange. He was usually the most patient person in the world. Still, after finishing up one sleeve, he grew irritated at how much time had passed.

The sound of keys rattled outside, and the front door swung open. Cathy was finally home. Sam used what seemed a fraction of his speed to bolt out of the bathroom and into his bedroom. Quickly, Sam shut his bedroom door and locked it. He hid the stuff he bought, the mask, and the sewing tools in the corner of his closet. He hoped she didn't check the closet or ask Sam why he acted suspiciously weird. A mother always knows.

When Cathy heard the door slam, she ran and knocked to check on her son.

"Sam? Is that you?" she called out behind the door.

She couldn't see it, but Sam struggled to take the top half off. "Yeah! It's me," he grunted.

"Are you okay?"

"Yeah!" Sam exclaimed, finally tugging the rest off of his body and tossing it into the closet. He debated on installing a zipper on it for easy access.

"Can you let me in? I haven't seen you all day. I've been worried sick."

"Yeah, just one sec!" Sam put on a black T-shirt he found on his floor (he didn't care if it was dirty) and unlocked and opened the door. His shoulders shrugged in confusion. "What are you worried about?"

From the shrug, Cathy looked at his palms and noticed the scrapes and little blood drops on his fingers.

"What happened? Where have you been?" she continued, "There was an attempted robbery at Beyrou's! Are you okay?!"

"Mom!" Sam yelled, getting her to be quiet momentarily to answer her questions. "I'm okay. And-" Sam desperately searched for a believable lie in his head before something could slip up, "No. No, I didn't go to the shop after all. The guys picked me up, and we just ate something and hung out for a bit. I was going out for a jog, and I slipped and scraped my palms."

Cathy took half a step back as she gently grabbed her son's arm to further examine, "Well-" she hesitated, "Let's get you fixed up, okay?"

"No, Mom. It's okay."

"Did you take your medicine, at least?"

"Uh. Yeah."

Cathy heard her son's answer, giving him a couple of bandages and wrappings. "Hey. You know you can tell me anything, right?"

"Yes?" Sam sounded confused, slightly annoyed by where his mother was going with their conversation. He continued to make his way toward his bedroom.

As she stared at her son walking away, she followed, folding her arms. "Look, I can't help but notice that you're lying to me."

Sam froze, not taking another step. He turned his torso around, looking back at his mother, and continued to lie, "I'm not, Mom. And even if I was, you've been lying too."

"What does that mean?" Cathy felt offended by the accusation from her son. She had no clue as to what he was talking about.

"Nothing... Never mind."

"I called the Sings. I called their mom. They didn't get into town until you left."

Sam rolled his eyes, trying to avoid serious eye contact as he returned to his room.

Cathy continued, slowly following her son, "You left way earlier than them... So what were you doing for the last six or seven hours since you claim you didn't go to Beyrou's?"

"Mom, I hung out with the guys. That's all! Just leave me alone."

"And I know!" Cathy emphasized. Sam paused for a while. That could mean anything. Does she know about the powers? Boots? Robbery?

"Know– What?" Sam hesitated, asking.

"I know you're not taking your damn meds! It's been almost 2 weeks, and the capsule should be empty now! I bet you even tried to throw them away!" Cathy grew louder, and Sam covered his ears. He felt that familiar, high-tensioned wave splash over his body, and his palms sweat more and more as his lies were now being uncovered. He only hoped that his biggest secret hadn't been exploited yet.

"MOM! STOP!" He screamed, slamming and locking the door in front of his mother's face.

Cathy started banging on the door, twisting the knob profusely, thinking she could open it. "Sam..." She sighed, leaning against the thin door, "Just talk to me. You can tell me anything! I'm your mother! Please!"

"Go away!" Sam yelled, breathing heavily and covering his tiny ears. He tried to stay focused and calm.

"I'm not upset with you! I'm worried! You're better than this- You're better than everything and everyone I've known! That also includes your father!" Cathy placed her palms on the base of the bedroom door. Cathy turned to emotion, saying things she didn't mean to and now ranting, "Don't be like him. Another thing I know is that you don't like whenever I bring him up. He's in your blood whether you like it or not! He existed in our lives, and now he's gone! He was always secluded and quiet. Please, Sam!" She begged.

Not being able to see her son's reaction to that comment, Sam lashed his voice like a whip through the door. "Don't! I don't want to hear that! Stop talking to me about that! This is why you're a liar!"

"What are you talking about, Sam?!"

The angry teenager opened the door. "We're doing this. Now."

"Doing what?" Cathy's eyes were filled with tears, and her throat was croaking from the realization that Sam knew the real truth about his mother and father.

"Why don't you just tell me the truth, huh?! Did you actually leave, Dad? Or did you cheat?"

"What?!" Sam's words made no sense to Cathy. Deep down, she knew that this conversation was going to take place, eventually. How later did she even want this to come out, anyway? It's been 18 years.

"Why don't you let me see him? Or talk about him? My grandparents, too!"

"Sam-"

"WHY?!" He bellowed.

"SAM! YOU DON'T-"

"WHHYYY?!"

"BECAUSE HE LEFT US! IS THAT WHAT YOU WANT TO HEAR?!" Cathy finally revealed the truth. It was about time.

Sam's screaming ceased. His eyes were puddling up. "What..."

"Fine! I'll tell you the truth! Your father, Tate- I didn't leave him when you were three because of some differences. No- He left me- us- right before you were born!... And I don't know where he is. I don't know if he's dead, missing, or moved halfway across the world. I don't know! He never wanted us in his life, and since then, it had been me and your grandparents raising you the best we could!"

The 18-year-old sobbed like a child throughout the entire explanation.

"Sam... I'm sorry you don't get the two-parent life. I'm sorry you have to live in this stupid apartment and that we had to live off of snacks and stale sandwiches for the first quarter of your life. I'M SORRY! But this is it. I wish I could've done better, but I'm doing the best I can..."

Sam trailed off to his bedroom. Cathy followed but got greeted with a slammed door to the face, calling it a rough night. Rough was an understatement. The boy witnessed a robbery, an acquaintance gone rogue, bad tension with the twins, and now being a bastard child. How much rougher could it get? Sam couldn't see his mother's face or hear her voice, but she was tearing up, too. She feared nearly losing her son from the accident, her and her son almost being a victim of a robbery, and now this devastating truth. Cathy slowly backed away from the bedroom door. Her mind raced with the repeated words: I'm so sorry. She wanted nothing more than to take away all of her son's pain and horrific fears, hoping to throw them all away someday.

Chapter 22
THE TRIAL

Everything looked atrocious at the Courthouse. A maple wood gavel echoed across the ears, tensing up the Jury of Dallas.

"ORDER!" Judge James' raspy voice had screamed. Each syllable spoken through his white, clicky teeth raised the tension across the courtroom. The trial was just beginning, and things weren't good for the defendants who remained behind the broad table. Even the comfort of the tall chairs didn't suffice for the tension that was brought upon them. Not to mention the money they had to provide for a fair lawyer. Scott Baron.

Fulton and the rest didn't believe in this guy. Not only because he was younger than most but because he seemed arrogant and misleading. His long, luscious hair was tied up in a bun, and he wore a neat, blue suit that wouldn't seem appropriate for this occasion. They also didn't understand why an excellent young man would vouch for an unusual bunch like them.

Eventually, Judge James read off the Arraignment. "Four counts of robbery, four counts of murder, two counts of attempted murder, aggravated assault of a deadly weapon. Each defendant was in possession of a deadly weapon..." the list kept going on.

Fulton pondered. Thinking of nothing but the money to save his mother. *This is it. It's all over. I failed you, mom...* He didn't know what scared him the most. The thought of losing his only family left, or the look on her face when she hears her son, is a deviant.

"These are grand charges for your clients, Mr. Baron. How does the defendant plead?"

For a moment, Baron was lost for words until he turned his head towards Fulton's depressed expression, explaining, "Your honor, my client took a vow of silence, but I assure you he would plead innocent as he has a reason for the commitment for the crime. Although it harms the people, the city's bank, the stores, and Mr. Beyrou's company. His intentions are not only misleading, but he admits his actions were undoubtedly wrong compared to his counterparts."

Judge James batted an eye at Mr. Baron before his eyes went toward the list of violence that followed. He turned his vision toward the couple behind Fulton, both Jo and Johnny. Nothing seemed to cross their minds but utter annoyance. Their faces would either tell you or the arbiter that this wasn't their first time being held up in court, or they could be simply put into a trance of boredom. The only thing they could do was just sit there and wait until this was all over.

"I'm sorry, ma," Fulton mumbled.

Baron turned his head again, staring at Fulton, confused at what he heard. He then focused his attention back on the front.

"Your Honor, I would like to call witness, clerk for Beyrou's, Sarah Lotwitz, to the stand."

"I'll allow it."

Quitely, Sarah walked to the witness stand, placed herself in the low chair, and cleared her throat into the microphone. The girl was practically shaking, riddled with fear, as her eyes pressed forward at Jo. Luckily, Jo didn't care enough to look her victim in the face. Too busy thinking she could be better off elsewhere.

Mr. Baron stood close, and Sarah could vividly smell the excess amounts of cologne on him. Too much for this man, she gathered as she waited for the statements that were provided directly to her. "Ms. Lotwitz. We, the court, and the jurors know you were held as a vital hostage in the assault at your work residence at uh- Beyrou's. Is that correct?"

She leaned in, speaking as clearly as crystals into the microphone, "Yes."

"Could you please explain the event on December 5th?"

Sarah was hesitant. Like someone was breathing down her neck or tickling her spine. That is the one day she would live to never forget. It's hard not to when one gets a barrel pointed in between their eyes. Her exhales were soothing as she sank into the rigid frame of her seat.

"I was assigned to work the day shift. Bright and early. Eight AM to five PM."

"What time did the robbery take action, Ms. Lotwitz?"

Biting her lip and reminiscing on that fateful day, she tried to pinpoint the estimated time of forsakenness. "Around ten to eleven o'clock, I believe."

For the brief seconds of silence between her statements, Baron looked at Judge James for reassurance of her continuance. "Your Honor?"

"You may continue, Ms. Lotwitz."

"Thank you, Your Honor." She said, "Before that hour had arrived, I was finishing up a few orders, getting off the phone with recurring clients, and such. Before the outbreak happened, I was assisting a customer—a young man who probably looked like a high school student. I was taking up his order, and when he finally had paid for his intended order, the three of them stormed in and took over the store!"

Turning his head at a slight angle, Baron used his peripheral vision to scan the Jury through the edge of his right eye. Not noticing a single adolescent face in the hall, "Uh, I'm sorry, your honor." he intruded, "Is this young man now present?"

Judge James noted this intriguing question, taking a quick moment to look through the Jury, "Will the young man present during the incident at Beyrou's please stand?"

There was no action considered, just the sound of flies buzzing across the ceiling's lights.

Baron questioned Ms. Lotwitz. May you provide the name of the young individual?"

"I don't recall his name."

Judge James noted the statement about the store's customer. Reminding himself to get that name soon. "Proceed, Ms. Lotwitz."

She cleared her throat, reaching forward to place her hands flat on the stand, attempting to stay restrained. "Half the store was forced to retreat to the storage room in the back of the store. No thanks to this man." She pointed out her thin index finger towards Johnny. "He was wearing this strange-looking mask and held a gun. The entrance to the store was being blocked off by his friend. And the woman, Georgia. She was keeping us quiet and on the ground. And-"

Suddenly, Sarah stopped speaking. Her anxiousness closed in as she remembered every detail, from the diameter of the barrel between her eyes.

Baron called out to her, "Ms. Lotwitz?"

Her mind flashed like a grenade, paralyzed by the memories that had taken her mindset. "She shoved her goddamn gun in my face!" she cried out, salty tears and snot running down her face. The justice community fell silent with no reaction, only internal sorrow and a slight twitch in the Judge's lip.

"Someone or something saved me!" she cried out.

"Ms. Lo–"

"And this crazy bitch tried to kill me!"

Judge James slammed his gambol on the dark platter, trying to alter the tension in the House of Justice. Sarah continued to burst out; she then aimed her attention with her fingers at Johnny. "I don't know who it was! But this person was wearing your mask!" Johnny grew confused at what she was going off about. He hardly remembered seeing someone with his mask. Slowly but surely, it was all coming back to him.

BANG! "Order! Ms. Lotwitz!" Judge James grunted, slamming the gambol down once again.

Baron declared in pure respect and concern for the witness, "Your Honor, I'll ask your permission from the court to take a recess."

Johnny and Jo just smirked, rolling their eyes, and were waiting for this session to be over. All the while, Fulton just stared into the solid marbled ground, tears rolling down his cheek.

"The defense rests; the court will take a ten-minute recess." BANG! The gambol screamed across the Jury. It is time to relieve and ascend into comfort for the time being. Jo started to sink into her seat, her head resting in her palms, combing her fingers into her golden hair. Jo slowly lifted her head up as the Jury scattered, eyeing Johnny's hairy face. "What?" He asked her. "Honestly, I'm just as confused as her. Who was she talking about? And why did this thing have my mask on?"

Jo threw him a slight answer. "Dunno. What do you remember, idiot?"

Johnny's eyes squinted, digging deep into his mind to remember what happened during their failed attempt to take over Beyrou's. "I remember taking a group of people to the back, trying to keep them down and quiet. I was about to take their shit before some dude knocked me out. When I woke up, my mask was gone, and I was all woozy. I remember seeing some figure standing before me, wearing something on their face. Unless the cops just confiscated it or something."

Jo rolled her eyes, straying away from her co-worker's face. "Then why would this girl claim to see someone else wearing it, huh?"

Ending the topic, Jo checked up on how Fulton was doing. He was still digging his head into his palms, dreading his mother's feelings. *Is she okay? Is she mad at me? Am I a disappointment?* All for his mother.

The ten-minute recess felt like four. (Ten minutes would've felt like twenty outside the lawful house.) The case continued. Soon, their judgment would be labeled over them, and justice would be served.

The authorities brought up a vast, black, 24-inch screen television. They slid in a videotape; it was the events of the robbery.

Fulton's jaw clenched, grinding his teeth and the tension in his forehead. He hoped that a good outcome would approach, and they'd let all of their incidents be put aside.

As the footage played on the jet-black screen, all eyes were glued in its direction, noting every detail down to the frame rate. The tape replayed that moment when Jo dragged the receptionist down to the ground, noting that Fulton could be seen guarding the front doors in his childish ski mask.

Now came the part where Jo was aiming her weapon at Sarah.

This part of the movie was a letdown. Jo thought to herself, wishing she had pulled the trigger immediately.

The Judge kept a stern, firm look on his face; he, too, was capturing every specific moment with his amber eyes. Even Johnny studied the recording, wanting to reminisce about what had happened at that moment. The room grew worried. Some were mentally preparing to see gore pop up so the queasy people could try to hold down their vomit. Thankfully, no life was taken on-screen. Instead, it looked like the footage had been tampered with. One moment, Jo stood up straight, firing a few shots to see the footage flash for a second. They noticed the hostage had not been harmed in any sort of way but also picked up on the position of Jo now being laid flat on the ground, with her gun missing from her grasp.

"Rewind that last bit, please?" Judge James requested help from the broad officer standing in the corner of the stand.

The officer rewinded the tape and then replayed that moment. There was no glitch, and nothing was tampered with. Everything was running smoothly.

James told the officer to slow the tape down, playing it only frame by frame. They then broke down the video display, figuring out what was happening with the blur between Jo and Sarah.

The last frame shown was the controversial blur. The tape provided a silhouette of a human figure. Unfortunately, the camera could not capture the remaining mysterious shape, only an arm and a side of the shape's head.

Johnny whispered, "What the..."

The Judge squinted his eyes, now putting on his thin glasses, hoping to spot more of what was now seen.

"I think that's my mask!" Johnny said aloud.

James shifted his head towards that comment at the last minute, noticing a matte black envelope resting on the edge of his desk. He reached for it, letting the recording continue frame by frame. The Jury watched, paying little attention to what Judge James focused on. His lips clicked as his eyes left the ominous note.

Judge James then announced, "I call this case... Dismissed!" Everyone's head turned forward. Reassuring themselves from what they had actually heard. James slammed the gavel on the wooden carved plate. There, he answered again, "Dismissed!"

Upon that word, Fulton fell to his knees, relieved. His heart still continued to pound profusely. Dismissed. The three got escorted out of the hall. Reporters and journalists from around the city huddled around them, wanting a spare comment from their peaky questions. Fulton kept thinking about his mama, wondering if she was okay.

Jo didn't mind flashing a finger or 2 to the press as she soaked up all the glory beneath her. Johnny walked with his hands in his jacket, still curious about the footage.

As odd as today was, things got more conventional. They were guided to a long, jet-black limousine. The kind that only wealthy or famous people would ride in. The inside of the limo looked like a narrow hallway. They could crouch and walk a few feet down to the other end. Jo fooled around like a toddler on a playground set. She ran back and forth until she got tuckered out, instantly grabbing some leftover champagne from the ice bucket on the floor. She chugged down whatever was left in it. Fulton and Johnny stayed seated, waiting for the chaperone to enter the fancy car. They did not know who this man was, but they could recognize from the file in his hand that he worked on the top floor of Summit Peaks. This didn't look good at all.

The man in the black suit pulled out a folded piece of paper, adjusted his metal-framed glasses, and read the note:

To the Employees of Summit-Peaks at the Texas Branch,

I have received news about the following disturbance down there. I am not pleased and distraught by your actions, disrespecting my company's name, and the use of company property. I have left 3 separate letters for each of you. Leaving me no choice but to pick the consequences ahead of you. But, given some of the reputation that has been built for some of you. Some will be terminated, suspended, or otherwise...

Flint Sichto. C.E.O. of Summit-Peaks Industries

The sharp man reached into his suit's jacket, handing out the 3 letters as stated. Each had their name printed beautifully onto the center in gold ink. As it said, their punishments were held in the palm of their hands. All of their outcomes were already written, and it was heavy to bear, like a teenager receiving his weekly grades from a school that had to be signed directly by the parents.

Johnny didn't give a rat's ass, ripping his seal open; reading aloud, "Mr. Plaza, your employment with Summit-Peaks is terminated and will cause your... detainment to the Dallas... Police... Department." his voice reduced, becoming more of a sad, gentle whisper. He crumpled the note, throwing it on the ground and spitting on it. "What is this bullshit?!" he exclaimed, tears filling his eyes.

"Mr. Plaza, we have records showing you have stolen property and money from our systems. Records have shown you have taken over three hundred thousand dollars. Not just directly from our branch but also from some safety deposit boxes. How you figured out they were Summits' is entirely unknown, but Mr. Sichto was not pleased."

Johnny was at a loss for words. He couldn't lie; the truth was already out. There was no backing down from this.

The man explained, "Mr. Sichto was unhappy when the files appeared on his desk yesterday morning. Coincidentally, given your current situation, termination for you was inevitable."

"My turn! My turn!" Jo squealed. "This is like opening an acceptance letter." She ripped the seal open, pulling the once clean sheet of paper out from its containment, covering the edges in spilled champagne. "Ms. Fezz. Blah, blah, blah. Inform you that your employment with Summit-Peaks is suspended.

Oh! It just says I'm suspended for a few months. Weird." It seems that killing civilians could go off with a slap on the wrist, but not when it came down to stealing from the company. Weird indeed.

It was Fulton's turn. All eyes fell on him; it was time to read. "Okay. Mr. Bruning, your employment with Summit-Peaks is now... terminated." Those last words were everything. Fulton had gone from being the newest manager to an unemployed nobody. There goes the Condo, the car, the money, the luxuries, treatments, everything.

"What else does it say?" asked Jo. Fulton couldn't read anymore. Passing it over to Jo's drenched fingers, she read:

We were informed that the heist plans were executed beneath Summit's warehouse department and used company property. Thank you for your service to our branch.

Best regards, Flint Sichto.

"He seems nice," she said sarcastically.

One by one, the limo driver dropped them off at their desired location. It didn't matter where or when they'd get there, as long as each had a place to go. Johnny was the first to get dropped off. He chose a bar, probably wanting to get drunk from some strong whiskey before being sent away.

Fulton was the next. He got dropped off at the Condo.

Meanwhile, Jo wanted to screw around, knowing this might be her only time in a limo. To her, there was no time like the present; make the most of it.

Fulton went to the elevators, thinking of what to say. *Did she see the news? Did she read the papers? Has someone already told her?!* Questions filled his stressed brain. An explanation was going to be provided. Donna might even disown her own child. After everything he'd done, there was no doubt about it.

DING! The elevator chimed, sliding its doors open for his desired floor. Fulton could see Gloria standing outside her door. As always, she could hear those things coming up or down, no matter the time of day.

This time, it wasn't one of those old friendly greetings but a sad one.

"Hey, Fulton."

"Hey."

She folded her soft arms, her bracelets clinging together in some type of synth. "I heard about what happened."

"Ya'. You an' everyone else, huh?" Fulton leaned towards the side of his door.

"No. Donna has heard nothing about that."

"How she holdin' up, Gloria?"

"I don't know. Donna was coughing really badly a couple of nights ago, and then she stopped for a while. Haven't heard much since yesterday morning."

"Alright. That's good, I guess."

Gloria shoved her hands to her side, addressing the giant elephant in the room, "Look, I know it's not my business, but–"

Fulton snapped, "It's not your business! I don't wanna talk about it."

"Okay then..." she murmured, heading back inside her home.

Fulton grew panicky as he turned the doorknob. He noticed something he should have seen a few moments ago: a FORECLOSURE note stapled across the peeping hole. A letter signed off by Summit. Fulton ripped the thing off, crumbling it into a messy ball before proceeding inside. The landlord knew of the message as well. That grouchy old woman didn't want a criminal living within the unit.

Fulton sighed, "There goes the Condo. What's next?" Walking further into the room, Fult saw that all the furniture had been removed. The TV and living room set were gone. The fridge and microwave were removed. Hell, even the decorative plants were abolished. What else was next? The car? His mother? He already lost his job.

Might as well take everything a man has.

Slamming the door shut, Fulton got a slight whiff of something rotten crawling up his nose. He covered his mouth and nose, gagging after each breath. "Ma?!" He called out. "I'm back! I'm home!"

There was no response; she had the door closed, locked.

"Hey, Ma! Aha! I guess you need that shower now?" he tried to push the door open, but it wouldn't budge.

"Ma...? Mom? Can you open the door?"

Again, he shoved the door, slamming his shoulder onto the surface. The door was creaking open, and the ends of the white wood broke.

"Mom?!" he shouted. Nothing but a dead response of tranquility.

Finally, he swiftly kicked the door, swinging it right open. A strong gust of the smell smacked the stupid man in the nose, and he vomited all over the nightstand.

There she lay... A lifeless mother. Laying stiff and gray, dead. What was worse was that she had something in one of her hands. It was her pills. Her delicate fingers could never get the capsule open. Fulton wasn't there to help her open them. He wasn't there to get her food; he wasn't there to take her to her appointments.

"No... No, no, no, no, no, no!" Fulton fell on his knees, his calves smothered against some of his vomit as he laid his head on her hardened side, "No...! Mom, I'm sorry, I'm sorry. Please! Please, no!" Tears and snot dripped onto her stone-cold hands; he squeezed them as if life was still remaining within her. "I'm sorry, Mom." Fulton reached for the orange capsule, throwing the bottle against the wall, creating a small dent in the panel. Another stage of grief was abroad, anger. He grabbed whatever was beside him. A blue lamp held the base of the light and smashed it against the wall, denting it even more. He even grabbed his mother's remote for the TV, throwing it against the screen, cracking the glass on impact.

After that moment of release, he couldn't help but cry. Nothing but to scream and cry. The smell of death didn't suffice; it only created more sadness for poor Fulton.

He mumbled, hysterically sobbing beside her bed, "I'm sorry, Mom. If I was- If I hadn't- I- this is- all my fault."

Chapter 23
A SUIT WITH NO TIE

Sam pulled a soft blue towel to his head, drying his wet hair from the steamy shower he took. He looked at himself in the mirror in his mid-thigh, black boxers. He glanced at the scars on his face and body, regarding that they had faded to nothing but minor marks in remembrance.

He chuckled at the scars. "Might as well add fast healing to the list, huh?"

It was time to get ready for school. The twins were picking him up this time. It'd been a while since he last hung out with them. Let alone finally acknowledge them. Sam was still caught up in his own little world. Some might say he was stuck in a fairyland, daydreaming about nothing.

Sam put on a black tee, dark gray denim jeans, and sneakers. It was a new day. Cathy sat on the couch in the living room. Sam avoided her. He needed time to process the truth about what happened between his mother and father.

Right outside, one twin honked the beefy horn, alerting their friend to come out. Sam could hear their radio blasting the same old country playlists they saved on their new phones.

"Just another day," he said, happy to continue living his regular schedule (with extra benefits).

Sam snagged his rucksack from the coat rack and opened the front door, ignoring his mother. She tried to wish a good day, but a hard slam from the door interrupted her. The rain was picking up more. Trevor stood outside the truck holding a black umbrella with the passenger door open, waiting for his friend. The truck had seen better days. The twins got only one headlight working, buffed out some scratches, and fixed one dent on the door panel. No tail lights, though. That was a rare part they had to find online somewhere.

Sam walked down the steps, feeling the patter of the drops hit his head. He didn't care if he got wet; he had too much on his mind. Reaching the truck, Trevor beckoned, emoting for Sam to get inside first.

Sam hopped in, scooting beside Garrett. "What's up?"

"Sup, Sam."

Trevor fastened his seatbelt. There was no intended rush; they didn't care if they were late. They were curious about what Sam had been up to and why he's been acting differently lately.

"What have you been up to, bud?" asked Trevor.

"Just working, school, helping my mom out with stuff. The usual."

"Working, huh?" Trevor repeated.

"We don't see you around much," said Garrett.

"I've just been busy, is all."

The rest of the drive was quiet. Quiet until Trevor brought up something he saw in the news about the attack at Beyrou's. "Did you hear about what happened in the city?"

"The robbery?" Sam raised.

"Yeah! The guys that robbed those stores, including Beyrou's, went to trial yesterday."

"Really? That fast? It's only been a few days." If Sam knew about the trial, he would've given a statement or at least caught the stream.

"Yeah. And get this, the Judge dismissed the case."

"What? Seriously?!" Sam's joy went out the window, knowing those maniacs were running around the city. They terrorized people and murdered a few, yet they're still roaming. Sam thought about Fulton and then about the why.

Why are they free? Why are they still out and about? Why were they doing these things?

Though it wasn't his business, he couldn't ignore it. They hassled his mother's workplace and killed people who didn't deserve what came to them.

Why, Fulton?

At West Made, Sam asked the twins if they could park on the side of the school near the Gymnasium.

"Why there?" they both questioned.

"I think I left some camera equipment in the locker room." Sam lied.

"I've never seen you go into the gym once," Trevor snickered.

"I can get it for you. Plus, I need to talk to Coach Martin about quitting the team," said Garrett.

"No. It's fine."

"Hey," Trevor called out to Sam before he took off. We're going to drop Sonny off at his internship next week. After that, Gar and I are going to Doe's. Can you come? We want to talk to you about something."

"Yeah. Sure." Sam nodded, rushing out of the red dame and speed walking towards the large, blue gym doors. The boy took a quick turn to see if anybody was around. No one was in sight. Perfect. In the distance, Garrett watched Sam go inside. He wondered why he was going there. They hadn't seen their pal in a while, and he came back acting strange.

The Gymnasium was wide open, and the roof had tight scaffolding carrying various balls between the crevices.

Probably because some lousy kids would just screw around and toss them as high as they could until one would get stuck. Only stupid.

The floor was sleek. The janitor had recently polished it during his morning shift. If anything could be labeled as sanitary, the gym's floor court was it. Definitely. Each footstep was a squeak, echoing throughout the room. Sam was eager to get into his new suit. He wanted to get some practice in, push its limits, and see how reliable everything was. Even if the suit was unreliable, it was too late to return the fabric.

In the shadows behind the stands, Sam monitored the basketball court in front of him, along with the exit doors and maintenance closet. It'd be embarrassing to get walked in on while changing. The first thing he pulled out of his bag was the bodysuit. It had been folded nicely and neatly, just enough to fit the rest of Sam's stuff in his bag. Next were the steel-toe boots. Sam bent and glued some of the tungsten rods along the rim of the shoes. He only hoped the super glue wouldn't give in or melt off during his speed. After the boots, he pulled out some gloves. They looked like thick, reasonably durable work gloves and navy blue like everything else.

Sam groaned, shoving each limb into the narrow sleeves. It's a bit of a tight squeeze.

It took a while for him to fit into his getup, but in the end, it was worth the wait. The last piece to the puzzle was the mask. The mask that belonged to Johnny was now Sam's. From outside eyes, no one could tell what Sam's expressions were. No eyes, skin color, boy, girl, adult, or hair color. Underneath the mask was a thrilled boy, wishing he could see himself. Sam checked himself out. His body was in a navy blue glory, and the small tungsten rods were glued and stitched onto the bodysuit. They lined up from his wrist to his shoulders, from the ankle of the dog boots, up to his neck. There wasn't much detail on his backside other than the same lining that went from the back of his wrist to the back of his shoulder. As for the blue balaclava, Sam had to change the lenses. He tore out the silly rainbow ones for a more reflective look, keeping the shape. They looked like mirrors that rested on his eyes. He also curved some rods and glued them along the lenses and down the side of his temples, wrapping all the way around his head. Thankfully, there were no rips or loose stitches displayed. Sam chuckled at the thought of a hole on his ass and everyone seeing his green boxers.

So far, so good. Nothing feels weird or off. Tight around my horn, but other than that, I'm fine.

Sam shuffled in his boots, getting used to the feel of the heavy ground. The weight from the tungsten and steel toe provided balance and reassurance that falling over wouldn't be too easy. "Now to test it."

Sam walked to the far end of the court. It was 95 feet long. The run was going to be quick. Sam fell into a running stance, bending his knees into place. BOOM! He thrust forward., touching the other side of the wall and running back within a couple of seconds. When Sam was boosted, the gym made a loud crashing sound, which was more audible than the hyperfrequency of a harrier jet. All the glass on the fluorescent bulbs above him shattered into pieces, and the floor on the court ripped and crumbled. Sam stopped momentarily, covering his ears and wondering why everything was so loud. Was it the outfit? Did the tungsten provide sound? He forgot to take it easy. That's what it was. The boy was too excited.

"Maybe I should try this outside..."

The football field was damp. Luckily, the rain came to a stop, and the sun was peaking through one of the thick gray clouds. He ran again. This time, he threw the boots off his feet to see if there was any difference. Again, BOOM! Sam bolted to the corner of the field. It was less loud. Sam felt his socks ripping as he slowed down. The boots had to come on again. Sam had to relax and take it one step at a time... literally.

Sam concentrated on the green grass, and his eyes flooded with that same electric blue. He took off faster than the eye could see. No loud noises, no broken floors, and, to a surprise, no friction burns. As Sam ran down Belknap Street, he constantly checked on the suit just to be sure. Nothing. No burns or tears. The suit was holding up well. As the kid ran on, he pointed his head down to see the boots. The rods were holding up nicely, and that damn glue wasn't lying about the extra hold. Sam had a bit on his fingertips, proof that that stuff wasn't coming off anytime soon.

Changing back into his clothes, Sam gave into his worry of further detention or suspension from school. 30 minutes into one lecture, Sam was tapping his foot in a hypermotion. To the average eye, they'd assume he had ADHD or needed to piss. But Sam grew increasingly impatient. Unknowingly, he thought he'd have a regular mad anxiety attack. This time, it wasn't an attack. He never felt such emotions before. This impatient irritation became agony.

Why? How come? He thought. Patience was always his strongest trait. He could wait hours and hours in the school without throwing a fit. Alas, he continued to tap his foot and groan into the desk. It had only been 30 minutes.

On his way to continuous lunch detentions, the room's silence became deadly. It awoke further impatience within the mind. Sam bit his nails to the rim, his thumb squeezing out a blob of blood from all the teething. Poor Sammy couldn't bother eating because he had a full stomach of fingernails. His mood was bipolar, from the joy of the suit to high impatience.

When the last bell rang, Sam immediately shoved the boots on his feet and took off back to the apartment. He didn't care if his shirt would rip or burn. He wasn't sure why this whole impatient attitude was coming to life. One thing for certain was that the moment he engaged his powers, that old irritating mood disappeared.

As Sam walked up the steps to his home, his eyes focused on a fire-orange Lamborghini parked in front of the unit. *Wow, that's nice. I wonder who it belongs to.*

Before unlocking the door, Sam overheard a couple of muffled voices inside. He didn't know if it was his mother and one of her friends or two random strangers intruding. Carefully, he placed the silver key into the rusty lock pad, turning it as quietly as it allowed and opening the door. At first, he couldn't quite make out who was in the kitchen, but he made out that it was a womanly figure standing next to the counter.

"Mom?" He called out, taking off his running boots. Sam overheard an eating utensil drop and hit the side of a plate as he walked closer to the source.

"Yes, sweetie?" Cathy answered, making herself known, "I'm here in the kitchen."

Something didn't feel right. Sam cautiously moved closer, tip-toeing to the room. When his frame was about in, his mother said, "I was waiting for you to get home."

Sam was about to ask if somebody else was in the room when the question was answered for himself. His eyes bugged, and his mouth dropped. All the air in his lungs drifted as he recognized that one. "I got to meet your new friend here. What's your name again, hon? Ellie Juniper, you said?"

"Oui."

Chapter 24
LETTING IT SINK

An EMT carried Fulton's mother out of the building. Others, inside and outside their homes, stood to see what was happening. The man heard murmurs and little whispers about him and his connection between Jo and Johnny. Some even muttered rumors he might have been holding his mother hostage or abusing her. Some had silly stories to say, like he and Jo were dating or that she was his sister.

Fulton clenched his fists, feeling nothing but pure pain and despair. Everything was taken away. Claps of thunder set the depressing mood. When the team carried Donna into the back of the vehicle, Fulton kept his hands by his sides, continuing to clench his bold fists. His head was throbbing from all the crying and muscle tension. He relieved himself by letting his hands go and keeping them in his pockets as one more tear rolled down his cheek.

"Goodbye, Mom," He said softly, walking away.

Upstairs, Fulton packed what he could. He couldn't stay there any longer. Not anymore. He didn't have any place to go. Nowhere else to stay that he could ever call home. Fulton grabbed one of his rolling suitcases, folding several pairs of clothes he had left. Gloria saw her neighbor through her peeping hole, not wanting to say a thing that could bother the sad man. Just talking to herself as if he were in front of her right now, *Goodbye, Fulton.* It was a shame. He hoped she'd come out one last time.

Rain washed on Fulton. He checked in the front to see about his car... That was gone, too. He knew nobody had stolen it. The Summit corporation had taken it like they took everything else he owned.

Stomping on the ground like a child, he screamed in frustration, "AHH!" He could do nothing but walk. He had no phone, so he couldn't call a driving service and he didn't want to stay at Jo's. He'd just have to walk until he could find a cheap motel.

After an hour of walking through the cold sprays, Fuller spotted a taxi at the next stoplight. He was so excited he ran, dragging his soaked luggage all the way there.

"Taxi!" He yelled, "TAXI!" He opened the door, entered, and squeezed his belongings tightly.

"Where to?" Asked the driver.

"Um– just the nearest motel– or hotel. Whatever's nearby and cheap. And take your time drivin'. It's cold as hell out there."

The driver looked like he was drunk or had just finished drinking. Fulton could smell the strong vodka from his breath, from the backseat. His brown handlebar mustache looked soaked from his last gulp. They drove around town for a few minutes. The only place nearby was that same motel that he, Jo, and Johnny used to plan the bank job. It was all he could afford.

Before exiting the taxi, Fulton identified a sticker on the edge of the window. It was a sticker of Summit-Peaks. The man couldn't bear it. He peeled the thing off with anger, holding nothing but remorse and utter shame for a place he once called work.

The man coughed like a broken whistle, attempting to talk. "Al- Alright- the total is fifteen thirty-five."

Fulton passed the old fellow a soaked 20. "Here."

The driver groaned, taking the wet bill and tossing it into the passenger seat, "Alright, get outta here."

Fulton hoped to God that he didn't get the same room as before. Then again, maybe all the rooms were like that—musty, gross, and not worth living. Fulton looked at the keys and read the room number: RM 200.

What are the odds? Fulton griped. *The same crappy room.*

As the depressed man unlocked the door, he trusted maybe they had tidied up the room, that they might have cleaned the beds, washed the carpet, and made it as good as new. Perhaps something that might remind him of home.

Turning on the lights, it was still a complete-and-utter shit hole. The room was still small, bleak, for that matter. He didn't know if it was him, but the bed seemed smaller than usual. The smell of mildew went wild because the AC was not being tended to. The room felt moist and wet, and there was a now leak in the ceiling.

Fulton sighed, tossing his luggage on the crusty, green carpet and sitting on the edge of the gross bed. He rubbed his cold palms over his short hair, and his fingers felt the tip of his ears, freezing at the touch. He just sat there... Almost like he was waiting for something. Waiting for something to happen but for nothing to happen. He fell into a deep depression. The kind where you can't cry or get pissed off- just to sit in a black hole of emptiness. Soon, Fulton laid his back on the bed. The sheets had pieces of hair sprayed on the pillows, making the drool stains pop out. He lay there for three hours straight. Not even deciding to get an ounce of shut-eye, laying there frozen with such horror riddling his mind. The rain continued with no claps of thunder. Just rain. Fulton stared at the drywall, listening to droplets smashing against the window and front door. The only time he moved was to switch positions, turning over.

Later, Fulton got the courage to take his mind off the current situation and turned on the TV on the wide, light-brown wooden dresser. How convenient was it that one of the paid promotions displayed on the screen was for Summit-Peaks? Within a microsecond, he slammed his fist on the monitor, grabbing it whole, his arms stretching wide around and slamming it on the floor. Fulton kicked the heavy box on the back end, stomping it until it shut off. Again, he lay on the bed for another three hours. The only sounds available to the cool ears were his heartbeat, his lips smacking, and the strong swallows of his saliva. His eyes caught sight of the ceiling fan, the only cleanest item in the room (brand new). Not a speck of dust flew off that thing. Fulton sat up, slowly admiring the built-in object resting on the ceiling. That beautiful black and white fan played like a movie. His dialed eyes spun in circles, attempting to follow its path. After his little game and fascination, he stood up on the bed and pulled the switch to shut it off.

"Cool." The man rolled his eyes and raised his hand to the blades, preventing them from moving any longer. He grew an idea- he tested its durability by grabbing the left side blade on the edge and pulling it down. It hardly shook, still stuck in place. Now, he seized on the right side, nearly dangling above the floor.

His remarkable hour passed. He hung from the fan, swinging on it like it was one of those jungle vines you'd see Tarzan swinging from; only this wasn't a jungle guy- this was a tough man. Less than that- he was a mama's-boy. Fulton then moved to his rolling case, pulling out a few sets of thin t-shirts. A black long-sleeve, a white short-sleeve v-neck, and a light crimson-red hoodie. His hands shook, and his jaw quivered as he tied them together.

About half an hour later, he formed the shape of a noose to fit the size of his bulky neck, clenching the end of the red jacket resting around his neck. Fulton threw the other lot of the shirts around the white mount on top of the fan, tying a solid knot around it. When he got the courage, he grabbed the desk chair beside him and jumped onto the seat to place his feet together, his shoes touching side-by-side.

It was time. It was time to let go... It was time to feel peace. It was time to not hurt anymore. Fulton couldn't think clearly. He could only focus on his pain, and to him, that was all he needed. Fulton didn't see any other choice. He couldn't find anyone or anything to blame or find any resources. Everything he owned and worked for, was taken away all within a day. The only soul he could blame was his...

He took a few deep breaths, examining the surrounding room before his big finale. His head turned to the ceiling, giving the custom noose a quick tug just to be sure. He tugged and tugged– it was tight and ready for use. Fulton exhaled, hopping off the chair, and gagged for air. For if there were any strangers, it'd be unsettling to witness. He didn't struggle. He didn't fight his choice, only keeping his arms behind himself, locking his fingers together. He squeezed until his air was gone. The shirts tightened together, holding the man's weight to great extremes. Fulton continued to choke, closing his eyes to the lullaby of the struggling shirts, only seeing the dark behind his eyelids and the dim-lit lamps on the nightstand next to the gross bed for one last time. Everything was over. Everything was over, and the rain finally stopped. He floated dead in the air. His body swung from left to right. Fuller R. Bruning was dead... for a few minutes.

The fan broke off the ceiling, tearing the drywall above and dusting over the carpet and shirts. The noose eased up, and Fulton's body smacked the ground. He screamed a tank of air, breathing like a demonic entity, cuffing his neck and pulling the tie off it. Fulton screamed in terror, crying again. He couldn't die- and he didn't want to live. His mind went insane for the moments he dreaded.

"WHY ME?!" He screamed. "JUST WHY?! ME?!" Why was he still alive? What was the point of it? For Fulton, that was the one question that's riddled his mind ever since his mother passed. His eyes poured into puddles, soaking the edge of the blankets. He curled up in a fetal position, holding himself, and gently massaged his neck. There were burns from the shirt's material.

Chapter 25
ELLIE

Hours before Fulton's suicide attempt, Sam was petrified to see Ellie. To see her in his kitchen, of all places, in his poor household. The model winked, then waved at Sam's eyes to knock him out of his trance. "Hello? Sammy?"

Cathy giggled, "Aww, that's cute. She calls you Sammy."

The kid blinked hard, knocking himself back into the present. "Hi? I don't mean to sound rude, but- what are you doing here?"

Ms. Juniper was eager to answer, nearly choking on her second cup of herbal tea. "I was nearby and hadn't seen you in a while, so I thought I would stop by. Your mother is so lovely, by the way." Cathy blushed, leaving the room so the two could catch up. Sam was afraid to make any movement, because he was embarrassed about his environment.

"Can we go outside?" Sam's voice trembled.

"Don't you want to put on shoes first?"

Sam gasped, looking around to find a decent pair nearby. He scooted his boots away. Blue boots were uncommon. Sam found an old pair of white sneakers pressed against the corner of the doorway.

"Lovely to meet you, Mrs. Clark."

"Her last name isn't the same as mine," corrected Sam.

"Oh. No?"

Cathy let out a light sigh. "No. My last name is Bakers. And I'm not married. Just Miss. I appreciate you being kind, though."

"Well, enchanté (nice to meet you), Ms. Bakers."

The two walked out and leaned against the balcony railing outside the unit. "Wow. This is nice," Ellie admired, glancing at the tall, lit-up buildings from afar. Her head then tilted up at the night sky. How far are you from the city? You don't seem too far out."

"You should see it from my room, haha," Sam grinned at the idea. "I'm about twenty to twenty-eight minutes away, depending on traffic."

Ellie looked over at him, staring into his eyes, unsure of what to say. He felt uneasy, making the tension awkward. "Sorry about my mom."

"Why sorry for?" she contested. "She's a nice mother compared to mine."

"I wouldn't know, haha. I'm sure she is nice, though."

"Well, I promise you, yours is way better."

"How so?"

"It's a boring story, Sammy. Plus, it's getting late."

"I don't have anywhere to be."

Ellie looked back at the front door, unsure if it was appropriate for Cathy to hear. If she could hear through the door, or if she was possibly eavesdropping. "Comment se porte votre français (How is your French)?"

Sam cleared his throat, remembering the French class he took in his sophomore year, "C'est bon (It's okay)."

Ms. Juniper explained she didn't want to appear disrespectful or whiny. She had a peculiar view of parents. Of course, the common term for that would be mommy and daddy issues, but Ellie didn't like that label. Ever since she was a child, the relationship between her and her parents (Anna and Henri) was far from perfect. Ellie also didn't want to sound ungrateful, but for a moment, she compared her life to Sam's and that not everyone is raised from privilege. Most kids don't grow up with a lot of money or two parents. In Ellie's case, she'd rather grow up without them. Her parents practically forced her into the modeling gig.

It was the spring of 1993. Ellie came home from elementary school, ready for her daily after-school snack of baby carrots and a piece of dark chocolate. Anna and Henri were desperate to make a buck. They both worked at a food market, living near the countryside of Bordeaux. Anna recalled an ad in the paper about a beauty pageant for kids, and she didn't hesitate to sign her daughter up for it. The reward for the first-place winner was five hundred euros. Second place was a hundred, and the third was fifty. The rest got nothing but a nice red ribbon for their designated outfits.

When the day of the pageant show came, Ellie became uncomfortable. She didn't enjoy what she was doing, and she had no clue what to do or how to appear confident. In a dark room with flashing lights and big cameras, it was hard to make out faces in the crowd. Ellie didn't understand her feelings, but the right word for this use was exploitation. She gained no pleasure out of being exploited or attracting lots of attention.

After the show, the judges rated her in second place. The Junipers were thrilled, happy that their daughter was a borderline star. They were so happy until the secondary emotions kicked in. Greed. It wasn't enough. One hundred euros was far from enough. They wanted more. Now, her parents were envious of the first-place winner.

As the years passed, Ellie was now thirteen years old. Her reputation grew, and more pageants passed, along with a handful of sponsorships. Her winning pattern shifted in rank. Sometimes, she'd win first, and most times, she'd win second.

You might wonder if this was enough for Anna and Henri. Did the years of money prizes, sponsors, and offers do the trick? Absolutely not. The lack of their child not being a constant first, the low prize money, all these trivial matters turned to blame. They blamed not only themselves but also their own daughter.

Anna would make comments here and there about how she wasn't pretty enough to win first place, and since then, Ellie had strived to be the best. She wanted to prove both her parents wrong. At first, she wanted out of that life. She wanted to steal all the money her parents hogged away from her winnings and run away and never see them again. This was mental torture for a teenager. Ellie couldn't even recall the last time she had a burger, what with all the diet restrictions enforced by her father.

Following up, Ellie's growth spurt twisted heads around. Puberty did a fine number on her as all the offers piled up, most of which originated from Los Angeles. Ellie heard about the famous stories of LA. Hollywood, Americans, celebrities, opportunity, fatty food. What could be better? Literally anything else. Anna and Henri used up their visas when visiting California. While the setting itself is beautiful, and the weather is always warm, the people there just weren't it. Ellie wanted to show her rebellious side, sneaking out of her temporary home to explore the city and meet some people. From there, she met a guy her age (18) and believed he was truly great. Ellie set herself up for disappointment. She often forgot how well-known she was in the world, and the boy was only interested in her in the hopes he'd get famous or at least say he got frisky with a model. This happened a couple more times until she realized that dating in a popular city like Los Angeles wasn't ideal. Environments change people, and city folks are usually assholes. Maybe it was the disdain for her parents that kept Ms. Juniper humble.

When Ellie turned 21, she stood up for herself, took back her money, and left a small cut for her parents to live off of. She never disclosed to Sam how much she exactly gave them, but let's just say it involved more than six zeros. She also got her citizenship (which took longer to process than most people who want to migrate to the United States).

"Qu'est-ce qui vous a amené au Texas (What brought you to Texas)?" Sam eagerly asked. He was stunned by her story. He had only heard rumors about her origins but never got the whole, detailed picture until tonight.

"Inférieur (Inferior)."

"T'es-tu déjà vengé de tes parents (Have you ever taken revenge on your parents)?"

Ellie explained that growing up, she truly hated her parents with every breath she took. Her original, vengeful plan was to find a way to make them go into debt or, by scaring them from dropping out of her career, make them fear being homeless and living on the streets. Anything, as long as she could make them feel everything she felt growing up... But Ellie looked back on her days in Bordeaux. The baby carrots and dark chocolate life before pageants and professional modeling. She overlooked those childish things and sat back. How was her living situation, really? Her parents couldn't keep up with their home, their job, and living expenses. Plus, adding a child on top means more spending. She relived her childhood in her head. She remembered a stack of letters in her living room. All were notices and bills, the fridge being empty on most days with nothing but milk, butter, and days-old fruit. The long walks to school because they didn't have a car. Ellie didn't need revenge. As she matured, she accepted them for who they were and their mistakes. She knew there was no reason to hold resentment because, despite her living situation, Ellie gathered they weren't doing this just for them, but they did it for her as well. They wanted their daughter to live without worry- to succeed- it was just a harsh way of teaching that lesson. Those snarky comments and harsh parenting style were a way to challenge her, not torment her. She didn't see it then, but she did now.

Ellie got teary-eyed, using her knuckle to catch the tear before it ruined her mascara. She stopped speaking in her native language and returned to English. "How are things with you and your mother?"

"Kind of a rough patch right now," Sam answered, falling silent after.

"Why?"

The boy shrugged. His throat bubbled up, and he tried to chuckle it off by how ridiculous he would look if he cried in front of a model.

"What's funny?"

"Nothing," Sam coughed, acting like something was stuck in his windpipe, "It's just... well- I don't want to give you all the details, but basically, my mom lied to me about my father and pretty much my life. Keeping secrets that shouldn't have been kept." (The irony of hiding things.)

"I'd say if she's lying or hiding things from you, it's because she cares."

"How?"

"She loves you, and the last thing she'd want is to hurt you. She cares about you, Sammy. I promise you. Just by the fifteen-minute interaction with your mother, I can tell she loves you and cares about you a lot, your feelings, your life, and the way you perceive her. You're growing up very fast, hon."

"Ms. Juniper-"

"Ellie. Call me Ellie." She insisted with a hint of annoyance.

Sam bit his lip. He was used to being respectful and showing politeness. "Ellie. Did you actually come here just to check up on me?"

"Oui (Yes), I did. You know I consider you a friend?"

"That's funny. I never thought I would be your friend."

Ellie raised a brow. "What did you think you'd be, then?"

"A stranger. Just another guy that'd be taking your photos."

"I'm more than a picture, Sam." Ellie patted his hand, nearly locking her fingers with his, and turned her attention back on the expansive view, "I can promise you that too." she said as she pulled her hair behind her small ear, revealing an exquisite, blue diamond piercing. "Maybe I'll see you during Christmas break, and we could get together?" she proposed.

Sam liked the sound of that. It'd be nice to bring more people into his life.

Chapter 26
MAMA'S BOY

Fulton took a cold shower, sitting naked on the wet floor, holding his legs to his chest until his skin pruned. He didn't know what would be next. What will he do now? Being homeless on the streets seemed to be the only option. Fulton got up, put on his spare trunk clothes, and packed his stuff. His eyes drifted towards the shirt noose, grabbing it. His hand trembled as he threw it into the case. Fulton fashioned a black tracksuit jacket to cover up his neck marks and left the motel.

Using the motel phone to call a taxi, Fulton kept thinking of the only place to go. The only person he'd ever consider a friend. Jo. The second he arrived, he ran up to the creaky patio, scooting past the broken dirt bikes and ATVs that leaned against the wall.

He banged on the screen door, "Jo!" he yelled, "Jo!" still knocking on the door.

She answered with thrill, happy to see him, "What's up, Fult'?" she smiled, scratching her forearms.

"Hey. Could I come in?"

"Oh- yeah! Yeah- I was going to ask that. What's up?!"

He brought in his luggage, rolling it inside the front entrance, "Is it okay If I–"

"Stay here?" she finished, "Yeah, sure. I kind of assumed you'd be out there. Ya' know– ever since we got caught."

"Yeah..." Fulton said with discontent.

She grabbed his bag, tossing it on the gray couch with subtle yellow stains. "You– can sleep here. Just don't barge into my room. Also, knock first! Don't forget that. The food's in the fridge. Last, don't make too much noise. It disturbs Grannie, and... that's about it."

Fulton clenched his jaw, getting a much more detailed look around the house. He never got a good look at the interior design of the home, only coming in when he needed something from her. The living room had a stale taste. Just the gray couch with a glass coffee table with granite legs. No TV, radio, or even a lamp. The only thing in that section of the room was a picture of Jo's grandmother. She looked old, wrinkly, and sad. Her face was white, causing the blush in her cheeks to stand out. The blush almost looked painted on, and her hair was almost platinum. Fulton focused hard on the picture, gathering that she was a former blonde like her granddaughter.

"Questions, mama's boy?" Jo raised.

"Nah', I'm fine. And don't call me that."

Jo leaned in close, noting red scrapes along the rim of his neck. "What happened to your neck?"

Fulton zipped up his jacket, popping up his collar. "Nothing."

Jo clicked her tongue, walking up to her room, "Alright, well- the food's in the fridge if you need any. Have a good day, Fult'."

When she ran upstairs, he took a tour of the kitchen. It was the only part of the house he hadn't explored. The room was elegant and white. Something about the theme felt home-like, more on the rural side. Fulton walked over to the round, gray fridge, got a cup of ice, and dropped it into a plastic sandwich bag, making an ice pack. His head throbbed from all the tears leaving his system. Fulton was done with the crying. He wanted to look for the answer to his question. Thinking couldn't help much. His headache was already kicking his ass.

Later, he searched the fridge, chucking down a carton of milk that held only about half a cup. Once finished, Jo ran down the steps, remembering she was late for a meeting. "Bye, Fult'! I'll be back soon. Gotta go to a meeting at my new job. I'll see ya later."

"Bye." he waved, watching her drive away in her black Chevy sedan.

Fulton rubbed his eyes, trailing off into the house, getting a good look at her and Grannie's decorations all over the place.

Nothing but off-brand paintings you'd usually see in convenience stores- nothing fancy. Fulton continued his exploring upstairs, passing through Jo's bedroom. There were only a few rules to follow, and Fulton couldn't resist. He stared down at the door, capturing every detail to its edge. She didn't get a lock on the door, leaving it easy enough for the guy to walk in. And with that in mind, he did. Fulton pushed that heavy door with one hand and swung it wide open.

The room was partially dark. Fulton had to walk in and flip the nearest switch available. When he did, it shocked his finger, marking a little cut on the tip of his finger. "Dammit." He shrieked. The lights flickered on, and the room was a mere mess. It was deemed more of a workshop than a bedroom compared to the last time he saw it. All things considered, it was a cute setup. Fulton tinkered around with the parts and brushed his hand through the debris, landing on a strange set. Two metal tubes set up on a tripod stand. He thought they were for decoration. After looking them over, he understood that something about the tubes was incomplete. Fulton paid closer attention to the detailing, following the wires scaled along its rims. He recognized some parts came from dirt bikes outside the house. The tubes followed up, leaving a gap in between, and attached to a thick metal plate the size of an average journal.

"Wait…" Fulton put pieces together like an advanced puzzle. That's why there were so many salvaged bikes out in the front. Still studying the mysterious tubes, hydraulics were added into the mix. "What the hell is she making?" Fulton shoved his eyes through its holes, capturing the scent of rubber and wax. "What's that?" Fulton reached his hand inside, grabbed hold of a smooth object, and pulled it upwards... it was a glove. A single black glove attached to a tube and wires. In front of the glove was a thick metal plate.

"What are these? Gauntlets?" His voice raised in confusion, reaching into the other set. For the other one- there was no sign of a glove attached, "I guess this one's finished," He scoffed. This was fascinating to Fulton. This was simple engineering. He expressed internal joy as he recalled all the hard work and studying he did to get that degree. *How could I forget?* Fulton spent so much time stealing money and settling for the warehouse that he forgot all about his major. He pictured a reality in which he continued to follow his dream of being a top-tier engineer at Summit Peaks or anywhere else. The man exhaled in melancholy. There was so much he had forgotten. His original plan.

Behind him, a voice called into the room, "Those are mine!" it said firmly. It was Jo, standing beside her door with her arms crossed. "What the hell are you doing in my room?"

"Uh..." Fulton was at a loss for words, looking around the room to make up an excuse, "I got lost?"

Jo couldn't help but cackle at that remark, rolling her eyes.

"How'd your meeting go?"

"It got canceled. What are you doing in here?" Jo's grin went away, turning blank.

"Just looking around, Jo. Honest."

As the woman uncrossed her arms, she unveiled a VHS tape and tossed it onto the table with the rest of the scraps.

"What do you think?" she wondered, toying around with one of the metal mitts.

"I don't know what to think. What are they?"

"They're gloves,"

"Oh? Really? I didn't know!" Fulton said in a sarcastic tone, eyes widened.

Jo reached over the workbench, slipping the gauntlet onto her slim wrist and strapping it firmly. "Do you wanna see what they can do?"

"They're not just a random pair of fancy-ass gloves?"

She shook her head, propping up a tall, empty bottle that once held a heavy amount of bourbon. You'd have to drop the thing about ten feet high just to get it to crack. Jo had almost forgotten something. Something essential to her invention: her airsoft face shield.

"What's that for?"

Jo strapped the visor onto her diamond-shaped face and explained, "This'll prevent any bits from hitting my face." Tightly clenching her petite fist and pulling back, Jo thrust her arm forward. The gauntlets' hydraulics kicked in, emitting a powerful- but mostly fast strike against the hard bottle, instantly breaking it into compact pieces. The gauntlets were so quick that Fulton barely registered her jab.

"Je- Jesus!, Son-of-a-bitch! Woah!" He gasped, raising his hands in astonishment.

"I know!" Jo hysterically laughed, throwing the glove off and placing it back on the tripod.

"I want it." He denoted, "I... want it."

After hearing the aggression in his voice, Jo became concerned. "What for?"

He shrugged, still amazed at her invention. "I don't know. Maybe something cool or some shit. I've never seen anythin' like that." Jo grew a smile, explaining the faults of the mechanics, "It works well. I just need to work on the other arm. It's kind of in the prototype stage."

"Can we get it done today?"

Her feelings increased at his curiosity. "Okay? Calm down there, mama's boy-"

"DON'T call me that!" Fulton shouted, causing Jo to jump in fear at the scream.

"Wh-what the hell is wrong with you? I- I would say that, and you've never thrown a fit!"

His throat ached. He cupped his throat and walked downstairs, heading outside to take his mind off the incoming stress. Unfortunately, the walk to blow off steam provided no aid. He threw up his arms and stomped his feet. "Mama's boy," he mocked, "Blah, blah, mama's boy." Fulton continued to walk until the evening. Eventually, calming down. Maybe he was just hungry? The man craved some good old chicken and waffles from Doe's but couldn't afford it. He had little money left in his pockets. Just a few tens and some lint. He returned to the house with the same empty stomach and bitter attitude.

Later that night, Fulton snored like a loud pig, dreaming of his mother's warm hands and heartfelt hugs. The dream slowly turned into a fatal nightmare- a terror of losing his life. Fulton could only grasp the hope that everything was just a long nightmare. The kind of terror that doesn't seem to have an end. He woke up breathing heavily to the sound of creaky stairs. It was Jo. She sat there, kneeling next to his tired body.

"Oh, my God!" He shook.

"I know," Jo said.

"Huh?" he groaned, wiping the crusty sleep from his eyes.

"I know what the red stuff is on your neck."

Fulton's face went from a tired squint to a straight frown, upset and embarrassed by her discovery.

"I've tried it myself. I died. Johnny found me and took me to the hospital. It's funny, I don't recall seeing a fiery hell or some stupid crap like that. I just felt cold. Cold like ice."

Fulton looked down, covering his neck. "I saw nothing. I just felt like I was floating."

Jo scoffed, not recalling that to herself. She pulled a pack of cigarettes from the coffee table behind her, lighting up one stick.

"Thanks, Jo... for letting me- ya' know. Stay here."

She grinned, staring at her friend, inhaling the strong nicotine. "I have something planned. I want you in on it. I also fixed up the gauntlets. Does that sound good?"

"Yeah."

"Alright. Sleep tight, boss."

Chapter 27
THE ATTACK AT SUMMIT PEAKS

Throughout the week, Sam took great advantage of his speed. Sometimes, he didn't plan on running into the city, mostly exploring certain parts he rarely visited. Now, it was lunchtime. He didn't crave a high-mighty breakfast meal from Doe's- no- he went to one of the finest pizzeria joints downtown, a simple place called Milano's Pizzeria. Sam brushed inside and drooled at the delicious menu, ordering a meat lover's slice that was toasted to the brim. He needed as much energy as he could get. As Sam's powers progressed, calories burned even faster than a protein beef-head or a fat chump trying keto. After purchasing the ten-inch slice, he bought two 24-ounce energy drinks. One cherry flavored and the other citrus punch. He sat by the front window eating his big meal, watching the city people walk by with their everyday lives. He took his time, savoring the nutrients in the greasy slice and sugary, caffeinated drinks. (If only Sam had received his powers earlier in the year, Thanksgiving would be a pretty satisfying feast.)

An alert sang on his phone. The twins set up a business call. RING-RING! It sang. RING-RING! Sam answered the call, bringing the phone up to his ear. "Hello?"

"Hey, Sam." The brothers greeted in sync.

"Not much. Just eating."

"Hey. Can we talk? It's finally time." Asked Garrett, clearing his throat into the speaker.

"Time for what?"

"The talk. Remember when I told you last week?" Said Trevor, trying to jog Sam's memory.

"Oh! Yeah, my bad."

"You forgot, didn't you?"

"No, no, no, I didn't forget. Um- when did y'all want to have the talk?"

"Now? If you can," Trevor said. "We're dropping Sonny off at the internship. It's at Summit-Peaks—or—at least, I think that's what it's called. Do you want us to pick you up? We're already on the way."

"I'm already in the city. I think I'm nearby Summit." Sam answered, stuffing his face with the pizza.

"Where at? Doe's?" Garrett turned up his radio to some early Tim McGraw.

"No, at Milano's. It's a small pizza joint on Raymond Street."

"Huh? Why there?" Trevor said in a slight, condescending tone, questioning there, of all places. It wasn't a bad spot; it was just strange to think of Sam roaming around the city without a source of transportation. And all things fair, Sam understood the confusion. Their usual spot was always Doe's, no matter the time of day. The Twins had no affection for pizza except for occasions like birthday parties or special events.

"Nevermind. I'll meet y'all at Doe's. I don't think I'm gonna eat there anyway," said Sam. "It's getting boring there."

"What?" Trevor whispered to his brother, then placed the phone back to his ear. "Okay. See ya there."

Sam crept into the alleyway behind the bistro, gulping down whatever was left of the cherry-flavored caffeine. When finished, he tossed the can into a nearby dumpster that smelled of skunk. It wasn't an adequate spot to change into the suit, but it was better than stripping on the sidewalk.

Easy. Sam grinned. It was getting easier to kick-start his speed. He'd only make it there in less than 15 seconds. His stomach nearly burned half the food he'd just consumed, forming a solid craving for Doe's. Alright... I guess I'm eating at Doe's after all.

The twins and Sonny arrived shortly. They placed Sonny in the middle seat, as usual, with guests hitching a ride. He seemed to have a great time, considering the massive smile on his face. He'd be jamming out with the guys. Any sort of music made that kid's head bop. He loved this country with all his heart, proclaiming to be a proud American.

"H-Hey, Samuel!" He waved, getting out of the truck.

Sam waved back, grinning at one of his lunch-table pals from West Made High.

The four gathered inside, walking to their usual booth. Sonny glanced around, blown away by the surrounding theme. "Wow. I-I've never been here be-before." He stuttered, his puppy dog eyes zooming to whatever came at him first. As always, Mrs. Buffers came out behind the counter and took the boys' orders, happy to see a new customer. She thought Sonny might be a new addition to their friend group.

"Hello, boys," she greeted, pulling up her list and ballpoint pen to take orders. Suddenly, her body shifted to the new kid, wanting to introduce herself, "Well, who are- you, cutie-pie?"

Sonny stopped looking around, shaking his head to her attention, "Oh- I-I'm Sonny. I'm new here."

"I can see that. You're looking everywhere, dear! I'm Mrs. Buffers. I'm the twins and Sam's usual server down here. Hell- sometimes I'm their mama!" She pushed out her thick hand, letting the new boy know she wanted to greet him with a handshake.

"Nice to meet you, Mrs. B-Buffers."

"It's nice to meet you too, Sonny. Also, if you don't mind me askin'- what accent is that from?" Her southern accent thickened.

"I'm from Colombia!"

"Oh, my! I've always wanted to go there!"

"No, you haven't," intruded Garrett, containing his snickering laugh. Trevor, too, held in his laughter as he elbowed his brother's arm.

"I–It's nice this time around. You'll love it." Sonny smiled, looking down at the menu. Mrs. Buffers clicked her chubby thumb in the pen, ready to take their orders, "Oh, I bet it is, sweetie! Now, what would y'all like to drink?"

After the hot, early dinner, the twins dropped off Sonny at the Summit building, running a cold two minutes late for work, no thanks to the two brothers dragging on their conversations about work, college, and who the prettiest girl at West Made was.

Before they drove to the front doors, the size of the property impressed Garrett. "Jeez. What floor do you work on, Sonny?"

"Twentieth."

"Wow. Good for you."

Sonny told the guys he'd been working on the middle floor, delivering coffee and office supplies for the last month. He hoped to get a job there one day as a supplier or maybe in customer service since he was bilingual. Before he could get distracted with further conversation, he sprinted out of the truck and into the establishment. Being late is not great, especially as an intern. Sam could finally relax now. It was already a tight squeeze with three in the truck, bad enough that there were now four present in the bench seat.

The three stepped out of the truck to stretch their legs. They promised to take Sonny back home after his shift. They didn't know how long their foreign friend would take. Garrett moved to the back and sat in the truck's bed. The chubby boy pulled out a fresh pack of minty cigarettes (the kind Sam had always liked), "Yo', Sam. Want one?"

"No. I'm fine." Sam started biting his nails, feeling that sting of impatience that he hoped was just a phase.

The boys felt off. It was a question of the matter. It was their usual thing to smoke a couple of cigs and ramble on about stupid things. Sure, cancer sticks aren't pleasant for kids their age, but it felt like a tradition to them.

"You okay?" asked Trevor.

Sam stopped biting at his nails, looking over. "Yeah. Why?" Sam tapped his foot along the floor.

"You seem tense. Also, that's the first time you've denied a smoke. We always smoke together." Said Garrett.

"I just don't like them anymore. I kinda grew off it."

Their eyes raised, amazed at how he suddenly became clean of them within a couple of weeks. Or at least to them, they assumed that's how long it took. "Damn. Just like that? I wish I could quit." Garrett laughed.

Sam left no response, biting his nails once more until they were on the rim of his skin. He stayed quiet, giving a little pace around the parking lot.

"Hey... are you okay?" one of them asked their friend.

Sam's breathing went on a bit of a spiral. "Yeah, I'm good. Are we gonna have the talk now, already, or?"

"Do you have somewhere to be?" Trevor questioned, staring.

"No. I guess I- uh... I don't know- just- carry on, I guess."

"Okay? Gar and I wanted to know if everything's good. Like- you've been distant lately and sometimes have been rude."

"What?!" Sam snapped in confusion. That's not at least how he saw it.

"Yeah." Garrett agreed. "We're not tryin' to confront you about this- at least I'm not tryin' to-."

"I'm not either, bro!" Trevor chimed, defending himself. "Look, you kinda left us in the dark. Like, right after the accident, you just disappeared. It feels like you're trying to avoid us. And the last couple times at Doe's, it seemed like you just wanted a free meal, then you up and left without saying bye."

Garrett then carried on the topic. "We're just sayin' that things have been weird with you. Not a good type of weird. You're weirder than usual."

Sam shook his head. His pacing grew longer, spacing out with larger breaths and higher impatience. "Is that all?"

Trevor then asked the question that cranked Sam's nerves, "Are you okay? Are you even listening, bro, or do you need a minute?"

"Yes!" He yelled, "Why do you keep asking?!"

"Really? You don't seem like it!" Trevor raised his tone higher than Sam's.

The kid felt that hot wave overcoming him, still pacing back and forth behind the truck, continuing to bite his nails. "Why do you care?!" Sam shouted, chewing on his thumb until it bled.

"We care because you're our friend!" Garrett hollered. "You're bitin' your damn nail– it's bleedin', for God's sake! What's the matter with ya'!"

Sam rolled his eyes, taking his windbreaker off and throwing it at the guys.

Trevor gasped, "The fu- ya' know, ever since you got back from London, you've become more of a dick!"

"Oh, yeah?!" Sam mocked.

"Trevor!" Garrett exclaimed, hoping to calm him down.

"YEAH!" His brother roared. "You hardly ever hang with us. You run around and leave us alone! You're becoming impatient by the day. You don't eat with us! You don't hang out or even sit with us at school! You don't smoke with us anymore! You ditch us and ask us for money! What the hell is wrong with you?!"

"Trevor, stop!" Garrett yelled, wanting his brother to quit it. "Both of you! Stop it!"

"Everything was going well until you went on that stupid trip! What's up with you?!"

"I DON'T KNOW!" Sam wailed, "I just- I don't know! Just leave me alone!" He began fanning himself by grabbing the center of his shirt. Sam felt like removing it to let the cold breeze fly down on him.

"Might as well be Felix." Said Trevor. "You keep this act going, and you'll be just like him!" Garrett wanted to avoid causing any attention in their area. The sun was dying down, and the dark purple skies were growing over. They all took a deep breath and calmed down. "Look..." the younger twin mumbled, "W-We wanna tell ya' something."

"What?" Suddenly, an itch spiked on Sam's head, and a couple of seconds later... BOOM! The tower shook and shrieked as glass fell from the sky, splashing along the area of the building. The three looked up in horror as the middle floors bathed in roaring flames.

"SONNY!" Garrett teared up in horror, covering his mouth, bestowed by the inflamed masses. The twins looked at each other, then back at Sam. They were in shock and unsure what to do besides having their mouths melt down their necks. Quickly, Sam ran to the passenger seat and grabbed his backpack.

"What are you doing?!" Trevor called out.

"I'm going to get help! Sonny is still in there! We need to leave now!"

Garrett got in the truck and called the fire department. The inside would help him concentrate and muffle out the sounds of the fire cracking and people screaming. The twin mistakenly grabbed the wrong phone, noticing he had Sam's phone instead of his. *If Sam was going to get help, then why did he forget his phone?* Garrett thought.

Sam jogged down the lot, building up his momentum while slipping his odd-looking mask on his face, dashing forward into the side entrance of Summit Peaks. This was similar to what happened at Beyrou's but far worse. Sam needed to help. As he ran on, his mind painted a mental picture of Sarah Lotwitz, the gun that fired towards her head. The people in there needed help. Sam didn't want to be selfish; he wanted to prevent people from getting hurt.

Inside, Sam had the rest of his suit on within seconds. He took advantage of the slow waves in his perception of time. It was hard to see with the polarized lenses, and he couldn't remove the mask unless he wanted to be coughing his lungs out. All around him were people screaming, crying, or laughing out of fear as they scattered around to look for help or an exit sign. Sam knew- he just knew Sonny was okay.

"Twentieth floor, just like he said." Sam repeated that number multiple times in his head. He just prayed that Sonny was still on that floor.

The fire exploded, lashing out like heavy whips against people trapped within the walls. Sam couldn't just get somebody and run them out. He didn't know what the effects of the aftermath would look like. As some of his hypothetical research said, one could get hurt from moving at such high speeds. Instead, Sam guided them one by one toward the nearest exit. He also used his speed to run back and forth from the stairwell to the elevators. When people are under duress or shock, everything they learn gets thrown out the window. Never use the elevators. Sam had to keep some people away from the elevators or near the fires. And like them, he couldn't see much. His lenses fogged up and collected flying bits of ash. Every other second, Sam had to constantly wipe the soot off his eyes.

The people in the building looked at the mysterious boy with such confusion. They reacted realistically. They didn't see a firefighter or police officer. They saw a random person—a vigilante helping—a stranger in a strange outfit. Sam moved carefully, covering the eyes on his mask from any more ash impacting his face. "Sonny!" he called out. "SONNY!"

A moment later, Sam was in the wild part of the flame. He stood slightly crouched in a room he couldn't recognize. If he could piece together the fragments of what it used to be, he'd say it was an office room, judging by the rows of desks and monitors scattered around. Sam was scared, but helping the people out mattered more than fear. He used his speed to check every corner of the room for any innocents. Eventually, he found Sonny knocked out cold and buried underneath a broken desk. Hot coffee got spilled all over his body, and blood poured from his head. Sam grabbed hold, pulling the desk off of him. It took time, but he got it. Sam had speed but didn't gain any super strength. Sonny remained unconscious.

The costumed kid was dragging his schoolmate away from the fiery madness, and Sam could barely make out the exit sign closest to the staircase. Thankfully, he got the attention of what seemed to be one worker. "Hey, you! Can you help me, please?!" He begged, but the worker ran off to save his skin.

"HELP!" Sam let out a gut-wrenching scream, "HELP ME!"

Another intern ran by, hearing the kid's cries, "Hey! Sir! Can you help him? Just get him out of here! Please! He's bleeding from his head!" Sam pleaded, relieved when the man wrapped Sonny's arm around his neck, dragging him down the steps carefully.

Just as Sam got his friend out, he heard a harsh rustle of furniture breaking. Another itch sparked in his head when he looked over to see what it might be. He moved out of the way in case any danger was lurking by - nothing. Another second passed, and a pillar slammed down on Sam's frame. The kid knew that he had to trust the itch. That was on the list of hypotheticals for a while. Whenever Sam received an itch on a particular area of his head, he knew he'd have to avoid anything happening in that direction. Soon, another itch came, and he acted too late. He received a swift punch to the face. The impact sent him about ten feet across the room in a twirl. Sam's eyes squinted, his vision blurred from the lenses, and the pain in his cheek throbbed. He couldn't quite make out what slammed him but noticed a tall, dark silhouette of what seemed to be a man. A man covered by a hood and shadows. The figure appeared to be shaking and out of breath. The moment Sam attempted to bring himself back up, the figure moved in, thrusting a substantial impact on his chest. This time, it was a robust and hefty punch, like a whip of metal pushing his body in. Sam would rather take shoves and slams from Felix than whatever this guy was giving him.

"God... what was that?" He grunted.

The hooded figure threw another punch. This time, Sam used his speed to swiftly dodge it just in time, but not before the mysterious thing countered and threw in a kick, pushing the boy back into a wall. The thing threw a strong punch into the ceiling, causing a cave-in right in front of him. A heavy lodge of scaffolding fell onto Sam's ankle. "AHHHHHH!" He wept., watching the mysterious figure vanish.

Before the roof fell, Sam got a glimpse of the silhouette's arm and what he was wearing. First, he noticed it looked like he had some strange hardware encasing around his fists. He didn't know what to call them, but it was proof of how he could punch his body almost halfway across the room like it was nothing. The last detail he got was the jacket he wore around himself. It looked familiar. It was some clothing he thought he'd just seen not too long ago. He remembered seeing a logo of some kind. It could be a letter or a symbol. Sam didn't mind it too much. His main priority was to get out. Sam pulled his leg out, limping his way outside to the stairwell, and clenched his chest to rub off the pain.

Sam made it outside to the front. His coughs were raspy, and his ankle still hurt. He stayed for a bit, watching the yellow blaze disintegrate the top side of the building. While citizens nearby were distracted by the catastrophe or recording it on their phones, poor, exhausted Sammy used this advantage to tread away to the parking lot. His eyes searched around, making out that the twins weren't there anymore. The only thing left behind was Sam's backpack. He slid his back down the side of a wall in pain. Sam's body turned frail as he took his costume off. When he removed his boots, he stared down at his ankle, bruised and strained at a high intensity. For Sam, it hurt like hell and was tender at the touch. Sirens wailed in, and helicopters were floating. Soon, this would make the front lines of all the news by morning. It was about time to leave.

No running this time, just a walk will have to do. Sam ambled through the block, feeling that sharp pain in his ankle, now alone. The van popped into his head once more. He remembered the crazy day at Beyrou's, which he ended up putting two and two together. *The van, Beyrou's, the jacket... the symbol on the jacket. What's-it-called? the– there was an 'F' symbol on the jacket!* Sam recalled the van again. "It was Fulton."

Chapter 28
KEEP YOUR ENEMIES CLOSE

Fire flew from above, and ash rose to the clouds. The moon looked gray, and despair was abroad. Everyone turned in worry and confusion, terrified by the blowup of the fire. Few barely made it out of Summit-Peaks alive as they coughed their lungs out until they puked chunks. Pedestrians would pull over to the side of the road just to get a decent view of the brightened skies. It looked like hell was taking over the earth, at least until the fire department arrived. This was a save-the-date type of night. A tragedy to remember.

December the 15th.

It was only a matter of time before this got to be burned into calendars to remember the fallen. Only some would find this event hilarious. Take it for crazy young Jo to laugh maniacally in the passenger seat of the van. She slammed her head against the dashboard, cackling more and more with Fulton. His laugh was more out of adrenaline than it was for hurting people. It was Fulton who'd invaded the industry, terrorizing the people and attacking a confused vigilante. It was stern, crazy Georgia that made the building blow up. Fire was her specialty, after all.

"Woah," Fulton gasped, "That was–"

"Awesome, right?!" Jo cheered.

"Heavenly." He exhaled through his teeth. Not realizing he was speeding, Fulton slowed down, trying to not draw much attention. They had already made it big on the news. There was no need to go bigger with this situation.

Jo then abruptly pulled her friend's face in and kissed his puffy lips, leaving a thick string of slobber between them. Fulton froze, tracing his eyes back to the road, barely registering the interaction. She tasted like corn and mint gum (not a tremendous mixed treat), but it didn't matter. She was still rocking out in her seat, ready to go home.

Shortly, the adrenaline wore off, ready to call it a night. Jo thought she could practically screw her buddy's brains from all the excitement. She'd been moist in the pants the second things went boom.

Jo understood the look on Fulton's face last week. She could tell he wanted to act upon vengeance- to take it out on the company. At first, she assumed he only wanted to blow off some steam, but this was more than that. He blamed Summit Peaks for taking everything he had just because they could. Now, he had nothing left to lose. Not anymore. His money is all gone, his job taken away, his home pulled out, his vehicle towed, and his mother dead... nothing.

"Hey, also, I saw somethin' weird on one of the floors?" said Fulton.

"Weird, how?"

"I don't know, but- this guy- I ran into this guy or somethin', and he looked like he was wearin' Johnny's old mask."

"Yeah, that's weird." She frowned, looking down at her lap. "We'll figure it out- tomorrow. Tonight, let's celebrate!"

At dawn, Fulton was up and early. His head throbbed from a hangover as he heated a fresh cup of coffee to start things off. While preparing the brew, Fulton ran over to the kitchen sink, puking bits of last night's pepperoni pizza and booze. He leaned against the counter, rubbing his sides in a circular motion, trying to find his balance. What made things worse was a questionable smell that burst into the kitchen. It'd smell of something foul, like a corpse was resting nearby. He continued to gag. From upstairs, he could hear loud, annoying banging from Jo's room. Fulton cuffed his ears, regurgitating and swallowing the aftertastes of his salty vomit. He wanted to go through her room to see what the commotion was about, and although he'd been through her room, he still had an ounce of proper manners to not barge in.

When the coffee was done, Fulton was feeling free. His headache was softening, and the cold winter breeze gave him the chills as he stepped onto the front patio. The main topic on his mind was those arms he used last night, practically dreaming of those things all the time. Eager to use them once more. Those gauntlets weren't his own, but he treated them like they were. Its power entranced Fulton. How hard would the punches impact with little effort? Ditching the hot mug, he jogged up the steps and into his friend's room, giving a couple of delicate knocks to let her know he'd be coming in.

"Come in!" Jo responded.

Fulton slightly groaned from the loud echoes in her voice. He wasn't fully cured just yet. He pushed the door open with his index finger, lightly lifting it with a creak. She'd been working on the gloves, tinkering around with its impulsive punches, attempting to make the thrust faster than most.

"Whatcha doin'?"

"Just messing around with my stuff. The gloves and all." Jo cranked the adjustments on the wrists, making it tighter and more stable for the next use.

My gloves. Fulton gradually became greedy over what he'd only used during practice and during last night's events. "Did you not get tipsy or anythin'? You seem energized as shit."

"Me? Drunk?!" Jo spoke in sharp wits of sarcasm, tending further on with her stuff. "I'm used to it. I drink and drink at least four times a week, so- I guess I'm just used to it. Good to know that I can out-drink you, haha!"

"Jesus..."

Jo dropped her tools on the table, eager to discuss something specific. "Hey, I uh- wanna talk to you."

"If you're going to talk about that kiss-"

"No! I was just excited. Meant nothing."

"'K, then? What?"

Jo grabbed one gauntlet, tossing it over to her partner in crime: "Well, first, I wanted to know how you're already so good at maneuvering around with this thing. I mean, I let you practice with it twice and then with last night, but how are you used to the weight, flexibility, and all that?"

Fulton laughed. "I used to take karate when I was a kid. I still remember a thing or two."

"Okay. Cool. Now, the other thing..." Jo grabbed a VHS tape from her dresser, twirling it around her fingers. It was the same one she threw on her table the other week. "I wanted to talk to you about this."

Fulton gestured to her to continue.

"When you brought up Johnny's mask, I kept reminding myself of the video we saw in court. So I went to the Dallas courthouse and-" Before continuing, she waved a videotape around his face like one would tease a child with a candy bar, "Don't ask me how I got this. It cost me a hand and a part to get this in my grasp. But I had to rewatch this... I think I should show you." Jo walked over to the other side of her room, peeking behind her TV, always keeping her VCR awkwardly stationed behind it, making no sense. Jo pushed the tape into the slot, pressing the big, green play button, showcasing a blurry lined video on the screen. "Why are tapes still around?" She grumbled.

The monitor crackled, and she slammed her palms against the box end of the TV. She repeatedly slapped her palm on it until it stopped. The footage played at total volume, not missing any trace of sound present while the two stood, watching closely. Fulton hadn't seen the video that day of the trial and could barely recall the incident during the robbery. He worried more about the consequences.

As the recording glitched, Fulton recollected everything bit-by-bit of the scenario that played out. His breathing became heavy, and his eyes filled with tears; he couldn't bear to not act out on emotion as he watched that strange boy in the mask getting in their way. It turns out it wasn't Summit's fault. It was that thing.

After 30 minutes of footage, he held himself as if his mother were hugging him. He thought of her hugs, kisses, and sassy attitude. He stared at the screen, thinking of the figure he saw last night. Fulton's mind switched to multiple thoughts at the speed of light. Jo leaned down, rubbing his shoulder with one hand with her other, and she pulled out a shiny piece of weakly magnetic steel from her pocket. "And then there's this." A rod of tungsten rolled on her palm, "I had time to give a hand job to a guy near the evidence room, and the first thing I saw near our stuff was this." Jo's hand poured, dropping the piece into Fulton's hand, and both observed it. "I don't know who it belongs to, but I know it's odd to carry a piece like that around. Strange, huh?"

Fulton squeezed the little rod. His palms made a stretch sound, clearly grasping the thing too tight. "You ever see that thing at the shop? The one that rammed into ya'."

"Not really. I was out."

He folded his lips, continuing to grasp them tightly. "I got an idea. I don't think it'll help, but- do you know any places or someone that sells this metal thing?"

Jo shrugged, coming up with the only answer she could come up with. "I'll call a few places. Don't get too excited, mama's-boy."

Fulton huffed, grabbing the two gauntlets and taking them outside to practice. He wanted to take his mind off things.

"Hey?!" Jo called out as he left the room, "I need to fix those!"

"I don't care!" Fulton slammed the door, walking out. As he exited the home, his nose caught a whiff of that foul smell, gagging again and holding his stomach.

Upstairs, Jo started a search on the internet, finding exclusive websites that offer sales on tungsten. Her dainty fingers typed along with the keyboard, running endless visits to various sites that offered all sorts of metal. Fake tungsten, molded, refurbished, melted. The list went on. It hadn't been long before she found a couple that sold precisely what she'd been looking for. She paused, taking a small break to look at Grannie. Jo opened the master bedroom's door, letting in a gust of that wretched smell Fulton had mentioned earlier. She stuck her fingers inside her nostrils, walking over to her grandmother, sitting still in her white rocking chair.

"Hey, grannie, it's Georgia!" She smiled, approaching closer by the syllable. "I'm gonna be busy for the next few hours, so I'll get back to you when I can. I love ya'!" Jo kneeled beside her stiff grandmother, giving a soft peck on her cheek. Dead. Dead long enough to create a foul, stenchy scent to the home. It wouldn't be long before the clothes and couches would reek of it. Jo continued to show love to the corpse, giving another quick kiss and running her hand along the hard shoulder, "Bye!" She waved, closing the door.

Outside, Fulton replayed the memories in his head, practicing efficiently with his gauntlets, ravaging the broken bikes on her property with immense pressure and force. As Fulton thrust his modified fist into a grom bike, it sent off a wild 18 feet into the backyard. After that, he took a break, inhaling deep wind into his lungs and breathing in from the nose. The cold made his nose run, wiping the snot off himself every couple of minutes.

Goddamn cold... "JO!" Fulton called out.

From inside, Jo scurried to the nearest window on the top floor, sliding the window wide open and sticking her blonde head out. "What's up?"

"Did ya' find anythin' yet?"

Jo groaned, slightly annoyed, "It's only been an hour, man. Calm down."

"Don't tell me to calm down! Now did your ass find anythin' or no!"

"I only found a couple of sites that sell these things. I made one phone call at the least."

"And?" Fulton waited.

"Someone bought around 30 pieces. All I got was a name. It might not even be the guy or thing we're looking for."

Fulton threw the gloves off, approaching the window. "Yeah? Who?"

"Someone named Samuel C. Clark II."

Chapter 29
INVESTIGATION

Across town, Sam needed to have a phone on him. He assumed it was lost in the twins' truck for the fifth time this year. Ever since the tragedy at Summit Peaks, Sam decided to hell with the cast, throwing it away in a random dumpster in town. No reason to fake an injury anymore. Speaking of injuries, his sprained ankle healed just five hours after the events that took place. The only thing left to memory was a bruise on his calf, and even then, that faded away.

On the bright side, Sam had a backup phone at Inferior. A work phone. It didn't have a carrier but could operate efficiently when connected to Wi-Fi. It was likely the only way to stay in contact and hopefully make amends with the twins. There was more than one situation to fix, other than the Sings. He still needed to talk to his mother and maybe get through to Fulton. This was a different type of loneliness for Sam. Sometimes, he had to face things alone, but not like this. This was out of his league. He shouldn't fear telling his friends or mom about the changes upon him or the crazy events ever since he came back from London. Everything was changing. He hadn't seen or heard from Trevor or Garrett in the last five days, and lord knows how hard he tried to avoid being seen by his own parent. Cathy was most likely overworked, and it didn't help to know Sam was adding to her stress from the sneaking around and the lack of communication. Christmas was nearing, and it was supposed to be the best time of the year. Time with family and friends. Not this year, I guess.

His work phone buzzed, catching up on the pile of unread notifications. Some were, of course, from Cathy, wondering where he had gone that night at Summit Peaks. One was from Mr. Grafton, most likely about the photos Sam had forgotten to send in.

In the meantime, Sam had to figure out how to work on his impatience, stress, anxiety, and overthinking. Granted, this only added to the thoughts, but it was the practice to take it one day at a time.

Christmas Eve. Sam still hadn't heard from the guys, not as much as a call or a stupid emoji. He realized how much he'd been taking them for granted, using them to get free meals, entertainment, and as a personal chauffeur. It wasn't fair. He was too selfish to see that their friendship was deteriorating and that he wouldn't tell them what was happening. They were the brothers in his life. They looked out for him when no one would. Sam desperately wanted to go to their house and make things right, but he worried that that would only worsen things. He couldn't call or text, not because he had no service, but because his backup phone only had Trevor's number, and knowing him, he always held a grudge. Regardless, it was a waiting game.

As for the situation with Fulton, Sam thought about contacting the authorities, but what would he tell them? *Hey, I ran into a burning building, and I saw a dude with these strange gloves and hoodie punch the shit out of me, who also was the one who robbed those stores, and a bank in the past month. How do I know? Oh! Because I have super speed! Stupid.* No. It didn't make sense. Where's the evidence? None. And if there were, Sam had too much on his mind to recall it. For now, nothing is what the evidence would be. Nothing.

Sam pleased himself with no rest. He sat at his desk for five hours, wondering why a man like that would even think about hurting people. The funny part is that Sam didn't know Fulton, other than a brief glimpse of his past, work ethic, and feelings since he told Sam about his sick mom.

Was that the reason? He queried to himself. Sam flashed back to the night they met. Moving back on everything from the man's rant. Ranting about life and work. Wait– that was it. Work. Sam was onto something. Fulton told him he was a manager at the warehouse for Summit. Why did you set the building on fire, though, Fulton? It was time to figure that out.

Sam made a quick run to the once-Summit Peaks industry, finding himself on the south side of the building. The warehouse wasn't hard to find—it was clear as day. The sight of everything looked depressing, with the whole place empty and the building burned half off. Sam didn't need to use his speed at the moment. He walked towards the loading dock, and on the wall parallel to him was the entrance to the depot.

Inside, Sam moved quietly. Each full-weight step, combined with the heftiness of the boots, made the whole place echo. Even more exaggerated now, knowing that not a single soul was in the department. Sam didn't want to risk having security come by to check for any intruders and get reported to the police. Sam put less weight on his footsteps, making a straight for what looked like the main office to him. It wasn't hard to miss in a standard warehouse. A thick white door beside a near bulletproof glass window to block out the outside noise and shades to minimize distractions. *Yep, it's an office, alright.*

The room was dark. The city had cut the power off to the whole property, including the light posts in the parking lot. Sam pulled his phone out of his backpack and turned the flashlight on. It was hard to see, and even more difficult with the mask. Sam yanked it off and brushed his hand through his hair to look neat.

What am I looking for? He wondered, investigating the office. His eyes read the nameplate on the dust-covered desk: Fulton R. Bruning. This was indeed the right place. Sam dropped his bag and mask on the floor, preparing for the possibility that he would be stuck in the office for a while, searching for any clues or whereabouts of Fulton.

The easiest and most accurate choice was to check the desk. Unfortunately, all the drawers were empty except for the last bottom slot. Nothing but old candy, gum wrappers, and some junk mail for furniture- wait- spam mail. Sam checked if the mail had a home address and not at the location he was currently in.

"Got it. 116 McKinnon Street. Number 75. I don't think that's far from here." The mail was there in the first place because Fulton had plans to use the paper shredder from his office. Sam gathered his belongings and fashioned the mask back on his face. His main objective was to find Fulton and figure out what was going on. Maybe he could talk to him, hear him out.

Sam sped to McKinnon Street, arriving about eighteen seconds in. It took him a while to find it. Running around a big city without having a sense of direction or knowing the specific names of streets wasn't as easy as people think. In our parents' early generation, it was a map, and now, for the next generation, it is still a map, just one designed for a phone. Sam had to take a few detours, running past McKinnon a few times before finding the street. If he knew where it was, he'd probably arrive sooner.

"Wow. Nice spot." Sam was amazed, leaning back and lifting his head in awe of the tall condo. "Number 75." He repeated, walking inside with his get-up still on. He could've removed it, but judging by the lack of cars around and the bleakness inside, almost everybody was either at work or gone for the holidays. Sam was gonna check real quick if Fulton was in his home, and if he were, he'd change back into his casual attire; if not– it was easier to just keep everything else on rather than having to change for the third time today.

Sam took the elevator, assuming each floor might have two to four rooms each. He pushed the number 15 button as an example to count the rooms and check for any numbers, if they were on a door, on a wall, or on a placard. Anything, as long as he was close.

On the 15th floor, Sam stepped out. On the wall beside him was a black-and-white plaque with engraved room numbers. He then counted the rooms on the level. There were three. It was now easy math: three rooms on each floor, 30 stories. Fulton should be on the 25th floor. Sam prepared himself. His palms were sweating under the football gloves, hoping that there'd be no confrontation or any type of hostility. He just wanted to figure out what was going on.

The home was empty. Sam felt disappointed. He didn't have to knock on the door. It was wide open, and there wasn't a single piece of furniture, decoration, or trash anywhere to be found. Scooped clean. Sam continued investigating anyway, finding himself in what used to be Donna's room. Nothing but dust and cold. Sam sighed, placing his hands on his hips to take a breather. Then, out of nowhere, an itch came on the back end of his head. A lady named Gloria Glenns, who was dressed in a pastel pink floral gown, attempted to swing on Sam with a black cooking pan. He dodged it right on his own time, scooting to the woman's right side, the pan grazing his left shoulder pad.

"Woah!" Sam yelped, "Hold on there–"

"Who are you?!" Gloria shouted, holding the pan like a baseball bat, ready to hit the figure in front of her out of the ballpark. "What are you doing here?!"

"I'm just-" Before Sam could explain himself, Gloria swung again, aiming for his head. The kid ducked down and jumped back to create distance. "Ma'am, hold on!"

"Ma'am?!" Gloria questioned, offended, "How old do you think I am?" The woman was ready to strike again until the person she deemed a home invader raised his hand to stop her. "Woah, woah, woah, woah! Hold on! I'm sorry- just hold on." Sam put his hand on the chin part of his mask, slowly pulling it up. Before he could show his whole face, he retreaded, hesitant about whether it was a good idea. "I don't think I can... I'm sorry."

"Why not?! Actually, why don't you just leave?!"

"I don't mean any harm. I just wanted to find the guy who lived here."

"Fulton?" Gloria queried.

"Yes. Fulton." Sam nodded, still keeping his one arm up.

"What do you want with Fulton?"

The two circled around the room. Gloria panted, remaining steady with her guard up, and Sam continued to show he meant no harm. "I just want to talk to him. To see if- he's okay and why he did all the things he did."

The woman lowered her silly-looking weapon. "I don't know where he is."

"Please, miss. I want to help him."

Gloria stared at him, studying him and his physique, and asked, "Why are you wearing a costume? Also, what's with the mask? Halloween ended two months ago."

"It's my suit."

"Funny suit." She replied, rolling her eyes.

"What happened with Fulton? Why did he commit all those robberies? Why are people getting killed?"

Gloria shook her head, avoiding the questions. Sam was desperate for the answer. He needed to know. Before anyone else gets hurt. The kid put his hand back on his face and took off his guise. Gloria's eyes turned big, dumbfounded by the reveal. "Holy shit. You're just a baby."

"I know."

"What's your name?" Gloria took a step closer. She knew he was being honest about there being no harm. The kid looked like he wouldn't hurt a spider.

"Um..."

"Come on," she lightly chuckled. You already showed your face, so you might as well say the name."

"Sam."

"Oh. I remember you. Fulton mentioned you once."

Sam raised a brow, finding that hard to believe. "He did?"

"He brought up the time y'all ran into each other in therapy."

"Right."

"Yeah," Gloria smiled, "He said you were a good kid. He could tell you were ambitious and a hard worker. He also said you were awkward."

"Yeah, I get some of those adjectives a lot." Sam brought up the questions again. "Do you know where Fulton is?"

"I don't. Sorry."

"Damn." Not the answer that Sam was hoping for.

"And if I did, I don't think it'll help. You don't know Fulton enough to get through to him. He mentioned you once, and that's that. He has a habit of not remembering everyone he meets. He's good with faces, though."

"So he might remember me?"

"Maybe. And to answer your other questions, he did all those things for his mom." Gloria explained what she knew. She didn't know the entire story, only fragments. She didn't know that Fulton had been robbing places until the trial. By then, she had pieced it all together. With her good ears and thin walls, she'd overheard her neighbor planning strange things. Talking about jobs, setups, guns. She guessed Fulton was just being boyish. She always believed he was a good man. Not whatever he is today. Moving on, she continued informing the kid, talking about Donna and parts about how tough it was for the two of them growing up and that the money was to provide a good life for her.

Sam found relatability with Fulton. Some of the way he grew up, the struggles of living every day with the weight of the world. The worries, burdens, and sacrifices. The only difference was that Fulton made a choice. He chose to steal and be selfish. In a twisted way, was it for a good cause? Maybe. It depends on how you look at it. But that doesn't mean the way he went about it was right. There's always a right and a wrong, no matter where you are or what you do.

Gloria mentioned to Sam that when Donna passed, a group of men who worked for Summit Peaks came into the building and took everything without warning. "The cruel part was that they left Donna here alone," said Gloria. "She died right here in this room."

Sam looked at the walls. He pictured where a mother would usually sleep. Finally, he pointed his head to the center wall near the bedroom door. That's where an adult would sleep. That's where Donna died.

At last, Sam got the answers he was looking for.

Chapter 30
SABOTAGE

Jo and Fulton spent the whole day in traffic. The holiday season was crazy—especially for the city. Every poor person planned on buying gifts at the last second and purchasing tickets for any events, mainly for Christmas light shows and family visits. Jo was happy to notify her partner that she had received more information on Sam. Fulton eased his concentration on the road, ready to listen. "I found an address. He's not too far out."

"Where at?"

"West side," she retorts. "I found a picture online. It's some small, crappy-looking apartment place."

"That all?"

"No. I also have the phone number."

"Bet. Let's give Sam a lil' visit."

If it wasn't transparent, the plan was to kill Sam. Fulton had it all planned out in his head. He wanted to torture him first. Scare him. He wanted to break down the door and give him a world of pain. Jo's idea was worse. She hoped Sam had a significant other, and she could torture them, too. Maybe she'd make the guy watch. Knowing that Fulton was in control, it was most likely that Jo's nefarious idea would never happen. The man wasn't evil.

At the apartments, Fulton scoped out the place, driving slowly around the block to study everything. If things went badly, his escape route was easy. Too easy since the gates around the property were already broken and wide open.

Fulton dropped off Jo at the main entrance, letting her find the unit while he cruised around still. It took Jo a minute to read the small numbers. She was searching for 2A. Anything that looked like it. She roamed through the parking lot, looking for it as hard as she could. Where are youuuuu?

"What's this?" Jo found 2B. Her head tilted up eerily to the second floor, where she found 2A. "There you are." She never wanted to take her eyes off the unit, immediately phoning for Fulton to park the car and come to her.

"This it?" Fulton put, popping the trunk open and putting on the gauntlets and airsoft shield.

"Yes, sir." Jo grinned, ready to cause chaos.

"Remember what I said. We go in, and I get him. Anyone else in there is all you."

"Easy." She agreed.

"Okay." Fulton pulled his arm back and gave the door a good punch. The glove jerked forward and popped the handle clean off. Jo shoved the door open, and the two entered. The place was dead. Nobody seemed to be home, and the place was boring. Jo expected to see a man that was ready for a fight. A certain man. Someone who keeps secrets and lives on the edge. Hell, she'd even take a family man, the type of guy to have a wife and kids, not someone who lives all normal and boring. "I don't think anyone's here."

Fulton took off one gauntlet, placing it on the brown couch. "Let's check the rooms." Jo went to the first room, the bathroom. Fulton checked the kitchen and the remaining area of the living room. Nothing. Fulton proceeded to the bedroom, unsettled by how blank it was. Just a bed on a frame, a wide charcoal dresser, and a white vanity mirror with makeup scattered on the table. Fulton assumed it was probably Sam's roommate, or perhaps it belonged to his wife or girlfriend.

When Jo went into the last room, she didn't understand it. This room looks like it belongs to a messy kid. She thought, disgusted by the piles of crumbled socks and stained shirts in the corner. The room wasn't organized and had a faint scent of sweat.

"You think this Sam has got a kid or a dirty roommate?!" Jo shouted, her voice echoing through the home.

"I don't know. He's not here."

Jo walked to Fulton's side. "So what do you want to do? Wait?"

"Nah." Fulton grabbed the other gauntlet, fashioning it on, "Let's fix it up."

"Great!" Jo's first instinct was to break the TV, and she would have until she overheard police sirens not too far away.

"I don't think they're here for us, Jo."

It was better to be safe than sorry. The woman's exhilaration walked out the door, including her body. She wanted to check and confirm that it wasn't for them. They were all on a probation period. The last thing they needed was to go to jail indefinitely, and it was looking to be true as the police got closer and closer. Jo looked around, thinking about how they knew there was a break-in. Sam didn't have an alarm or any cameras lying around. What Jo didn't know was that ever since the tenants around experienced weird activity in their neighborhood (Sam's loud speed), one neighbor became a little nosy. Even nosier after overhearing another loud sound in the night from Fulton's punch to the door. The police were already on their way the moment that door opened.

"We have to go!" Jo exclaimed, making a run for the car.

"What?!" Fulton raised, about to punch a wall in, until he saw Jo runoff. He had second thoughts about this failed attempt at sabotage, thinking maybe this might not have been such a good idea. Thank God that nothing got damaged today and that nobody was home during the invasion.

The two criminals drove out of the county, near downtown. It was time for another plan. Fulton wanted to contact Sam and meet him face-to-face. Before taking any other drastic measures, Fulton's stomach growled. *When was the last time I ate?* He searched around, peeking over the highway bridge to find any grub. Fulton wasn't in the mood for burgers or pizza. He wanted something that took the edge off. Something that could calm him down.

Still on Interstate 30, Jo pointed out Doe's. It was coming up on the next exit. At first, Fulton denied it, but as he neared, he thought of the chicken and waffles.

Man. The last time I got Doe's was... oh. Fulton's mind went blank. He knew the waterworks were bound to creep up, but this time they didn't. It was as if they had dried up. He, then ignored his silly emotions. No more crying. It was time to be a big boy.

While at Doe's eating a full plate of chicken tenders and syrup-soaked waffles, Fulton restarted, building up a new plan. He asked Jo for the number and contacted him via text message. It wasn't difficult, but now the hard part was trying to get the stranger to meet with him.

"Do you think he'll respond?" Jo asked, sipping her cup of hot coffee with six sugars and three vanilla creamers.

"He better."

"Where would y'all meet? Can't exactly have a showdown at a diner."

"I don't care. I could if I really wanted."

"No. Bad idea," Jo rebut. "Unless you want more cops showing up or for some brave soul to stop you, then you better find someplace else."

"Whatever. You're no help." The phone on the table buzzed, a response from what seemed to be Sam. Fulton grabbed it, eager to get things done, hiding the screen away from Jo.

Jo put down her coffee, asking a serious question, "Why do you want this guy so bad? Like- actually. I don't think it's a big deal anymore. We're out. We're free. All our charges got magically dropped-"

Fulton cut her off, answering her question. "I'm goin' to kill him, Jo. If it wasn't for him intervenin' at Beyrou's, we would've walked away with the money and ended it all. But no. Because of him, my ma is dead."

"Or maybe because it was you." She mumbled under her breath.

"What'd you say?!"

Jo jumped in her seat, her eyes getting big, and she wondered if he was actually asking or being rhetorical. "Nothing. Nothing.

I was just joking," she said, nervously laughing. "Nothing—I was just wondering why."

"Now ya' know." Fulton sent one more text and dropped his head into his hands, seeking a moment of solace. A lot has happened since mid-November.

Mrs. Buffers swung by the table, holding a fresh pot for refills. "How's everything going tonight, y'all? Need a filler up, hon?" She happily offered.

"No. We're good here, thanks. Actually, could we just get the check? That'll be great." Jo smiled, pulling out her leather wallet.

"Yes, ma'am. I'll get that for you real quick."

Another text vibrated the table. Fulton dropped his hands and snatched the phone as if someone were about to take it away. Jo watched Fulton type and read aggressively for the next two minutes.

"Also, how can you be sure that he was the guy? For all we know, the tungsten might've belonged to some old lady or a child who found it in the street."

"I just know, Jo. I don't know what else to tell ya'. I just know." Just then, the memory of Beyrou's came back. *Beyrou's. That's it.* Fulton thought loud, "I know where he can meet me." The man dropped a pin where the store lived. It was time to move.

Mrs. Buffers returned with the bill. Jo was ready, handing over eighteen dollars and a five-dollar tip. "Thanks, " Jo said, leaving.

"The once" was" tailor shop was a few blocks out. Fulton grabbed what was needed from the trunk of the car and got into gear. The mechanical gloves worked fine, and the helmet was still the same. Just a thick piece of black plastic attached to shiny goggles.

Beyrou's looked like it was not planning on making a comeback anytime soon. The glass remained shattered; the hole was covered with plastic and police tape. The inside collected dust. Dust all over the shelves, desks, and tables, complimented with trash on the floor. The tape, locked exits, and plastic didn't prevent kids from vandalizing the walls with cheap graffiti or the homeless from leaving their sleeping bags in between the racks. The city shut off power to the building; no point in wasting energy on a shutdown business, even though it was only shut down for now.

"He's on the way." Notified Fulton. "You're all good."

Jo stood awkwardly near Fulton, not knowing what to do with her hands, fidgeting around. "What do you need me to do?"

"What do you mean? You're good."

"Like... what?"

"You're good to go, Jo. I don't need you."

"I can help. I can." Jo insisted, begging.

"No."

Jo's jaw fell, and she wondered where this was coming from. She didn't believe it. Fulton always said he never wanted help or to pull jobs anymore, but in the end, he'd always come running back like a desperate ex. "Come on, Fult, let me help."

"No!" the geared-up man yelled.

"You always say that, but then you need me." Jo then rested her hand on his shoulder, rubbing it. "Just like any other job, right? Come on, mama's-boy-"

Without hesitation, Fulton swung on her, slapping her across the face, the end of the metal plate bumping against the woman's cheek. "GET OUT! GO!"

Jo held the side of her head with both hands, one eye opened, jolted by what he did. She froze, still holding on as her open eye turned pink, tears flooding under the bottom lid. Fulton showed no remorse for his actions. Maybe he had zero remorse for anything he'd done.

Jo stormed out the front doors of Beyrou's and never looked back.

Chapter 31
IF THIS BE MY DESTINY

After the interaction with Gloria, Sam found himself at the usual booth at Doe's, rethinking every decision that led him to today. This wasn't normal. Ironically, nothing had ever been normal since day one. Hopefully, after finding Fulton, things will be better. Better with his mom (even though he was still holding resentment), the twins, work, and everything.

People came in and out of Doe's, asking if they had holiday specials on the meals. The only treat they had for the week was a little sale on pancakes. *Buy two pancakes and get one for free! Get it now for $4.99!* The sign displayed.

Sam wasn't at Doe's for the food. He was there for the Wi-Fi. He was tired of waiting and wanted to fix things ASAP. He dialed Trevor, hoping he'd pick up. At first, he thought it'd go to voicemail until he heard the call go through, followed by some low breathing on the other line.

"Hello?" By the tone of Trevor's voice, he seemed upset or annoyed. It was hard to tell. "Hello?!" Trevor repeated, clearly pissed.

"Trevor?! Oh, thank God."

"What is it, Sam?"

"Yes- yeah- I'm calling from my work phone. I- I wanted to call a few days ago, but-"

"I get it."

"Also, I don't have Garrett's number on this phone. Could you maybe- send me his?" Sam asked, hoping for a positive answer.

"Garrett got a new phone a few days ago. I'll ask him once he gets back. I don't remember the new one. For now, I'll just give him yours."

"Thank you." Sam grinned. "Can we talk real quick?"

"We already are," Trevor said blankly.

"Could we talk about the other night? When we were at Summit Peaks."

"Look, Sam... we're busy right now. We're at a funeral, and I don't have time to deal with this. You need to get your act together because all this is bullshit."

"You're at a funeral? What happened? Who passed?"

Trevor pulled away from his phone, his voice fading. "Don't worry about it. We'll text you later. Bye." Without another second or a glimpse of hesitation, Trevor hung up. Sam looked down at the phone, sliding it into his pocket.

Before settling down and ordering a plate, Sam's phone twitched on his thigh. He presumed it to be another text from his mother or Garrett reaching out. Or maybe it was an email about a new life insurance policy. You know- the ones that keep popping up that you happen to not give a damn about. Unsubscribe.

This wasn't the case. There was no pointless email or family reaching out. It was an unknown number. The text simply said, "Hello, Sam."

The boy ignored it for now. His focus was on reminiscing about the fun times he had with the twins. To think, it had only been a month and some change since London.

Since then, things have been a wild rollercoaster. Both physical and mental. He pondered if he really was becoming someone else. The argument between the three was the first and worst interaction. Each word stuck in Sam's mind. Was he really that bad? Becoming arrogant, selfish, alienated, all of those things? Using the Twins for free food just to keep his power steady? Or how about the way he never even bothered to tell them or his remaining parent what was happening? Was this the way things were gonna be from here on out?

"I have to fix these things..." Sam told himself. "I have to." This wasn't him. He was just a kid that was trying to get by. Work, school, life, and maybe one day, love. The speed was only adding to the negatives. But was it really, though? Or did it just reveal what was buried within? A boy who was so low that he couldn't wait to be on top. No. This wasn't him. This will all pass.

Sam finally responded to the text. *Who is this?*

Right after, another text from the stranger followed:

Do you own any tungsten? I think I have one of your pieces.

Sam's face squinted with uncertainty. He was aware of what he owned, but the question was—how did this person know it belonged to him? "Who is this?" he texted.

When Mrs. Buffers stepped out of the kitchen with her blue pen and notepad, she took heed that something might be wrong with her favorite customer.

"The usual, hun?" She teased, her hand resting on her lumpy waist.

"Hey, Mrs. B."

"What's wrong? Where're the boys?"

Sam shrugged his shoulders. Mrs. B wasn't having it with the silence, "Honey! You're gonna have to talk to me. I can't read your mind."

"They're busy."

Mrs. Buffers walked away to the kitchen, bringing her young, favorite customer a tall glass of chocolate milk on the house. "Here you go, sweetie."

"Thank you." Although it looked good, Sam didn't bother to take one sip. Instead, he toyed with the thick milk with his straw, stirring it around endlessly.

"Now, why aren't you with them?"

Sam fell quiet, giving nothing.

"May I?" Mrs. B asked, tilting her head at the empty seat.

"Sure."

The big girl had to squeeze herself into the narrow booth, pushing her stomach into an uncomfortable position. Her breathing became heavy, and her voice tended to a slight rasp. Sam had never experienced her from such a close distance. For the last couple of years, he'd always sat down and stared up at her. The tension between him and her was personal—as if he were talking with Cathy.

Mrs. Buffers held his wrist, making firm eye contact with the boy. "What's wrong? Did something happen between you and the boys?"

Sam got another message. Paying no mind to it now. It was rude to space out while someone was talking to you. "Yeah.

We're not talking. I haven't seen them in a while. It's been about a week and counting."

Her eyes twitched, thinking back to the last time they were together, "I know school is out, but other than that, I usually see y'all here almost every day after y'all get out. Sometimes, I can't wait to see you there."

"I know. But it's complicated now."

"And why's that, hon'?"

As he sat there, Sam curled his lips and strayed away. Tears bubbled in his eyes, turning pink from the strain and pain he endured. Mrs. B could tell he had no intention of explaining the situation, placing her warm hand onto his, and sympathizing with the lonely child.

"It'll be alright. I promise," she assured him, patting his fingers, "Here. I'll fix you something warm. On the house."

"Oh- Mrs. B, you don't have to-"

"No-no. It's alright. You just sit there now."

"No, it's okay. Really. I think I'm gonna head home."

Buffers understood, nodding her head. "If you change your mind, let me know."

"Thank you."

Sam went back to the message, reading it. "Just someone that wants to help." Sam came back with another:

But what's your name? How'd you know it belongs to me?

After sending, Sam's eyes followed Mrs. Buffer's path. He might just reconsider that free meal. It was funny to see how Sam's hunger died the moment his eyes landed on Fulton at the other end of the diner. Mrs. Buffers walked over with a pot full of coffee in her hand. Sam and Fulton made a half-second of eye contact, causing the kid to duck down under the table. Luckily, Fulton was too focused on his phone.

Fulton. The next text said.

Mrs. Buffers asked one person in the booth if they were up for another refill. She declined. Sam couldn't ID the blonde girl sitting in front of Fulton, and it didn't matter. His focus was on the man, not the woman. The scared boy peaked up from the table, keeping a close eye on him, and continued communicating, asking if there was a place he'd like to meet.

Was he sitting there the whole time? Sam thought, his heart pounding like a drum. *I pray he didn't see me.* Sam wasn't more so scared of Fulton recognizing him, but at the fact that he was nothing more but scared. This was intense, trying to reason with a criminal who might want to kill him.

Sam received the next and final text message: *Meet me at Beyrou's.*

The two got up and left, and Sam followed, keeping a great distance. He witnessed them getting into a car and driving off. The boy's heart continued beating, and a mini itch formed on his forehead. This time, he didn't need an itch to tell him something was up. Sam moved to the nearest secluded area to change.

Half a block away from the shop, Sam braked behind a dumpster, covering his nose from the stench of the muck, piss, and rat shit swarming all over it. He waited until he arrived, watching cars pass on until it was time. Sam had to guess whether the blonde woman would join in on the conversation. There were no guesses on who she was.

Once again, Sam took time to reflect on the memories, wondering how he got to be here. Instead of relying on the negative, he turned to the positive. Soon, he thought of the good but felt overshadowed by the bad. His head took over, closing his eyes and thinking of the good, welcomed thoughts that led him here. Even though his powers brought such disaster to his work, school, and home life, he never thought he'd experience something so raw and intense. The only words he could tell the twins were, I'm sorry. After that, he can explain everything.

Peaking around the corner, Sam kept a watch, waiting for the two to show up. While standing by, His breathing became hyper, and his shoulders hung low. Sam could not pinpoint the difference between nerves and a panic attack. This was the consequence of not taking the medicine anymore. No meds mean free use of powers but with occasional anxiety. Meds meant being free from his diagnosis, but no more special powers.

When Fulton and Jo arrived, Sam's eyes popped, and his itch turned into a sharp ant bite. Watching them roll in a black Chevy, he wished he was he was looking at the twins' cherry-red Ford instead. They parked diagonally in front of the shop. Fulton got his gloves from the trunk, ready to head inside. Sam recognized those things. This would not be a conflict resolution talk. This was a fight. Sam retreated against a clay-red brick wall, wanting to cry like a baby. It was all scary. It was all too surreal.

There's no way this is happening! Why is this all happening to me?! Sam screamed internally. The kid took a deep breath. Possibly the last deep breath he'll ever have, or it could be his calling, a cliche strike of fate. Everything happens for a reason. Sam had to take responsibility. There was no time to be scared. His life didn't get easier the moment he gained his speed, and it wasn't easier back then. He made a choice to let it coexist with him. He made it an option to keep using it. He had this, and now it was time to own up to it. Sam took the time to grow a pair, removing his gloves for the last time to wipe the sweat off his palms and walk onto that street. The anticipation would kill him before Fulton would. Deep down, he hoped it would.

It was clear Fulton wanted a fight. He didn't drive all the way, just give him a damn rod. If this is it, so be it. For once, Sam wanted to be a better use. He was being selfish, arrogant, and whatever poor, bad character descriptions out there that painted him in a lousy picture. This was a privilege. Maybe he could even help Fulton... if it wasn't too late already.

Sam didn't want to stretch out the time. It was already eleven o'clock, and waiting until they'd driven away was unlikely. Now that they had his information, they would never leave the boy alone. They got his number, name, and most likely his address (little did he know). Sam's mind raced to high school, thinking about how he'd rather take harsh shoves and beatings from Felix than an angry criminal with powerful arms.

Before he took another step, someone rushed out of Beyrou's. It was the blonde woman Sam had seen earlier. (Jo.) He witnessed her getting into the Chevy, starting up the engine, pulling out, and driving away. Sam had a questionable gut feeling that this wouldn't be the last time he would see her again. He digressed, moved on, and focused on what was in front of him, gently pulling the store's front door open and entering.

Inside, it was cold and quiet. All the products were taken off the shelves. Sam noticed the glass palette on the counter that the clerk used to ask the boy what color he wanted. Before the chaos happened. He sighed.

Looking away from the counter, Sam's eyes could hardly adjust. Everything was still dark, and only the city's lights could provide a form of a nightlight as they'd flash through the windows and backdoor exit.

"Hello?" Sam called out. The silence grew louder, and the anticipation became deadlier, not knowing what lurked beneath the dark. Sam could hear his own heartbeat and the clicks of his tongue ambling into the empty abyss of a shop.

"Fulton?!" He finally yelled, hoping to get any response, even as little as a tap of a foot or something falling over to the ground. Something to break the tension.

"Hello!" a voice echoed. Sam couldn't figure out where the voice was coming from. He lurked around, spinning like a scared cat.

"Is that you, Fulton?!" Again. No response. Nothing but a bad itch to the back of his head and a quick jolt to Sam's back. That same strong, forceful thrust he felt back at Summit Peaks had pushed him lightly off his feet, slamming against one shelf bolted into the wall.

"What's up, Sam?" Fulton smiled behind his face cover.

The teenager cautiously got back up, resting on his knees and leaning against the wall. Both the moonlight and city lights cast a spotlight on Fulton, showcasing the man of interest. "It's good to see you again. I don't know if you remember me, but we met at this store."

After saying so, Fulton gave another quick thrust to Sam's chest, sending him back to the other wall behind him as his suit formed scrapes and collections of dust from all surfaces. His whole costume went from looking navy blue to a faded azure.

Sam held his chest, on the verge of coughing blood through his mask. He couldn't fight, but he could run.

Without a thought, he jolted forward to pass by Fulton, but he received another forceful punch to the gut, sending him back into the wall again. The drywall was bending. After another hit or two, Sam would fall right through.

"Listen to me, I don't wanna fight you. Please." Sam begged.

Another modified punch was thrown, and Sammy was lucky to dodge it, ducking below. After his dodge, Fulton followed it with a swift kick, sending Sam to fall through the wall, his back turning near white and gray from the powder of the broken drywall. He crawled away like a turtle, not making it far enough to avoid Fulton's kicks to his ribs.

"Please!" Sam begged again, "Please!"

Fulton stood him on his feet, giving the boy a combo he'd feel in the morning, using both gauntlets to form a powerful punch to his chest. Doing so made him fly off his feet and through the glass doors. Sam's back ripped, his skin tearing and bleeding down his spine.

This time, they were out in the open. Cars were passing by, and people were staring, admiring the epic showdown, and watching from their phones. Sam dodged a couple more licks, leaning back and ducking again. Each back-bending maneuver stretched the cuts on his back and caused it to drip more blood.

His back was not only white but also mixed red, making the powder turn mushy like dough.

It took a lot of work to use his gifts. He needed strong attention to awaken his powers for protective use. The itches that developed alongside his head were irrelevant. He couldn't follow or scratch them if he tried. It only brought an agitating annoyance to the mix.

"Fight me!" Fulton yelled, slamming his fists together, denting the gloves.

"I won't! Please! Just Stop!" cried Sam. Somehow, Fulton got a firm hold on him, slamming his head into the side of a cab, showering his top half with glass, and soaking up with blood. Now, his mask was damaged. One lens broke, revealing his cinnamon eye, and the top corner of the fabric was ripped, unveiling a piece of his dark brown wavy hair.

Both grew fatigued yet still fighting, causing a commotion from the streets. Sirens were wailing in for help. They'd be there any minute...

Now, the showdown was turning ugly. Fulton threw him back into the store, tossing him over the front counter and tussling with him. Sam wanted him to stop but couldn't fight. He tried to run, but Fulton would eventually catch him. There was no point.

So Sam used most of his energy and focused on the detailed moments between the fists that impacted his anatomy, swiftly moving to the actions and grabbing one gauntlet. Sam focused his ability on his arm, quickly ripping one tube and bending the man's arm back, breaking it before Fulton could realize.

When the pain finally registered, he screamed and backed away, but not before landing a solid jab to Sam's right kneecap. Sounds of bones were crumbling, scrapes were singing with pain, and there was no escape. He still had another hand left. Sam could no longer run or use his powers. He'd just have to accept the welts. From what he could sense, the fight was nearly over.

The mechanized fighter's broken arm was winging around like a wet noodle while his left hand was still intact, and he swung it around every chance he got. He broke a couple of Sam's ribs and sprained his leg. It was now Sam's turn to return the favor, grabbing a hold of the gauntlet on his working hand and tearing it off his arm. In doing so, it also tore off about nine inches of Fulton's skin. It dangled on like a piece of ripped paper, presenting the pink underlayers of his skin.

"AHH!" he screamed, "You asshole! You stupid- ass-" There were no words. It's just pain. "You ruined my life!" he yelled, grabbing Sam's arm, twisting it behind his back, and dislocating it. He fell on his last given knee, tired and suffering. He was on the verge of counting sheep or possibly seeing the stairway of heaven, but not before the guy delivered one last naked blow to his face and pulled the kid's mask off. Sam quickly turned over, hiding.

Both leaned against opposite sides of the front desk, facing each other in a broken and beaten slump. Sam lay down on the floor while Fulton sat up. They huffed and puffed their lungs, spitting blood on the dirty floor. The sirens remained, alarming the outside public to stand aside to handle the situation.

Fulton threw off his airsoft mask, drenched in sweat, with hardly a scratch on his face. Sam turned over, and parts of his face swelled and bruised with blood on top. He was beaten. Over.

"It... it- it was your fault. You took away my ma. My job. My life!" He wheezed.

"I... didn't." Sam groaned, whispering in agony.

"Yes, you did. Yes..."

"No. You did..." When Sam turned to look at the man, Fulton's eyes twitched, noticing his familiar look. An old stranger was lying in front of him.

"What- you?!" Fulton shrieked. He didn't realize the person he was tumbling around with was just a kid. A kid who would partake in multiple therapy sessions, a kid facing heavy amounts of trauma, a kid who would sit and listen to his sob stories. A kid that Fulton forgot about.

"Hey, Fulton... it's- good to see you again," He smiled.

Retreating, Fulton sat fully upright, facing the bloody child. "Hey, Sam."

Were they simply strangers? Yes. However, within those small conversations, Fulton knew that the kid was special. He couldn't apologize or fix what he'd done. His only regrets were failing his mother and not remembering Sam. Was it the hair? Or the silly costume? Or maybe the beaten-in face?

"I'm- I'm sorry that I-I got in your way. But I didn't intend t-to bring-g any harm to-"

"I know, man." Fulton interrupted, leaning over and picking up one glove. "I know."

The two stayed on the ground, sitting in pure silence. They wanted to say nothing else but sorry. The police came in closer. People stood around still, recording from their phones, hoping at least one of them would come out to bring more entertainment.

"You shouldn't have gotten involved, kid," said Fulton.

"I know... I don't know what I'm doing. I have zero clue." Sam coughed, attempting to sit comfortably on the broken glass floor.

Fulton looked around. He didn't want to look the teenager in the eye, but it was as if he was getting tugged in his direction. Fulton believed this was a sweet kid. He reminded him of himself. The man had to bite down, swallow his pride, and admit the painful truth. "No. I don't know what I'm doing. You were right to stop me..."

"No." Sam kept his modesty. "I should be home, playing some stupid video game. I should be doing my homework and wasting my life away. It's not my responsibility to protect people. I... never should've done this."

"Sam!" Fulton raised. "You did the right thing."

"How?!"

"I'm sorry things had to go this way... I made all these mistakes growin' up, and you were the one brave person to stop it. Most people here in places like Dallas– are selfish, but not you, kid... You were brave and selfless." Fulton spat some blood, snickering. "Ah. I think you broke a tooth."

Sam tried laughing, but his lungs were hurt, "Heh. I think you broke my leg."

Fulton returned to the serious topic. "I never wanted people to die. I attacked Summit because of what they took from me... those deaths weren't from me. But I know the blood is on my hands. I know I won't be forgiven for those things, but I just want to say again that I am sorry. I don't want anyone else to end up like me..."

The injured kid understood. He let the man rant on again like he did the first time. "I'm sorry for what happened to your mom."

Fulton slowly looked up at Sam. That was the first time anyone had shown sympathy for what happened to Donna. His eyes flowed with uncontrollable tears, and there was no way to make them stop, no matter how much Fulton tried to wipe them away. "Oh. Speaking of which." Fulton wanted to bring it up before he forgot, "I broke into your apartment... sorry about that. Who's big room is that?"

"My mom's." Answered Sam.

"Right... Keep her safe, kid. My only regret was not spendin' enough time with mine before she... ya' know..."

"Yeah."

Fulton stood up, his body shifting towards his right, holding his broken arm carefully. The man took one more glance at the broken boy on the floor. *Damn...* He thought.

"I actually have homework to do," Sam mumbled, watching Fulton eventually get up, removing his signature jacket and carefully placing it on his abused torso like a warm blanket. "Here, Sam..."

"What?"

"A long ass time ago, my ma made me this... I don't think I need it anymore." Fulton struggled to get the last sleeve off. His arm twitched at the slightest touch. "I want you to have it. I don't deserve to wear it anymore. It should go to someone that's a better man."

"I don't think-"

"You are." Said Fulton. "You're a good kid." Tears flooded the broken man's eyes as he limped away, shoving his forearm into his nose to block the runny snot. This was an odd way for the man to take accountability. He never fully explained why he gave Sammy the jacket.

Was it because Fulton was learning to accept what he'd done and moved on from his ma? Was it a comforting item that could mentally help Sam during his troubled times, just as it did for Fulton? Or was it a gift out of guilt? That was something that the boy had to decide. They didn't know each other well enough to conclude that, but they knew each other's situations. The victory went to Fulton. A Pyrrhic victory. After all of that, it was now over.

Chapter 32
KEEP YOUR FRIENDS CLOSER

Before the cops rolled in, Sam crawled awkwardly towards the back exit, holding onto his mask, new jacket, and the other gauntlet. Along the slow path, his dislocated arm popped back into place. After groaning through the sudden stings of the pain, the teen could now move a little quicker than earlier. As he continued, tears rolled down his face, wanting to go home. He thought of Christmas. He thought again about making amends with the boys, especially with his mom.

Inching closer, he noticed something through the back exit. It was precisely what he was thinking: something big, luscious, and red. It was them, the twins. The best pairs in town, driving up to the back alley in their large beauty. Sam reached the doorway, waving his arms to catch their attention as they passed. The tires screeched, coming to a quick and complete stop. It's probably because the boys saw him last minute through the rearview mirror.

The heavy door opened, revealing only one twin present. Garrett. Trevor wasn't in the truck. Just himself and the red dame. Garrett rushed to Sam, dropping to the floor and gently helping him up. He didn't know what part of Sam's body was in pain or wonder why Sam was wearing a full bodysuit.

Sam no longer wanted to move. He held him close and cried into his big shoulders, sobbing and clenching onto his hoodie as he held him up.

"I got you," the twin assured. Garrett drove Sam to the hospital, unsure where to start with the questions until Sam cleared up from crying and asked the first one himself. "How'd you find me?" He sniffled. Garrett passed Sam his phone, trying to make his friend feel better with a sly inside joke, "Fifth time."

"Heh." Sam scoffed.

"Trevor gave me your number. When I tried calling you, nothing was coming up. And knowing you, you're always wanting to fix things with us, so I knew something was up when you didn't answer. I checked your location and saw that you also synched your location for the other phone. I saw where you were and came to you... You should really put a password on your phone, man."

"I know." Sam agreed, picking it up to see 15 missed calls from Cathy and two messages from Sonny and Alexus.

"Where's Trevor?"

"You know how he gets," he answered. "I think it's deep this time."

"Oh..." Sam lowered his head, wondering if things would ever go back to normal.

"Give him some time. I'm sure he'll come around."

"Yeah."

Now it was time for Garrett to ask the serious questions. "Your turn. What's been goin' on with you? You've been different since you got back."

"It's hard to explain. I-"

"Just say it!" Garrett exclaimed. "At this point, I don't care if you're on drugs or somethin'. Just tell me."

"After the accident in London, I felt strange. It started in the hospital when my heart rate was too high and my perception of time was low. At first, I thought it was just in my head or that I was dreaming. Then the day came when I went back to school, and that same feeling came back again."

"And then?" Garrett beckoned, wanting the explanation to continue.

"I can now run faster than anyone can possibly imagine. I have super speed." Sam summed up.

"And this costume you're wearing?" Garrett pointed.

"It's able to sort of- withstand my speed. It's a lot of physics and too much to explain right now. I'll maybe break down the science for you one day, but- yeah... ever since I got this new thing, it's been changing me. For the better and for the worse, I guess." Garrett continued to drive, not knowing what to make of the answer. It seemed better for Sam to lie and say he was on various drugs, but it was time for the lies to be over.

"You sure you're not on drugs?" Garrett queried.

"I'm sure. At the moment, I wish I was."

"We're almost at the hospital."

"Hospital?" Sam said, "I can't go there."

Garrett's eyes widened. "You're bleedin' everywhere! Your leg is bendin' in an odd direction, and you're obviously not in the best condition. I'd know. Trust me."

Sam signed, trying to get himself out of his outfit before people started asking questions or putting things together about what happened at Beyrou's.

"What are you doing?"

"Trying to get out of this," Sam answered, pointing to the ripped suit on him. Garrett pulled some of Trevor's extra clothes from under the seat for Sam to wear for now. The red and black flannel shirt was going to fit loosely on the kid, and the shirt and denim pants were just fine. The sun was coming up soon, and Sam wanted to take advantage of whatever night was left so no one could see him changing.

When they pulled up to the hospital, Sam was almost immediately tended to. Thankfully, his legs weren't severely damaged. His left arm, hand, and right foot were sprained, along with seven stitches on his back—nothing too bad. His fast healing was starting to pay off, and thankfully, his ribs healed, but it was clearly going to be some time before he was in good shape again.

"This hospital bill's gonna kill me," the boy groaned. *I hope I have enough of the money Ms. Juniper gave me.*

Later in the afternoon, Garrett drove to the apartments to drop Sam off. Everything seemed fine for now.

"Do you really have super speed?" Garrett had raised, growing curious about the world around him, thinking about whether superpowers or superhuman-like gifts were really among society.

"I'd show you if I could, Gar."

"I'm just curious if it's real. Also, it's concerning to me that one would have a cool power, yet you got your ass handed to?" the twin sassed.

"Heh... It's complicated. I'm still figuring this out. It's only been a month since I've had this."

Garrett nodded, looking glum.

"Which reminds me. Can you keep this glove?" Sam flashed the hunky modified thing in his face.

"So that's what this is, huh? Why can't you take it?"

"Mom would notice. I'll pick it up when I have the chance. Please?"

Garrett agreed, impressed by its rigid design. "You know I have to tell Trevor now."

"About what?"

"Everything."

"Yeah." Sam agreed.

"Later, though. Right now, he needs to just be by himself. He'll come around... You know you're both still friends, Sam, right? It's just the way he is. Some people just take things personally. He just so happens to be one of those people. It happens."

The kid sighed, "I know. I know. Now that all the craziness is over, I was hoping that things would go back to normal."

"They will. I'm sure."

Sam got out of the red dame, held onto his backpack, which contained his damaged costume, and walked to the house. Suddenly, Garrett called out to Sam before he got too far. "Hey! Does your mom know?"

"No. At least I don't think so?"

"Are you gonna tell her?" He asked in a concerned tone.

"I will. Tonight's not good. I don't want her to worry more than she has tonight... Another problem to add to the list, I guess..."

"Hey! Chin up, Guy! You're a superhero!" Garrett laughed as he drove off.

Sam's face puzzled. "Hero? Huh?" He liked the sound of that. It could be a bit of a reach, but it would come with the territory if he wanted to take responsibility.

Sam carried himself up the stairs, tiptoeing along the rugged, rocky concrete that led afloat. He didn't bother needing a key. When he stood before the door, he looked at the knob and side frame of the door, damaged from what Fulton had referenced earlier.

He wasn't lying when he said he was broken in.

When the boy walked inside, Cathy stood across the counter with her arms crossed but tossed them low when she double-took another look. Cathy jogged across the room to take another glance at her son. Both didn't squeak a word, not even a breath.

She studied the swollen cheek, the cuts on his face, and the black eye forming. Cathy then slapped her son and followed through with a tight bear hug. Sam understood why she did that and that he deserved it. He held on to her. "I'm sorry... I'm so sorry."

Cathy's eyes were filled. She didn't need to say a thing. The moment already spoke for itself. She pulled away, combing the dirty hair away from her son's eyebrows, staring deep into his soul. She couldn't see it but felt the pain that washed over her child. She, too, was in similar situations of horror. She reached in and kissed his pink cheek, then his scratched-up forehead.

"I love you, mom."

"I love you too."

He let out a sigh and sniffled, "Grounded?"

"Grounded." she smiled, letting out a soft laugh, hugging him once again.

Christmas wasn't over yet. Sam's leg started coming around, and his arm felt sore. Mr. Grafton gave him a few days off to restore his health. Otherwise, he'd be fired.

Sam spent the rest of the day with Cathy, having a marathon of Christmas movies. The twins had their little get-togethers down in Houston. Sam was never invited, and it was fair. It was the time for family.

Later, both Cathy and Sam put on their traditional crappy Christmas sweaters. She wore a bright red and green one with a Santa face stitched onto the front and back. Sam wore a dark blue sweater with Frosty and Rudolph stitched on the front with gold trimmings and sat on the couch to continue the movie marathon. He couldn't help but savor the moment.

Moments like this reminded him of how he took his mother for granted. Took everyone for granted. Every once in a while, he'd have to stop and thank her for everything she's sacrificed for him. All the time, money, weight, patience, and opportunities. Maybe something different would have come if his father had stayed... or if they'd possibly used protection. One could wonder about the possibilities.

From across the apartment, a gentle knock came at the front door. Sam turned to his parent to let her know he'd get it. As he answered the door, he beamed. It was the one and only Ms. Juniper. She stood in a gorgeous, ruby-red dress wrapped around her body, and her earrings sparkled like fire. She had no jacket; it was a miracle she wasn't freezing. Not a muscle in her was twitching. In her hands, she held something. Her fingers were interlinked, carrying a cardboard paper bag with a red and green bow wrapped around the handles.

"Hi, Sammy." she grinned. Her expression then dropped, finally seeing the cuts and bruises on his face. "What- What happened?" She asked, covering her mouth.

"I just- got into a fight. That's all. I'm doing better, in case you're wondering."

Sam stepped outside, closing the door behind him, "I'd offer you to come inside, but- I'm kinda in trouble, so..."

"No, it's fine. Just glad you're okay."

He looked down at her hands. "You got presents?"

She shook her head, returning to her smiley expression. "No. They're for you and your mom." Her hands raised, she lifted the bag and gave them over. "Appréciez (Enjoy)."

Like the last visit, they leaned against the railing on the balcony, looking out towards the flashy city. Everyone was home for the holidays, spending their love and time with each other. Sam pitied Fulton. He felt terrible that he didn't have a proper home to go to nor a family member he could spend the holidays with. His eyes turned to notice Ellie was shaking from the cold.

Quickly, Sam rushed inside to grab a coat, draping his olive-green windbreaker over her shoulders. Her cheeks blushed as she acknowledged his care. Ellie turned, facing towards him. The tension was perfect. They could almost hear Christmas carolers singing around the block, practically smelling the warm cocoa they'd been handing out.

Sam leaned in, and Ms. Juniper closed her eyes, puckering her soft-looking lips... instead of something so lovely, the boy hugged her tightly. A hug that was not only a letdown for her but something welcoming. She felt warmer than the jacket and more warmth in her heart. Sam would never engage in her little hugs. She knew he'd keep his arms low and hang to the ground. Her cheeks turned red, and she wrapped her arms around his shoulders.

She leaned towards his ears, letting out a gentle whisper. "Merry Christmas, Sammy."

"Merry Christmas."

New year. The start of 2016. A new beginning for Sam. Nothing had changed anyway. The last semester of school was here, work at Inferior had to get done, more work-life balancing, and yet to talk with Trevor and Cathy about his little secret. Garrett wanted to tell his brother, but it wasn't his place to talk. Everything was going to change the more Sam widened his circle. It was a beautiful, cold day. Sam was up and at it, making a hot breakfast of scrambled eggs, extra slices of bacon, two cups of orange juice, sweet tea, and an energy drink. All his energy restored like a full battery.

Garrett picked up Sam (not with Trevor). He sighed, having hope for his best friend. Not everybody gets a happy ending. Sometimes, things will always stay the same.

"Give it time," said Garrett, patting his friend on the back.

Sam and his friend group reunited at the cafeteria before school started. Kids were running around, showing off their new Christmas presents. Their latest shoes, hoodies, or their over-the-top stylish backpacks. Sam looked around the cafeteria, hoping to spot his friend. His eyes scanned again and saw how he was sitting far away. Trevor ate mini pancakes with chocolate milk. He didn't look around or seem lonely. He appeared to be blank. His face had no emotion, just a blank grim. He no longer wanted to sit near Sam or anyone in the friend group.

Was I bad? Sam thought. *Did neglecting him really make things end?*

Garrett patted Sam again, messing with his hair to distract him away from his brother. "I know he's stretching this out, man. I'll go talk to him later."

"He's never gotten this bad, though."

"Don't worry about it," Garrett dismissed. "How are you feeling?"

"Better." Sam took one last look at Trevor. Their eyes locked, and Trevor was still chewing away at his breakfast. The stare was intense and seemed to carry on for a minute. Sam nodded his head, a small gesture for his friend. Trevor looked back, quickly nodded, then stared back down, not looking at him again for the rest of the day. Progress. Sonny, Heather, and Carissa chatted about the rest of the semester before graduation. Sam never gave his future a thought. It was strange to be back in the rhythm. Other than that, it was another day at school.

Back home. Sam sat at his desk, turned his lamp on, and reanimated his suit. He sewed away, occasionally picking his fingers with the needle. "Ow." He hissed, continuing. The poking mattered little. He simply admired the outfit and fixed it. The teenager stayed up almost all night to fix every rip, dent, and crack. Sam grabbed his mask, observing the damage. One lens needed to be replaced. Scratch that- both of them needed to be replaced.

The boy glanced at it, wondering what would happen next now that Fulton was gone. The man's signature jacket rested on the twin bed, and Sam hung it in the closet. It was too valuable to be damaged. Maybe someday Sam will find him and really work things out. Until then, it had to be put in the past. Speaking of the past, Sam's family record book was just below. His thin fingers picked it up and flipped through the pages, his eyes staring at that interesting Albanian word again. Zhivë.

Chapter 33
EPILOGUE

While Sam was spending half of his Christmas in the hospital, Jo drove back to her home. She was distressed and confused about Fulton. Her thoughts ranged from working together, kissing him, to being hit. She never heard from her partner. She assumed he got arrested, ran away, or worse, killed.

Her mind spiraled, jumping from one overbearing thought to the next. She, too, had the mindset of a child and the overfill of emotions like any woman. She thought about the gauntlets, the money, the trial. All of it. Soon, she was finally at peace of mind. All of those thoughts jumped and were suddenly gone. She was crazy. Jo realized she didn't need Fulton anymore and was unlikely to see him again.

Good!

Christmas was a specific holiday she wanted to avoid. She wasn't happy around her family, hating most of them. It didn't matter if they were immediate family or late. The only few who cared for her were her nephews and sister. Every holiday season, she'd receive a call from them, letting her know they missed her and wished to spend time with her and Grannie. Of course, Jo had to make a call. She couldn't keep her withering grandmother in the home to rot forever.

Jo never attended her funeral. She overtook the country home and trashed most of the living area. It was in her plans that her family would never visit the horrendous property. Jo drove her car to the backyard, got out, and pulled out a metal baseball bat.

The thoughts were all coming back, but it wasn't about Fulton, the gauntlets, or the work this time. She replayed her childhood (something she sincerely wanted to forget) and slammed the side mirrors. She hit the front and back windshield to bits, taking all her anger out on the vehicle. Now, she was trying to forget about Fulton and Johnny. She, too, could say goodbye to the gauntlets she made, realizing she would not see those again, either.

Fortunately, she had another project to work on. She didn't have so many lighters lying around just to burn herself; she used the coils, oil, and cotton stored within. She had a secret idea—wanting to wait to work on it until the right time.

After her little tantrum, she threw the bat off into the yard, looking at the surrounding forest. She did not know what was going to happen next. Maybe she'd experiment with fire or diddle around with herself. Maybe. Jo rubbed her scarred arms, warming herself up in the cold wind as she sat on her back patio. A sudden buzz tickled her left thigh: a phone call. She reached into her blue jeans and pulled out the device. The call was from one of her nephews. The screen displayed a name. *Trevor.*

She answered it, holding it to her round ear, "Hello?"

"Hey, Auntie Jo! Merry Christmas!" He cheered.

Jo rolled her eyes, "Yeah. Yeah. Good holidays to you, little guy." She sat on a rusty lawn chair, kicking back and soaking up the cheesy vibes. "Whatcha up to, bud?"

"Oh, nothing much. Are you going to Houston with us for Uncle Dan's party? I would really appreciate it if you'd drop by."

Jo shook her head, contemplating it for a moment. "No. It's fine. How's Garrett?"

"He's good... listen- I know what happened between the stuff you and your crew did."

"You do?" She questioned, sitting up straight and holding the phone closer to herself. She grew embarrassed and self-conscious about the revelation.

"Don't worry. I'm not gonna judge you," said Trevor, "I still- I just want to let you know I miss you and love you. It's been a while since we last talked."

"Two years... I know." She sighed.

Trevor explained he was running to the party late. It was a three-and-a-half-hour drive from Dallas to Houston. Not enough time to get tipsy from all the mixed eggnog and drive back home.

"Why so late? Y'all gotta be on the road right now. The traffic is bad."

"I know. I know. Garrett was busy helping a friend. He had to go to the hospital this morning for some reason. Garrett doesn't know either."

"Is your friend okay?"

"I guess?" Trevor's voice shook. He sounded puzzled and careless.

"You haven't checked up on him? Trevor, you must check up on him if you consider him a friend."

"I know." He repeated. "It's just not a good time right now. I've been pissed with him lately."

"Do you wanna talk about it?" Jo's voice went from aunt to motherly. She was always Trevor's favorite person in the entire world. When he was little, he'd stay up with her playing board games, and she always gave him the most gifts out of everyone in the family.

"It's a lot to talk about. He borrowed money from me and Garrett for whatever reason, and he showed up late to school and work, and not to mention he left the room when his arm broke and never said bye-"

Suddenly, Jo interjected. "Wait. Wait. Wait."

"What?"

"He was there when Garrett got his arm messed up?"

"Yeah." He replied. "What? You didn't see him?"

"No." She scoffed. "I think I'd remember. What's his name?"

"I gotta go, Auntie. It was nice talking to you again. I miss you. I hope to see you soon. Gar and I gotta hit the road."

"Wait- really quick- what's his name?" Jo leaned forward, almost out of her chair. She grew curious about something.

"Sam."

Jo's lips widened into an evil smirk. There was one last question on her mind. "Does his name happen to be Samuel Clark?"

ARTWORK

Samuel Connie Clark 11

Fulton Rockefeller Bruning

Cathy Bakers

Trevor Sings

Garrett Sings

Georgia "Jo" Fezz

Donna Bruning

Johnny Plaza Jr.

Ms. Ellie Juniper

Samuel Connie Clark 11 (After Accident)

Zhivë

Rockefeller

www.ingramcontent.com/pod-product-compliance
Lightning Source LLC
Chambersburg PA
CBHW070158310726
48976CB00001B/134